Making Waves

Liz Allen w.
She graduat
before joinir
secretary, wh
as Alan Plate
first articles p
BBC for Inde
worked as Pr ... resenter of a nightly music and chat programme. After a season working on cruise liners she returned to England and began work on *Making Waves*. In 1979 she moved to London and joined Radio Two, where she presented the live middle of the night show. She is married, with one son, and lives in Buckinghamshire.

LIZ ALLEN

Making Waves

FONTANA PAPERBACKS

First published in 1984 by Fontana Paperbacks

Made and printed in Great Britain by
William Collins Sons & Co. Ltd, Glasgow

TO MALCOLM

PART ONE

CHAPTER ONE

You can't funk making decisions all your life and keep on getting away with it. No matter how fatalistic you are, how strong your belief in what will be will be, or won't, sooner or later you're going to be landed right in it.

I was furious. Damn Joe! Where the hell had he got to this time? And damn myself, too, for being fool enough to hang around waiting for him to come home. I glanced at my watch. I had about fifteen minutes to get to work, get my things together and get behind the microphone and by my normal driving standards I was still a good twenty minutes away. I changed down into third and shoved my foot hard to the floor. I cleared the lorry with a yard to spare, scaring myself witless in the process, and sped on towards Dringley as the night darkened around me.

True to form, somewhere on the road between home and 2D Radio, I underwent a sort of Jekyll and Hyde transformation. From being me I turned into the lady on the radio, though I was never sure which one was Jekyll and which was Hyde. By the time I was on the dual carriageway down the hill into the city it was complete – I'd forgotten Joe's absence and my anger as if they'd never been. And I'd forgotten me, too. For the next few hours I'd be the late night radio deejay, the warm voice on the airwaves comforting others through their night, helping some along with their fantasies as they looked at a grubby publicity photo of me with a potted biography, mostly lies, on the back. I'd give background music to soft lovers' murmurings or loud cries of passion, hate, fear, anger, boredom and sighs of apathy. I'd probably even accompany a suicide or an attempted one, the odd car crash with blood and twisted metal and the voice on the car radio still chattering over the shocked silence. My voice. It all happened out there while I was working and I never saw it, never met them, never got to know them, the ones who listened. But they thought they knew me. I was their property to be turned on or off at the touch of a button.

But it wasn't really *me*. The lady on the radio was smiling, confident, beautiful. She had everything she could wish for: fame, glamour, money, respect, any man she wanted. That lady got to meet famous people, interview them on her own ground, had hundreds of free LPs, tickets to McCartney concerts, and love letters from men she had never even met. That lady was envied. She'd made it.

But it had nothing to do with *me*. I was the one who'd sit in the soundproofed studio with a splitting headache feeling knackered. I was the one in faded jeans and an old T-shirt whose husband didn't understand her, so she'd turn the lighting right down low so Nigel on the switchboard through the double glass opposite couldn't see her red-rimmed eyes. I was the lady whose smile would automatically switch on with the movement of the microphone fader because smiling alters the mouth cavity so the voice comes out warmer. The smile would disappear as the fader slid shut. I was the one who'd sit there like an automaton operating the equipment, playing records, programming commercials, firing jingles, pressing buttons, cueing tapes, talking and smiling. Close the microphone, stop smiling now and wonder if Joe was home safe in bed yet, where he'd been, who he'd been with, and was he perhaps listening to me on some transistor radio in some room somewhere? Perhaps he'd be thinking proudly, 'that's my wife'. Or perhaps he'd turn me off.

I sometimes wondered if I should walk out and to hell with it all and so what if at the end of that record there'd be just a steady click click click of the stylus instead of another two hours' entertainment? Because if I did there'd be no magic to make a radio show, no stand-by presenter, no stand-by tape, only me in the whole hibernating building except for Nigel who answered the phones and relayed badly written messages to Sandra from Terry who said thank you for a *wonderful* evening, so the whole of Dringley and North Yorkshire thought they'd been screwing each other. Lucky Sandra and Terry, I'd think, as I interviewed some moronic rock star whose total vocabulary consisted of, 'Well (pause) er (pause) yeh man (silence)', and wishing, oh God wishing, I was home in bed with Joe. And I was the lady who still wouldn't have changed her job for the world if she could help it.

I loved it because at that time there were only about six other female radio deejays in the rest of the country so it felt like a fantastic achievement. And I hated it because it was the late night programme which meant, it being 'live', that I worked late nights.

Joe, on the other hand, rose early and worked through the day at the regional TV studios as script-editor of a soap opera, whilst writing in his spare time whatever other one-off things he could get commissioned for. He thought he was selling his artistic integrity down the drain by writing for money. I think he really would have been happy as a sand-boy if he could have starved in a dusty garret for the sake of his art. Foolish attitude. I liked my stomach well filled, so consequently I earned more than he did by producing and presenting my own nightly three-hour programme. We met up for a couple of hours in the evening, Joe exhausted at the end of his work, me on edge about to begin the main part of mine.

We soon began to begrudge each other the large portion of our selves that we gave to our careers so we made a pact that in our precious hours together each evening we'd try not to talk about work. It seemed like a good idea. In practice, communication ceased. Not that we really noticed most of the time. Except for times like tonight. The strain of our daily round of his work, my work, and hardly ever meeting each other in the middle even though we lived in the same house, was beginning to tell. More and more these days I found myself thinking that perhaps we should never have got married at all, we were so different. But you know what they say about opposites attracting . . .

Joe had gone to Westminster and up to Oxford to read Classics. I went to the local girls' grammar, secretarial college and Leeds University where I just scraped a degree in English Lit. Joe's family was very rich – father in politics, period country house and gardens with an 's'. I'd grown up in a semi with a front garden and a back yard. When he left Oxford Joe launched himself straight into the world of 'The Theatre' and lived with actors and writers and directors, and whatever you've heard about these arty types is all true. I was into a first marriage before I'd even graduated or had a job or lived away from my parents' home. I became a Drama Production Secretary (Radio) at a BBC northern outpost, had an affair with a bloke in the next office (which was the first time I discovered that sex could be fun), got divorced, screwed selectively and then met Joe. He had discovered sex at an early age (twelve, he said), liked it and screwed his way through life ever since with whomever, whenever and wherever he got the opportunity, which, him being an attractive sort of person when he wants to be, was quite often. We used to joke about my relative virginity but underneath the smile I strongly resented the sheer difference in numbers between people 'fucked' by Joe and people 'slept with' by Alison.

The other big difference between us was in our attitudes towards sexual fidelity. For Joe, having sex with somebody was 'just like shaking hands, only more fun', and if you wanted to do it you did it and it was nobody's business but yours. If I fancied somebody, Joe expected me to follow it through and insisted that he'd feel absolutely no degree of sexual jealousy at the thought of it. If I were to come home one night reeking of stale semen and covered in love-bites, his only concern would be that I'd enjoyed it. He said. So long as there is no *emotional* infidelity then do what, or rather who, you like. He certainly would if he wanted to and therefore I should if I wanted to. Emotional infidelity was the only sin in his book. It all sounds fine in theory. But then, so does communism.

My view was, and still is, that if you love somebody you don't leap into bed with somebody else. And if by chance you should fall from grace then you keep very quiet about it so's not to hurt. I believed him when he said he hadn't so far because he hadn't wanted to so far. But hot on the heels of such statements would always be the reminder that he would if he wanted to and it was really none of my business so long as his emotions, if not his cock, were pointed in my direction. Because I loved him and was terrified of losing him I tried to accept his point of view even if I couldn't agree with it. So I'd make a point of never asking him who he'd been with because that was his business, and if he wanted me to know then he'd volunteer the information. If he went into another room to make a phone call instead of doing it in front of me I'd never ask him who he was ringing. If he got a letter and didn't show it to me or say who it was from, I'd never ask. All this so he wouldn't think me jealous, possessive, clinging. It would never have occurred to him that I might simply be dying of *curiosity*. In consequence there was a lot about Joe that I didn't know, that he didn't share.

That's why him staying out without telling me had really got to me. Echoes of 'he would if he wanted to' came bouncing off the windscreen at me because it looked like, at last, he might just want to. Where the hell was he? And who was he with?

CHAPTER TWO

It isn't really surprising that Joe and I began to lose each other somewhere along the way. Or, to be more precise, that we were already well into the loss. It had been going on for months already without either of us allowing ourselves to notice it. To acknowledge it might mean that we'd already lost and I was far too afraid of the possible consequences to allow that. So instead of recognising it I compensated for it. By falling in love. Frequently.

I spent most of our marriage being in love with somebody or other (than Joe). But I was never in real love, and I knew it. That I suffered countless schoolgirl spasms of ecstasy over this man or that was irrelevant because Joe was the only one who really mattered to me. He was my core.

To use sixties jargon I had crushes on people. It was exactly the same feeling I'd had for Agnes Graham, the Head Girl at school when I was a twelve-year-old first-former; Cliff Richard, who stole my heart when I was thirteen; George Harrison when I was fifteen; and Kenny Higgins, who played the drums at the Locarno when I was fifteen and a half. And, just as with all those others, nothing ever came of my crushes. They lasted a couple of weeks or so and then they'd stop. It was all very anticlimactic because they never even had the integrity to stop with a drama, they just . . . stopped. Ceased to be there. I'd go to work one afternoon, see the object of my desires and think: oh, there's so-and-so, and the passion would expire, like a leaky balloon, with a damp fart. Until someone else came along.

They were fun, those little secret passions – and very little and very secret they were too. I'd go home, say not a word about it, and happily work out my lust upon my husband. That way my marriage got all the sparkle that a clandestine relationship gives, but none of the danger. That was until I met Joss Jordan.

Really. Joss Jordan. The name was genuine but it should have belonged to a comic-strip hero, or a forties film star, or a champion racing driver. Instead it belonged to Joss, newest recruit in the newsroom, trainee radio journalist, nineteen years old and reincarnation of my idea of what a Greek God *should* have looked like. I almost keeled over the first time I saw him, and again when I found out he was still a mere teenager. Nineteen, for God's sake! There was I, twenty-eight years old, married twice and almost old enough – if you *really* stretch a point – to be his mother. There was I, late night radio fantasy of thousands, lusting after a teenage cub reporter. Ridiculous. But very exciting.

One afternoon shortly after Joss had joined the staff I happened to be following him down the corridor from the tea-making machine, euphemistically referred to as the canteen, to the newsroom, when I was struck by the delectableness of his bottom.

I've never been surprised at the number of women who delight in a good male posterior, but continually surprised at the number of men, particularly in the north, who seem not to believe that women have such thoughts about the male form. In consequence, sadly, they do nothing to enhance the impression given by their own, usually beer-gutted and slack-arsed bodies, thinking that simply by virtue of their being the glorious male they need do nothing to make their appearance pleasing to the female. Joss, however, was not one of these.

He had a splendid rear end. And he knew it. And he knew how to make the most of it. It was small and round and neat and firm and clad in tight denim which never showed a ridge of underpants beneath. I found it most intriguing.

I did something then which I've only rarely done before and which has invariably got me into trouble. I gave in to an impulse. Approaching this for-all-practical-purposes stranger from behind, I stroked the relevant part of his anatomy and said, 'Lovely bottom you've got. Very nice.' And then I stroked it *again*.

Female chauvinism? Sexual harassment? Who cares? Joss didn't. He simply turned around and, looking into my face with an oh so serious expression on his, placed both hands on my somewhat more ample buttocks and stroked them ever so erotically. 'So've you,' he said. 'I'll show you mine if you'll show me yours.'

Call My Bluff. Now Get Out Of That. Well, I'd asked for it, I suppose. But what I hadn't expected to get was the jelly where my kneecaps used to be and the sudden surge of warmth at the crotch. We stood there in the middle of the corridor outside the record library, each with hands on the other's bottom, and both of us trying not to be the first to back down. I was the one who gave in and giggled. 'Nice idea,' I said, 'but not now, love, I'm far too busy.'

'When then?' he said, but I was already half-way along my strategic retreat to the presenters' room so I got away without having to answer.

After that I caught myself working out devious methods to meet him accidentally. My tea consumption rose dramatically because the hot water machine was situated along the corridor just past the open newsroom door. When I had a tape to edit it seemed easier to nip into the newsroom to see if any of their editing machines were free instead of going into Studio B, as had been my wont. I developed a habit of rising a bit earlier than usual and getting to work just before lunchtime so I could go up to the Admiral for a half of lager and a ham sandwich with the rest of the guys from work. There would be Joss, leaning on the bar with a pint of Guinness, his delectable behind clad as ever in tight denim or cord. I'd arrive and join the crowd, and somehow, I was never sure whether it was my engineering or his, Joss and I would end up sandwiched together in a corner.

Don't misunderstand me. I wasn't contemplating actually having an affair with the boy. No matter how steadfastly Joe put forth his liberated views on sexual fidelity I couldn't let myself accept their veracity. And neither was I prepared to rock the marital boat by putting them to the test. Not in actuality. But I could fantasise, couldn't I? And besides, Joss did my ego a power of good.

My husband, grabbing a handful of my flesh, would say, 'Why don't you go on a diet? You're getting fat.'

I'd reply, 'Yes I know, I'm sorry. I will, I will.'

Joss used to say, 'I love it when you wear those tight jeans, Alison. You've a fantastic figure. When are you going to let me see it properly?'

Joe, tugging a strand of my hair, would say, 'Did you know you're going grey? You'll be reaching for the Grecian 2000 before long.'

Me, flying to a mirror, 'Where? Liar. I'm not, am I?'

Joss used to say, 'Twenty-eight? I don't believe you. You're not a day over twenty.'

Joe would say, 'Who? What d'you mean, "Nigh-tch-ky"? I thought you went to university. It's pronounced Neet-sha, Neet-sha!'

I'd reply, 'How was I to know how to say it when I only ever saw it written down? It was a good guess.'

Joss used to say, 'You amaze me sometimes. You're so clever. How do you know so much about so much?'

I liked it when somebody liked me.

So Joss and I became workplace buddies. June had spreadeagled itself into a long, hot summer and lunchtimes became a glorious hour of sitting on the grass outside the pub with Joss and occasionally my friend Carol, who found herself at a loose end during the university summer recess, along with one or two variables from 2D Radio. We'd lean back on our elbows and watch the lorries rumble up the hill and the kids running about in the school playground over the road. I abandoned jeans and took to wearing loose, swishy skirts which I'd hitch up to bare my legs to the sun. The blokes would strip off their shirts and we'd all gleefully have contests over whose skin was the darkest shade of pale. I'd restrain myself from putting my hands on Joss's bare back – even when Carol wasn't present.

I drove on, grateful for the fact that when you work my kind of hours at least you miss out on rush hours and traffic jams. 'Unsocial' is the term used, and it's pretty accurate. My social life these days seemed to consist solely of those lunches at the Admiral.

This lunchtime it had been just me and Carol. No Joss. I was playing it very cool so she wouldn't notice that every time the pub door opened I glanced across to see if Joss would emerge.

Then she said, 'Joss's late today.'

'Is he? I hadn't noticed.'

'Come off it!' There was a pregnant pause. 'Ali,' she went on casually, 'say it's none of my business if you like, but . . . '

Oh-oh. The standard preface to sticking your nose in where it's not wanted. But I was curious. 'Go on. But what?'

'People are beginning to talk, you know.'

'Oh? What about?'

'You and Joss.'

'What?'

'People aren't blind, you know. I just thought you ought to know that – well, everybody knows.'

Innocently, 'Carol, what on earth are you going on about? And anyway, what "people"? Everybody knows what?'

'You don't need to play games with me, Ali,' she said. 'I know you too well.'

I doubted that. In my book we hardly knew each other at all really. But she was younger than me and very open and head-first about everything. That's why Joe and I liked her.

We'd met a few months ago when the university drama group had asked Joe to write a play for them. That made him Joe the Writer, not Joe the Hack, so he was predisposed to like the director, Simon, who was a lecturer at an affiliated college of education. His girlfriend, Carol, was a bright-eyed sociology undergraduate at the university proper, and was to take the leading role. The four of us had quickly become as firm friends as respective timetables and programme schedules would permit. Nonetheless, there were some things – like my feelings for Joss, for example – that I could hardly be expected to share with her.

I focused on a small black ant crawling over my index finger. I squashed it. I looked at Carol. She was studying me. I shrugged.

'I'll take your silence as an admission of guilt,' she went on.

'I admit nothing except ignorance,' I said. 'I'm not clear exactly what it is I'm being accused of.'

'Oh, come on!' She was losing patience. 'You and Joss. It's obvious. You two only have to *look* at each other.'

I used my matter-of-fact voice. 'So. I fancy him. So what? I fancy lots of people.' Why did it come out sounding defensive?

'Not the way it is between you two,' she said. 'Talk about lust? Christ, the air fairly bristles with it! You could practically reach out and touch it.'

I laughed. 'I wouldn't mind the chance!'

'Neither would I,' she said, 'but . . . ' She stopped in mid-flow. Then, 'You mean you *haven't* actually . . . er . . . ?'

'No!' I was still laughing. 'We haven't actually, er.'

'Oh.' She thought for a moment and then became rushingly earnest again. 'Then that's exactly what I mean! For Christ's sake, why don't you just screw each other and have done?'

'What?'

'You heard. Get on with it and get him out of your system.'

'Carol, I'm shocked at you.' I was, too, because I regarded her as belonging firmly to my 'I'm Mrs Joe' persona. Yet here she was, leaping across from being 'our' friend to being 'my' confidante, encouraging me to infidelity. It was uncomfortable. I reminded her that I was married, that I happened to love my husband, and that Joss was a mere nineteen-year-old boy. 'What do you take me for?' I ended, feeling more and more like the Player Queen.

'What's any of that got to do with it?' she asked. 'Look Ali, it's like there's a piece of elastic between the two of you and it's stretched and stretched and if you don't watch out it's going to snap and ping you one right in the eyeball. So why don't you just . . . well, take the pressure off it? I would. He's gorgeous.'

'Yes, he is, but that's beside the point. There's a hell of a difference between a harmless flirtation and a full-bodied affair. Excuse my pun.' God, I was sounding older and more housewifely by the second.

'But it's not just a harmless flirtation, is it?' she said, worrying at it, terrier-like. 'And it's not fair on Joss, either. The poor lad's in it up to here,' she said, indicating somewhere about two feet above her head. 'You wouldn't notice of course . . . ' she said, 'but it's the way he watches you when you're not looking.'

I sat in silence pulling at bits of grass so she could go on and tell me more about the way he looks at me when I'm not looking. Please.

She gave an exasperated little cough. 'It's not fair on him because he's in love with you and you're wearing it like some kind of medal! So why don't you just go ahead and put him out of his misery? Joe wouldn't mind,' she added.

Ouch. How did she know? The trouble was, she was right. So why didn't I just go ahead? I took a drink and then leaned back on my elbows putting my face into the sun. I closed my eyes and tried to set out my feelings in a mental list.

One: because I love Joe. Real love. He's the one, he's the centre, if I had to choose, I'd choose Joe, no hesitation.

Two: I don't half fancy young Joss, though. Oh, to have my way with his perfect young body! Unfulfilled lust is unhealthy, ergo screwing Joss would be therapeutic. Medicinal. And for Joss too – let's not be selfish or one-sided about this. One good session to get it out of our systems and then that'd be the end of it.

Three: since I've been married to Joe I've not had anybody else. I *couldn't* with anybody else. I mean, if you love somebody, you just don't do it. And I love Joe. So I won't do it.

Four: but Joe says it's all right to do it with whoever you want so long as your emotions remain faithful. Therefore if me and Joss made love together I wouldn't be being unfaithful because I still love Joe, put him first in my life.

Four. No, five: those are Joe's terms, damn it, not mine! What about integrity? Honesty? Dignity? What about being faithful to *my* principles?

Six: (so change your principles, Alison.) But that one stayed in brackets. I pretended I hadn't thought it.

‘Come on,’ I said after a long silence. I opened my eyes again and sat up straight. ‘Time I got back to work.’

We took our empty glasses back inside the pub and left . . . at the very moment Joss walked in.

‘Oh, just off, Alison?’ he said as if Carol weren’t even there.

My ego allowed itself a little preen. I desperately wanted to hug him. But, resolute, I waved him goodbye and set off down the hill to work, silently talking myself into doing without my daily lunchtime fix of Joss Jordan.

I was really proud of myself all afternoon. I didn’t make one mug of tea. My only trip to the loo was a real demonstration of will because my head didn’t even twitch as I passed the newsroom door. I got through my work quickly, and as the ‘live’ studio guest for that night was already on tape, all I had to do was check the duration and in and out cues, and I was away off home by half past three. I called in at the village butcher on the way, shoved a rather exotic casserole into the oven for Joe’s later delight, had a bath, washed my hair, and prepared to seduce him on the carpet as soon as he got back.

But Joe hadn’t come back. At least, not before I had to set off for work again, leaving a brown and sorry ex-casserole congealing in the fridge.

CHAPTER THREE

I drove the rest of the way like a lunatic, determined not to be late but not looking forward to the hours ahead. The mood I was in it looked like it was going to be a bad night. It wasn't fair. The least Joe could have done was let me know he'd be late. All my delicious plans for a cosy evening *à deux* ruined. And after I'd denied myself a lunchtime's flirting with Joss, too.

I unlocked the door and let myself into the radio station. It was practically deserted. It had an atmosphere all of its own at that time of night with the daylight gone and the striplights quietly humming. The offices were empty and littered with the fag ends of a busy day which the cleaners would get rid of early in the morning. It was all a bit desolate and was a perfect match for my feelings.

'That you, Alison?' called Nigel from down the corridor.

'Yes.' I went into the presenters' room and dumped my box of records, took off my coat.

'You're cutting it a bit fine aren't you?' he said, appearing in the doorway.

'Yes,' I said curtly. Then added contritely, 'Sorry, Nigel.' After all, it wasn't his fault.

'By the way,' he said. 'Joe rang – said he's going to be late home and not to worry. He got held up with the drama group.'

That bloody play of his! *Now* he tells me. He could at least have timed it so's to tell me in person. I sighed. 'Who's on late news?' I asked. 'Has he arrived yet?'

'Yes. Joss.'

I felt as though I'd been thumped in the solar plexus. Then I told myself: so it's Joss. So what?

'Can I ask a favour, Alison?' said Nigel. 'Would you mind if I left early? Irene's got 'flu and Joss says he doesn't mind staying behind until closedown.'

'Oh.'

'If that's all right with you I'll go after the phone-in. I'll make sure you've got plenty of deddies to see you through before I close the switchboard.'

'Yes. Yes, 'course it's okay, love, you get off back to Irene. Sure that's all right with Joss, though? Him hanging around all that time?' It was a regulation. No one was supposed to be alone in the building working electrical equipment. And the management said they were happier if someone else was around to offset the chance of their only female star being molested or raped when she went out into the backstreets in the early hours. Not that Nigel would have been much protection. But it was a gesture. And about the only gentlemanly thing they ever did.

'Yes. He's got a lot of stuff to get ready for tomorrow's early shift so it's no bother.'

'Right then,' and I added as an afterthought, 'Sorry about Irene. Give her my best.'

Nigel is going home early. Joss is staying behind. This will be a building with just me and Joss in it, I thought. So up yours, Joe.

I looked at the clock. Four minutes to go. 'Better make a start I suppose.' My programme began at ten o'clock. Precisely. At ten-thirty whoever was on the late news shift would come into the studio, sit on the other side of the desk facing me and read a five-minute summary of the day's local news. Tonight it would be Joss facing me. And then he wouldn't be going straight home.

I picked up a pile of LPs and letters and checked that I'd got the right guest tape. I walked quickly along the corridor and caught a glimpse of Joss typing frantically in the newsroom, scowling beautifully in concentration. I struggled through the two sets of double soundproofed doors to the studio area. They were about three inches thick and might have been filled with concrete, I was always suffering sprained wrists from pushing and pulling at them. The red light outside the studio itself wasn't lit so I could go straight in without having to tiptoe or whisper. Ahmed, the Asian presenter who did the programme before mine, looked up as I entered and beamed at me. He was small and dumpling plump, and always smiling. 'This one is going to be my last record,' he said. 'Is it going to be long enough before the Independent Radio News?'

IRN comes up the line on the second. Usually. I had to press the buttons and slide the faders while Ahmed cleared his stuff from the studio and got the hell out during the news, to leave me in sole occupation by the time the three-minute summary had ended. It was known as a hot-seat changeover. I glanced at the clock. It was 2159.07. I checked the record on the turntable. There was a good half-inch left to play. 'Yes,' I said, 'should do it fine.' And anyway, if it looked like running out before it was supposed to I could always bang in a jingle. 'Said your goodbyes?' I asked.

'Oh, yes yes. I have done that before this record.'

'Right, love, I'll take over now then, shall I?'

Ahmed stood up and handed over the headphones. They smelled of Brylcreme and felt a bit greasy. I put them on and sat while he busied about putting commercials back into the carousel rack and picking up records and squiggled-on pieces of paper which he always dropped on the floor instead of into the bin when he'd done with them. I chose my first record and quickly cued it up ready to come in with it as soon as I heard the out-cue from IRN. My eyes darted between the second hand on the clock and the stylus of Ahmed's record. Yes. It would just last out the time nicely. I watched the second hand, the red one, fingers ready to fade out the record, other hand poised over the button to fire the news jingle and then dart to another fader to bring in the voice of the London-based newsreader. Ten seconds to ten, started to fade music. Five seconds to, fired jingle, lost the music and switched cans over to pre-fade with speakers on output so I could hear what was going on at the other end of the line as well as the stuff that we were transmitting. On the dot, flicked open the IRN fader, one second past, newsreader began on cue, switched cans back to output and we were all systems go.

I always allowed myself a sigh of relief at that point. It was now all mine. Nigel held the doors open for Ahmed and then, bless him, brought in the first of many mugs of tea. He left well before my first link and half a minute later appeared behind the double glass window into the room known as Master Control, which housed, as well as a multitude of equipment that I didn't understand, the phone-in switchboard. He opened up the lines and gave a thumbs-up sign and I could see the little flashing lights reflected in his spectacles. The messages began to roll in and Nigel scribbled them down to bring them through in batches as the programme went on.

The first half-hour flew by. Commercials, jingles, records, dedications, talk a bit and hardly have time to sit down until the local news summary. Certainly no time to concern myself over Joe's behaviour or Joss's staying till closedown. The programme always comes first.

I had my head buried behind the controls, cueing up a record, cans on, deaf to any other sound when I looked up and Joss was sitting there opposite me, obliterating Nigel from view. Obliterating anything from view. All I saw was Joss's face. His mouth moved.

'What?' I said, slipping headphones back off one ear.

'I said watch the clock! Ten seconds!'

'Shit.' I shoved the news ident jingle into the cart machine, faded the record, opened the mic and said a few words, fired the jingle, opened Joss's microphone while closing mine, and he started to read the news. He wasn't very good, a bit fluffy, but he still suffered from nerves. He'd get better. As quietly and as quickly as I could during the first story I pushed the cartridges he'd brought with him into an empty triple-stack. I heard him say ' . . . Fiona Cooke reports,' and he pointed at me. I automatically pushed the right button and opened the right fader and Fiona Cooke reported. I closed Joss's mic and said, 'Jesus, that was close. Sorry,' wiping imaginary sweat from my forehead.

He cleared his throat loudly, twice, and said, 'Coming up.'

I listened for the out-cue on Fiona's cart. It came up. I opened Joss's mic and off we went again.

I was a bit thrown by all this and felt bad about it. I shouldn't have got caught out like that, I should have been ready. If the news had been messed up it would have been my fault. Unprofessional. So much for the programme always coming first. It was worrying that Joss should have such an effect on me.

But the rest of the show went without a hitch. I brought in the next IRN summary exactly on the second, the recorded interview sounded as if it was happening right then and there in the studio, none of the records stuck half way through, and the quiz contestant was bright and amusing but didn't win. That meant I wouldn't have to bother scrounging around the management for a decent prize, parcelling it up and sending it off.

As soon as I was into the first disc after the phone-in Nigel came in to say goodnight and deliver the last small pile of torn-off scraps of paper bearing messages to be relayed across Dringley and district. 'I'll tell Joss I'm off then, on my way out.'

'Okay. And thanks a lot, Nigel.'

'See you tomorrow,' and he left, closing the door just before I opened the microphone to smile the next bit of late night chatter at the unseen thousands. I was beginning to feel tired. It was approaching half-past midnight. I put on a good long album track, six or seven minutes' worth, and sat back to enjoy it, cans off, speakers up good and loud. The door opened, I looked round, and Joss walked in. My tummy did a cartwheel.

'Nigel's gone. Everything okay?' he said, moving to stand behind my chair.

'Fine.'

'You went home early this afternoon.' He started to massage my neck and shoulders, oh so gently, through my T-shirt.

'Did I?' I squeaked.

'Relax, or this won't do any good. Relax, woman.' His fingers moved to a patch of bare neck under my hair and my muscles tensed involuntarily. 'That's better,' he said. 'Long track?'

'About another four or five minutes.'

'Lean back then.'

I slithered down into the chair. The back of my head rested on Joss's tummy. Hard, firm tummy. He started stroking my forehead.

'Close your eyes,' he said. 'I'll watch the clock for you.'

So I closed my eyes and concentrated on the feel of his fingers on my face. Long sweeping caresses over forehead, on cheeks, under chin, over throat. Bliss. The whole of my head became an erogenous zone. He could have made a living at it. 'Better check your record now,' he said and took away his magician fingers.

I felt bereft. I looked at the stylus. It was getting very close to the end of the track. Just enough time to whip off the single I had ready on the other turntable and substitute an LP. I opened the microphone and leaned into it saying softly that now, as a special treat, we were going to have a three-in-a-row golden goody from the Moody Blues. I sneaked the music under as I was talking, then closed the fader and sank back into the glories of *Nights in White Satin*. Joss resumed his caresses. The whole of side one was segued and I allowed the music to play on and on. It would last nicely through to goodnights and closedown and I was very sorry that there were some dedications I hadn't managed to squeeze in but, you see, there was this beautiful young man standing behind me who was just starting to stroke my neck again and I would have found it very dif . . . difficult . . . to talk . . . coh . . . coherently.

Joss had mesmeric fingers. They traced delicate patterns over my face, my eyelids, my lips. I kissed them spontaneously, my eyes still closed, and listened appreciatively to Joss quietly singing along in perfect harmony with Justin Hayward. Joss had a good voice. I opened my eyes and told him so. It broke the spell. His fingers left my face and he came from round the back to crouch beside my chair. 'They're good, the Moodies,' he said.

'Yes. They don't make 'em like that anymore.' My voice was fighting the session musicians as they worked up to a glorious orchestral climax from the stereo speakers on either side of us. It was like having our heads together in the middle of a musical orgasm.

Joss didn't say anything. And I didn't really want to launch into a discussion on different eras of rock music – not when he was there beside me looking unflinchingly into my eyes. I met his gaze. Then he took a strand of my hair and kissed it. I wasn't sure I was really there, that this was happening. The spell had reasserted itself, it was like a Dali dream. My hand went out and stroked his hair. At last, the first time I'd ever allowed myself to touch it. Soft. He closed his eyes and moved in closer, leaning his face against my breasts. I held his head there, not daring to move, hardly breathing, thinking: he must be able to hear my heart thumping.

'I can hear your heart beating,' he muttered into my left nipple.

Oh. Ooh. 'Can you?'

'Mm. Why's it thumping so hard?'

'Stupid,' I said. I held his head away from me and looked straight into his eyes. 'Why d'you think?' And then I kissed him, ever so chastely, on the mouth. That wouldn't have been so bad except that I did it again. And again. And Joss kissed me back, not quite so chastely. His tongue parted my lips and mine met it. We stayed like that for ages, just kissing, until eventually I pulled away. We were well into the third track and the hands on the clock were very close to one a.m. The radio programme was about to take me over again, and I had to let it.

'Don't,' said Joss as I moved. 'Don't go away from me. Please. I l . . . '

I put a finger across his lips. 'Sssh. No words, Joss.' I ran the finger softly across his cheek. Then I turned back to the desk, set everything for the closing sig and the last news, put my cans back on and tried to say goodnight properly while Joss naughtily started to play with my throat and I ached for his fingers to roam lower.

The news finished. I fired the closedown jingle, shut all the faders and switched off the machines. I bounced up from the chair not knowing quite how to cope with the changed relationship. How to get out of the building with my principles intact when all I really wanted was for Joss to make love to me then and there on the studio floor?

I became bright and breezy and businesslike. Joss carried a pile of records back to the office for me and turned off the lights along the corridor behind us.

'That's it then,' I said chirpily, 'another one finished.'

He didn't speak, just came closer and helped me on with my coat. His fingers briefly brushed against my neck. It was like an electric shock. We walked towards the door, both of us intensely aware of the space between us and the silence in the air.

'See you tomorrow then?' he asked.

'Yes.'

'Lunchtime? Admiral?'

'Yes,' I said after a slight pause in which my few remaining good resolutions vanished. 'Yes, I'll be in at lunchtime.'

'Good,' he said.

I set the burglar alarm then we went outside together into the dark, sleeping backstreets of Dringley city centre. I locked the door behind us and walked to my car. I was starting to get in when Joss took hold of my shoulder from behind. I turned to face him. 'Goodnight then,' I said.

He let go. 'Goodnight.' He said it quietly and looked down at the pavement.

I was struck by how terribly young and vulnerable he suddenly seemed. I wanted to take him in my arms and rock him. But I knew that if I touched him now I wouldn't go home. The keys to that empty building were burning in my pocket. Quickly, I got into the car, started the engine and waved as I drove off along the street. I looked in the rear-view mirror to see him still standing where I'd left him, making no move. I turned the corner and sped furiously up the hill.

I didn't really think about much on the way home. The car knew its own way and I drove back on automatic pilot finding, when I arrived, that I hadn't remembered anything about the journey at all. It was quite worrying.

I registered the fact that Joe's motorbike was parked outside and the house was dark behind drawn curtains. He'd finally come home then, and hadn't bothered to wait up for me. I went inside and quietly up the stairs, undressed and got into bed. Joe changed position but didn't wake up.

'Joe,' I said softly, touching his shoulder. 'Joe, I love you.' I wasn't sure why I felt the need to say it – to reassure him or myself, or to make him feel guilty, or to ease my own burgeoning feelings of guilt? Whatever the motives, I said it again, 'I love you, I really do.'

He turned towards me and sleepily murmured, 'of course you do,' then he put his arm around me, cuddled me into him and started snoring.

That did it. I resented the fact that he could drop straight off to sleep again when I was on the brink of an emotional crisis and it was all his fault. After all, if Joe had come home when he should have done I'd have given young Joss short shrift. Wouldn't I?

I nudged him. 'So what happened to you this evening, then?' I asked. 'Why did you stand me up?'

No response.

'Damn it, wake up!' I said, shaking his shoulder.

'What the hell . . . ? What's the matter? Let me get some sleep, will you? Some of us have to get up for work in the morning.'

'Fine. And what do you suppose I've been doing all night, while you've been out God knows where?'

'Not a lot if your last half-hour was anything to go by. Call that working for a living, end-to-end Moody Blues? Great radio show, Alison,' he said, voice dripping sarcasm.

'Don't you criticise my work,' I said. 'Fat lot you know about it. You stick to your job and I'll stick to mine. And stop evading the issue.'

'What issue?'

'Where were you tonight? I waited and waited and I'd cooked a special meal for us and it was ruined and you could at least have phoned to let me know where you were or that you'd be late . . . ' It all came rushing out of me.

Joe sat up in bed and yanked on the light cord. 'Jesus! What is this, some kind of inquisition? I left a message at 2D, didn't I?'

'It was a bit late by then, wasn't it?'

'Look. Just because I married you doesn't mean you own me. I'll do as I damn well please.' He thumped his pillow and flung himself down on to it, back towards me, rigid.

'Joe?' I put my hand on his shoulder. He shrugged it away. 'Come on, Joe, don't be like that. I'm sorry.' Why is it that when Joe is quite blatantly in the wrong, *I*'m the one who feels guilty and apologises? Still no response. 'Oh, all right, be like that. Sulk if you must,' I said and switched off the light. I burrowed down under the duvet and turned my back to his. I didn't get to sleep for hours.

The situation with Joe was precarious enough without me complicating it any further, so after that white satin night in the studio I held back from Joss.

It got more and more difficult. But I kept on saying no and kicking myself as I said it. I used all the old arguments about how it would be a good thing to just do it and get it over with, get him out of my system, and how going on like this – wanting to but not doing – couldn't possibly be good for me. Or for him, or even Joe for that matter. But the longer I held off, the more he needled into my mind, became a part of me. And now that the physical barrier had already been crossed there seemed no valid reason to say no to more kisses and hugs and strokes. And Joss took to working the late shift regularly.

Nigel never said much about it. I don't know if he was being tactful or merely naive, but he'd use Joss's willing presence as an excuse for going home early whenever he could. Neither Joss nor I complained. We didn't even try to avoid the gossip because everybody was convinced that he and I were at it like rabbits anyway, any time and any place that we could. Knowing looks abounded. Everybody thought we were, so why not have the fun as well as the reputation, I kept asking myself? And Carol.

'Quite,' she said. 'Go on. If you can't leave off him, then for heaven's sake stop agonising and just do it. Joe'll never know. And if he did he wouldn't care, so what's the problem?'

I thought: thanks for nothing, friend.

Even though she was probably right I stuck at it. In the middle of a late night clinch I'd say, 'No, Joss, no we mustn't.' 'Please (sigh) don't.' 'Joss, no, I'm married and I'm *not* going to be unfaithful to Joe.' And so on. If you can say one thing for Joss it's that he was persistent. His sheer devotion to the cause was extremely flattering. And he kept saying that he loved me which is a powerful aphrodisiac. I'm amazed that I resisted for so long. He began to do little things for me to make my work easier. He'd do silly, romantic things like slipping a note saying 'I love you' in amongst the dedications. I loved it! I loved Joe. I loved, in a different way, Joss. But I still couldn't let go. Something inside me said, 'if you do then Joe will start screwing around too. He might not find out about you and Joss but he'll start screwing, just you see.' Like not stepping on the cracks in the pavement when you were a kid – 'if I step on that crack, mother will die.'

My annual holiday was due in the first two weeks of September. It had been organised for months, programme schedules carefully planned, stand-ins booked, no alterations allowed unless for life and death emergencies.

June: 'Where would you like to go for our holidays this year, Joe?'

'Oh, God knows. Plenty time yet. No hassle.'

July: 'How d'you fancy camping in southern Ireland, Joe?'

'Maybe. We'll see. When did you say your two weeks are?'

August: 'We really ought to think about our holidays. My leave is only a month away.'

'Is it really? First fortnight in September? I can't take time off then, lovey. Impossible. Why didn't you give me more notice? Can't you change it?'

'You know I can't. And I've been telling you for months.'

'You'll have to go by yourself then if you want to go away. Sorry,' he said.

The problem was that damned play he was writing for the drama group. He was obsessed with it – and them. The first draft was almost finished and he couldn't possibly leave it now. Half of me understood, sympathised and supported him, the other half pleaded and argued that a break would do him the world of good. But Joe was adamant and I was faced with the prospect of two weeks' holiday on my own. He urged me to go away somewhere, not spend the time in

Dringley just because he was there. He wouldn't have much time for me anyway, what with working during the day and writing or meeting the group in the evenings. It was his way of telling me I'd only be in the way.

I thought, hell, why not? and reached a compromise with myself – a week at home so Joe and I would at least be able to share a bed for the same eight hours each night, and then a week away somewhere by myself. I rang a travel agent and asked for any cancellations. I was offered Greece.

Athens and the Acropolis. Sunshine and souvlakia. I booked, feeling slightly apprehensive because I'd never been away by myself before, and Joe said 'well done' and that I'd cope perfectly well on my own. I began to really look forward to it. I did need the break. I felt physically exhausted and emotionally drained by the end of that summer, and, Garboesque, I wanted time to be alone. To be away from Joss, Joe, everything. I needed sunshine and somewhere to lie around, not thinking, and sweat. Time to take stock.

CHAPTER FOUR

I spent the first week's leave packing and re-packing, making lists of things I'd need, watching TV alone in the evenings while the typewriter clacked away upstairs, making love with Joe at night, and driving into Dringley to the Admiral at lunchtimes. Joss was always there. I talked about the forthcoming trip and he looked on enviously. We said goodbye the day before I was due to go. We were both feeling just a tiny bit wistful. 'What train are you catching?' he asked.

'Two-fifteen. The fast one.'

'I'll be thinking of you. Will you think of me?'

'A bit. Probably.'

'I'll miss you, Alison.'

Sweet, I thought, and we indulged in a parting squeeze of hands and a touch of footsy under the pub table.

But on the drive back home that afternoon I felt relieved. A week away from it all was bound to get him out of my system. I'd come back and my tummy would stay put instead of cartwheeling at the sight of him, and I'd no longer look forward to each day just because it contained a tiny fragment that had Joss in it. I'd no longer make passionate love to Joe while wondering what it would be like if he were Joss.

Joe drove me to the railway station the next afternoon. I'd stay the night with my old friend, Sally, before catching the morning flight. I was a bit tearful when I left Joe sitting in the car outside the station. He didn't believe in platform farewells. 'Will you miss me a bit?' I asked.

''Course not.'

'I'm going to miss *you*, Joe.'

'Don't be silly. You'll have a wonderful time. Do what you like and enjoy yourself. I shall.' That's my Joe. He gets so sentimental at partings.

I trudged along the platform, casing the train until I

found a second-class smoking compartment with only three or four passengers in it. Then I climbed aboard, sagged into a seat leaving my suitcase in the aisle, and looked out of the window. It was open at the top and a waft of station smells came in, diesel oil and dust. I closed it. I was feeling dejected and just a little apprehensive. Incongruous for someone about to set off on holiday. But I was already missing my husband, worrying about just *how* good a time he was going to have without me, and confused about the Joss non-affair. It was going to be a week's therapy rather than a week's holiday and I wasn't filled with excitement at the prospect.

There was one bright star on the horizon, though, and that was the thought of seeing Sally in a few hours. Dear Sally. I'd known her since schooldays and we'd seen each other through every female crisis from first tampons, through first loves, and into swilling down our first contraceptive pills together with a bottle of champagne. Sally was the one who'd supported me through my brief first marriage, who'd listened and said 'there, there' when necessary, who'd helped me to find out for myself the wrongness of it, and given me the courage to leave it when I had to. I'd only seen her twice since she'd moved down to London but though we rarely wrote each other letters or even spoke on the phone it didn't make any difference. We both knew that the other would come running if there was any need. Special friends. Yes, I was definitely looking forward to seeing Sally and to an all-night session of girl-talk. I wondered what she'd make of Joss/Joe, yes/no.

I took *Pride and Prejudice* out of my handbag and settled back into my seat listening to the solid 'thunk' of doors being closed along the length of the train. Just as the whistle blew I caught a glimpse of a figure belting past the window. The train jerked forward and stopped again. A door opened then slammed and the train shuddered into motion once more. I shook my head over that tardy passenger and couldn't help feeling a little bit smug about my habit of always getting to wherever I'm supposed to be on time, whatever the problems involved.

I opened the book and sank with pleasure into Miss

Austen's description of the Bennet family, feeling relieved that no one had come to sit by, or opposite me. I wanted no distraction, no discomfort. From here until we pulled into King's Cross I wanted to be alone inside my head so I could concentrate on imagining myself as the delightfully sensible Elizabeth Bennet. *She'd* have had no truck with a nineteen-year-old cub reporter, no matter how attractive.

Plunged into this flight of self-indulgence, my mind barely registered the carriage door sliding open and shut. But it became more aware and sank as a shadow fell across the pages and my suitcase was heaved up on to the rack.

'If this is yours, it's in the way,' said a grumpy and breathless voice as its owner flumped down next to me making me bounce in my seat. I shifted myself closer to the window, prepared a suitable scowl and then glared at the intruder.

He was grinning from ear to ear. 'Hello,' he said brightly. 'It's me! Nearly missed it.'

Stunned silence.

'Aren't you talking to me then?'

I managed, 'Hello.'

'Buffet car open yet? I've a hell of a thirst.'

'What are *you* doing here?'

'Same as you, I should think. Going to London. Gracious me, what a coincidence!'

I ignored his theatrical attempt at humour. 'Why?' I asked bluntly.

'No law against it, is there?'

'No.'

He touched my hand, then took it in his, kissed it, squeezed it and gave it back.

'Joss, come *on*,' I said, totally befuddled, 'what are you *doing* here, why aren't you at work?'

'I've told you. I'm coming with you.'

'You're mad!'

'Quite possibly.'

'This has to be a bad dream.'

'Aw, don't be like that. I love you,' and he shut me up with a kiss.

I pushed him off. 'Oh, Joss, you're crazy!'

'Yup.'

'You really can't do this.'

'I'm doing it.'

'No!' I said with as much firmness as I could muster.

'Okay.'

That pulled me up short. 'Pardon?'

'I said "okay". I'll get off then,' and he stood up and made for the door, hanging on to the seat backs.

'Fine,' I said. ''Bye then.' And I turned back to my book.

'I mean it,' he said from the end of the carriage. 'I'll get off *now*.' We were swaying along at who knows how many miles an hour. 'I love you, Alison,' he said far too loudly in a matter-of-fact voice, 'and if you don't want me I'll throw myself off this train. This minute.' Of course he didn't mean it. He was smiling. But the few other occupants of the carriage had overcome their British reserve and were staring at us openly. Tomato-faced and squirming with embarrassment I got up and quickly followed him. He'd gone through to the connecting passageway and had his hand on the outside-door handle. 'Well?' he said.

'You're being silly now,' I responded, sounding like a nanny. I put my hand over his, knowing that he wouldn't *really* open the door, but I wanted to be on the safe side – *I* didn't want to fall out. 'And anyway, I give in.'

'You do?' His hand tightened over the handle and he looked at me suspiciously. 'Honest injun?'

I sighed. 'Yes all right, honest injun. Now come and sit down.'

He let go, and keeping a firm hold of his hand I led him back to our seat, steadfastly ignoring the other passengers.

'Do you have to be so embarrassing?' I asked.

'It worked though, didn't it?' he said grinning. It was an infuriating smile. So damned sexy.

We sat for a few minutes not talking to each other, Joss no doubt happy in his little victory, me trying to get the situation sorted out in my head, Elizabeth Bennet long since abandoned. There was I, fleeing on a train from Joe, Dringley and Joss, and there was Joss, following me relentlessly. I was horrified by it, I loved it, I was outraged,

I was immensely flattered, I was insulted, and I was joyous. I burst out laughing. 'You're mad!'

'I think you've already said that.'

'Probably. So . . . what am I going to do with you?'

'Take me to bed without any supper?'

Had he any idea how very tempting that was? With great effort of will I replied, 'Certainly not. Look, the buffet car should be open.' I took out my purse and gave him a pound. 'Here, go and cool off and fetch me a cup of tea, will you?'

He took the money and I watched him until he was out of sight then I thought of gathering my things together and hiding. Instead I turned to gaze out of the window at the sunny September countryside flashing past. Me and Joss? If I wanted to, it would be so easy now. But no, this latest escapade of his, flattering and giddy and delicious as it was, only strengthened my resolve. It was at best inconvenient and at worse, if not worst, it was blocking my escape route. He was robbing me of the space I needed, forcing me into accepting a *fait accompli*. Oh, how lovely it would have been not to have had to decide at all, just to carry on dipping into, tasting, the excitement of him whenever I wanted to without it intruding on the rest off my life. And here he was, insufferable and irresistible as ever, intruding with a vengeance. I'd been waiting for some sort of catalyst to make me decide one way or the other, but I never expected that the catalyst would be Joss himself.

Decision time. I spread the remaining options over the speeding landscape. I could climb inside a rainbowed bubble with Joss, suspended somewhere above the rest of the world, my marriage, the radio station, everyone I knew. I could cut myself off from everything that might bring on an attack of guilt and then launch into an outrageous affair. I could revel in it. Pretend I was someone else. Oh, it was tempting.

Could I say all that, even consider all that, and still say in all honesty that I loved my husband, that he was my centre, what mattered? Yes. But I couldn't *do* it. Joe was the foundation of my life and I was tied there. And I needed that base too much to risk it.

There was the difference. I needed Joe, the security that

just being married to him gave me. Joss gave me fantasies and excitement and an ego-tripping adoration. And I loved him for it. But I didn't need him. I had to choose Joe and, with all its headaches, reality.

Joss returned with a tea, a lager and a ham sandwich, and settled in next to me again, our thighs touching. I took the plastic lid off my cup and sipped at the scalding liquid. The train lurched and some of the tea slurped hotly on to my hand. I put the lid back on and wiped my hand on my jeans. Then Joss took it and without saying anything kissed it better and held on to it. It was just a gesture. But Joe wouldn't have made it. Then again, I reminded myself, neither would Joe have put me in this position in the first place. He was as considerate of my personal space as he was jealous of his own. Resent it as I might, he was only giving me what I'd wanted all my life – total freedom. It wasn't Joe's fault I was having difficulty coping with it.

So many contradictory thoughts and feelings were going through my mind as the train hurtled its prisoners south. Joss was still holding my hand and his touch still affected me like a match to a sparkler. It had to stop.

The train stopped. Doncaster. 'Joss, don't you think you should get off here?' I suggested.

'No,' he replied. 'You're stuck with me. All the way.'

'Okay, so then what?' I said, not bothering to hide my exasperation, but dropping my voice to a stage whisper. 'You know bloody well I'm not going to bed with you. I've told you often enough . . .'

'I'm patient and I'm stubborn and I can live in hope. One day you'll give in,' he said, and started to nibble my ear, ' . . . if only to get rid of me!'

Ooh, it was nice. 'Stop it,' I said. More passengers were getting on and our compartment was filling up. 'Be sensible and go home.' It was the last reasonable chance. The next stop wasn't until Peterborough.

'No.'

I turned away from him and finished my tea while the train was stationary. It had cooled off a bit. It was about the only thing that had. 'Look,' I said as we moved off again, 'I don't know why you're bothering. It's not even as if I'm free tonight.'

'Oh yes, that friend of yours.'

'Sally. And tomorrow I'm off to Athens. You weren't thinking of following me there as well were you?'

'Yes. But I didn't have the money.'

'Thank the Lord for small mercies,' I said grimly. 'At least I won't be stuck with you.'

He looked away when I said that, past me and out of the window. 'Do you enjoy hurting me?' he said quietly, the jokiness all gone. He meant it. I *had* hurt him.

'Oh, baby, I'm sorry,' I said, turning to put my arms around him. I stroked his hair. 'Poor Joss. It's a mess, isn't it?' He just nodded. 'That's why we mustn't see each other anymore,' I continued. 'It's got to end.'

'It doesn't have to,' he said. 'If only you . . . '

I let go of him. 'Yes. Well, life's full of "if only's". I guess we've just added another to the list.'

We lapsed into a silence which must have lasted for a good fifty miles.

We were approaching Peterborough when he said, quite brightly, 'All right, how do you fancy a night on the town and then I'll get the last train back up north tonight?'

'And what about Sally?'

'Ring her from the station and tell her you'll be a bit late, that's all.'

'I can't just do that!'

'Why not?'

'All sorts of reasons. I don't cancel out on my commitments, for one thing. She's expecting me, she'll have made plans, I've been looking forward to seeing her . . . '

'But you still would,' he said. 'A bit later on, that's all.' He put the back of his hand against my cheek and gave me a look that would have melted a polar icecap. 'Please. All I'm asking for is a few more *hours*, Alison. Then I'll go. For good, if that's what you really want,' he added quietly.

I put my hand on his and pressed it against my face. 'Dear Joss,' I said and closed my eyes because I didn't want him to see how close, suddenly, I was to crying. Who for? Him, me, us? No, for Abelard and Héloïse, Heathcliffe and

Cathy, Romeo and Juliet, any other damned pair of star-crossed lovers. But not us. We hadn't been star-crossed, we'd just been stupid. Shouldn't have let it happen in the first place. I opened up again. 'Okay. You've got this evening. Then it's the last train back, you promise?'

'Promise.'

'And you won't give me any more hassle?'

'Can't promise.'

I gave him a look.

'But I'll try,' he smiled.

When we got to King's Cross I left him to look after my suitcase and find out about train times back to Dringley while I waited for an empty telephone bubble. When I got my turn at a phone I explained what had happened as briefly as I could, aware of the other people waiting their turn and spicing up the boredom with a dash of eavesdropping. I needn't have worried about Sally's reaction. 'God, you don't change, do you?' she said. 'You're still living your life as if it's a Jilly Cooper novel.'

'Sorry.'

'What for? I wouldn't be. I'm just jealous! Have a nice time. Be good. Then get rid of him and come and tell me all about it.'

I smiled. Sally hadn't changed much, either.

'What time shall I expect you then?' she asked.

'Dunno. Depends. Let's just say if I'm not there by two o'clock you can give me up as a fallen woman.'

'Don't weaken. One-night stands aren't worth it.'

'No, but it'd be more than that.'

'All the more reason for not weakening then. You just get yourself over here, no matter what time it is. And if you come broken-hearted, don't worry, you can have my full sympathy – but only in exchange for all the details, remember!'

I laughed. 'You're on. See you later then.'

'Okay.'

'And, Sally . . . ?'

'Yes?'

'Oh nothing . . . just, thanks for being a pal.'

'Oh piss off back to your baby-snatching, woman.'

I hung up smiling and went back into the jumbling crowd to look for Joss. He found me. He approached from behind and put his arms around me, pinning mine to my sides. 'Gotcha,' he said. 'Mine, all mine!'

'Not for long if you carry on like this, my lad,' I said, wriggling round, still pinioned, to face him. 'Hey, what have you done with my case?'

'If you squeeze your hand right down into one of my front trouser pockets, you'll find a key to a left-luggage locker,' he said mischievously. 'But I'm not telling you which pocket. You'll have to try them both.'

'Difficult,' I said. 'I'm trapped.'

'Aw, go on, try.'

I could feel his penis hard against my abdomen. I was sorely tempted to follow instructions. 'I'll just take your word for it,' I said, unable to prevent a smile.

'Spoilsport.' Then he kissed me, a long, languorous, sensual kiss, before he set me free.

'Right,' I said, businesslike, 'the evening is before us. Where shall we go?'

'How about getting ourselves lost in Sin City, never to be found again?'

'How about a stroll in Regent's Park?'

I had promised myself that this was the end of my non-affair with Joss. I hadn't actually resolved my inner confusion so much as locked it away in a cupboard, but by locking it away I'd come down on the side of Joe, reality and prudence. Therefore, I reasoned, using a much practised system of converse logic, for the next six or seven hours I could say 'to hell with common sense' and be totally, gloriously and innocently, head over heels in love. At midnight, or thereabouts, this too would go into the cupboard and then we'd all live sensibly ever after.

The feeling of surrender was sheer heaven. Joss and I enjoyed a multitude of ordinary little experiences which were totally new to us: holding hands as we walked along the road without worrying that we'd bump into someone we knew, walking into Capital Radio and asking for a car-sticker, slipping into a shop doorway for a kiss –

something Joe and I had stopped doing long ago – then, when we got to the park, lying down together under a tree and having a necking session in full view of the rest of the world.

As the twilight approached and softened the edges of the day we left the park and crossed Marylebone Road to look at the symmetrical, creamy elegance of Park Crescent, half of it in deep shadow, the other half washed peach by the setting sun. 'If these were still private houses,' said Joss, 'and if one was for sale, and if I were rich, and if you'd come and live with me, I'd buy one for us. Would you like that?'

I smiled and put my arm around his waist. 'Yes,' I said. 'If.'

We walked down Portland Place and sat for a moment on the circle of steps outside All Souls' Church, looking at Broadcasting House. I could see why people had described the building as a ship; its rounded end like the stern of some great liner sailing away from us, sailing away on the airwaves, out of reach. I flared with ambition. 'One day,' I said, more to myself than to Joss, 'I'm going to work there. BBC. Top of the tree . . . Or Capital, or Radio South. One of the Big Three.'

'Watch out, Jimmy Wogan, Tony Aspel, Alison is coming!'

'Something like that,' I replied. 'One day.'

'I'd better have your autograph now, then, while you're still humble like me.' He took a ball-point pen out of his jacket pocket and handed it to me, then he rolled up his sleeve. 'Sign here, please. Put "To Joss, with all my love, from Alison".'

I laughed. 'Don't be silly!'

'Go on,' he said. 'I mean it. And don't forget to put some kisses on.'

So I signed his forearm.

'Thank you, miss,' he said, tugging at an imaginary forelock and with a sheepish I'll-be-your-fan-forever look on his face. 'I'll never wash it again. Never.'

I gave him back his pen.

He held it reverently. 'Or this,' he said. 'I'll never wash this again, either.'

We both burst into a gale of giggles, and then kissed. Eventually I said, 'My bum's getting cold. And can we go and find somewhere to eat? I'm starving.'

'What do you fancy? Chinese, Indian, Italian . . . ?'

'Greek,' I said. 'Get into practice.'

'Charlotte Street then,' said Joss, impressing me with his knowledge.

I was curious. 'Know the area well, do you?'

He shrugged. 'I did a little research. Just in case . . . '

'Be prepared, huh?'

He took my hand and helped me to my feet saying, 'It's not far; we can walk it if you like.'

I groaned. I felt as though I'd walked miles already. 'Oh no,' I said, 'I haven't the energy. And I'm too hungry. I need food *now*. Let's get a taxi.'

He shook his head. 'Not very juicy,' he said as if giving serious consideration, 'and I don't think the driver would be too happy about it. Here,' he held a finger to my mouth, 'chew on this in the meantime.'

I had a strong desire to say 'oh, I *love* you!' Instead I went to the kerb and looked for a cab. Joss stood by my side, spotted one before I did, put his arm out and the car drew up. The driver leaned across and opened the window.

'This lady,' said Joss, still ever so seriously, 'is the famous Alison Wonderland. And she'll disappear if she isn't fed before eight o'clock. Charlotte Street please.'

The driver gave us a look that said: 'I meet all types in this job but you take the biscuit,' and muttered, 'Hardly worth it.'

Then Joss added, 'And an extra quid over the meter if you get us there inside five minutes.'

'Which end?' was the more favourable response.

'The middle.'

It was one hell of a taxi ride.

Houmus, six kebabs, some sticky Shreddies and a bottle of wine later, we were replete and holding hands on the table cloth, gazing at each other silently over a flickering candle. I remembered Kate Bush's song about the man with the child in his eyes and I thought she must have met Joss. The restaurant was fairly empty by now. It was getting late. A small and gentle panic was germinating within me and I couldn't stop it. I didn't want this time with Joss to end, I wanted it to begin all over again, in a different time and place, somewhere uncluttered where it could grow and consummate and continue. I smiled at myself. I guess I really did want to be Alison Wonderland.

'Penny for them,' said Joss softly.

'Sorry,' I said. 'Worth a million.'

'Take a cheque?'

I took a breath, held it for a couple of seconds, then exhaled, shaking my head.

'Go on. What were you going to say?'

I considered, then thought: sod it, and began, 'I don't know whether this will help or hurt but . . . ' I hesitated again.

He squeezed my hand. 'Go on.'

'Sorry, I'm not feeling too coherent. The wine.' I smiled across at him. 'That's my excuse, anyway . . . What I want to say is, I'm a lot older than you and I'm married and I fancy you like mad and I'm not going to do anything about it . . . and I want to. I'm sorry and it was foolish to even begin to get involved and I didn't think anybody'd be hurt and . . . ' I faltered to a stop and picked at a drip of wax petrified on the cloth.

'But I know all that,' he said. He reached across and put his finger under my chin, tilting my face up again. 'Hey,' he said, 'look at me.'

I did. Then I took another deep breath and said, ' . . . and I love you.'

Then Joss was the one to avoid *my* gaze. He closed his eyes. When he opened them again the child in them had gone. 'You've never said that before.'

'I know. And I don't think I should have said it now.'

'I'm glad you did.'

'It doesn't change anything,' I said. 'It just hurts.'

'I know,' he said quietly.

I looked at my watch. It was time to go. We settled the bill, went out into the dark and walked, not too briskly, back towards Euston Road, looking in shop windows, pointing out the presents we'd buy for each other 'if only'. We didn't say much.

Railway stations at night are depressing places to be, even the modernised, computerised, sanitised ones like King's Cross. They seem dirtier than during the day.

We hid ourselves in the cafeteria and made strangely polite conversation about the bitter tasting, overstewed tea and the thick, chipped-round-the-edges cups. There was something to be said, after all, for avoiding station farewells. A pseudo-snooty female voice came over the tannoy with 'The next train to depart from platform eleven will be the oh-one-twenty-five to Dringley, calling at Hatfield, Stevenage, Peterborough, Grantham, Newark, Retford, Doncaster, Wakefield, Leeds, Harrogate and Dringley.'

'Christ,' I said when she'd finished, 'you didn't tell me it was the milk train. It'll take hours.'

'I don't mind,' he replied. 'You're worth it.'

'Bet you won't think that by the time you get back,' I said, trying to introduce a little light-heartedness. 'On your feet, boy, time to be off.'

'I know.' But neither of us moved.

'Come on then,' I said, still not getting up.

'Yes.' He pushed back his chair. The noise of it sawed on my nerve endings. We went out on to the platform. Station-smells, stains of oil, discarded chewing gum splattered black on the platform, crumpled crisp packets. We walked the length of the train looking for a cheerful compartment. We reached the engine. I was thinking: I don't want him to go, I want to get it over with. We didn't speak. We turned and started back again and I opened the first carriage door we came to. Then I gave him a small hug and pointed him towards the door. He turned back to me, feeling in his trouser pocket. 'Don't forget your suitcase,' he said, handing me the key to the left-luggage locker.

I took it. 'Thanks.' It was the last thing on my mind.

'You'll be all right?' he asked. 'Into a taxi and straight to Sally's.'

'I'll be fine,' I said with a smile. 'I'm a big girl now. Go on, get in.'

He did, and I closed the door on him. He slid the window down and leaned out of it and we held hands. I was thinking: I will not cry, I will *not* cry – as my throat clenched tight and Joss's face became moistly blurred around the edges. I blinked hard and it cleared again. A whistle blew and my heart lurched. Joss grabbed my head and kissed me furiously. I lost myself in him. Then I gently pushed him away. 'No more, Joss,' I said.

He smiled, a bit crooked. 'That's it, then?'

'Yes. Back to our lives.'

'No,' he said quickly. 'It's not as easy as that! What about me? I love you. You love me, damn you!'

I flinched.

'You can't just calmly walk back into your life as if nothing has happened.'

'Nothing has! Joss, don't . . . ' The train's threatening departure was making us both sound frantic.

'Life's not that simple. You can't just take a chunk out of it, live it, enjoy it, and then chuck it away as if you'd just eaten a good meal and then put the dirty plate in the sink!'

He was right, of course. 'I'm sorry, Joss. Please . . . ' I don't know what I was pleading for, what it was that I wanted.

'Oh shit,' he said quietly. 'I'm sorry.'

The train jerked once and then started to move slowly but relentlessly. Joss stayed at the open window. I grabbed for his hand again and walked alongside. 'Take care,' I said, then I let go of him and stood still.

'You too,' he said. Then, louder, 'Remember that I love you!' Then, 'I'll be waiting,' he shouted as he was carried further and faster from me.

I stayed there until the train had completely disappeared, and then some more, before I turned to go. Then I walked quickly and fairly rigidly to the Ladies' Room where I locked myself in a cubicle and sat on the edge of the seat. And then I cried.

CHAPTER FIVE

But not for long. Mascara can be very inhibiting. I fished around in my bag for a Kleenex, found one and carefully used it like blotting paper. Then I had a good sniff, flushed the soggy tissue down the lavatory and stopped off at a mirror on my way out. I'm always checking on my reflection – in mirrors, shop windows, shiny car doors. Joe, so careless of his own appearance that I sometimes wonder if the dishevelled mess is carefully cultivated in secret, found the habit totally infuriating. He called me vain and tinged with pathos as I'm no great beauty, but he was wrong about the reason behind my fondness for reflective surfaces. Vanity it was not – more a dislike of feeling conspicuous. I only feel relaxed and comfortable if I'm not singled out for attention. I like to blend with my background. Clothes, for me, mean camouflage rather than adornment. Unless I'm dressed in the accepted uniform of my peers, like the ubiquitous jeans and T-shirt at work, then I tend to choose muted colours, beiges, browns. 'A walking cowpat' was how Joe put it once. He followed it up by presenting me with a shocking-pink, skin-tight jumpsuit which I loathed on sight and only wore once before splitting a seam.

I leaned over the hand basin and examined my reflection. I'm fairly tidy when it comes to crying, and apart from having washed away my lower eyelashes I reckoned I'd just about pass muster to face the outside world with, so out I went to retrieve my suitcase.

Three-quarters of an hour later I was sitting cross-legged on a king-size beanbag in front of a burning gas fire cuddling a mug of tea between both palms, and Sally was curled up opposite me in a lumpy armchair, dressing gown and slippers. I felt secure for the first time in months. There wasn't much to her little flat but it had a good atmosphere. Two rooms and its own shower room, with the kitchen sink, a tiny fridge and worn-out gas stove along one wall of the living room. The opposite wall, painted a stark white, was covered with about two dozen block-mounted black and white photographic prints of Sally's own creation. As I hadn't seen her since she'd moved flats, the first thing on the agenda had been a guided tour. It took about thirty seconds to glance at the shower and bedroom, then with a flourish she drew a curtain across the front of the sink/cooker wall. 'I put that up so I don't have to live with the dirty dishes. Would you believe the agent had the nerve to call that a kitchenette?' she said. She swept her hand over the curtain. 'All my own work!'

It was exquisite. White cotton with great swirls of hand-painted pastel flowers peeking from a field of beige-green grasses. 'Beautiful,' I said. 'That cloth must have cost a bomb.'

'Very expensive,' she said, nodding. Then her eyes twinkled. 'Two old sheets from a jumble sale at ten pence each, a kid's box of poster paints and an old make-up brush. Not bad, huh?' she said proudly.

'Only sheer genius.'

'God knows what I'll do when it needs a wash, though. Change flats again I suppose. And now I've shown it off to advantage . . . ' she pulled it open again, 'I'll put the kettle on.'

I poked around the room while she was making tea and picked up hardback photo books of the coffee-table kind, rifling through the glossy pictures. 'One of these days, kiddo,' I said, 'it'll be *your* name on the cover.' I nodded towards the far wall. 'They're very good.' I had much admiration for my friend. She'd trained as a secretary after leaving university because she still didn't know what she wanted to be, and had spent the next three or four years temping until she found out what that elusive something was. It turned out, to everyone's surprise including hers, that she wanted to be a photographer. She had no training and little money but she had one hell of an eye for shape, composition, texture, light, shadow and so forth. So she joined the local library, read all the photography books from cover to cover, bought a third-hand manual SLR, and she took photographs. Thousands of photographs. All in black and white, all self processed and printed and from the first, though technically not all that good, there was something about them that grabbed you. 'But how on earth do you manage a darkroom in this place? There's no room, surely?' I continued.

'Ah,' she said. 'Come with me. I just hope you don't actually want a shower tonight.' She took my hand and led me into the shower then drew back the shower curtain. Inside the cubicle was not soap and shampoo or anything so mundane, but a squarish, wooden bedside cabinet on top of which stood an enlarger. She opened the cupboard door below to reveal various bits of photographic paraphernalia: bottles of chemicals, boxes of paper, plastic trays, all piled in neatly on top of one another. Then she closed the tiny window curtain showing me that it was lined in a heavy black material and demonstrated the velcro strips down the edges and along the bottom. 'Now all you have to do is put the living-room light out, close the door and you have a perfect black-out. Well, at night, anyway. The developer tray goes on the floor, stop bath on the loo cistern and fixer on the seat.'

'What do you do if you want to use the loo?'

'Cross my legs,' she said. 'Anyway, to continue . . . the prints sit in the hand basin till I take them through for a proper wash in the kitchen sink, then I peg them on a piece of string in the living room to dry. With a red bulb in the socket and the enlarger plugged into the extension lead – there you have it!'

'Ingenious,' I said. 'Didn't understand a word of it. Is it safe?'

'Probably contravenes every home safety regulation in the book,' she replied. 'But so long as you make sure the shower doesn't drip . . . I tie a plastic bag round the nozzle just to make sure. One of these days I'll be able to afford my own place with a proper studio and a real darkroom.'

I looked at her quizzically.

'Well I can live in hope, can't I?'

'Don't we all,' I said. 'And in the meantime you're still typing by day and flashing by night?'

She grinned. 'You have a wonderful turn of phrase.' The kettle started to hiss so we went back into the living room.

'But seriously, Sally, how's it coming along? Published anything yet? Got your portfolio together?'

'Almost, to the last question and would you believe, yes, three, to the first!'

'Sally!' I squeaked and hugged her. 'That's wonderful! You mean they paid you real money for them?'

'Not a lot,' she said and handed me a mug of tea. 'But it's a start. I'll show you them later but not yet 'cos it's you first, we made a bargain, remember, and you're not going to wriggle out of it. Now then, this young Adonis of yours – sit down and tell me *all* about it.'

So I did just that. The sense of release was wonderful, at last being able to really spill it all out without any thought of an image to keep up or any fear of judgement. Here in London with Sally there was no reticence. Just an unconditional acceptance of each other as we happened to be at the time. 'It's ridiculous,' I said. 'To feel so starry-eyed and desperately in love. He's only a teenager. I'm pushing thirty . . . '

'Stretching a point,' she said.

'And I thought I'd got over all this kind of thing in my teens. You know – mixed up, confused, unsure of what you want or who you are, all that kind of thing. And suddenly here I am again feeling just like a custard pie somebody's scored a direct hit with!'

'You know, this is just like old times,' she said, leaning back in her chair and smiling contentedly.

'Oh Sally, do you think we ever get to grow up?'

'God, I hope not!' she said. 'Come on, do you really want to be staid and responsible and always totally *sure*?'

'It'd make a nice change.'

'You'd soon be crawling up the walls, and you know it.'

'But I'm crawling up the walls now!'

'No you're not. Not if you stop and work it out for a second.'

'But I've been trying for ages and I can't seem to come up with answers. Joe, Joss, me, life . . . '

'The universe and everything,' she nodded sagely. 'So

what's new? If you haven't any answers it's only because you're asking yourself the wrong questions.'

'Glib.'

'Maybe. But if you think it through you haven't a problem. Not any more – you've come out the other end of it already.'

'I don't see it.'

'Look, you've got a husband but been tempted by a gorgeous third party. You said "no" with a lot of agonising, which is typically you,' she said smiling, then continued quickly before I could protest, 'and you've come through with marriage unsullied and reputation intact. Well, almost. See? No problem.'

'Then why do I feel like this?'

'Like what? Describe. Briefly. I know we've got all night but you've already had a great chunk out of it.'

I felt guilty again for agreeing to spend the evening with Joss. I sighed. 'Okay, I'll try.' Then I was silent for a moment, thinking hard, trying to put it into an objective list. 'I'm hurting, I feel confused. Pulled in two directions. I miss Joe and wish he were coming on holiday with me – but I'm dreading going back to him. I miss Joss as well. I wanted to take him in my arms and keep him with me and run off with him into the wild blue yonder. It could have been like a fairy tale.' I paused, trying really hard to be honest. 'Yet I'm relieved that he's gone. But, oh Sally, I do wish I *had* gone to bed with him.'

'That's your fantasies talking. Come down to earth and really look at it. He's nineteen and randy. He'd probably have lunged at you with all the finesse of a bull in a field full of cows, come in three seconds flat, then lunged again five minutes later. Quantity maybe, but no quality. Do you really want to be *practised* on? Because that's what it would have been like.'

'I'm not so sure,' I said, remembering the way he used to massage my neck and shoulders in the studio, the gentle, almost teasing way he used to kiss me sometimes, the way my body responded if he so much as accidentally brushed my skin with his fingertips.

'Your ego's been flattered, that's all. But look at you,

you're nowhere near old enough to play Léa – the older woman fantasy just isn't you, Alison. Be realistic. And anyway, you wouldn't really want that, would you? They always get dumped on in the end, you know.'

'I suppose you're right,' I agreed. Verbally. But not inside my head.

'Of course I am,' she said. 'So now that we've sorted out this Joss business, do you want another drink before I start on Joe or after?'

'Big subject. Refreshments now, I think. Got any alcohol?'

Sally stretched, cat-like, then settled herself deeper into the armchair. 'Mm. You get it. Whisky's in the cupboard under the sink. Next to the Vim.'

'Fine hostess *you* are,' I grumbled and struggled out of the beanbag. I retrieved the whisky bottle and straightened up. 'Where do you keep your glasses?' I asked, looking around and only seeing two half-pint beer mugs upturned on the drainer. 'Don't tell me – under the bed?'

'You're looking at them,' she said, twisting round. 'Those are my only two.'

I made a mental note to present Sally with a proper set of drinking glasses as a late flat warming gift, then poured out a goodly measure each. 'Want anything with it?' I asked.

'As the choice is water or water, I'll have water,' she said. 'But don't drown it.'

I let the cold tap run for a few seconds then gave it a one-second burst into her glass. I took mine neat and returned to the enveloping comfort of the bag on the floor. I squirmed around to remould it to my shape then held out my glass and said, 'Cheers.'

'Cheers. Here's to getting what we want.'

'Seconded.' We both drank to it.

I watched Sally swirling the liquor round in her glass. 'So,' she said, looking back at me speculatively, her eyes narrowed, 'what exactly *do* you want, Alison? I don't mean life in general, but specifically, now, out of this Joss and Joe business?' I took a breath but before I could answer she continued, 'And don't say "I don't know". That's a cop out. This is me, Sally, remember.'

'Okay. I want to be two people at the same time,' I said. 'I want to be in love with Joss who would be even more in love with me than me with him, and I want to sleep with him, live with him, look after him, play with him – like we were kids. And I want to be Joe's wife, and for Joe to love me all the time, and to sit with him, talking about things, in front of the fire like we were allies instead of warring factions. I want to be with Joe like I am with you. Only with sex thrown in as well, of course,' I added. 'And I want both lives simultaneously without either intruding on the other. And without any subterfuge. And without feeling guilty. There. Satisfied?'

She laughed. 'You don't want much, do you?'

I shrugged. 'Ask a silly question . . . ' We lapsed into a cosy silence interrupted only by the hiss of the gas jets and the occasional, quiet, satisfied slurping noises as we slowly transferred the whisky from glasses to stomachs.

Then Sally poked my shoulder. 'Hey, I thought we were going to start on Joe?'

'Oh all right then,' I said reluctantly. I was, at last, beginning to wind down properly and a deliciously hazy glow, a mixture of tiredness, comfort and alcohol, was turning all my hard edges into a gradual fade-out. I could hardly tell where I left off and the air around me began.

'I take it you love your husband?' she asked.

'Of course.'

'There's no "of course" about it, under the circumstances.'

'Will a straight "yes" do, then?'

'And you want to stay together?'

'Of . . . yes.'

'Then how can you say you love Joss?' she demanded.

'So who said you could only love one person at a time?' I replied. 'It's stupid, that a language as rich as ours should only have the one word for all that emotion! I mean I "love" my parents, I "loved" my grandad, I "love" you, I even "love" *me* sometimes. So: I "love" Joe. I "love" Joss.'

'But there must be a difference. Try and explain it to me.'

I sighed and leaned back again, closing my eyes. It all

seemed like a lot of hard work. I made the effort. 'Joss thrills me. He makes me tingle all over when he touches me, it's as if I'm a black and white telly and he switches on the colour. He makes me feel I'm seventeen again and everything's possible.'

'Doesn't sound like love to me. Infatuation maybe, not love. Love's more like a pair of comfy slippers.'

She said that just as I was taking another drink and I laughed and it went down the wrong way. 'Barbara Cartland . . . ' cough, choke, 'you will never . . . ' choke, splutter, ' . . . be, my friend!'

She got up and thumped my back, hard. 'Better?'

'No, stop it!' I said, still choking and giggling at the same time. 'It's a myth! All that does is hurt!'

'Sorry.' She stopped, allowed me all of thirty seconds to recover, then started on Joe, how did *he* make me feel?

'Scared,' I said without thinking. 'Scared of losing him, scared he'll stop loving me, scared, sometimes, that he already has. But not often,' I added quickly. 'That's just me being insecure. As ever.'

'Not scared of losing young Joss then? Or giving him up?'

'No, I wouldn't say scared. Just don't *want* to.'

'Selfish cow,' she said affectionately. 'So if you had to choose, or rather *when* you do, you'll choose Joe,' she continued, very baldly. 'In fact, you already have, mentally. All you've got to do when you go home is have a firm and final little talk with Joss and then get on with the rest of your life. And there you are, problems solved. Cheers,' she raised her glass in another toast. 'Easy really, wasn't it?'

I considered. Then I said, 'No.' I drank. I could feel an attack of philosophy coming on. I gave in to it. 'Is losing a hand less painful than losing an arm, simply because it's the smaller part of your body?' I asked, quite proud of the analogy.

'Smart arse. Just so long as you don't lose your head, my dear,' she countered, with the wiggle of an admonitory finger. 'You've come very close to it, you know.'

'I know.' The picture of Joss looking at me over the restaurant table when I said I loved him. The way he said 'then I'll go. For good if that's what you really want,' earlier, on the train. Saying goodbye, holding on to each other. Him leaning out of the carriage and getting littler and littler, calling out, 'Remember that I love you.' All these images came into my mind at once and I felt tears coming. I didn't try to stop them because there was no need, not with Sally. I just said, 'Have you got a hanky, please? I think I'm dripping.'

'Hey, what's all this?' she said, voice suddenly full of concern. 'Come on, there, that's right,' she soothed, stroking my hair. 'You have a good cry, love. It's all all right.'

I had a good sniff and wiped at my wet cheeks with my fingers. 'Sorry,' I said. 'It's just that . . . ' I sniffed again.

'I know. It's all right. Here.' She delved around in her handbag and came up with a hanky. 'It's a bit dusty, but I haven't used it. Have a good blow.'

My tears had stopped as suddenly as they'd started. I shook out the handkerchief and blew my nose. 'Thanks.'

'Better now?'

'Actually, not a lot,' I said, managing a limp smile. 'Bang goes another myth.'

Sally put a comforting hand on my shoulder. 'Never mind, we'll have another drink.' She fetched the bottle and emptied it into our glasses. 'It'll all sort itself out, you'll see. Drink up.'

I took a large gulp.

'And if it doesn't . . . ' She patted the top of my head. 'Well, just remember that no problem is so big or so complicated that it can't be run away from!'

CHAPTER SIX

Oh, what can you say about Athens in September when you're taking time off from your life to play the role of playing no role at all? Just simply being, and only doing when inclined. I didn't even send any postcards, just spent days in the sun almost naked on the rooftop by the pool. Evenings under the spectacle of a floodlit Acropolis. Ambling through the Plaka, bouzouki music clashing from different bars. Sleeping deep and heavy under a single sheet in a single bed. And thinking very little at all. That could wait till later. The seven days seemed like a lifetime and passed as quickly as a dream.

I was so relaxed and comfortable with myself by the end of the holiday that I began the return journey with wings on my feet and a shining confidence that the gods, or whoever, were finally on my side. Problems, what problems? But somewhere in the sky between Athens and Heathrow an invidious metamorphosis began. By the time I'd fought for the last empty seat on the train from King's Cross back to Dringley it was complete. The shine had tarnished, my winged feet seemed well and truly hobbled and the gods had turned into little darting demons. I told them to piss off and leave me alone. I'd already faced the situation hadn't I? I'd sent Joss back up to Dringley. I'd gone away alone, I'd remained the faithful wife in the face of overwhelming temptation. I had, in the end, stuck to my principles rather than Joe's. Common sense had won a victory over fantasy, close fought maybe, but still a victory. I should have been feeling proud of myself and virtuous. So how come all I felt was hemmed in, depressed and cheated?

I sighed, shifted in the seat slightly to ease the ache that was beginning in the small of my back and tried not to think about how Joss would have offered to cure it. A short pang. I surveyed my fellow passengers in preparation for a quiet game of guess which one's the Russian spy, the sugar daddy's plaything, the mass murderer, or the eccentric millionaire, but the material just wasn't there. A right dismal lot they looked. I'll bet none of them ever had a breathless and beautiful youth threatening to jump off a train for the sake of them, I thought smugly. But that brought on another quick, sharp pang, so I rummaged around in the duty free airport carrier bag stuffed down by my legs and dragged out a bottle of Ouzo. Not bothering about the disapproving sniff from the gentleman opposite who then steadfastly stared out the window, I broke the seal and took a deep draught straight from the bottle. Then I choked. I wasn't very practised at drinking neat Ouzo. The heat edged its way down my chest and burned into my guts. A bit better. Not much, but a bit. I finished coughing then took another swig before putting the bottle back again. It was rotten of me to open it. It was supposed to be a present for Joe, and Ouzo, like Pernod, isn't exactly the easiest of liquors to water down.

The next thing to see the light of day was the scruffy little notebook which lives permanently in my handbag as part of my survival kit. I've kept a notebook like this since I was sixteen or thereabouts. It's not a diary as such, or rather, *they're* not diaries, there must have been eight or nine of them altogether, hidden away in the cellar at home. All my crises from sixteen until Joe, poured into the private notebooks as into the ear of a pet dog or god if you believe in one. Meant for no eyes but my own, those ecstasies and desperations, big thoughts and little thoughts, fantasies, hopes, grudges, poems I never showed anybody, thoughts I never shared, even with Sally, great diatribes against the injustices of life. I couldn't bear for anyone to read them, but how could I throw them out? So I unclipped the biro which lived permanently with the book, turned to an empty page and prepared to write.

I use the notebooks like other people might go for a work-out in the gym or a ten-mile jog. They keep me healthy, give me release, help me to see things in perspective. Surprisingly, there was very little written in there about the Joe versus Joss dilemma. Did that mean that the whole thing was really not very important, or that it was too important? I decided the question was irrelevant, as I'd already made the decision. All it needed was a little strengthening and the best way to achieve that was to summarise as much as I could remember of what Sally had said about the whole thing, get it down on paper. It may be illogical but there's still that unreasoning belief lurking somewhere inside that if it's written down it must be true. I covered three pages and came almost to the end of the book. I felt so much better when I'd done that I practically laughed out loud at myself – all that agonising for all those weeks, when all I had to do was gently but firmly tell Joss that, apart from an unavoidable working relationship, I didn't want to see him again. So what if he was physically attractive? He was also very immature and inexperienced and why on earth should I need any of that when I already had an ideal sexual partner and intellectually stimulating mate waiting for me at home? A rare and valuable thing, according to Sally, and not to be dispensed with or trifled with lightly. I closed the book and sent off a mental memo to myself to remind me to get a new one, then I put it back into my bag. Thank God I'd married the kind of guy who wouldn't dream of delving into the mysteries of a lady's handbag.

I smiled, feeling comfortable with myself once more, and leaned my head back against the seat closing my eyes against the rest of the world. The sounds and vibrations of the moving train were soporific and I drifted into that slightly dizzy feeling you get when you're hovering half way between full consciousness and sleep. 'Home to Joe, home to Joe, home to Joe,' sang the wheels on the track as they carried me back to Dringley, and I rolled the words around on my tongue tasting all their different meanings.

Home. The word itself is comfortable, warm. Joe. The name is homely but the man it belongs to is not. The trouble with Joe is that he's incapable of apathy, or appears to be. The trouble with trying to nurture a stable relationship with him is that he gets into a panic at the very concept of stability. When these two facts co-exist you can get problems. I got a husband who loved me sometimes, and other times I could feel waves of hate pointed in my direction like somebody had a blowlamp aimed at my face. And oh, how he took pride in being honest about it.

'I can't stand the sight of you.' 'I feel invaded by your presence.' 'I really don't want you with me at the moment.' All, with many other variations, spoken with a real cold steel edge to his voice. Sometimes I could positively feel him not wanting me in the same town with him, let alone the same building, the same room; not wanting me to touch him, talk to him, even breathe the same air. His silences were the loudest things I have ever heard.

I'm not a dedicated masochist, so what was it that held me there? It was the other Joe, the other face of him, which was equally, if not more, intense. When he loved me he was the most loving – and lovable – person I've ever met or even imagined. 'You're the best thing that could ever happen in my life.' 'You are my most precious possession.' 'Fuck the meal, I want you to fuck *me*! Now!' Oh, Joe when he loved me pushed anything else out of my head. My past, my future, my present, my selfness, were all Joe.

It wasn't an easy road to travel. Some people can't differentiate between red and green, others can't hear a sharp or a flat. On a similar, very basic level, Joe has no capacity for indifference. He clutched me to him or threw me away from him but he couldn't cope with us existing comfortably side by side. It scared him: comfort equals stagnation, gradual change equals boredom. He would change from loving to hating between one goodbye and the next hello. It used to hurt terribly at first, after he'd moved up north and we were living together. That was when I first became aware of it, but by the time its full significance had sunk in it was too late. I was deeply and desperately in love, we were married, and it was too late to opt out, too late to want to. So I learned to cope. I quite simply got the hell out of the way and left the hating bits to pass over my head, which I knew they would because they always did. Sometimes it took a couple of hours, sometimes it lasted one or two days. When the black moods were on him I could sense it within seconds. The air around us bristled with it like in an electrical storm. He had real, Lutheran, dark nights of the soul, and during them I kept out of the way as much as I could, practised being inconspicuous till I'd got it down to a fine art. It was worth it. Afterwards he'd suddenly open up, blossom like a desert flower after rain, and I'd be engulfed in the heady magic of him. I wondered which Joe would be meeting me at Dringley station.

He was waiting at the other side of the ticket barrier. 'Hello, pet,' he said, giving me a peck on the cheek. 'Last again as usual.'

I put the case down, put my arms around his neck and kissed him properly. He tasted good.

'Come on then, car's over the road.' He turned to lead the way, and with a small, exasperated shake of my head, I picked up the suitcase again and followed.

Just as our farewells were rather staid and restrained, so we never had grand reunions either. It was as if there was some rule that said we were in official limbo until we were both actually back inside our house. The conversation in the car was polite, both of us feeling around each other, making sure of ground, sniffing for familiarities, reassurance that the other was still the same person.

'Had a good time then?' he asked.

'Mm, lovely. Didn't do a darned thing. Just sunbathed, ate and slept.'

'You mean you didn't have lots of outrageous affairs with Greek Adonises? Shame on you.'

I laughed and put my hand on his thigh. 'Joe, really!' He changed gear and I felt his muscle flex and harden under my fingers. Nice. 'How about you? Play coming on well?'

'Fine.'

'Good.'

A few more miles of fairly easy silence and we were home. Joe carried my case into the house and dumped it in the hall at the bottom of the stairs. 'I suppose you're dying for a cup of tea?'

'Oh, please,' I said, and collapsed into the nearest armchair.

Then he said, 'I've missed you such a lot.'

My heart leaped.

'And now you're home,' he continued, 'it's such an anticlimax.'

Thud.

He disappeared into the kitchen.

As you might have gathered, I'm the sort of person who's quite happy to drift along the stream of life. I'm not a woman who can batter at life, grab things from it, knock holes through barriers with a sledgehammer. But sometimes you learn how to keep something only by losing it. You understand something only through tearing it to pieces. I wish I could have battered at Joe sometimes but the habit of waiting patiently in the background for things to pass over had become too strong and I continued to avoid direct confrontation while he continued his efforts to demand it. 'And now you're back it's such an anticlimax,' was just such a provocation. I tried to avoid it but it wasn't to be. Joe hadn't been lying when he said he'd missed me – he really had. He'd been without his whipping boy for a whole week.

'How on earth anyone could be so lazy, timid and uninterested as to spend a whole week in a place like Athens and do practically nothing amazes me,' he said, conversationally, from the kitchen. 'You'd daydream your life away if you were left to your own devices. You never actually *do* anything, do you?'

'That's not fair,' I called back. I must admit, even though I was used to this kind of conversation, I hadn't expected one so soon on my return. Trust me to time my arrival so it was slap bang in the middle of one of his moods.

'I expected you to come back bubbling over with new experiences, and just look at you,' he said, coming back into the living room. 'Flaked out in a chair and waiting for a bloody cup of tea.'

'You offered it!'

He ignored that and went on, 'You're just the *same*.'

'Well what did you expect? Of course I am. So are you for that matter.' I accompanied that with what I hoped was a defusing smile. It wasn't.

The kettle clicked off and we both ignored it. 'Oh well,' he said, 'at least you managed to get yourself a tan. It suits you.'

'Thanks.'

'But when are you going to do something about your hair? It's a mess.'

It was, I admit, looking pretty ratty and in need of a wash. 'I thought you liked it long,' I said.

'It's boring. Why don't you have it cut? Really short. Or dye it or something. Make yourself look different. I'm bored with the way you look. You've only been back an hour and I'm bored with *you*. Bored, bored, bored.'

It worked. He finally got me riled. I flung his insults straight back at him saying *he* was boring, and arrogant, insufferable, a bully, a nagger, the most self-opinionated man I'd ever come across, and it was my hair and I liked it long.

'Listen to her,' he said. 'Can't even think up an original insult. Why didn't I marry someone who's at least my intellectual *equal*?'

'You merely have a wider vocabulary than me,' I said in as supercilious a tone as I could manage. 'Anyone can read a dictionary.'

'Why don't you then? Look, you can't even hold an intelligent discussion without getting all whiny and whingey.'

'This isn't an intelligent discussion, it's a list of personal insults.'

'Well for God's sake fight back then!'

'I thought I had been doing!' I wailed, and to my horror burst into tears of tiredness, frustration and feelings of inadequacy.

I could see that Joe was trying not to laugh as he said, 'Poor Alison. I'm sorry. There, there, pet. There's nothing to cry about.'

'I'm not crying.'

He held both his hands up, palms towards me and said, 'Okay, fine, you're not crying.' Then he laughed. 'But you are funny when you get yourself all screwed up like this!' He came over to sit on the edge of my chair and put his arm around my shoulders. 'There, there,' he said again, infuriatingly. 'I love you.'

I pulled away from him. 'Can't think why, considering everything else you've just said you feel about me.'

'Stop putting yourself down,' he replied, assuming that I agreed with all the things he'd just said.

'You're a shit.'

'Yes, I know I am. Can't think why you put up with me.' He hugged me again and kissed the top of my head.

I let him. 'If you know it, why don't you stop it? Stop always criticising me.'

'But you know me. That's just the way I am, lovey.'

(That's right, this is me, I won't change, you must.) 'You're a bastard,' I said quietly. I pulled his shirt loose from his jeans and wiped my eyes on it.

'Yes, that too.' He smiled. 'You look awful. Your face is all blotchy and your eyes are red.'

'Thanks.'

'Come on. Let's go to the pub.'

'I can't go looking like this!'

'Sure you can. Stop worrying about what other people think of you. Damn what you look like! You've got to learn to face the world and yell at it "okay, this is me, go screw yourself if you don't like it".'

'So go screw yourself, Joe.'

'That's better,' he said, smiling. 'Come on, let's go.'

So I got up, splashed cold water on my face and wiped it dry, glad I hadn't bothered with any make-up for my return journey, and went with him, out into the world with a red and blotchy face thinking: why am I doing this? It's what *he* wants again. But I went anyway. Normal service had been resumed as soon as possible and before I'd even had a cup of tea.

As the evening progressed I began to mellow and Joe, feeling contrite, had decided that perhaps I wasn't so bad after all. He was kind to me, and charming, attentive and amusing, so that by the time we got back from the pub I was as ready as he was to fall into bed, make love and let bygones be bygones. I lay awake long into the night with him quietly snoring beside me and cuddling me in his sleep. I was thinking back, not just over this argument, but over all the others, the way our marriage was shaping, and what I could do about it. If I agreed with all his criticisms of me it would be easy to say, like he did, 'Yes, this is me, take it or leave it.' He would have approved of that attitude. But because I want to believe I can be bright, attractive, beautiful, sexy, amusing, intelligent, interesting and vivacious, I denied his criticisms, which made me defensive – an attitude he did not approve of.

Underneath all that aggro, how could that thread of attraction still join us? It did though. Opposites may clash but they do attract. What was that indefinable thing about him that made me want to hold on to him so much? What was it in me that attracted him in the first place? He liked his ladies tall, slim, flat-bellied, long-legged, aggressive and independent and he told me so frequently. I'm small, with a complex about my convex tummy and short legs, only aggressive when I'm pushed to the choice between self-survival or suicide, and I like to feel that somewhere there's somebody I can lean on. My life's unsolvable puzzle: what connected me and Joe? He was the centre, the base, and God knows why or how it should be so, but it was so.

That's why the very openness of Joss's admiration had been such a contrast. And a relief. Christ knows, I often needed it – living with Joe was like trying to fall asleep on a tight-rope. Joss was a reaffirmation of my self-image, an exciting secret that I took out and hugged to myself when Joe and I were in conflict. He was an extra prod to my blossoming when Joe and I were in love. I knew he was a foolish mistake which I wasn't coping with at all well but, logic and common sense to one side, I still didn't want to let go of him because he was the safety valve I'd come to rely on – if Joe ever decided to leave me I could always run to Joss. How easily resolutions weaken in the middle of the night!

With all this going round in my head it was impossible to sleep so I gave it up as a bad job around dawn and went downstairs to make myself a cup of tea. When it was ready I sat down, lit a cigarette and took the notebook out of my handbag. I read through everything I'd written on the train the day before. It was practically illegible, but once deciphered, packed full of forthright common sense. Good old Sally. I may have problems every now and then in my relationship with Joe, but having a full-scale affair with a nineteen-year-old was certainly not the way to resolve them. I closed the book, symbolically closing myself off from Joss for good, and went down into the cellar to put it (and him) away with the other books and memorabilia of my past that were hidden there amongst the rubbish.

But when I switched the light on I had a nasty shock. The cellar was tidy, practically empty. My heart missed a beat. Joe must have had a clear-out while I'd been away. Oh God, please let him not have found my secret hoard, thrown it out. It could easily have been mistaken as junk – hell, it was designed to be – a cardboard box inside a black plastic dustbin liner sealed with a paper-covered wire twist to keep out mould and mildew. But inside it were untold treasures: an old red leather attaché case with my collection of notebooks locked inside it. And the rest of the stuff – all sorts of bits and pieces of my past. The odd love-letter, photos of old boyfriends, birthday cards from once special people, defunct invitations to this or that, a mummified red rose still inside its cellophane coffin, a lock of blond hair secured with a paper clip . . . a private junky clutter which was nice to keep, even though I rarely rummaged through it.

I looked round again, more thoroughly this time, but it wasn't anywhere to be seen. Gone. Lying on a tip somewhere or already destroyed in the Council incinerator. I sat down on the stone steps, heedless of the cold, and put my head in my hands feeling quite numb. I couldn't even be angry with Joe for chucking it out. He wasn't to know it was anything other than the rubbish it appeared to be. Then I thought, he could have looked, checked first, swiftly followed by, I hope he didn't.

I heard his footsteps on the stairs above me. 'Alison? Is that you? Or are you a burglar?' he called out in a voice which implied confidence that it was only me. He appeared at the cellar door. 'What on earth are you doing down there?'

I stood up, rubbing my cold buttocks. 'I was just looking for something,' I said, as if it was the most normal thing in the world for me to be in the cellar when the sun had hardly finished rising. I went up to him having totally forgotten about the notebook still in my hand. 'I see you cleaned out the cellar.'

'I had to shift a writer's block,' he said. 'But I never realised you were such a magpie.'

We were both back in the living room. 'You didn't by any chance throw out a black dustbin bag did you?' I asked casually.

'Oh that,' he said. Then he noticed the notebook I was clutching. 'Ah! The latest chapter!'

I turned to stone. 'What?'

'Your little black books.'

My stomach lurched. 'What have you done with my things?' I asked calmly.

'Don't worry. I didn't chuck them out. You'll find it all safe and sound in the bottom of the wardrobe.'

I rushed up to the bedroom, wrenched open the wardrobe door and dragged the bag out, spilling its contents on to the carpet. The attaché case was there, lock broken, fastening bent and twisted. I looked at it in horror.

Joe appeared in the doorway behind me. 'It made perfect bedtime reading while you were away. I never realised you were such an insecure little thing. And so romantic.'

'You broke the lock,' I said in quiet outrage. 'Why? How could you? How *dare* you?'

'I had to check there was nothing valuable in there, didn't I? I couldn't throw it out without checking.'

I flew at him in a rage, screaming, 'You bastard!' as I started pummelling at him with curled-up fists.

He warded off the blows and fought to grasp my wrists, holding them in a vice-like grip which would have hurt except I was too angry to feel it. 'What on earth's the matter with you?' he said in what sounded like genuine surprise. 'What are you so upset for? It's only an old case. So I broke the lock, so what? It's only a *thing*, it's not important!'

'No it isn't! Yes it is!' I yelled, quivering and confused. 'And you read them. How could you?'

'Why not? They were most entertaining. And a red leather case to keep them in, too. How appropriate.'

I broke away from him and flung myself on the bed. I felt

exposed. Raped. All my deepdown private, personal things, Joe had held them up to the light and devoured them all. I raged and stormed at him, went on about privacy and deceit and how could he go on reading them once he realised how personal they were?

He sat on the very edge of the bed, keeping a reasonably safe distance from me, and very calmly said he wanted to know about me and if I never told him my thoughts but preferred to write them down, then how else was he to get to know me? If I hadn't wanted him to read them I shouldn't have left them lying around. If I felt bad, it must be my guilt at what was written. He refused to feel guilty for reading: I was, after all, his wife and he had a right to know me through and through. And all this from the guy who'd carry the phone into the airing-cupboard so his wife couldn't overhear the conversation.

By this time I was sitting in a morose and quivering lump on the opposite edge of the bed with nothing to say to him. I was trying hard to reconcile my outrage and humiliation with the fact that in a way he was justified. He was my husband, did have a right to know about me. But all the thoughts and feelings in those books, all those old letters, that was different. He had no right to scrutinise those, no one had. They weren't on offer. But Joe had stolen them, admitted it brazenly, and he really couldn't see what all the fuss was about or the hypocrisy of 'I have a right to know' coming from the lips of the world's greatest defender of his own personal space.

I turned to look at him and flung the remaining notebook on the bed between us. 'There,' I said. 'You may as well read that one too. Finish the story.'

'No way. Not if you're going to make this kind of fuss. You keep your little secrets.' He stood up and left the room, adding as a parting shot, 'And I'll keep mine.' He clattered angrily down the stairs.

I took a few deep breaths, willing myself to calm down, then I began slowly and methodically to tidy up. Each precious memento was gently placed back inside the cardboard box. The final book was added to the others and stacked in three neat little piles inside the case, which was in turn put into the box with everything else. Then I shrouded the lot in its black plastic and put it back into the wardrobe. All the while I told myself it didn't matter, it might even be better this way, they were only objects, not important. You could only be outraged and humiliated and violated if you allowed yourself to *feel* those things. I stolidly pushed those feelings away, shoved them into the bag in the bottom of the wardrobe along with the rest of it, and determined to carry on as if nothing had happened.

But in the space of those few minutes I'd grown one more layer to the protective shell which surrounded me. Another boulder had been added to the wall which was growing between Joe and me.

I closed the wardrobe door and went back to bed. At least, now, I felt exhausted enough to maybe get some sleep. I wanted to. Block everything out for a while. And the final thought that came into my mind before I sank into a comforting oblivion was that as soon as I got the opportunity I was going to fuck the living daylights out of Joss Jordan and the hell with principles, common sense, virtue, morals, everything. The hell with Joe.

It must have been about lunchtime when he decided it was time I was up and about and facing the world. He brought me a cup of tea and some jam on toast, kissed me on the cheek and said, 'Peace offering. Come on, don't just lie there like a slug when I'm trying to apologise!'

I had to fight my way into wakefulness through a long black tunnel of treacle and I emerged with sticky eyes and a mind full of goo. I yawned hugely. 'Sorry I thumped you.'

'Forget it. Drink your tea.'

I heaved my reluctant body into a semi-upright position and drank. He sat on the edge of the bed watching me then he took the mug and toast from my hands, set them down and gave me a hug. 'I'm sorry you felt I invaded your little secrets.'

An interesting apology – not sorry for the act, only for its effect. 'S'all right. Doesn't matter,' I said, reclaiming the tea and toast and re-erecting them as a barrier between us. I wasn't lying, it didn't matter to me anymore because I had

Joss for my fully-fledged lover (or at least I would have within a very few days). It evened up the score, turned my self-image into that of equal combatant instead of impotent victim. I wondered if and when I would ever tell Joe about it.

He stood up, crossed to the window and flung back the curtains to reveal the epitome of a perfect autumn day – blue sky, little white puffy clouds, brilliant white sunlight. It hurt my eyes. 'What shall we do, then?' he asked bracingly. 'Picnic? Excursion to the seaside? Long walk?' It was the kind of day when he suggested that sort of thing.

I groaned quietly. 'How about just sitting outside on the grass?'

'Not a chance. Come on, you little snail, up you get, we're going to *do* something!' With that he yanked the covers off the bed leaving me exposed and terminally goose-pimpled and threw a pair of knickers at me.

I got up. Half an hour later I was a vibrating bundle of anorak, jeans and sturdy boots with one gloved hand lightly on Joe's waist and the other clamped rigidly to the parcel rack on the back of the Suzuki as we buzzed along the A59 like a hump-backed wasp heading for Bolton Abbey and a healthy trek. I endured it, superimposing on the Dales scenery the different settings and scripts for my imminent capitulation into the loving and lusty arms of my adoring young slave-lover.

None of the imaginary excursions had the remotest resemblance to the actual event. On Monday morning, after I'd seen Joe safely off to work, I spent a self-indulgent two or three hours luxuriating in the bath, washing my hair and drying it carefully so it was a straight and silky curtain, making up my face with more care than usual and wriggling on the floor to zip up the newly washed jeans I'd been saving for my first day back at work. I drove into Dringley feeling a rush of nervous anticipation similar to those of seventeen before the first Saturday night out with a new boyfriend, only more pleasurable because at twenty-eight there's the added rarity value. I parked outside the Admiral, made a final check on my reflection in the rear-view mirror, took a deep breath to ensure that the confident, attractive magnetic persona was firmly in place, then breezed into the pub, smiling to greet my colleagues without a doubt that Joss would be among them having nervously watched the door for my entrance for at least the last half-hour.

Except that he wasn't. Just my luck that he'd be doing the lunchtime cover on my first day back, I thought. That was the only explanation for his absence. Bang went at least three of the scenarios. I couldn't very well just turn round and leave, so I graciously accepted the half of lager generously proffered by Frank, the Programme Supervisor and, as such, my immediate superior, and squeezed in round the pushed together tables with him, his secretary, two journalists, one record company rep, the morning-show jock, and a station engineer.

I finished my drink as quickly as was politely acceptable, and with the excuse that I'd have a lot to do for tonight's show, and a huge backlog of records and mail to catch up on after two weeks' absence, I left. I walked briskly but steadily down the hill to the station (I didn't want to appear breathless at Joss's feet) and wondered how I was going to get him alone so I could hint delicately that his waiting game had paid off and he was about to get the prize. I also wondered why the hell he hadn't manoeuvred himself on to the late shift. But first things first, and first thing was to find him, so I dumped my coat and bag in the presenters' room then wandered off down the corridor ostensibly heading for the ladies'. I glanced in the newsroom on my way past but he wasn't there. I looked at my watch. No, he wouldn't be in the studio either at this time. He wasn't at the tea machine. Maybe he was in the gents'? The lager was making its presence felt so I paid a quick visit to the loo then lingered over making myself a cup of tea but no one emerged. He must be out on a story. He could be back in five minutes or it could be ages. I was longing to see him by now, practically hopping from foot to foot, but I couldn't very well just come out with it and ask somebody where he was. Too obvious. Too dangerous, considering that from now on any rumours about us would be true. I took the tea back to my desk, and resigned myself to having to wait a little longer. The tingling anticipation had turned to annoyed frustration.

I wheeled the gram deck across the room, plugged it in, put on headphones, plugged them into the deck, and started to work my way through the records. Actually, you don't listen to them, you sample them. Stylus on the beginning for a few seconds, a couple of hops and skips in the middle and then a burst at the end are enough to give you a fair idea of whether you're going to like it or not. If you don't, that's it and it goes into a box for a few weeks just in case it turns out to be a hit, before you give it away as a prize or to a youth club. If you do like it, you start again and listen to it until at least half way through then you programme it. It seems a bit heartless when you think of the time, money and hopeful dreams spent on producing the thing in the first place, but there are so many new records released each week that you have to be ruthless about it or you'd do nothing but listen to records twenty-four hours a day.

In and amongst the record sorting I started on the post. There weren't all that many dedications because most people phoned them in on the night, but there were one or two really nice letters saying, 'the late show's not the same, I'll be glad when you're back', and that kind of thing. I kept those in a file marked 'Nice ones', not just to flatter my ego but as future ammunition in case it ever should be needed and I'd be able to say 'but you can't fire me, the listeners like me'. As I read I sorted the letters into piles: dedications for specific programmes, send photos and/or reply, and no action necessary. Then I opened a letter which wouldn't fit into any category at all. It was typed and it was inside an envelope which was addressed simply to 'Alison' with 'Personal' on the top right-hand corner in red. It was from Joss.

'Dear Alison,' it began. 'By the time you read this . . . ' I turned cold, skimmed through the note quickly, then read it again, carefully, word by lacerating word. He'd gone. He'd quit. He'd left town. He couldn't face seeing me again knowing I could never be his. It was better this way. He would always love me . . .

How *dare* he! I screwed the note into a tight little ball and clutched it in my shaking fist. How dare he deny me the right to change my mind. How dare he deny me the chance to love him back.

I yanked off the headphones, and marched, furious, through into reception. With a tight smile at the receptionist I said, 'Hi. I've just heard. Where's young Joss gone off to then?'

'Dunno,' she said, hardly raising her eyes from her knitting. 'It was last Monday. He came in with a rucksack, collected his stuff, went up to see Digby and left.'

'Just like that?'

'Mm. No forwarding address, no notice, no nothing. Damn, I've dropped a stitch.' She peered concentratedly at the work in hand and rescued it.

'How come?'

She shrugged. 'Dunno.'

'And you say he didn't leave a forwarding address?' I asked, just to make sure.

She looked up at me, curious. 'No, why?'

'Oh, just wondered,' I said casually. 'Catching up on the gossip.'

'Mm. Oh well, he always was a bit headstrong. Very young,' she said, shaking her head. 'Got a new one starting next week.'

'That's quick.'

'Well,' she said, gesturing with needles and wool at the grubby paintwork and full ashtrays, 'it's the glamour, isn't it?' She grinned, bowed her head and went back to work.

I went back to the gram deck, turned the volume up and hid my head inside the cans again. I carefully smoothed out the limp and creased scrap of paper and read it through once more. 'I'll always love you.' Fat lot of use that was if he wasn't going to be around for me to take him up on it. Why did he have to leave *now*, just when I'd finally decided to dive in head first? Oh Joss, my young and beautiful almost-but-not-quite lover, why did you have to leave me now? Now that I need you.

I folded up his letter and put it away inside my handbag. I lit a cigarette. I listened to more records. When I'd sorted out the ones I needed for that night I didn't find it at all surprising that most of the songs I'd chosen fell firmly into the agonised and lovelorn category. I switched off, tidied up, left the programme material in a neat pile with a note on top saying 'Tonight's Late Show. Please do not disturb', and then walked slowly back up the hill to the Admiral car park thinking things like: it's all for the best, just as well, and why does it always happen to *me*?

When I got home I went straight upstairs and buried Joss's note deep in the cardboard box in the black plastic dustbin liner in the bottom of the wardrobe, then I made a cup of tea, reached for a book and sat down in front of the fire. The book was *Sense and Sensibility*.

CHAPTER SEVEN

Of course I was filled with curiosity as to where he'd gone, what he was doing, and concern – would he be all right? And, oh, how I missed seeing his face, hearing his voice, touching him. Going to work was suddenly flat, routine, nothing in particular to look forward to. There was no one to replace him. I stopped, after a while, thinking of him at least once in every ten minutes. It dwindled to every half-hour or so, then maybe once in an hour, until sometimes a whole day might have passed without him popping into my thoughts at all. Joss never, to my knowledge, tried to get in touch with me, and apart from the immediate and brief interrogation of our receptionist I never tried to find out where he was. I became occupied, a little bit too frequently, with wondering where my husband was.

Joe had finished the official first draft of his play and the idea now was for it to undergo various stages of re-writes based on the young actors' improvisations in rehearsal, before entering it in the national student drama festival. Because his work at the TV studios occupied him during the day, rehearsals had to take place in the evenings. So the time Joe and I had to share, little enough already, was reduced even further.

When he got back from rehearsals I'd already have left for work. If he was excited and wanting to discuss what had come out of the latest session I wasn't there for him to talk to – he could only hear my voice talking at him if he bothered to switch on the radio. Big deal. When we eventually did see each other the immediacy and the enthusiasm had gone.

Much as he loved motorbiking, even Joe admitted it wasn't much fun in the rain. So when it was wet I'd drive into Dringley early taking him with me in the mini before I tore off again for the radio station, mind on my work.

Sometimes, if the weather was dry, Joe would call into the studio on his way back from rehearsal and have a cup of coffee before setting off for home on his bike. In one way it was good to see him there, in another, it wasn't.

It's very difficult trying to concentrate on presenting a radio programme when there's somebody else, it doesn't matter who, in the studio with you. Conversations are determined by the length of records and then broken off in mid-sentence as you dive for a fader or select a jingle or say 'Sssh' before you open the microphone and start talking to unseen strangers about something totally unconnected with what you've just been saying to your visitor. Whoever it is in there with you they can't help but feel in the way because no matter how much you want them there they actually *are* in the way.

I was just going into the eleven o'clock news one night when the studio door opened and Joe walked in. I had to wait a full twenty-five seconds before I could get up and hug him, or even say hello. That sort of situation doesn't exactly encourage spontaneity. When the unseen newsreader in London was safely being transmitted through my lines and faders I stood up and gave Joe a hug. We had about two minutes to talk to each other before my next microphone link. I was pleased to see him.

'How did it go?' I asked.

'Fine.'

'Good. Hang on a sec.' I cued up the next record quickly. 'There.'

Silence from Joe.

'Is anything the matter?' I asked.

'No, I'm all right,' he said as if the weight of the world was on his shoulders.

'Come on, what is it?'

'Hadn't you better keep your eye on the clock?'

'Mm.' I got ready to lose the news and read out the weather forecast. That done I started the record, selected another and cued it up. It was a full minute before I got back to Joe. 'Come on, what's up?'

'Well if you must know, all this is,' he said, sweeping his hand through the air. 'I never see you. I've been out and

I've had a good rehearsal and I've been to the pub and I've been with friends and you weren't there. I never see you when we're with other people. It's always only when there's just the two of us. I want to see you in a group. I've forgotten how you react.'

I pointed out that I'd been in the pub with him and the crowd only last evening before work.

'Your body was,' he replied. 'You weren't. Eyes on the fucking clock, terrified of being a second late.'

'I have to be, Joe!'

'Yes, I know.'

'Come on, give me a hug.' I took hold of his hand.

'No.' He took his hand away. 'You'll get caught with your turntables down.'

'Don't be like that. Please.'

'Your record's finishing.'

I closed the appropriate fader and segued into the next disc.

'What, no dedications?' he said with thinly disguised sarcasm.

I ignored it, cued up another record and pushed some commercials into the cart machine. 'I'm sorry, Joe, but it *is* my work. I don't come down to the telly studios while you're working, do I?'

'I'll go then.'

'I didn't mean that. Don't.'

He was half way out of the door when he turned round. 'I want a wife back,' he said, and then he was gone.

'Joe . . . ' I said, but there were already two sets of double soundproofed doors between us.

He hadn't said it vindictively or anything. Just quietly, flatly. 'I want a wife back.'

He had a point. All the months we'd been together but not really together. The silences. The wall between us. All the reasons for Joss. I hadn't lost my head over Joss, nor, with or without help, ever lost sight of Joe being my base, my centre, my reason for being. I had stayed Joe's property. But still my desire for Joss *had been*.

I went through the rest of the show like a robot. 'I want a wife back' in that small, flat voice went echoing through my head all night long. But I still didn't wake him when I got home.

We bumbled along together with little conflict and a considerable amount of hurried lovemaking for a while after that so the immediacy of his statement faded. But I kept on thinking about it, trying to work out a way round it that wouldn't involve me dramatically chucking in my job 'for the sake of my marriage'. Anyway, why the hell should I? My career was just as important as his. I could see only one solution – to somehow get myself off the late night show and on to another time slot. If only I could do a different programme, either during the day or even early evenings, then we'd be able to spend more time together and lead a more normal social life. At the moment my social life was a non-existent joke. Oh, the thought of being able to do something ordinary like go to the pictures on a weekday night, or sit in a pub at closing time or even just sit at home and watch closedown on the telly!

I put it to Joe, being very careful not to give him any suspicion I'd be doing it mainly for him – he was always so adamant about my doing things for my own sake, never for his, to show I was independent and not leaning on him. So I emphasised the social side of it, that I was tired of working constant late nights, that I wanted a normal life/work style for a change, and that a daytime programme would be a new professional challenge – different audience, different pace.

He agreed it would be a good idea but added, 'Do what *you* want to do. It's your job. But whatever you decide, just make sure you do it for your own sake.'

I started dropping large hints around the management like 'Can I do a daytime programme please?' but I was totally unprepared for the management's reaction to my suggestion.

I started with Frank, the Programme Supervisor. He was a weedy little man, a year or so younger than me, who thought his Mexican-bandit moustache made him look sexy. You know the type – always looks heavily in thought even when smiling, sits with elbows on desk and fingers steepled, and takes cricket very seriously.

'I want to come off the late night show,' I said, subtle as ever.

'This comes as, er, a bit of a surprise,' he said, lying.

'Oh, come off it! When I first started doing it you said it would only be for six months or so. That was two years ago.'

'Yes!' His eyes lit up. 'Yes! That's because you're doing such a marvellous, er, job of it!' Such enthusiasm. Such sincerity.

'I'm bored with it, Frank. I need a new challenge.'

'Understandable. But, er, there aren't any off-air jobs going at the, er, moment.'

'Pardon? Off-air?'

'Well, I mean to say, you couldn't do a daytime show, er, too good where you are.'

'Frank,' I said with admirable patience, 'I could do a wonderful afternoon show if you'd give me the chance. Just what the housewives want. A woman on the radio. Someone to identify with.'

'Ah,' he said slowly. 'No. Oh no, no. Er, you've got it a bit, er, wrong. You don't understand scheduling, Alison. That's exactly what the, er, housewife for want of a better word *doesn't* want. I mean she'd rather listen to a man, really she would. All our research indicates . . . '

'Bollocks,' I said. 'Who did the research, anyway?'

'Er . . . researchers.'

'Male ones?' I had him there. I knew. He and Digby Richards did it way back when they were angling for the franchise.

'That's not the point, Alison,' Frank was now being the patient party. 'You're needed where you are. You've really built up the late night slot and we can't, er, afford to take you off it now.'

'But, Frank . . . '

'And you can't really have thought it through. The implications. It's a very different, er, kettle of fish you know, daytime programming. Different pace. Different audience. Different content. You'd lose your musical freedom you know. Er, have to stick to the playlist. Rigidly. No more side one of the Moody Blues for instance.' A sly dig.

'I wouldn't mind that. I need a new challenge, something different.'

'No, it's out of the question. Besides,' he added, 'you've never done a daytime show. Er, have you? So how could I take that gamble?'

'I'd never done *any* kind of a radio programme when you took me on. You gambled on me then, didn't you? It paid off, didn't it? You've just said.'

'Ah, but that's different. Er . . . not such a big, how can I put this, risk. Not many people listen at night.'

I was approaching eruption but I held it in check and said very calmly, 'Stuff and nonsense. I get as much mail as anybody else on this station and you know it. Even the breakfast show. All I'm saying, Frank, is that I could do with a change for a while. I'm getting stale.'

He leaned back in his chair. 'What you need,' he said as if the thought had just struck him, 'is a change.'

'Now why didn't I think of that?'

'Yes, you're working too hard. Your lifestyle's all cock-eyed. You should take things a bit easier, try and work out a normal home/work routine. Stay at home all day, for example, then come to the station around six and work straight through like the rest of us do. Then it'd be more like a normal working day and the rest of your time would be your own.'

My jaw was beginning to twitch. I unclenched my teeth and said, 'Sorry, no good. I'd never see my husband at all if I did it like that.'

'Oh. Er, yes, I suppose you wouldn't. Well now, let's see . . . ' He paused for thought. Then he leaned forward and beamed. 'Yes, that's it! I've got it! Christmas.'

'Christmas?'

'I'll take you off the Christmas schedules.'

Magnanimous. 'You mean you were going to have me working all through this Christmas when I did it last year and the year before?'

'Well, we have to give priority to those with families, don't we?'

'But *I* have a family! You know – husband, parents, brother – that kind of thing.'

'You know what I mean, Alison, don't split hairs.'

My mouth was open but no sound was coming out.

'So. You'll work on Christmas Eve then don't come back until, er, New Year's Eve. How about that?'

'Wonderful,' I said flatly. 'A whole week.'

'With pay, of course.'

'Oh, of course.' I hardened my resolve. 'And we'll make that two, eh? Two weeks.'

'Oh. I see. Well, er, I'm not too sure we could, er, spare you for that long.'

'Two weeks with pay,' I said, then added for good measure, 'You'll have to. You owe it. It's in my contract.'

I made a mug of tea and retired to a corner of the record library to drink it. I wonder what it is that gives a library that distinctive atmosphere. It doesn't matter whether it's filled with old books or new LPs, whether it's a vaulted hall or, as in this case, a glorified cupboard, but there's something about a library which offers respite. I took it along with my tea and planned the next stage in the campaign. Strike while the iron is hot, they say, or in my case, before you lose your nerve, so as soon as I felt fit, I trotted off upstairs to see the Managing Director.

I gave a peremptory knock and walked straight in, seeing as how he was always going on about his door always being open to his employees. He liked to think of himself as a father-figure, even when the Union (I was shop steward) was hammering on his door (locked).

Digby was fat, middle-aged, and thirty-four years old. He put the phone down as I strode in.

'Ah, Alison my dear, I was expecting you. That was Frank,' he said, nodding at the telephone.

I pulled up a chair and sat down.

'Sit down, my dear, and let's have a little chat, shall we? Now then, what's the problem?' He was smiling. It looked fixed in place with superglue giving him an expression reminiscent of Little Red Riding Hood's wolf.

'I want a daytime programme.'

'So I gather. But it's not quite as easy as that, is it?' he said, being reasonable. 'We'd have to move one of the other jocks to your slot, wouldn't we?'

'Logical,' I conceded.

'But we can't just shift our presenters around like that, you know.' He tried to snap finger and thumb together. He failed. 'It's not fair to your audience. And,' Digby was being emphatic, 'it's not fair on your colleagues. We can't just take somebody off a daytime show and tell him he's got to work late nights, unsocial hours, just like that.'

'Why? *I* work late nights, unsocial hours, just like that.'

'Yes but you see, my dear, it is *your* programme, after all.'

'But, Digby,' I said, leaning forward over his desk and trying to look a bit pathetic. 'I'm asking you to try and put yourself in my place. I'm trying to run a home and look after my husband . . . '

'Your personal life isn't exactly *my* concern as your employer, now dear, is it?'

More soft soap was needed. 'Digby,' I said with a sniff, 'I can't go on like this. It's wrecking my marriage!' I looked down at my hands and put them on his desk where he could see them looking, I hoped, small and helpless.

He leaned over and covered one of them with his pudgy paw. It felt sweaty. 'There, there, dear, it's not as bad as all that, surely now, is it?'

'Yes it is,' I said. 'I'm not asking this lightly, Digby. I can't see any other answer. I've given it a lot of thought. I must have a daytime programme. At least for a while.'

'But we can't put you on in the daytime as easily as that, my dear.' He leaned back and smiled harder. 'After all, Alison, you're a woman.'

So, he'd finally admitted it out loud. And I finally exploded. 'What do you mean I'm a woman?'

'Now then, calm down, dear, don't let's have any hysterics. I know you're very women's lib and all that but . . . '

'I am *not* being hysterical and I am *not* very women's lib, I just want equality!'

'Calm down.'

'I am calm.' I took a deep breath.

'There, that's better,' said Digby. 'Now. What I meant to

say was . . . ' he was trying ever so hard to be tactful, 'women are lovely on the radio. Just what I want to hear when I'm going to bed. But I wouldn't want to hear one when I'm having my breakfast.'

'You mean women are fine to go to bed with but not to get up with?'

He didn't notice the sarcasm. He breathed a sigh of relief. 'Exactly, my dear.'

I wanted to scream but I was silent. Numb.

'Now then,' he continued, 'I'm sure we can work something out. Can't have unhappy presenters on my station. Basically, it's your marriage, am I right?'

'Partly, but essentially it's the late . . . '

'Your marriage, yes.'

I could practically see his brains skittering about behind the creases on his forehead. Almost absently he said, 'My marriage went through a little bit of a sticky patch, you know. A couple of years ago.'

'Really?' My voice was flat.

'Yes. Oh yes. Wouldn't think it now, of course, but it was. Very sticky. And then,' he said with a flourish, 'we had a baby! Little Damian. We've never looked back since.'

'That's nice,' I said, hoping he wasn't going to bring out his photographs. I thought how wonderful it must be to have a wife-person at home to produce meals and babies when required. Somehow, I couldn't see Joe settling down as a housewife.

'Yes,' he agreed, 'it is nice.' Then he leaned across the desk, looking his most paternal, and patted me on the wrist. 'Why don't you have a baby, dear?' He was serious.

I pulled my hand out from under his. 'Listen, Digby,' I said, voice rising; to hell with martyrdom, 'there's one thing you ought to get straight. I'm not a woman disc jockey, I'm a disc jockey who just *happens* to be a woman! There's a difference! And I'll thank you to keep your nose out of my sex life!' I stormed out of his office and forgot, in my fury, to slam the door.

I was still angry by the time I got home, but the anger was turned on myself. There was no chance now that I'd ever get that pig-headed set of male chauvinists to give me a daytime programme. There was no point in fighting because I knew I couldn't win. You can't batter a way through that sort of bigotry because the more you batter, the more you seem to them to prove their point. I could only see one way off the late night slot and that was to quit. Finito. I didn't want to resign. I loved the job, I got a lot from it, enjoyed it all. Only the hours were wrong. But then again, I loved Joe, I got a lot from him and I enjoyed our relationship. Only the hours were wrong.

CHAPTER EIGHT

When I got back to work in the New Year I made a last all-out onslaught on Frank and Digby about getting a daytime programme. This time I got arguments about rearranging the schedules for the sake of the one against the benefit of the many. And then it was back to the old bone about women deejays on the radio.

'Women don't want to hear another woman on the radio,' said Digby.

'I'm a woman and I do.'

'But you're not hard enough to do a daytime show. Your style is too, er . . .' Frank was thinking hard, '. . . soft.'

'I can change it to suit.'

'I doubt that very much, my dear,' said Digby, condescending.

'How do you know if you never try me?'

'We couldn't do that – you've no, er, experience of a daytime slot,' said Frank.

'Give me some then!'

'No way, lady,' they chirped in unison.

Stale or Check, but either way – Mate. Stay or get out but there would be no compromise.

Decision time. Out with the notebook again. You can always tell when my life's having a crisis by looking at the notebooks. Whenever there's a spate of entries it's crisis time.

The newish book was practically falling apart from overuse.

Entry:
January 28. Effect of Job on Life.
Pros:
 1) glamorous job – fame (?) perks prestige
 2) money good
 3) it's fun

4) it's a great ego trip
Cons:
1) unsocial hours
2) tired
3) hard work
4) male chauvinist pig headed management
5) don't see enough of Joe
6) tired and floppy and boring when I do see him
7) Joe and me don't make enough love
8) too involved in my job. talk about little else
9) suspect Joe resents my career
10) I'm bored. want a new challenge. same every night
11) money's not *that* good
Possible results if I quit:
1) lose immediate financial independence
2) find another job? Be a secretary again?
3) be a housewife? (No, never, no no)
4) see lots of Joe
5) me and Joe happy together
6) social life reborn
7) sex life ditto
Summary of above:
fairly obvious now I've written it all down. I shall hand in my resignation.
End of entry.

I woke Joe when I got home from my Friday night/Saturday morning stint, regardless of his resistance. 'I'm thinking of handing in my notice,' I said, just a little too brightly.

'Mm?' came his sleepy voice, 'you what?'

'I said I'm thinking of quitting. Work. Radio. You know.'

He woke up. 'What's brought all this on?'

Remembering that I was supposed to be an independent person and that just because I happened to love him, or he me, and be married to him, and that I must not use him as my life's prop, I couldn't say to him, melodramatically, 'I'm thinking of throwing in my job to save our marriage.' He would have interpreted that (correctly) as 'look, I'm making this sacrifice for your sake'. So I said things like I wasn't happy in the job, it didn't challenge me anymore – all the 'cons' section of my notes came reeling out.

'Well if you've thought about it . . . do whatever you want.' He was silent for a moment. Then, 'You're not doing it because of me, are you? You know, because I've sometimes grumbled about never seeing you?'

'Whatever gave you that idea?'

'Good,' he said. 'I just wanted to be sure.'

'I'll quit then,' I said, feeling a little resentful that a) he hadn't seen through my subterfuge and b) if he had done he would've been angry.

'Well, whatever you do, just so long as you do it for your own sake,' he said. 'Now give me a cuddle and let's go to sleep.' End of conversation.

I don't know what the opposite of male chauvinism is called but it can be taken too far. I snuggled down under the quilt feeling cheated and then he put his arm around me and pulled me into his side. Aw, I thought soppily, he does understand really, he just doesn't want to say it. I kissed him in the dark.

'You smell like an old ashtray,' he said. 'Why don't you quit smoking as well while you're at it.'

The weekend was before us. Joe woke up feeling randy. I never feel randy till I've been to the loo and cleaned my teeth and had two cups of tea and even then I have to work at it. We cuddled sleepily and didn't kiss, Joe stroking my thighs and then quickly on to higher things. My body was irritated, rather than pleased by his touch.

'I'll have to go for a pee,' I said.

Joe rolled away from me. 'Christ, you really know how to ruin a mood, don't you?'

'Would you rather I wet the bed?' I said, crawling out from under the warm quilt, body shocked by the cold air in the room. Breath came out like steam and I switched on the fan heater. It whirred into life with a hot, dry smell. When I came back from the bathroom Joe was out of bed and dressing.

'Oh,' I said. 'I thought . . . '

'Don't feel like it now,' he said, pulling on brown

corduroy trousers. 'I'll make some tea.'

'I'm sorry,' I said, coming up behind him and putting my arms around his waist. It was like hugging a tree. I let go and began to dress. He went downstairs.

'I suppose one of us ought to do a shopping list,' I said a few minutes later when I'd joined him.

'You do it.' He handed me a steaming mug of tea.

'Ta.' I slurped at it and began to feel very slightly more alive. 'Mm. That's good. Don't feel like doing the shopping, though.'

'Me neither. But we've got to eat.'

'Tell you what,' I said, 'let's go now, as soon as we've finished this, get it over with all in one go at the market, then go off somewhere for the day. We could go away for the weekend even. Stay overnight in a little pub somewhere. Dales, p'raps? What do you think?'

'We're meeting Simon and Carol later. I told you. Or have you forgotten?'

'No you didn't. It's the first I've heard of it.'

'I did tell you. You've just forgotten. You never *listen* do you? Wrapped up in your own head.'

Silence from me. I could have sworn he never told me. But perhaps he had. I honestly didn't remember it. 'Tell me again, then,' I said. 'What time? Where are we going?'

'Eight o'clock,' Joe replied with strained patience, 'at the Crown and Anchor. Then we all go and eat somewhere. Remember now? That I told you?'

'No.'

'Well I did.'

The pub was packed with students when we arrived. I felt all of my twenty-eight years. Hot and steamy atmosphere and I couldn't see over the heads of people, just bodies and armpits in my nose. Joe forged his way through, me following as best I could, wanting to hang on to his hand, little girl in shopping crowds frightened of losing mummy. We found Simon and Carol sitting on a bench behind a wet and beery table, ashtrays full of fag ends and peanut packets. I secured a couple of empty stools for me and Joe. He squeezed on to the bench next to Carol. I sat on one of the stools facing the other three and lit a cigarette. I felt out of place in my fur-collared coat next to all those anoraks.

It's about time Carol had a proper description. She was twenty-one and consequently her laughter lines had not yet sharpened into wrinkles. Being a sociology undergraduate she had to be very earnest about everything she did, from eating a corned beef sandwich to beating Simon at chess. She had thin lank hair which hung in tongues around her shoulders. Her skin was pale, the sort that Jane Austen's heroines were careful to preserve, and her eyes were an ordinary bluish colour. I always thought of her as the kind of girl described as 'almost pretty' on a good day, except that sometimes she had an uncanny knack of looking a bit like Popeye's Olive Oyl. This is a totally sexist viewpoint, of course. Male eyes saw her differently. She never used make-up or cigarettes, never bothered to do anything with her hair except wash it, wore old jeans and tatty pumps, and still managed to collect a group of men around her wherever she went and without appearing to notice the fact at all. I decided it was her enthusiasm that drew them. She was always bright and bouncy, bubbling over with energy, yet she was soft and understanding, sympathetic to fellow students with problems, puppies with cut paws, and me. Carol was the sort of person people loved, whether they be male or female, and I can testify to it because even though she had long legs and big tits, I loved her too. Carol was a leading lady. She was telling Joe how much she loved her part in his play, how clever and subtle it was. Joe took the compliments casually, glowing inside with the praise because he respected her opinion. They began to talk about the importance of performance to the written arts and how the actor can bring out new aspects that the writer didn't see were in the words he'd written. Joe complimented Carol on her interpretation. Carol complimented Joe on the tools he'd given her to work with.

Simon, the director, looked across the table at me and said, 'What about the director then?'

'What about the live-in support and comfort?' I smiled back at him.

Joe and Carol, deep in their mutual admiration society, didn't hear us.

Driving home much much later on that dark and rainy night I said to Joe, 'Do you fancy Carol?'

''Course I do,' he replied. 'You know me, I fancy the pants off everybody. Don't you fancy Simon?'

I thought of Simon, plump, pale-lashed and balding on top. 'No. Not a bit. I often wonder what she sees in him.'

'So do I,' said Joe. We drove on in silence for a couple of miles. Then he said, 'You were very quiet tonight.'

'Was I? I was listening. To you and Carol. It was interesting.'

'I wish you'd join in sometimes. Say something. Show a bit of enthusiasm.'

'I enjoy listening,' I said. 'Besides, you were going on about Theatre-with-a-capital-T again. How can I join in when I've never seen any of the plays you were talking about?'

'You *never* join in though. Not just about Theatre, about anything. I wish you would.'

'I do. I can talk you under the table about rock music. You just say I'm boring.'

Joe ignored this point. 'You make me feel responsible for you. Sitting there in silence. As if you're not enjoying yourself and it's my fault, and I ought to do something about it.'

I thought: perhaps you should. I said, 'But I was having a lovely time. I've told you, Joe, I enjoy listening to other people's arguments – just as well married to somebody like you,' I added in a smaller voice.

'You put a damper on everybody.'

'I'm sorry, I'll stay at home next time then.'

'God, can't I talk to you about anything without you taking it as a personal criticism? You're so bloody egocentric.'

'Wasn't it a personal criticism? Why can't I enjoy myself my way? Why should I have to enjoy myself the way you think I should?'

'But it's so dull when you're like that. You're dull, Alison.'

'Have you ever stopped to think that people might think you and Carol dull, the way you hang on each other?' I said, feeling bitchy.

'Don't be stupid,' he replied. Then, 'I think that's your trouble, you know.'

'What?'

'It's not just laziness that makes you sit back and watch instead of joining in . . . '

'Who said anything about laziness?'

'It's simply that you're stupid.'

'Don't be so arrogant.'

'That's right,' said Joe, 'fall back on your usual defence. Call me names like a three-year-old.'

'You started it!' I yelled.

'See? You're being childish!'

'I'm not being childish!'

'Don't just deny! Argue with me for God's sake!'

I took a deep breath and tried to be calm. 'Look,' I said, 'let's just forget it, shall we? We're both . . . oh I don't know.'

'Just like you – "forget it". I don't want to forget it. I want to talk about it. Talk to you. Talk. Say something.'

I couldn't think of a darned thing to say. My mind went a complete blank. 'I've nothing to say.'

'I believe you,' he said.

A long silence.

'Joe . . . ' tentatively, 'I know things are bad at the moment. But it'll be better. It'll get better. We'll have more time together soon. It's what we need. When I've finished at 2D, when I've stopped work.'

'Oh, that,' he said dismissively.

'We'll be able to do things together more often. I'll be able to share your world a bit more.'

'Just so long as you don't turn into a parasite,' he said. 'And have you thought about what you're going to do? Or are you just going to sit around at home all day waiting for me?'

'That's not fair, Joe.'

'Who's talking about being fair?' he said. 'Why do you always talk in clichés? Can't you say anything out of your own head? What are you thinking? I want to know what you think about. Do you think?'

I was thinking: how can I get close to him again? Why is he so antagonistic? What's wrong with me? Then: why do I believe it must all be my fault?

'Well go on then,' he said, 'aren't you going to say anything? Tell me something interesting. You must be able to think of something!'

'Stop it, Joe. Why are you always attacking me?'

'Because,' he said, voice cool, 'it's the only way I can get any sort of reaction from you. I can't stand you just sitting there, loving me, comfortably. I want you to excite me!'

'Like Carol does?'

'*Yes*, like Carol! I want to bounce my ideas off you. I want you sometimes, just sometimes, to have the guts to tell me I'm wrong.'

'Well you are wrong!' I said. 'About me.'

'That's right, I tell you to tell me I'm wrong so you do as I tell you just like that and tell me I'm wrong.'

I tried to work out the syntax of his sentence.

'You really are stupid, aren't you?' he continued. 'Thick.'

We finished the rest of the drive in silence. When we got inside the house I busied around making tea till he eventually asked me why I didn't go to bed.

'Aren't you coming?' I said.

'I'll be up in a minute. Do we have to do everything together? Can't I just sit here for a while without you worrying at me?'

I shrugged and went upstairs taking my tea, a book and my grudges with me. The black mood was surging from him in tidal waves. How long was it going to last this time? Minutes? Hours? Days, even? I sat in bed consoling my feet, if not my feelings, with a hot water bottle, book open on my lap, not reading a word. I was thinking over the evening and wondering how it had all come to this. What exactly had gone wrong, what particular incident had started it off? But I couldn't find one. Would quitting work really turn out to be the panacea, or only partial? Maybe it was already too late and spending more time with each other would only mean more of times like this.

About an hour after I'd gone to bed I heard him come up the stairs. He came into the room and sat on the edge of the bed. So I said hello. It seemed a logical way of re-opening communication channels.

He put his arm round my neck and pulled me towards him, squashing my nose against his shoulder. 'I'm sorry, Alison, you shouldn't let me be such a shit.'

'So it's my fault you're a shit?' I said, smiling at him.

He smiled back. 'That's just the way I am. Can I come into bed with you?'

'Please.'

Joe took his clothes off and I watched him. He got into bed and cuddled up close to me, my breasts against his chest. We held each other, not talking, just holding and stroking. His penis became hard against my belly and I ran my hands down his back, over his buttocks, inside his thighs. We made love. It was nice. But it wasn't very exciting.

Almost immediately afterwards Joe went to sleep. I lay there for a long while, on the wet patch (how come *I* always got the wet patch?), not sleeping. Where had all the excitement gone? What had happened to the Joe who used to be? What had happened to the me who used to be? Whatever happened to the young freelance radio producer and the ambitious and frustrated BBC secretary? Had I changed, or had Joe changed, or was it both of us? I found no answer. Why didn't I cut my losses and leave him? I'd done it before, walked out on a marriage. Why not again? Because I love the bastard, I thought, turning to look at him. There was no answer to that either. So I made plans, there in the warm bed in the dark room, next to a sleeping Joe. Once I'd quit work there were endless possibilities to my life. It wouldn't be so much the end of something as the beginning of other things. I could learn classical guitar, write songs, take up potting, change my appearance, seduce Joe in the mornings, join the drama group, write a book, get enthusiastic over politics, read the paper all the way through every day, argue forthrightly about anything and everything. I'd fascinate Joe all-the-way-home. When I'd quit.

On the Monday morning I got up early, went in to work, handed in my resignation, phoned Carol, left work and met her for lunch. We met outside a little pub close to the university and much frequented by the students because of its cheap and delicious roast beef sandwiches with plates and plates of crispy pickled onions. I waited in the doorway for about ten minutes until Carol turned up. She wasn't late. I was early: Punctual to a fault. Carol arrived looking worried and a bit out of breath.

'Oh, am I late?' she panted. 'I saw you from up the street so I ran.'

'Daft old thing,' I said, giving her a friendly punch, 'I was early. Come on, I'll get the first round and you can sit and get your breath back.'

Carol found an empty table while I bought drinks and food. Then we sat down and small-talked for a few minutes while we ate our sandwiches, me feeling guilty at every mouthful. Food and guilt, guilt and food.

'Okay,' Carol said, butting into my thoughts and looking straight at me with her concerned social-worker-to-be face on, 'what's up?'

'Is it that obvious?'

'Yes.' Blunt, uncomplicated, straight to the heart of the matter, Carol.

'Carol,' I took a deep breath. 'I'm in a mess.'

She waited for a second or two. 'Well. Go on. I'm not a mind reader. What is it?'

'It's Joe. Me and Joe, so I've quit. This morning. Handed in my notice.'

'Christ,' she said quietly. 'You've *quit*?'

'Yes.'

'Well, go on. What brought all this on?'

So out it all came. She was always a good listener. But I wished she were Sally.

'God, I'm sorry,' she said when I finally trailed to a halt. 'I didn't think it would come to this.'

'What do you mean?'

'Sorry for you,' she said. 'I mean I've seen there's been a bit of a strain between you and Joe for a while now, but I never thought . . . '

'Trouble is . . . ' I said slowly, thinking: don't say it, don't say it, ' . . . I know that Joe fancies you.' I watched her reaction to this very closely. 'You're my friend but you're also my biggest threat.' There. It was out.

'Oh come on, Alison, don't be daft. Me? That's silly. Anyway, even if he did you've nothing to worry about from me. You're my friend, for Christ's sake. So is Joe, and I love you both very much, but Joe's your husband. What do you take me for? You can trust me, surely?'

She loves us *both* very much. Ergo, she loves Joe. No, both of us, a pair. 'I'm sorry, I didn't mean that I thought that you . . . ' I fibbed. 'It's Joe I'm worried about.'

'I think you're reading far too much into everything. You're just going through a bad patch that's all. Everybody has them. But don't you think you've been a bit drastic? Quitting and all.'

'No I don't. I think it is that serious.'

'Poor Alison. It's not that bad, surely. You're just a bit fraught and everything is assuming a far greater importance than it actually has.'

I wrapped both hands around my glass and somehow wished it was her neck. Illogical. She hadn't done anything. 'But when I stop work Joe and I will be able to spend so much more time together. I'll be able to come to the rehearsals, for instance.'

'That'll be nice.'

'Anyway, it's done now. No going back.'

'But what are you going to do? Sit at home?'

'That's what Joe said.'

'It's a fairly natural response.' Why was she defending him? 'Will you look for another job?' she asked.

'Not right away. I just want to spend more time with Joe.'

'Well . . . ' she said it like a magistrate summing up, ' . . . I'm going to be honest with you . . . '

'You always are, aren't you?'

' . . . I think you've been a bit rash. Chucking in a job like yours. Why, I'd give my right arm for it. But you've done what you think's best so I'm right behind you. You can count on me. And if Joe starts to grumble at you about it then you just send him to me, right? I'll tell him what for.'

I smiled. She must be joking. 'Okay,' I said.

'Good. And anytime it seems to get too much for you, you know where I am. If you just want to talk it all out with somebody, you know I'll be here and that I understand. Right?' She put her hand on my arm and squeezed.

'Thanks.'

'Well, that's what friends are for, isn't it? You'd do the same for me.'

I had thoughts upon the subject of friendship. We smiled at each other for a couple of minutes.

'At least you're both aware of the problems,' she said then, 'so that's a start, isn't it?'

'Both aware?'

'Well, Joe talks to me a bit about it all too, you know. Just call on Carol, universal aunt.'

'Does he? When? What has he said . . . ?'

'Not much. Hardly anything really,' she smiled at me affectionately. 'And however bad things might seem sometimes, they're not really, you know. He does love you. At least there's that. And it's a very big "at least". He's always talking about you to me.'

'Is he?'

'So stop being silly, pull yourself together, and *be positive*,' she finished.

'Yes. You're right. Thanks, Carol.' I lit a cigarette. 'So. How are you? How's Simon?'

'Oh, he's fine.'

'Seeing him tonight?'

'No, not tonight, he's in London.'

'Oh? Deserted you has he? What will you do with yourself?'

'I'll have a good time,' she laughed. 'I've got a friend coming round.'

CHAPTER NINE

That same night I came home after the programme to find that Joe wasn't there. No motorbike, no lights, no husband asleep upstairs. The emptiness and quiet of the house practically shouted at me. I wondered where he could be.

I flopped into a chair. Adrenalin had deserted me for the night and I was too tired even to put the kettle on. I thought about going up to bed but there seemed no point if Joe wasn't in it. I put my head back and closed my eyes noticing again how quiet it all was, not even any traffic noise.

I wasn't really worried but I was curious as to his whereabouts. I knew there'd been no rehearsal because of Simon's trip to London and Joe had said earlier that he was looking forward to a quiet night in. The minutes ticked by very slowly and still no sign of him. Anxiety set in. Horrible imaginings started to flash through my mind – visions of him in bloody pieces spread over a road somewhere. I was just beginning seriously to consider calling the police to check if there'd been any murders or motorbike crashes when I heard his bike. In a couple of minutes the door opened and in he came, waterproofed, booted, gloved and helmeted, a Michelin man in black. He took off the helmet and left it on the dining table saying, 'Oh, hello. You're back already.'

''Course. It's gone two o'clock.'

'Is it really? Oh.'

'You went out after all then?' I asked lightly, longing to know where he'd been and who he'd been with and why he was so late, but not asking him because I couldn't face an accusation that I was being possessive. I hadn't the stamina for a fight.

'Yes,' was all he said.

I waited for him to volunteer a little more information. He didn't. So I gave in and asked him where he'd been.

'Just out.'

‘Anybody I know?’ I asked, again trying to keep it inconsequential.

He hesitated briefly then said, ‘No, don’t think so.’

‘Oh. Want a cup of tea?’

‘No.’

‘Shall we go to bed then?’

‘You go on up. I won’t be long. Might have a bath first.’

So I went up to bed by myself knowing I should have persisted with the questions, demanded to know where he’d been, who he’d been with, insisted he come to bed with me, told me about his evening, shared his life with me, his wife, just a little. But I hadn’t the energy. I lay there, the bed cold, thinking: don’t worry, it won’t be long now, only a couple more weeks then everything will be all right again and you won’t have to fight to share Joe’s life. No radio show, no stress, lots of time together, lots of fun, lots of love, Yours Faithfully.

I had to work out two weeks’ notice. I was beginning to wish I hadn’t been quite so drastic as to actually give up my job, but that’s me all over: dither for ages but then once I’ve decided something I go the whole hog. Anyway, it was done now, a replacement producer/presenter for the late night show, *my* show, was ready to take over and there was no going back.

So I put on a smiling face and became secretly sentimental and self-sacrificing over the career I’d donated to the worthy cause of marriage. The listeners became ‘my’ listeners as I counted the number of programmes left to do before I finished making airwaves forever and hurt a little bit more as the number inexorably decreased each night. I dug out favourite album tracks to play, replied to fan letters by hand and sent a special card to faithful Mabel of Knearsby. I even became punctilious about little details like using the correct colour leader tape and logging the timing of records accurately instead of just guessing. I resumed lunches at the Admiral and looked back with fond wistfulness at the sunshine of last summer, the memory of Joss. Everything became unbearably dear to me. I even began to stay behind for a little while when I’d finished the show and after Nigel had gone home, just to be in the building alone, prove to it that it was still mine.

Every time I came home from work a little later than usual I'd excuse it to Joe by saying that there was a lot of winding up to do and not to worry, it wouldn't be long now. Not that I needed to – he rarely noticed that I was late, and when he did, he didn't seem bothered. He was too involved in final rehearsals and the excitement of the imminent festival to notice much else at all.

The nights passed. The finale arrived with champagne splashes and giggles and I was surprised when I played the closedown jingle for the last time to feel no regrets, no sadness, not even anticlimax. I just drove home as usual, not actually believing that I wouldn't be repeating the journey tomorrow night and the night after and the night after that. I closed the door quietly, crept upstairs, undressed in the dark and eased myself into bed beside the sleeping Joe. After taking all that care out of habit not to wake him up I then grasped his shoulder and shook him. 'Joe. Come on, you. Wake up. I'm home.'

'Hello, smelly,' he muttered fondly.

'Hello,' I said, kissing him. Then with a vigorous hug, 'Hey, I'm *home*!'

And there was no difference.

The National Student Drama Festival began in a couple of days up in St Andrews in Scotland, so I finished work on the Friday night, spent Saturday packing for both of us and being supportive and on Sunday we hit the road. Joe the author, Simon the director, Carol and the rest of the cast were excited, apprehensive, proud, nervous, the honour of the drama group at stake. And I, the wife, was carried along with it too – excited, apprehensive, proud, nervous, the reputation of My Husband The Writer at stake. But I felt hopelessly outside it all, the bridesmaid on the wedding night. I helped to stage-manage, checking on props, ironing costumes, following the script, helping Carol to dress and make up, typing the programme, shifting the chairs. I never felt really accepted as part of the *bona fide* drama group, though. I was not an artiste, you see, merely a keen supporter, secretary of the fan club, the wife. I wasn't used to being The Wife.

Joe's play was received very well. The church hall was full every night. Not 'standing room only', there wasn't even standing room. It was a funny play, you see, and had songs in it, and was a lovely change from Brecht. Joe hung around the exit at the end of each performance eavesdropping on comments as the student audience trooped out. Most of them loved it, a lot of them liked it, none of them hated it. He was very upset by one overheard comment: 'It was very good! But it's not really *Theatre*, is it?' Poor Joe.

I was immensely proud of him and of the whole group. But there was something between us, Joe and me, that hurt. Everything was strained, he never touched me. We were never together, even when we were alone, just the two of us. 'Worlds apart' wasn't just a meaningless phrase anymore. Joe and I were living it in the most literal sense. It was so obvious, so huge, that we couldn't even mention it to each other. While it remained unspoken there was just a chance that it was all in my imagination, but if I shaped it into spoken words I'd be vesting it with reality. I daren't even tell it to my notebook, all I could do was lecture myself with common sense: give it time, give us time, you can't expect a magic wand to sprinkle glittering moondust over your life in seconds. It's only been a few days, it'll get better. After all, we've a lot of ground to make up, we have to grow back together again after living virtually separate lives for so long. All we need is time.

But there wasn't any. We came back home, play over, festival over, no more evening rehearsals, and I launched myself wholeheartedly into a schedule which included things like dieting to get slim for Joe, making nice meals to delight him, experimenting with my appearance to surprise him. The aim was to please. I even made the supreme gesture and had my hair cut short. I hated it. It felt odd. The image reflected in the mirror didn't match my self-image anymore and I felt an uncomfortable shock every time I saw it. A displaced person. All Joe said about it was 'Mm. P'raps you were right. Maybe it was better long.' I could have strangled him.

He started calling in for a drink after work and therefore coming home later and later in the evenings, and then, when he got home, he'd eat in silence then go off for a long walk by himself saying he wanted to be alone. He'd erected a glass shield around him which was brittle with jagged edges, at the same time as being utterly unbreakable. Even someone as stubbornly blinkered as me couldn't ignore the warning signals anymore, no matter how much I wanted to, because even when I resolutely shut my eyes against them they were still there branded red on the back of my eyelids.

This went on for seventeen days after I finished work: seventeen days of loving Joe, of him being the focal point in my life, him being my new career, of me trying everything I could think of to turn our cohabitation back into a marriage. But after only seventeen days he quit. Resigned. Joe was now the one to hand in his resignation.

It was Monday evening. He was sitting in a pile of cushions not speaking, eyes focused at infinity, pale face which showed the pull of gravity. That was nothing unusual these days. I went over to him and knelt on the floor putting my arms around his knees. 'What's the matter, lovey? What are you thinking about?'

'Us,' he said flatly and followed it with a long silence.

Eventually I broke it. 'Go on. What were you thinking about us?' I said it very lightly, with a smile, and reached to smooth the hair back from his forehead.

He jerked his head away with shocking violence, leaving my hand foolishly stranded. 'Go on then,' I said again. I almost held my breath, suddenly not wanting him to answer.

'I was thinking . . . I don't . . . love you anymore.'

He might as well have slapped me in the face. I just sat there with my mouth open, not able to say anything.

So Joe said more. 'I want children.'

My voice came back. 'But you just said . . . '

'But I don't want *you* to have my babies.' A verbal kick in the stomach.

'Oh,' I said. What a useful little word that is. So I used it again. 'Oh,' just like that, sounding calm as anything. 'It's bad, then, isn't it?'

''Fraid so.'

But I couldn't actually believe it. 'Oh, Joe . . . don't you think you're being a little dramatic? Don't be hasty. You've got to give it time, you know. We've hardly had any yet. Only seventeen days,' I said reasonably.

'Seventeen days of nothing,' he replied, voice still flat. 'I expected it to be wonderful, having you around more. But it's not. It's just like it was before only there's more of it.'

'Thanks.'

'I'm sorry, but that's how I feel. I can't in all honesty say that I love you.'

'And you always were the great one for honesty, weren't you?' I said. The strange thing was I didn't even feel like crying. I merely stayed where I was, still hugging his knees, not really believing the conversation. I wasn't part of this, I was just an eavesdropper. Eventually an alien voice, not mine but coming from my mouth, asked, 'What do you want to do then? Do you want a divorce?'

'No.' The reply was too quick. He thought a little and changed it to, 'I don't know.'

'I see,' I said, though I didn't at all. 'Then answer me this,' I continued. My voice was tiny but at least it was recognisably my own again, 'and I want the truth . . . '

'Of course. What?'

I hesitated, then jumped in. 'Is there somebody else?'

'No.'

I believed him.

'The trouble is,' he continued, 'there isn't *you* either.'

'Yet you don't want a divorce?' I wondered why I asked it again, risking a different answer from the last.

'No.'

'Why?'

'Because . . . I suppose I don't want to lose you, us. I don't love you. But I might. I'd like to. I don't. But I might again one day.'

'You mean you don't want a divorce yet, just in case.'

'Something like that.' Then he continued quietly, even kindly, 'But I don't hold out much hope. I'm sorry. Poor

Alison.' The concern in his voice, the pity there, crumpled me.

That was when the tears started. All I could think was: Joe does not love me. He wants babies, but not with me. He might love me again one day, but he has little hope of that. Damn it, why do I always have to believe what he tells me?

My life's base went plummeting down through the cellar floor and down and down and down. 'Joe,' I said. 'Hold me. Please.'

'No. I can't. It would be dishonest.'

'Damn your honesty!' I cried.

He got up and walked miles away from me across the room to look out of the window at the distant orange lights of Dringley. I slumped into the cushions which were still warm from his body.

'I'm sorry,' he said across the space which divided us. 'I didn't think you'd take it so hard.'

'Pardon?' I said, incredulous. 'Jesus, what did you expect? That I'd laugh? I *love* you, damn it!'

'I'm sorry.'

'You and me both,' I said with an edge of bitterness. I wiped away the tears angrily, had a hearty sniff and tried very hard to be practical and unemotional. 'So. What do we do now?'

'I don't know.'

'Nor me.' Not caring how ludicrous it was, with our marriage in bits about my feet and no glue, I continued, 'How about a cup of tea?'

He didn't answer so I patted the cushion, stood up, dusted myself off and went into the kitchen to fill the kettle. Hell, I needed some even if he didn't. I couldn't hold on to myself for very long though.

'But what do you want to *do*?' I burst out when the kettle began to hiss.

'If I knew that it wouldn't be so fucking difficult, would it?' his voice came back full of frustration and anguish.

I was glad it was hurting him too, if only a little bit. 'Do you want to leave?' I called out as the kettle boiled.

'No.'

'You want to stay then,' I put a teabag into a mug and

scalded it, boiling water splashing all over the worktop.

'No.'

'Jesus Christ, what do you want?' I squashed the teabag sadistically. 'And do you want some tea or don't you?' I was almost, but not quite, shouting.

'Fuck tea,' he said quietly. 'And fuck it, I don't *know* what I want!'

'All right,' I said, heaping in some sugar and a dollop of milk. I carried the mug back into the living room and went to stand by him. But not too close. 'Let's try and look at it from the outside. You don't love me.'

'No.'

'But you'd like to.'

'Yes.'

'And therefore you don't want to move out?'

'No.'

'But you don't want to stay.'

Then Joe cried out, 'For God's sake stop being so fucking logical about it all!'

'Don't *swear* at me!' I shouted, banging the mug down on the table and bouncing tea up into the air. The hot liquid landed on my hand, scalding it. 'Now look what you've done,' I muttered, hand in mouth, sucking it, tears pricking at me again. It was a ridiculous scene. If it hadn't been so true I would have been laughing. But it was true, all of it, and I couldn't see the joke. I sucked my hand for a long time after the pain had left it, not knowing what else to do, or what to say. I knew that as soon as I took the hand out of my mouth I'd have to say something, but I wasn't even thinking at that point. Just standing there sucking my hand and floundering.

Joe spoke. 'I know all this must have come very suddenly for you.'

I nodded, still mute, still sucking.

'But is it really so unexpected? We've both felt things were wrong, you must have felt it.'

I stopping sucking. 'Of course I did! Why do you think I quit my job for Christ's sake? I didn't expect this. Not that it had come to this. I knew it would take time to get back to how we were, and I was giving it time, but seventeen days, Joe?'

'Stop going on about seventeen days as if you finishing your job was everything. That doesn't *matter*! Can't you see?'

'Sure. I can see that it's bad. But I didn't think it was this bad. I never stopped loving you, Joe,' I said, not wanting to look at him but not being able to help it. I knew there was love in my eyes. And hurt and bewilderment too.

'Don't throw your love at me like a weapon.'

'I'm not. It's simply a fact. I love you. That's my hard luck, isn't it?' I said.

'Do you think I'm enjoying this any more than you are? Do you think I want to feel this way? Shit, can't you see that at least I'm being honest with you? Grant me that.'

There it was again. Honesty. The deadliest weapon of them all and the most comforting self-justifier. 'I wish you'd lie then,' I said.

There was another silence. It said everything, but gave no answers. I drank some tea, then tried again. 'So what now? What do we do now?'

'I don't know.'

'Stop saying you don't know!' My voice was rising again.

'But I don't!'

'Then what's the point of all . . . this? Why the drama? Why say any of it at all if you don't know what you want?'

'Because I know what I *don't* want.'

I had to say it: 'And you don't want me.'

'I don't know!' Joe screamed, arms flinging upwards, hands grasping his head.

'You bastard,' I said quietly. Then I went upstairs, got into bed keeping all my clothes on, closed my eyes, shivered and tried to assimilate all that Joe felt, prevarications included, with all that I felt. My reaction remained, unreasonably in the face of such overwhelming contradiction, one of stubborn disbelief. And rising anger. Don't lose your cool, I told myself, don't think. Just breathe, deep and slow. Count. One . . . in . . . two . . . out . . . three . . .

CHAPTER TEN

Beginnings and endings are always confused, mingled into each other, and you can no more separate them than you can separate the fat and the flour in pastry. But that doesn't stop the pastry from crumbling, does it? So the next two or three weeks were a kind of limbo, existing somewhere between two states of certainty. At one end of the scale was the concrete platform of marriage and at the other was a concrete platform of being one in the world instead of half of a pair. The limbo state was no base, the amber light on the traffic lights, not starting, not stopped and yet not moving. I had nothing to stand on. Joe wouldn't let go, wouldn't acknowledge that 'we' were over, whilst denying that 'we' still functioned, or that he even wanted us to function. Put simply: I was married to Joe but he wasn't married to me. 'Don't know' was the only thing I could get out of him. Not: 'Okay, that's it, we're finished,' but this: 'I'm not sure of my feelings,' and this: 'Don't give up on us because I might come back to loving you again.' So I zoomed in on that word 'might' and I hoped. But I could find no true direction because he didn't want me, or love me, or need me but he wouldn't let go. And I couldn't let go.

We lived in the same house, shared the same bathtub (separately), ate the same meals (occasionally), and slept between the same sheets (alone, on alternate nights, one upstairs in the bed, the other downstairs in a sleeping bag. Scrupulously, laughably fair).

I turned to a new notebook and filled it with questions. I turned to music and totally identified with the lyrics in sad songs. Why did the industry have to choose that particular time to release nothing but sad ones? Every time I switched on the radio the music would have something to do with left, bereft lovers, partings, passions and pain. To say nothing of the paralysis resulting therefrom. And the medium itself held its own special pain for me – I didn't even have a job anymore that I could throw myself into. In the absence of anything more constructive I spent self-indulgent hours wallowing through my record collection, intentionally, masochistically, homing in on the agonised ones and aching over the lyrics, my body resonating to a weeping guitar or the passionate cry of a tenor sax. Oh, there's nothing to beat a bit of emotional masturbation when you feel you've been emotionally raped.

And of course Carol was close at hand so I used the shoulder she proffered, spreading out my pain upon it, sticky as marmalade, sharp as paper. She listened with care in her eyes, care for me, care for Joe and me. 'I wish you could be stronger, that you wouldn't squirm so much,' she said. 'Are you sure you love him and aren't yourself just hanging on for the sake of it?'

'Yes! I love him. I wish to God I didn't but I do. I never quite realised how much until all this happened. It hurts so much. I can't tell you. If he leaves me I don't think I'll be able to bear it.'

'Alison, you must be strong.' She paused, then said, 'If you really love him you must let him go.'

'Agony column clichés don't work in real life. I'm damned if I'll just let him go. He's my husband. I want him. I love him. I won't just leave. He'll have to make the decision.'

She sighed. 'The ball doesn't have to be in his court. You really should put yourself first for a change, think of yourself.'

'But that's what I'm doing. I want Joe, I want us together, so I am putting myself first.'

'Poor Alison,' she said, 'I don't know what to say to you. Except that if I were you I'd leave him.'

'But you're not me.'

'No,' she replied, looking away and frowning. After a moment or two of sympathetic silence she resumed. 'He's not good enough for you, you know. You'd be better off without him. You should finish it now, once and for all.'

I smiled a watery smile and thanked her for her loyalty. 'I know,' I said, 'and I can't.'

The inaction, the uncertainty, was beginning to drive me nuts. I had to do something, get away, distance myself for a little while at least. I thought if I were absent for a few days it might help Joe too, help him to come down on one side or the other of his interminable indecision. Maybe he'd miss me. Or maybe he'd simply feel light-headedly free of me? It was a chance I had to take. I wrote a note for him saying I was off to Sally's for a couple of days, and putting down her phone number just in case. I packed an overnight bag, checked my dwindling current account, left the note on the table and locked the door behind me before I had a chance to change my mind. I wanted to be gone before he got home from work. I filled the petrol tank and headed for the M1 thinking: that'll show him. At least he'll see that I am capable of independent action. And I hope it pisses down all weekend – if he doesn't miss me, at least he might miss my car.

Dringley to London is a long and harrowing drive, but luckily I'd timed it so that my arrival at the other end was well clear of the rush hour, and I'd already got the route to Sally's flat imprinted on my mind as well as arrowed in red on the pages of the *A to Z* which was lying open on the passenger seat. Sally greeted me with 'I like your hair!', a bear-hug and oodles of tea and sympathy. But I was twitchy. 'I'd better phone home,' I said when I'd only been there about five minutes. 'Let him know I got here okay.'

'Shall I? Would you rather I talked to the bastard?' asked Sally.

I smiled. 'No thanks. I think I'd better do it.' So I picked up the phone, dialled the number and listened to it ringing at the other end. And ringing and ringing. I dialled again just in case the first time had been a wrong number. But no reply, no Joe.

'Never mind,' Sally said, 'you can try again later. Try all night if you want. Maybe you'll be lucky and get him out of bed.'

'I daren't leave it too late.'

'Why on earth not? Good God, woman, he can hardly lean over and clobber you – he's over two hundred miles away!'

'I know, it's just that . . . well, suppose I ring at three in the morning and he's not there? Or he's . . . maybe he's . . .'

'Busy?' she said, carefully. 'Do you think that's it, that there's somebody else?'

'I don't know, I don't want to think about it. I couldn't stand the thought of him . . . naked and making love with somebody else. That's special. It's private. It's ours! I know I had my little fling with Joss and all that last year, but we never, in the end I didn't . . . Oh Sally, I just can't cope with the thought of it. It's the sort of thing that, you know, like cancer or something, I have to believe that it can't happen to me. I suppose when we get down to the nitty gritty I'm not as modern as I like to think. "Keep thee only unto him" and all that. I need that. I believe it. He's my husband!'

Sally just nodded, understanding.

'Oh God, I hope it isn't that. But then, why not? He's always said he would if he wanted to. He's always been quite open and honest with me about it.'

'What are you trying to do, defend the sod? Honesty! Huh! I think it's about time you started being honest with him. Go home, catch him in the act and kill him. I'll help.' She looked as though she meant it too.

I lit a cigarette and started pacing the floor. 'Oh, I don't know. There probably isn't anyone. Just me and my lurid imagination. It makes for a simple explanation that's all. I mean, if you just stop loving somebody, without something happening to cause it, some sort of catalyst, then it can only mean that it's me, that I'm not worth loving . . . ' The thought was too heavy for my fragile ego to bear, and my voice broke. I started to cry.

'Hey, come on, is this the girl who had a teenager pursuing her half way across the world for love?'

In spite of the exaggeration it didn't help. I sat, face

hidden in my hands, and Sally sat on the arm of the chair and put her arm around my shoulders.

'I'm sorry,' I sobbed, 'I just don't understand what's happening. I don't know what to do, how to get through it, who to fight. I feel so lost.'

'There, there,' she said, stroking my hair. 'Come on, don't be so negative. There's lots you can do.'

I didn't believe her. 'Like what?' I sniffed.

'Well if there is another woman . . . '

'No.' I didn't want to think about that.

Sally made me. 'I said *if* there is, then you find out who it is and you play dirty. Or honestly if you prefer. Same difference.'

'Oh yeh? How? Just supposing I had the guts.'

'Well for a start, you meet her and you face her with it. Odds are just knowing that you know and that you're prepared to fight her for him would scare her off.'

'Not her . . . ' I replied, shaking my head, and realising as I said it that I was actually admitting to myself for the first time the real possibility that Joe's other woman, if he had one, had to be . . .

'Who?' asked Sally.

'Carol.'

'That student friend of yours, the one I'd get on with like a house on fire?' Sally could be very sarcastic.

'That's the one.'

'So face her with it. And if that doesn't work, tell her you're pregnant. Or that Joe's got syphilis. You'll be able to think of something.'

'Easier said than done,' I replied, despairing.

'You can do it. Come on, chin up,' she said whilst giving me a big hug which made her instructions physically impossible. 'Besides, maybe you won't have to do a thing. There's probably no one else at all and it's just Joe throwing one of his wobblies. It'll all turn out all right and in a few days he'll come bouncing in just like his old bumptious self saying "where's my fucking dinner and get your clothes off"!'

The mimicry was so accurate that I had to laugh in spite

of everything. It felt so bloody *good* to have someone so totally and unquestioningly on my side.

'That's more like it.' She patted the top of my head and stood up, hands on hips, looking resolute. 'So, when you get back what are you going to do?'

'Ride it out. Scintillate Joe all the way home – and check up on Carol.'

'That's my girl. Now wash your face and in the morning we'll play with make-up and you can be my first cover-girl guinea pig.'

I stayed for two days and she did a terrific job of making me feel valuable again. I left with a couple of black and white portraits of myself, my resolutions strengthened, claws sharpened up a bit and ego nicely patched.

The resolutions lasted about as far as Leicester Forest Services. With every mile I drove after that I just became more and more nervous. Would he be there when I got home? Would he be pleased to see me? Would I walk in and find him in bed with – somebody? Would he hug me and say it had all been a stupid mistake and he'd missed me? I rehearsed thousands of opening lines for when I walked into our house and imagined a thousand different welcoming and not so welcoming responses from Joe. It was a pretty useless exercise because he wasn't even at home when I got back. Only an empty house and a sink full of dirty dishes. From which I took a squalid comfort: at least he hadn't moved out.

I took my overnight bag upstairs and unpacked it. I made the bed, and while I was at it checked the sheets for any tell-tale signs of double occupancy. There were none and I was ashamed of myself. I went downstairs again, washed and dried the dishes and put them away. I dragged the vacuum cleaner out and did the carpet. Then I went upstairs again and cleaned the bath. Then down again to make a cup of tea because I couldn't think of anything else to do. I wished I'd stayed with Sally for a little while longer. I opened the evening paper and started to look through the Situations Vacant. Hell, why not? The Grand Gesture hadn't made much impact.

It was after midnight when Joe came home and there was no pleasure in his eyes at seeing me there. He paused in the doorway. I got up from the chair, crossed the room towards him and held out a hand. He side-stepped, and not touching me, he walked further into the room and sat down in the chair I had recently occupied. He picked up the paper, still open at the jobs page and, noting the circles I'd made round one or two of the advertisements, said, 'Job hunting already? You can't stick with anything for more than a few days, can you? Not even being out of work.'

He hadn't even said 'hello'. I sighed. How could we find our way through this? 'What are we going to do, Joe?' I asked, touched by a real despair.

'I don't know.'

'Surprise, surprise,' I said, despair turning to sarcasm. 'Well at the very least we have to talk about it. It's ridiculous to go on like this.'

'Okay. You start.' He sounded as if he didn't care one way or the other. He probably didn't.

But I wasn't going to let him off the hook so easily. I was determined to have it all out in the open, get myself some kind of footing, even if it meant the end of me and Joe forever. So I started the ball rolling. After what seemed an eternity of trying to delve into the reasons behind it all, digging around in my open wound searching for the canker in it and getting nowhere, I plucked up the nerve and laid myself, and my fears, absolutely open. 'Is there someone else?'

'No.'

'Really?'

'I said no, didn't I?'

Even Joe couldn't lie that well, that blatantly, without a flinch. Not to me. Filled with relief I went on, 'I love you. I want our marriage to work, I want to grow old with you.' I felt illogically stronger by spreading my vulnerability before him. I was daring him to hurt me, confident that he couldn't do it in the face of all that love. I went on boldly, 'You must have some feelings left for me. Can't you open your mind just a little bit to the possibility that you might still love me? Try pretending for a while. If you pretend hard enough, really act the part, it might turn from pretence back to reality.' I was sinking fast, beginning to plead. Wish hard enough for something and it will come true. I didn't believe that myself anymore. How could I expect him to?

'Stop it,' he said. 'I won't pretend. At least I've got enough respect left for you not to do that. Just give me more time. Wait. Be patient.'

Short of urging him to get it over with and leave me for good there was only one thing left that I could do, could offer. 'I'm going up to bed. Will you come?' I asked in a small voice trying not to make it sound too much like I was begging. What I meant was: I'm crossing more than half way, holding out my hand in the shape of my body, please take it. Please.

He said, 'Goodnight then. I'll see you in the morning,' and he unfolded the sleeping bag.

I saw him only briefly the next morning. I came down to find him dressed in waterproofs and packing his saddlebags. My hopes both soared and plummeted simultaneously. He's leaving! He's not leaving?

He looked up as I entered the room and said, vaguely apologetic, 'I guess now I'm the one who needs to get away for a couple of days.'

'What about work?'

'Sod that. I'll call in sick.'

'Oh.' This must be really serious then. He'd normally struggle along with pneumonia if he had to, because that's showbiz. 'Where will you go?' I asked.

'I'm not honestly sure. Might go to the seaside; Whitby or somewhere. Might just ride around. Don't know where I'll be.'

'Call me?'

'If you like.'

'Please.'

'Okay.' He hefted the bags over his shoulder, picked up helmet and gauntlets and left.

'Take care,' I said to the closing door.

It was Tuesday morning. I phoned Sally, knowing that she'd have already gone to work by now, but I tried anyway, needed a booster injection before I called Carol. Neither friend was at home. I wondered if perhaps Carol had gone away for a few days too? Had she got her own crash helmet by now? Was she on the back of the bike, arms clinging round my husband and riding off into the wild blue yonder? I stopped myself before it got any further, any worse, and thought: stupid! She's a full-time student. So she'll be at a lecture or something, that's all.

But I had to see her. Soon. Now, today. Face her with it. Get it over with. I decided to take myself out for lunch. If I went to the beef and pickled onion pub by the university there was a good chance that Carol would show up. This decided, I went upstairs to prepare myself with infinitely more care than if I'd simply been meeting a man.

It was about twelve-thirty when I entered the pub. It wasn't too crowded and I saw at a glance that Carol wasn't there. I got myself a glass of wine, it suiting today's image better than a half of lager, and sat down at a table in full view of the entrance so I'd be sure not to miss her if she turned up. I was feeling distinctly uncourageous. It was a lot easier talking about 'facing her with it' back in Sally's flat in London than it was to actually do it in a pub in Dringley on a Tuesday lunchtime. But again, I told myself I was being stupid. It was probably all in my imagination and I was wronging Carol terribly by even suspecting her of having an affair with my husband. She was my friend. I didn't have too much time to mull over the rights and wrongs of my suspicions because she arrived with a group of other students before I'd made any kind of impact on my drink. As soon as she saw me, she smiled, waved, had a brief word with her friends then came straight over. I felt better already. She certainly wasn't trying to avoid me.

'Hi. What are you doing here?' she asked brightly. 'Thought you'd gone away for a bit.'

'Only a couple of days,' I replied. Then, 'News travels

fast. You must've seen Joe then?'

'Mm. Friday or Saturday, I can't remember which. Did you have a good time?'

'Yes, lovely, thanks. Well, actually, no, not really.' I took a fortifying sip. 'To be honest, things are bloody awful. That's why I'm here. I needed to talk to someone.' Correction, 'To talk to *you*.'

He face fell. 'Oh, poor Alison,' she said, sounding concerned. 'Hang on, let me get myself a drink then you can tell me what's the matter.' She seemed innocent enough. She went to the bar and returned quickly with a pint of draught cider which went very well with her jeans, sweatshirt and training pumps. I wished I'd worn the right uniform. I was feeling very conspicuous in eyeshadow and high heels. So much for giving her something to contend with! The only thing to do was play it to the hilt, so I re-crossed my legs, straightened my spine, and thought myself into being cool and elegant. Or tried to.

'So,' she said, once she'd settled herself in, 'what's up? Come on, tell Aunty Carol all about it.'

I took a deep breath and thought: come on, girl, get it over with, straight between the eyes. Then I said, 'I think Joe might be having an affair.' I looked her full in the face. She didn't flinch. She didn't answer, either. Nothing. So I continued, choosing the words carefully, 'I'm sure he's screwing around.'

'Poor Alison,' she replied, dropping her gaze to the ring-stained table. 'Are you certain?'

'Almost,' which was true by this time. Unreasoningly. I was talking myself into believing it, and believing it was her.

'Screwing around?' she echoed. 'Surely not. It would be more than that for Joe, wouldn't it?' She went on quickly, 'Oh I'm sorry, that was tactless.'

That's the trouble with playing cat and mouse. You never know when you're suddenly going to turn into the mouse. 'I really don't know,' I replied.

'Poor Alison,' she said again. 'But I'm sure you're imagining it. Really.' She took a long drink from her glass then continued with a change of tone, almost conversationally, 'How would you feel if he was, though?'

I couldn't keep it up. Honesty won through. 'Devastated,' I said.

'Oh.'

I reached my hand across the table and touched hers. 'Carol, you're Joe's friend too, as well as mine. Tell me honestly,' I looked her full in the face again, 'do you think he's got a lover? Has he said anything to you?'

'I'm sure he hasn't,' she said, giving my hand an answering squeeze. 'But he'd hardly be likely to confide in me about it, would he?'

Thanks for nothing. I lapsed into silence. Where to go from here? I'd faced her with it and she'd either faced me out or was totally innocent. I chose to believe the latter. After all, next to Sally she was my closest friend. Innocent until proven guilty. Certainly nothing approaching proof here. If anyone were guilty it had to be me, for doubting her. I eased my shame a little, mentally apologised to her, by heaping my hurts upon her shoulders, telling her how much I loved Joe, how I desperately wanted our marriage to survive. 'I feel so helpless,' I said. 'I don't know what to do. I don't even know where he is now, or when he's coming back.' It came out like a graceless whimper but I couldn't stop it.

Carol looked away, obviously feeling uncomfortable, an unwilling witness to my pain. 'I don't know what to say,' was all she said.

Poor Carol. The burdens we inflict upon our friends, new friends, old friends. I pulled myself up straight again, gathered up the dregs of my dignity and said, 'Sorry. I didn't intend to go like that, to let go on like that. Sorry.'

'Don't apologise,' she said. 'It's all right. Really.'

But I could tell it wasn't. She'd changed since those days a lifetime ago when we'd argued about Joss last summer. 'Oh well,' I said. 'Just put me down as a rehearsal for when you're a fully qualified social worker.' I smiled brightly at her. It was very difficult. 'So forget it, eh? I'm just being pre-menstrual,' which was a lie.

'Poor you,' she said. 'Have you tried vitamin B6? Or calcium tablets are supposed to be very good.'
I drove home meditating on vitamin and mineral deficiencies being the cause of irretrievable breakdowns of mental health and marriage.

Joe's 'couple of days' dragged into three and then four and then five and I spent them and their accompanying nights not going out, not wanting to move too far away from the telephone, waiting for it to ring. I left the bathroom door open and shivered wetly naked so's I'd be sure to hear it if it did. I found myself staring at it, willing it to ring, shouting at it as if it were Joe himself, 'Ring, you bastard, ring, ring, phone me damn you, I need you. I hate you. I love you. Please phone me. Ring!' But it didn't, not once.
It was a very sunny Saturday afternoon when he came back. One of those perfect spring days which are a prelude to summer, a foretaste of what's to come. Blue sky, little white clouds in puffs here and there, trees becoming frilly with green again and grass stretching upwards after its winter sleep. I was sitting on the lawn, just sitting feeling the sunlight massage the creases from my face. The neighbours were quietly chattering, their voices mingling with birds and wind in leaves. Then the throb of Joe's motorbike drowned out the other sounds. I hardly dared turn to look at him. It was too nice a day for anything bad to happen but it seemed inevitable. Now that he was here I didn't want to see him. Limbo seemed safer.
He took off his crash helmet and gauntlets and left them on the seat of the bike then came across the grass towards me, his thick leather boots squashing the daisies. He sat down next to me without saying anything, not even 'hello, how are you?' I was pulling tufts out of the lawn, gritty bits of dirt getting under my fingernails. Joe put his hand on mine to still it. It was our first physical contact for ages. We looked at each other.
'I'm back,' he said.

'Obviously. How was it?'
'Okay.'
'You didn't phone.'
'No.'
I was acutely conscious of the birds and the neighbours and the wind, as if the volume had been turned up two or three d.b.'s.
'Alison, we've got to talk.' 'There's something you've got to know.'
Oh God, this is it, it's coming, I thought. But I couldn't bear not knowing any longer so I asked. 'You said before that there wasn't anybody else. I believed you. I'll ask you again. Is there?'
'Yes,' he said, very softly, quiet and gentle. 'I don't have to tell you who it is, do I?' Perceptive, knowing, or at least hoping, that I already knew.
I did, of course. I didn't want to believe it, didn't want to say her name out loud, but I knew I had to, so I did.
'Yes,' he said. 'Carol.'
'I see. Of course, it had to be didn't it?' My voice had an awful calm to it. 'Have you and she . . . '
'That's not important.'
'It is to me. I want to know. I have a right to know. Tell me.'
'Yes. We have.'
'When?'
'The first time . . . last weekend. When you were in London.'
'But I asked you then, when I got back, and you said no. You *lied* to me! You both lied.'
Joe didn't answer.
'Where?' I looked up at him, squinting through the ridiculous sunshine, quite dry eyed. 'Not in our bed?'
'No. Not here. What do you take me for?'
'You don't really want me to answer that do you?' After a brief pause I asked, 'Do you love her then?'
'I don't know.'
Dear Joe. What else should I expect him to say? But it lit the touch paper. He'd once said that he wished I would

react to things a bit more. Well at last I gave him what he wanted, even if I did go completely over the top. I flung myself at him bodily, in a virulent passion against the unfairness of it all. How dare he be unfaithful to me! How could he screw my friend! How dare Fate deny me Joss and then allow this! What happened to the rules? I felt like a blind and trusting victim of the ultimate betrayal. My fault, anybody's fault? Irrelevant. I'd loved where none was returned, and been allowed, nay, encouraged, to hope against all reason. I'd trusted where there was only betrayal. Not just Joe – I'd never really trusted him anyway – but Carol! Whom I'd called friend. Who'd listened to me, taken it all in, sympathised, advised. Carol smashed the rules. She took my confidences, my vulnerabilities, and wrapped them around herself like armour, using them to infiltrate the enemy's (my) camp and carry off the booty (my husband).

All the pain, anger, and futile hope of the last few weeks congealed into one great lump of rage as I flew at him, arms flailing, heedless of the neighbours and their hopes of a peaceful afternoon in the garden. I didn't care. I just yelled and shouted and sobbed and swore, regardless of the fact that it was only Joe who was being bombarded and not Carol too. It amounted to the same thing. They were partners in crime.

Poor Joe, much in need of armour plating himself, just sat on the grass with my blows raining down upon him and waiting for the storm to blow itself out. He didn't have to wait long. I soon turned from a screaming virago into a sobbing and exhausted heap, stripped of dignity, of pride, of any of those other stalwart virtues that you're supposed to fall back on if you want to keep your self-respect. I had nothing left, certainly not self-respect.

Joe watched me warily, then deciding it was safe now, put his arms around me and held me quivering against his chest until I was quiet. Then he said, 'I'm sorry. I never meant to love her.'

'You do then?' I managed.

'I think so. I don't know. But it's so astonishingly *intense*.'

It would be. It wasn't the fact that they had made love – and I didn't doubt that it was that, and not just screwing – it was that so many rules had been broken: you don't betray a trust, you don't take your friend's man, you don't inflict a wound with one hand and stroke it better with the other. And even Joe. He'd broken the cardinal rule, his rule. He had lost his head. I was no longer his centre, but Carol. Emotional infidelity the only sin – Joe's pledge, broken. I felt as if all my life I'd lived by the principle that green is green and suddenly I'd found out that it was red. Rules didn't count for anything anymore.

'And what about me?' I asked. 'Do you care for me at all, even just a little bit?'

He hugged me. I recoiled. 'Of course I do,' he said. 'I care for you. But not enough.'

I wasn't quite ready to let him go. There must be something I could salvage. 'Joe,' I said, attempting to breathe steadily, 'I can share your body, I think. Even with her, if I have to . . . ' I knew that was a lie, even as I said it, but any old port in a storm. 'I can't share your emotions as well, though.' What I meant was: choose, you bastard, I love you but it's me or her.

'Don't say that.' There was something in his voice, careful, quiet, almost threatening, that I couldn't quite make out the meaning of. He made it clear. 'If you make me choose, I'll choose her.'

'You *bastard*!' With that I slapped him across the cheek. As hard as I could. My hand stung with it. Then I turned my back on him, and making my voice as cold and hard as possible I said, 'You'd better go then, hadn't you?'

He went.

I didn't move, didn't turn to watch him, just sat where he'd left me on the grass in the (how could it still be shining?) sun. I was emptied, numb, blood boiling ice, wondering vaguely when this long and ridiculous nightmare would finish so's I could wake up again and carry on with Joe where we left off, somewhere around last Christmas, probably. I had to wake up sometime, because we couldn't really be just figments of each other's past, could we? Not me and Joe. The very idea was just too silly.

Eventually I stood up, pains stabbing at various bits of me and pins and needles in my legs. I stamped back inside the house and closed the door. It seemed very dark inside, my eyes not adjusting after the sharp sunlight. I shut the window and sat at the table, slumping over it, head cradled in my arms. After a while I noticed that my sleeves were becoming damp. I thought: I can't stand women who cry all the time. Then I carried on crying. Loudly. There was a glorious kind of release in it, in totally letting go. I was enjoying it. So I stayed there until the sun went out, then I drew the curtains and went up to bed.

Joe called in to see me the following day. I didn't ask where he'd spent the night and he didn't tell me. He simply asked, 'Do you want me to go? I mean move out?'

'What else?' I replied. 'You don't expect to go on living here with me, do you, while still carrying on with your little fancy woman?'

He didn't like the way I referred to his lady-love. 'Don't you criticise her!' he said, leaping metaphorically to her side.

'Why the hell shouldn't I? What is it that's so special about her? What has she got that you can just chuck away everything we had? What is it now – three, four years? How long before she wears out your imagination too? Or haven't you thought that one through yet?'

He remained silent.

I sighed. 'You want it both ways, don't you?'

Still no response.

'Oh why don't you just fuck off?' I said quietly and even politely. 'I'm going over to see my parents tomorrow and I'll be gone all day. You can come and get your things then. And leave the key. And the car key.'

'If that's what you want,' he said. Then, 'You'll be all right?'

I smiled at his attack of gallantry. Or was it conscience? 'I'll be terrific,' I said. 'No need to worry yourself about me. How about you? Where will you go?' I thought I knew the answer but I was wrong.

'Oh, I'll find somewhere I suppose. I'm quite good at sleeping on people's floors.'

'Not to Carol then?'

'No. There's Simon. He doesn't know.' Joe looked sheepish.

I was silent while the full meaning of that simple statement began to sink in. Then, 'You mean she hasn't even had the decency to tell Simon? She can muck up my life, our life, your life, Joe, but she hasn't told Simon? Simon doesn't know?'

'No. Why should he get hurt?'

'God! All this, all this and you're just her bit on the side?'

'Don't!, he said, 'it's not like that. She's not like that, she just doesn't want to hurt anybody.'

'Pardon?' I said, not believing that Joe could be so taken in. 'Doesn't want to hurt anybody?' I parroted. 'What the hell does she think she's done to me?'

'Don't be vindictive, Alison, it doesn't suit you. Carol never meant to harm you. In fact she said last night she was sorry she might end up losing a friend.'

'Is that meant to be some sort of vindication, to make everything all right? She's sorry! She *might* end up losing a friend? Oh, poor little Carol.'

'We couldn't help it. She didn't mean it to happen. You mustn't blame her, Alison.'

'Fat lot you know about it. About all those times I was crying on her shoulder, trusting her, and she was . . . ' I was filling up with anger again, and hatred, and I wanted Joe to realise exactly what she'd done to me. But I couldn't find the words, my anger was making me verbally impotent, and if I carried on I'd only cry. The last thing I needed. So I shut up.

'If you're going to be like that,' he replied with an attempt at dignity, 'I'm going.'

'Thank God for that,' I said, and turned away from him. I heard the door open and close, the motorbike start up and Joe drove off. He was gone. Again.

I pondered over what he'd said. Poor, innocent, loving and lovable, don't-want-to-hurt-anybody Carol. I took out the notebook and my hatred for her spilled all over its pages in red ball-point. I felt strong with it, with the desire for rightful revenge. Until I remembered that there was absolutely nothing, short of murder, that I could do to her. I threw the book and biro at the wall with all the force I could muster, clenched my fists in the air and let out the rage, the frustration, my seething, struggling helplessness, in one long, mighty, scream.

PART TWO

CHAPTER ELEVEN

I had no idea what time of day it was when Joe left me and I started screaming. Morning or afternoon, it was the beginning of my own Lutheran dark night of the soul. I felt totally alone. Not just lonely, but alone. It didn't matter that I had a family looking forward to seeing me tomorrow. It didn't matter that I had a dear friend in London looking forward to seeing me anytime. They didn't exist because my reality was suddenly contracted into four walls with a scream inside.

On one of those walls was a framed print, one of M.C. Escher's graphics, 'Band van Möbius I', a kind of simple knot with no ends, just going round and about and in on itself, no starting place, no ending place, continuous and eternal. It reflected my emotions. Anger, impotence, pain, hate, love, despair, loss, anger, impotence, pain, hate, love, despair, loss, round and round, blending into and out of each other with no edges, no ends, no beginnings.

I remembered some lines in a poem about loss where the poet had said that loss was quite ordinary and now it was his turn to be touched by it. I thought, yes, it is an ordinary thing. It happens to lots of people lots of the time. And now it's my turn. So ordinary a thing. But the poet's got it wrong. It doesn't touch, it batters.

Such tiny, ordinary memories of Joe loving me tumbled around my mind weaving in and out of the Möbius Band. Joe, sitting on the bed in my old flat with a cassette recorder on his knee dictating his adaptation of a novel, looking up and saying, 'Hello, can I have a kiss please?' then carrying on talking to the machine. Joe and me rolling down a grass-covered slag heap laughing in slow motion how many sunny afternoons ago? Joe leaving a stolen daffodil in a milk bottle for me when I got home and a note saying, 'A flower for a flower.' Joe sitting beneath the cracks in the ceiling by the damp patch on the wall with coffee spilt on his trousers and burnt toast on the table and a fried tomato slithering down the wall just beside his head, yet saying he loved me. Ordinary miracles, Joe loving me. Not ordinary; so very precious, so lost.

I spent the day, the night, wandering through the house touching things. Finding his clothes still in the airing cupboard, a T-shirt, an old pair of underpants, a sock, red with a hole in the toe. I never did darn his socks, saying he could use a needle as well as I could, so he bought new ones. He must have possessed more socks than anybody else in the world. Piles of socks, odd socks, separate socks, almost matching but not quite. They had a talent for divorcing themselves from conventional pair bonds. Like Joe and me now. Separate. A wrong match. I caught myself hugging the red sock with the hole in the toe to my cheek. Disgusted with myself I flung it in the dustbin.

It was dark outside, and cold now. I shivered and went back inside, turned the gas fire on and contemplated briefly whether I should bother actually lighting it or if it wouldn't be easier just to sit in front of it, doors and windows closed, and be gently eased into a permanent sleep by the toxic fumes. I lit the fire quickly but the train of thought continued. The serrated edge of the bread knife grinned at me from the kitchen. The thin covering of skin over wrist would score through quite easily. But it would hurt. And I turn squishy at the sight of my own blood. And it would mess up the carpet. An overdose, then, I wondered? But they say it gives you stomach pains and makes you throw up. You die in a puddle of vomit. Yuck. Besides, overdose of what? There was one old Mogadon and three aspirins in the house and that was it. There was the car, of course. I could drive it into a brick wall or poison myself with the exhaust fumes inside a sealed-up garage. But I didn't have a garage and the car would probably run out of petrol before it completed the job. I went through all the various methods I could think of for committing suicide: electrocution, drowning, throwing myself off the roof? It'd serve them all right if I did. Then they'd be sorry, Joe would be. It'd ruin his new love affair. A sweet revenge. But then, what's the point if I wouldn't be there to see it? It would be no revenge at all. Should I bother killing myself, then? Damned if I will. Murder somebody else, Carol or Joe possibly, but myself, never!

I stomped up to bed. One day, I promised myself, I'd be rich, famous, respected, desired, and Joe would come crawling to me on hands and knees begging forgiveness, begging me to take him back, promising to cherish and worship me forever more. That would be my revenge. The fantasy was a balm to my soul and I fell asleep embroidering in its details with multicoloured silks, unable to decide whether on that glorious day I'd take him in my arms or kick him in the balls.

I woke up the next morning with a throbbing ache in my head and a lump of ice where my soul used to be. Aspirins eased the former but I didn't know how to melt the ice, or even if I wanted to. If it went away I might find that there was nothing left in its place. Half-heartedly I got myself ready to go out into the world, set foot beyond the walls of my house which had become a kind of sanctuary overnight, a cocoon. I'd be stepping outside as a deserted wife, a rejected lover, incomplete and undefined, merely the remaining half of a once whole pair. But it had to be done, my parents were expecting me, and when I returned, tonight or tomorrow morning, it would be different. The limbo would be incontrovertibly over. Joe's possessions would be gone and his keys would be pushed through the letterbox. The thought spurred me into activity. I didn't know what time he'd turn up, but I didn't want to be here when he did.

I got in the car and headed towards the Pennines feeling a little apprehensive because I had no idea what kind of reception I'd get. I felt sorry for my parents, for the things I'd already put them through, and here I was doing it again. If I'd been born with a penis instead of a vagina I think they might have coped with me a little better. I mean, you expect a certain amount of hassle from a boy. But all they ever wanted for me was that I should get married to a nice husband who had a nice job like a bank manager or a schoolteacher, who would provide me with a nice semi-detached house with a nice garden wherein I could play with my couple or three nice children who would do very nicely at a nice school, thank you very much.

But my mother's only daughter got her sex mixed up and acted rashly, like a man. Daddy's little angel singed her wings, threw away her halo. Oh, I started off on the right track, went to university, then got married to a nice boy. My mother sat back, content to contemplate her daughter's rosy pink tomorrows while my father calculated the cost of the goodies and decided I'd done okay. Then the shock waves zapped through the family as I socked them at ground zero and upped and walked out on it all with only a sleeping bag under one arm and a bottle of brandy under the other. I couldn't see any rosy pink tomorrows, only an endless stretch of dull grey, so I left a letter for the nice husband on the nice mantelpiece in the nice front room of the nice (but very dusty) house. And nobody, least of all my parents, could understand why.

Why is it that when parents, particularly mothers, say 'I just want you to be happy,' what they really mean is, 'I want you to be *my* idea of happy'? Poor Mum. Poor Dad. Their eyes showed bewilderment, worry, care. But worst of all they looked betrayed, as if by rejecting all their sacred teachings I had thus rejected them. Not true.

Neither of them could understand why I walked out on that 'ideal' marriage. That was partly my own fault because I never even attempted to really help them understand it, or me. I just acted. I rented a small, bare flat and furnished it with painted beer-crates instead of a three-piece suite.

Dad, offering money: 'Here, love, go and buy yourself a nice, comfortable sofa.'

I painted the bathroom walls dark brown and splurged a jungle of white silk-finish flowers all over them.

Mum: 'It's a bit . . . er . . . different, isn't it? Why don't you paint it all magnolia? I'll help you.'

I spent Dad's present on a cream, furry, toe-wiggling wool carpet for the bedroom, leaving the rest of the floors naked.

Mum: 'It feels so bare. Echoey. Why didn't you buy cheap carpeting for all the rooms instead of splurging it all on this one? It'll show the dirt.'

Then with the divorce settlement money I left the flat and bought a little cottage with crooked walls and uneven floors and Joe moved in.

Mum: 'You haven't actually bought it? Sell it again! I'm not having any daughter of mine living in a slum. What was wrong with your nice modern flat? And when's he going to marry you?'

Then I stopped being a secretary at the BBC and became a commercial radio programme presenter mingling with outlandish people like pop singers and rock musicians.

Dad: 'Alison, my daughter, used to work at the BBC. But now she's disc-jockeying or something.'

Joe and I got married.

Both: 'I think she's beginning to settle down at last.'

But I kept on working, and working late nights at that, even though Joe had got himself a 'proper job'.

Mum: 'Are you sure you want to keep on working, Alison? Can't Joe keep you now that he's earning? Be a wife to him, cook his meals, have babies.'

And then . . . twenty-eight years old and still no children and this second marriage crunched to a halt. I drove over the Pennines to the arms of my parents remembering all that I'd put them through and thinking they'd be thinking: What's wrong with her that she can't keep a husband? Where did we go wrong?

How we misjudge our parents! It was a strange and paradoxically wonderful afternoon, the first time ever that I saw them as people rather than as my mother and father, the first time they talked to me as a woman, not just as an erring daughter. We talked for hours. We talked through their life and my life and three-quarters of a bottle of brandy. We talked of endings and beginnings and they guided me out of the swamp of my pain and pointed to the beginnings that could lie on the edge of it. Their conversation was, as usual, liberally laced with maxims and platitudes, but instead of closing my ears in an instant dismissal as I usually did, this time I allowed myself to listen to them, to absorb the wisdom which lay behind the hackneyed vocabulary.

But I still had to put up a token resistance. 'That's all very well, easy for you to say, but I've got no husband, no money, no job, nothing . . . '

'Don't talk rubbish, lass,' said Dad. 'You've got the whole world if you want it. It's all out there. Get up off your backside and go and take a look at it. What's to stop you? You're lucky!'

'Lucky?'

Mum, more gently, 'Your Dad's right, love. You're young, aren't you? Not like us. You've got brains, and you're pretty. Aim high. It's all there for the taking, all you have to do is grab at it, go and see the world.'

'You didn't and you've done okay.'

Dad said, 'Oh aye?' and Mum quietly snorted.

'Well you haven't done badly,' I said.

'Listen,' said Mum, 'if I'd had your opportunities I'd never have married your father for one thing.'

'I'd never have asked you,' he countered.

'Oh, don't start. Please.' They were turning into parents again which turned me into their child and I didn't want that. I was enjoying the new, adult closeness between us, revelling in it, and I wanted it back. So I plonked a bit of practicality down on the table as a diversionary measure. 'See the world indeed! Easier said than done.'

'Well why not?' said Dad. 'You youngsters have all sorts of opportunities that we never had, what with the War and everything.'

Mum nodded sagely. 'You'll find, once you get to our age, that the only things in life that you really regret are the things you didn't do, not the things that you did.'

I was sure I'd heard that line in a Joan Crawford movie on the television once, but I didn't pursue it.

'Aye,' said Dad. 'You shouldn't be asking yourself "why?" Only ask "why not?"'

'All right,' I said, rising to the challenge. 'Money. I haven't got any. A job. I haven't got one of those either. How's that for starters?'

'Pathetic. You'll have to do better than that. Get a job. Go be a croupier in Monte Carlo or go do your disc-jockeying on a cruise liner . . . ' He trailed to a finish under the admonitory look that Mum was giving him.

'Well, perhaps you don't need to go quite so far,' she said, 'but your Dad's right in principle.'

But the spark had caught and my imagination flared into action. 'Mm. I could, couldn't I? Why not?' I burst into song with a quick chorus of 'A life on the ocean wave' and then collapsed, giggling. The brandy was having its effect. Another first – I'd never been intoxicated in front of them either.

Dad laughed. 'Our Alison running away to sea! I like it.' His eyes were sparkling. He could see himself in my place, and I knew then, watching him, that if he had the opportunity, if he were younger, free, he'd be off like a shot. Mum saw it too. 'Stop it, Dad,' she said. 'Don't encourage her. Be sensible and calm down. Besides, Alison's not a boy.'

I giggled again and wiggled my finger at her. 'Irrelevant. Besides, you're the one who said I should go and see the world,' I reminded her.

'I didn't mean it literally.'

'Ah, but *I* do,' I said, and gave her a hug. 'Don't worry, Mum, I'll be okay, honest. And you never know, I might bewitch an Arab prince who'll whisk me away to the Kasbah!'

She shuddered. 'Don't say things like that. That's just what I'm afraid of.'

'Oh, all right, how about a lonely Texas millionaire, then?'

Mum smiled a grudging smile, Dad laughed and said, 'That's the spirit!' and our conversation turned to the more immediate practicalities of would I be able to pay the next gas bill.

I didn't stay the night. I wanted to get back to my own home, empty as it was, and begin my new beginning as soon as possible. Although the conversation about Monte Carlo, the world and ocean liners had been half joking, I found myself considering it very seriously. There was nothing for me here – no Joe, not even a job to drown my sorrows in. Why not run away to sea? Hell, I needed to run somewhere, away from Joe's keys glaring at me from the table.

But how did you set about it, where did you get the basic information? I didn't think shipping lines would be listed in the Dringley and District Yellow Pages. So I sat down and thought hard, looked at the problem from the other end. Suppose, oh glorious fantasy, I were rich enough to be thinking of a Mediterranean cruise. Where would I start looking at what's available? A travel agent, right? But I can't go into a big glossy travel agent's, cap in hand, telling them I want to nick their free brochures because I'm looking for a job, because I'd feel humble and I'd had enough of that recently. So bluff it, lie, pretend you're idle rich and looking for amusement!

I did exactly that the next morning and had a ball, raking through my wardrobe and yanking out the classy BBC secretary uniform that I hadn't worn for ages, dusting off the gold jewellery that Joe had despised, playing with make-up and hair-styles until the image was just right.

I left the travel agent with arms full of slithering, shiny brochures and their exotic, brightly coloured photographs of cruises from anywhere to everywhere. The world was quite literally within my grasp. I got back home, still buoyed up by the fantasy, searched out the all important head office addresses lurking at the end of the euphemistic literature and carefully composed the master copy of the can-I-have-a-job-please-anything-will-do letter along with an updated version of my old curriculum vitae, its truths carefully twisted to suit a life at sea. I typed out the letters and got them in the post just as the red GPO van came driving up the street to empty the pillar box on the corner.

I returned empty-handed to my empty little house and the fantasies and plans which had kept me shored up for the last couple of days fizzled into emptiness beneath me. I didn't actually want to run away to sea to see the world, I wanted Joe, here and loving me. But he wasn't, wouldn't be, didn't and couldn't and there was just me and the house was silent. It was a bit scary. Not the house, but the world outside it. Just suppose, I asked myself, that one of those shipping lines actually took me on? Unlikely in the extreme, of course, and I'd probably spend the rest of my days miserably broke and unemployed, but supposing they did, what then? Christ, I'd be whisked away on a ship, not knowing anybody, not knowing any of the rules, without even the familiar small comforts of my books, records and accumulated paraphernalia to cushion me against the shocks! I might be perpetually seasick. I might not make any friends. I might never come home again, I might fall overboard and drown. I considered the latter possibility and took comfort. Yes, there was always that to resort to – if I didn't like it I could always fling myself over the ship's rail. That pulled me up short. Pathetic, defeatist, whining little worm! The whole idea of running away to sea or somewhere was to save myself from drowning! Hadn't Joe once said that I spent all my energies on daydreams so I had none left over to set about achieving them? I had to prove him wrong. And I'd do it too. If not at sea then somewhere, somehow, else.

The evening paper flopped through the letterbox, so I dashed for it, hastily turned to the situations vacant page, spread it over the table and commenced a close scrutiny. Just in case all my shipping lines went under.

As things turned out I'd have been better off scrutinising the state of my wardrobe and practising a confident, friendly smile. Within three days of posting off the letters the phone rang and a voice on the line said, 'Can you be in Southampton by tomorrow afternoon?'

The voice went on to explain that they didn't normally employ people in this manner, without proper application forms and references and interviews and so on and so forth, but one of the Cruise Staff girls had radio'd her notice and was going to walk out as soon as the ship docked. As it sailed again almost immediately and my letter was there on her desk, how about it, on a short, trial contract? Could I get there?

I asked myself 'Why not?' Not a thought was given to whether there'd be a train or a plane or anything between Dringley and Southampton. I simply said, 'Yes.'

I spent a hectic afternoon buying clothes and a new, big suitcase and all sorts of things that I might or might not find necessary on a cruise liner. Then I phoned Mum. I couldn't cope with long explanations, I was too excited and had too much to do, too much not to think about, so I just said, 'I've done it. I'm going to be Cruise Staff, a sort of hostess. I'm off to New York tomorrow. Not for long, a couple of weeks or so. No time to talk now. Tell you all about it when I get back.' Poor Mum. Then I phoned Sally and said much the same to her.

She whistled in disbelief. 'You jammy beggar! Talk about falling on your feet! See if there's a job for me too, will you? They might want a spare photographer?'

So, I was round the other side of the S-bend, shaken, scarred and bleeding a bit, but still functioning and the scars were on the inside where they didn't show too much. It could have been worse.

It nearly was. That evening I was up in the bedroom with the radio on full blast, madly flinging things into the suitcase with one hand and pulling them out again with the other when someone banged lustily on the door. Wind and rain were lashing against the windowpane in a fury but I opened it and leaned out. Best to check it's not a likely rapist before letting them in. It was Joe. He peered up at me and lifted his rain-spattered visor. 'For God's sake let me in, I'm soaked. I've been knocking for ages!'

I slammed the window shut. What the hell did he want? I was tempted to leave him dripping on the doorstep but decided I was above that kind of pettiness. Besides, what could he do to me now? I was immune to him. I had a job again, a label, somewhere exciting to go, something exciting to do. I could define myself without any reference to him. The world was about to spread itself at my feet. I couldn't prevent the fleeting hope that maybe *he* was, too, as I raced down the stairs to open the door.

He came in, wet, bedraggled, slopping puddles on the floor. 'Leave your crash helmet in the hall,' I said as he was making for the table with it. (Proprietorial, this is *my* home now, not yours.) 'What do you want?' If he'd come to beg me to take him back, I wasn't going to make it that easy for him.

'I left my thesaurus and dictionary behind. I was passing so I thought I may as well collect them.'

'Oh.'

'How are you?' he asked.

I told him I was fine and that I was leaving tomorrow. I mentioned the job casually, not making a big thing of it, sounding as if hopping on a liner across the Atlantic was the easiest thing in the world and the sort of thing I'd have done every day if I hadn't been tied.

He looked genuinely pleased for me. 'Oh, well done,' he said. 'You see, I knew you had it in you! All you needed was a little push.' Trust him to turn it to his own credit, to refer to his despicable actions as 'a little push'. The nerve!

But I wasn't going to let him rile me, so I just smiled and said, 'How about you? Have you found anywhere to live yet or are you still camping out?'

'I'm still looking.' He paused and glanced around the room. 'Alison . . . Seeing as you're going to be away for a while . . . ' He hesitated.

The thought had struck me too. I had nothing to lose and everything to gain by being generous. 'Would you like to stay here?' I asked, then quickly continued, 'Not now, of course, but while I'm away. It would give you a breathing space while you look for somewhere decent.'

'Oh, if I could that would be marvellous. Thanks.'

'May as well take the spare keys now then,' I said, nodding to his old set still on the table. 'It'll only be two or three weeks, though, four at the most. I'll let you know when I'm coming back. Of course you'll have to go then, even if you haven't found anywhere.'

'Of course. Would you like me to pay you rent?' he asked, no barb intended, I'm sure, but one taken.

'Just your share of the bills will do,' I replied. 'You can use the car as well, if you like.'

'There's no need. I've got the bike.'

'For when it rains, then.'

'Thanks.'

'You can come tomorrow evening. I'll be gone by then. And I'll let you know exactly when I'll be back as soon as I know.' No harm in hoping the trial contract would expand into something worthwhile, is there?

'Fine,' he said. 'And, thanks, Alison. I really mean that.' He took a step towards me, holding out his hand as if he were about to offer a caress.

I stepped back. 'That's okay,' I replied, smiling. 'Just so long as you wash the sheets and things before you leave.'

He took it like a man, as they say. 'I suppose I deserved that.'

'I suppose you do,' was my reply. I didn't ask him about her at all and he didn't mention her. We had nothing more to say for the moment so he thanked me again for my generosity and took his leave. I closed the door behind him and listened to the throb of his motorbike getting fainter as he rode away. 'Damn you!' I shouted out loud, cursing both him and myself at the same time.

So much for my newborn equilibrium.

CHAPTER TWELVE

At four-thirty the following afternoon I was walking along the dock, unable to believe that a floating object could be so big. It wouldn't even have fit into Dringley High Street, for example. Oxford Street in London maybe? I was also unable to believe that I was actually there, standing next to it, looking up at it, and about to wave goodbye to England and life as I knew it. The only emotion I felt at the prospect, if you can justify calling it an emotion, was indifference. Considering that in only a week, if that, I'd gone from being a deceived wife on the green grass outside my house in Dringley to being a smiling hostess on a liner on the grey ocean heading for America, I suppose it's only reasonable to be suffering from some form of shellshock.

Until now the nearest I'd ever come to being on a ship was the cross-Channel ferry from Dover to Calais and I used to think that was pretty big. But comparing the ferry to the sweeping, graceful curve of metal soaring above me was a bit like calling the Pennines 'mountains' once you'd seen the Himalayas. Boats and ships, ships and boats, the dividing line between the two is vague and impossible to define. It isn't necessarily just to do with size. Function, grace and style come into it too. For example the largest of the cross-Channel ferries would still be a boat, whereas the royal yacht *Britannia* could never be anything but a ship.

I embarked. There could be no doubt that I was now on a 'ship'. And what a ship! She was big – even to my inexperienced eyes – and for some reason I've never been able to fathom, like any other water-borne vessel she was also female. This ship would be described as a woman rather than a lady, female rather than feminine, glamorous rather than pretty or beautiful. She'd be the sort of woman who wears false eyelashes and puts lacquer on her hair, uses an uplift bra to enhance her already well-endowed bosom, and would choose gold lamé for evening wear in preference to white silk. But because of her class and her style, she would never quite be described as brash.

It was a case of love at first sight. From the very outset she was 'my' ship, with pride. Not quite the *QE2* or *Canberra* perhaps, but good enough for me. She was to be my home, workplace, social outlet, prison, countryside and personal *Perfumed Garden* for the next four months. Initial fears about sharing a poky cubbyhole with complete strangers had been allayed by a young man in the Purser's Office who doled out the keys. He had half a stripe round the cuff of his jacket and pimples on his chin and he leered at me in a pathetic but infuriating manner which combined lust with condescension. 'Cruise Staff, eh?' he said. 'I can see you'll be popular in the Ward Room.'

'What's the Ward Room?'

'My dear girl . . . ' he said, unprepared for such naivety. 'You'll learn. Here's your key. I'd keep the door locked if I were you.'

'Am I sharing?'

'Cruise Staff don't share cabins,' he said. 'Unless they're in luck. 5122. I'll remember your number.' Smirk. (Schmuk.)

I had a double cabin to myself. 'Double' was a euphemism. Twin beds with a drawer unit separating them, a fitted wardrobe and a cupboard with shower, washbasin and loo inside it. That's all. It made Sally's flat seem like a mansion. I unpacked the gigantic suitcase I'd bought the day before which I could hardly lift when empty let alone full. It was a big mistake buying that case. Literally. I put toothbrush and paste in a glass in the 'bathroom' and picked up three hairpins and one used elastoplast left by the previous occupants and ignored by the steward. I allocated a place for everything, and put everything in it. Then I had a shower, much needed after hours on British Rail and multitudinous losing battles with the simulated leather elephant. The big question was what to do next. It was only seven o'clock and I didn't report for actual Cruise Staff duty until nine the following morning. We were to set sail with the noon tide. So the evening was before me. I didn't know anybody, the few people I'd seen had been heading off the ship rather than staying on it, and I'm not the type to latch on to total strangers just for company. Neither did I feel like exploring the streets of Southampton alone at night in search of excitement, or even food. I hadn't bothered to bring a radio with me on the principle that not many stations broadcast to the Atlantic Ocean and I didn't feel like reading. So I sat on the bed and indulged in a little misery. I tried it out for a few minutes but I couldn't keep it up, I was too restless. And hungry. Nothing, not even misery, can come between me and my stomach. It was time to explore.

A combined lesson in geography and semantics: my cabin was down on Five Deck at the front (for'ard) on the left (port) side of the corridor if you're facing the pointed end (bows) on the right-hand (starboard) side of the ship. Which means it was an inside cabin and its walls (bulkheads) had no windows (portholes). Five Deck, although fairly low down in the ship, was just above the waterline. I thanked Neptune for small mercies.

Taking cigarettes and doorkey with me I headed down the corridor towards the back or rounded end (stern) to see what I might see. I felt like Judy Garland setting out along the yellow brick road. Five minutes of walking in a straight line brought me to the end of the corridor. As the only way to go now was up – because I certainly wasn't prepared to go down below the waterline, even though we were still safely at anchor – I found a lift and pressed the top button which was mysteriously marked 'Q'. On arrival I went through a couple of heavy doors and found myself outside on the open deck. It would be reasonable to assume, wouldn't it, that having pressed the top lift button, you'd be at the top of the ship? Wrong. I looked skywards and the view was edged by three more decks above me making a giant's staircase towards a big, black and grey, spotlit funnel. How on earth was one supposed to go up there if the lifts didn't? I discovered later that there were many other lifts and not all of them went from bottom to top or even from top to bottom. In fact, only one of them went all the way. The system was a relic left over from the days when the ship was more firmly rooted in class distinction than it was now – when the humble members of Tourist Class couldn't even sneak into the First Class areas because the lifts and stairways wouldn't let them. It was still difficult, but at least these days you could get hold of a map to guide you through the maze. But on that first night aboard I didn't know that.

So I wandered around the public rooms gaining orientation and losing it again just as quickly, recognising places I'd been in half an hour ago but not knowing where they were or how I'd got there again. And I didn't meet a soul. It was really spooky. Like exploring an updated and hugely magnified *Marie Célèste*. There I was wandering around this enormous, luxurious ship which had everything from a shopping centre to three swimming pools and a morgue (somebody told me later), feeling more and more like the sole survivor of the holocaust. And getting more and more hungry. My feet were aching from the miles of thick carpet and I was in desperate need of a cup of tea and something solid to wash down with it. I had to be braver. So, arguing with myself that I was officially 'crew' I tentatively began to push on doors marked 'Crew Only. No Admittance' until one of them actually admitted me. That was how I got my first view of a pantry.

Now to me, a pantry was always somewhere where old ladies keep pots of home-made jam and bottles of elderberry wine on stone shelves. I collided with yet another new definition: a ship's pantry is a kind of big, stainless steel kitchen where waiters make crustless smoked salmon sandwiches and cups of bouillon for American tourists who are likely to give them large tips. I was dazzled by the white walls and shining expanses of cupboards, worktops, everything stainless steel, in a room larger than the total square yardage of my house up in Dringley. It seemed silly to hope that a place such as this could contain anything so mundane as a teabag and kettle.

Suddenly the far door opened. A large, auburn-haired, sun tanned man walked in, and I froze. I knew I shouldn't have gone in there. I felt like a burglar caught in the act. He looked me up and down. 'Who on earth are you? What are you doing in here?'

'Er, Cruise Staff,' I replied. 'I've just joined. I'm sorry if I'm not allowed in here. I think I'm lost.'

'My dear,' he said, 'how nice to meet you!' and his face broke into a beaming smile. It really broke – cracked into a road map of gulleyed flesh. He came at me round the central unit holding out his hand. 'I'm Sylvester, fellow dogsbody.'

I must have looked very blank.

'Dogsbody, drudge, flunkey, bondservant, skivvy, and general pimp – in other words, Cruise Staff, my dear, like you,' he explained.

'Oh.' I must admit I was a bit taken aback by the job-description.

'You must be the new girl. At least I assume you're not the new boy – we're expecting one of each.'

That was comforting. At least I wouldn't be the only rookie then. I smiled at him and took his outstretched hand. 'Pleased to meet you, my name's Alison.' We squeezed hands and I said 'Ouch!' as something rough and metallic bit into my fingers.

'Sorry,' he said and waved his hand in front of my face flashing an enormous gold lion's head which I took to be a ring. 'Tiddles didn't mean to bite you. Do you like him?' he asked, displaying it some more.

'It's very . . . big,' I said with as much enthusiasm as I could muster. I'd never seen anything which so aptly fit the word 'vulgar'.

'Mm, lovely, isn't it? Used to be a Dunhill lighter. But then a friend gave me a Cartier so I had it melted down into this old blob.'

'Very nice.'

Picking up where we left off before Tiddles interrupted us he said, 'So you're lost, eh? Not surprised, dear, on this old barge. What were you looking for?'

'A cup of tea?' I answered hopefully. Sylvester seemed the type who would know how to acquire such things.

'At last, a fellow tea drinker!' he exclaimed. 'I *adore* you already.' He hugged my startled frame. Then he released me and began to poke around in cupboards, filling his pockets with teabags, sugar lumps, and a teaspoon. 'That's why Americans are so absolutely unbearable, you know. All that disgusting coffee they consume. Come on down to my house and I'll brew up for you. Grab some biscuits. In that cupboard there,' he said, pointing to the one I was leaning against.

I opened it but could only see jumbo-sized catering tins, all firmly sealed. Was there nothing of ordinary, human dimensions on this ship? 'But none of them have been opened yet,' I pointed out.

'Bring the tin, my darling,' he said as if I should have known better. 'Can't let the punters have all the goodies, can we?'

He left the pantry and I quickly followed, trying my best to look inconspicuous as I hurried along behind him through doors, down stairways and along corridors with a ruddy great catering tin of stolen goods under my arm. I hadn't a clue where we were. As we progressed he explained the system of survival on the ship. Quite simply, you borrow things. Tea, coffee, milk, sugar, teapots, vases, knives, plates and whisky miniatures if you're good at it.

We arrived at a cabin door somewhere downwards and near the back. He took out a bunch of keys held together on a chain fastened with a solid gold clasp in the form of a lover's knot. I didn't even try to imagine what that might have been in a previous existence. He unlocked the door, pushed it open with a flourish and stood back to let me pass first. 'Welcome to my house!' he said. 'Make yourself at home.'

Home it was, though it was even smaller than my cabin – a single bed against the wall with a bunk bed folded away above it. A mirror was prettily framed by little stick-on flowers of pink, blue and yellow, and there was a handful of vividly coloured ostrich plumes in a vase on a coffee table which was covered by a hand-crocheted cloth. 'That's pretty,' I said.

'Yes, isn't it,' he said, visibly growing an inch taller with pride. 'I made that on last year's world cruise.'

One wall was covered with framed photographs of attractive, rugged looking men, some artistically posed nude, most of them signed to Sylvester with love. I recognised a couple of famous faces among them. 'Happy passengers,' he said with a delightfully smug smile, and he kicked a stuffed green felt snake against the bottom of the door. 'That's Freddie,' he said, pointing at it. 'They won't let me bring Ermintrude, the rotten bastards.'

'Who's Ermintrude?'

'My guard dog. Do you want to see my pickies of her?' and he pulled a little leather wallet out of his pocket without waiting for an answer. Very proudly he showed pictures of himself with a python draped around his shoulders! 'Isn't she beautiful?'

'Very,' I said. I was beginning to realise that Sylvester was no ordinary sailor.

I perched on the edge of the bed while he opened a drawer and took out a kettle, a teapot, a milk jug with milk in it and a sugar bowl containing loose sugar and a silver spoon. Two cups and saucers followed. This was much better service than I gave myself at home. He filled the kettle while I registered more details of his 'house'. The mirror gleamed, the air smelled of polish and Eau Sauvage, and a fresh red rose with a ribbon tied round it was propped up against a photograph which stood at the head of the bed. An exceedingly handsome, blond-haired, butch and athletic looking chap in his late thirties probably, smiled out at me from the frame. 'He looks nice,' I said. 'Who is he?'

'My husband,' answered Sylvester proudly, his face breaking up into a smile again and his eyes taking on a dreamy look. 'I miss him already. Are you married?'

'Yes,' was my first answer, quickly adjusted to, 'No . . . Well I'm not really sure.'

'Oh, not to worry,' he said briskly. 'You'll soon get boxed off on here.'

'Pardon?'

But the kettle boiled and my host became too involved in brewing up to explain. I didn't pursue it because I'd already showed far too much ignorance for my liking. Instead I commented on how empty the ship was.

'Of course,' he said. 'We're in port, aren't we?'

'Oh, of course.'

He took pity. 'Everybody's off on exercises, petal. At home with wifey while their ship-board girlfriends are exercising their on-shore boyfriends. Or their on-ship boyfriends are screwing their on-shore girlfriends. Or the other way round. Or all together. Or something. You only get one night here in every ten so you've got to make the most of it.'

I gave in. 'So what's boxed off?'

He handed me a cup of deliciously steaming tea and a plate piled with biscuits. 'Don't worry, you'll soon learn all our little tribal customs.'

I sipped the tea. Nectar.

'It means you have a friend,' he continued. 'Screwing somebody. And the sole aim of each trip is to get boxed off. As many times as you can. We have a points system for it, but I'll go into that another time. Eat up your biscuits like a good girl, you're looking pale. Only two rules to remember . . . ' He raised a finger in warning and with a wink that cracked his face even more than his smile, he said, 'No poaching – murder has been committed for less – and be discreet. Apart from that – enjoy!' He delivered the last word as if it were Life's Golden Rule. Sounded like a philosophy worth trying out.

I left Sylvester's cabin loaded with the box of biscuits, a packet of cornflakes, sugar, a spoon, a bowl, and instructions on how to find the pantry nearest to my own cabin where I could get milk supplies and anything else I needed so long as I slipped the resident steward a dollar if he happened to catch me borrowing. I made up my mind to swap most of my pounds sterling for the much more useful US dollars first thing in the morning.

When I got 'home' I sat on the bed, lit a cigarette and tried to sort out everything I'd learned so far. It had been quite an educational evening. If I played the next two or three weeks by the new book, it looked like I might have a very good time indeed, not to mention getting a kind of revenge on Joe. It all boiled down to Sex with an intentional capital 'S'. Sex and all its possible variations between all the possible sexes. Life at sea revolved around it. It might take love to make the world go round, but sex, it seemed, was what kept cruise ships afloat. I was a bit shocked by the laxity, the *laissez-faire* of it all, but as I turned out the light and closed my eyes I found myself being more and more seduced by the idea. I think I even went to sleep with a smile on my face.

When the alarm went off at half past seven the next morning the last thing I felt like doing was smiling. I groaned. Half past seven was practically in the middle of the night as far as my biorhythms were concerned. I fell out of bed and into the shower, got dried, dressed and ventured along the corridor to the pantry which was empty of life so I quickly borrowed a glass of milk and scurried away again to eat my cornflakes. Once passengers were on board, the ship started to function properly and I'd be able to take my meals in one of the restaurants.

Then, because I was nervous and not too sure of the way to the Cruise Director's suite, I set off far too early for my nine o'clock appointment and arrived outside the door at ten to. At five to I knocked. When a voice called out, 'Come in,' I went in. The bathroom of the suite was situated right next to the entrance door. I walked in and the bathroom door was wide open giving a full view of the Cruise Director (I assumed) seated and straining on the lavatory. I did a double take. He looked up and said, quite unconcerned, 'Go right in, I won't be long.'

Dringley and life as I knew it was getting further away by the minute. I went on through into the main part of the room, sat on a sofa, spied an ashtray full of stubs so lit myself a cigarette and tried not to listen to the farting noises issuing through the still open bathroom door. The lavatory flushed.

'I take it you're Alison?' said my new boss when he emerged, yawning. 'Nothing like a good crap to start off the day, eh?' He held out his hand in greeting and I wondered if he'd washed it. 'Jim Thrippleton's the name,' he said. 'To rhyme with nipple. You can call me Jim.'

I said hello, still embarrassed by the vivid picture of his straining face and the bare buttocks drooping over the side of the lavatory seat. I offered him a cigarette. He coughed and took one, lit it and took a long deep drag from it. Then he coughed again, longer this time. 'Ah, that's better,' he said. 'Now. Ever worked on a ship before?'

'I'm afraid not. I'm finding it all rather strange.'

'Hm.' He thought for a minute. 'You've a lot to learn then. Right, first thing is . . . ' and he started marking off the points on his fingers, 'you don't sleep with waiters, stewards or ABs. Officers, entertainers and passengers only. Oh, and not forgetting your boss, the Cruise Director, i.e. – me.' He yawned again and scratched under his armpit.

Tricky, I thought. He sat down next to me on the couch, making sure his thigh touched mine. I edged slightly away from him trying to disguise the action by smoothing down my skirt. I smiled at him and thought very quickly. Inspiration. Innocently I said, 'But wouldn't that be in breach of my contract, Mr Thrippleton?'

'Jim.'

'Jim. I mean, doesn't it say something about "Cruise Staff will not entertain members of the opposite sex (passenger or crew) in their accommodation"?' Funny how that sort of clause always sticks in your mind. Useful.

'Does it?'

'I believe so. And besides, I don't even know what an AB is.'

'Able bodied seaman. Sailor. The blokes who keep the ship afloat and moving.'

'Ah, the VIPs,' I said, nodding wisely.

'The lowest of the low,' replied Thrippleton.

My first lesson on the importance of class, not 'First' or 'Tourist', but among the crew. I crossed my legs and tried to look demure and efficient. 'So what exactly will my duties be?'

'Smile a lot,' he said through another long yawn. 'I'll put you with Wendy for the first couple of days. You'll meet her in a minute. We have a full meeting every morning at half past nine prompt. I'll introduce you to the mob. There's only six of us at the moment. A bit short staffed. You and the new boy will make eight. Not that either of you will be much use straight off, being trainees, so to speak.' He sounded very disheartened. He looked at his watch.

'Where is he anyway? Have you seen him?'

'No. I've only met Sylvester so far.'

Jim Thrippleton laughed. 'I won't ask about your first impressions then!'

'He seemed very nice,' I said, practising diplomacy.

'Raving old queen. Heart of gold though. Most other things too, or so I'm told!' He nudged me in the ribs, a little too high and to the front for comfort. It was getting tricky again. Perhaps if I'd been able to find within myself the slightest spark of sexual attraction for my new boss the situation might have been a little more acceptable. He was smallish and on the heavy side, though you wouldn't quite describe him as fat. His coal-black hair was short and slightly greasy and still spiky from sleep. His shirt tail was hanging over the back of his trousers and he wore sandals over his socks instead of shoes. He had mild halitosis, or perhaps he just hadn't got round to cleaning his teeth yet. There is a line somewhere which divides the frank and broad-minded and it's-all-a-bit-of-fun type from the downright coarse and obscene. Jim Thrippleton stood unequivocally on the latter side of it.

I crossed my arms. 'So I'll go round with Wendy?' I said, trying to get him back to business. 'And do what?'

'Just watch, help out when she wants you to, do as she tells you, find your way round the ship, and be nice to the passengers.'

'Doesn't sound too difficult,' I said, my spirits rising.

'Don't you believe it.'

A knock at the door interrupted the conversation and that was when Elliott walked into my life, flustered, lost and late. My fellow neophyte and instant friend. Introductions were performed, Elliott was given a brief outline of his duties, similar to mine except that he was allocated to somebody called Phil, and very soon after that the rest of the Cruise Staff, all bleary-eyed and yawning, trickled in for the morning meeting. Further introductions were performed. I forgot the names almost immediately, of course, except for Sylvester and Wendy who was easy, being the only other female member of the company.

As soon as everyone had found a space to park, Jim

opened the meeting. 'Right now, kiddie-winkies, everybody comfortable? Then we'll begin.' Elliott and I looked at each other in mutual apprehension from opposite ends of the room as the boss handed round copies of a glossy pamphlet entitled 'For your Pleasure and Leisure'. It was the programme of entertainments for the day. 'It'll be your job,' said Thrippleton as he handed me my copy, 'to bring a dozen or so of these programmes to me every night before you go to bed. And if I'm not too busy,' here he grinned and squeezed my kneecap in passing, 'I might even let you stay.'

I had strong suspicions now as to why the previous occupant of my post had left. She obviously had good sense. I smiled weakly and as soon as his back was turned I whispered to Sylvester who was sitting next to me, 'Is he always like this?'

'Always, even with me, ducks. But don't worry about it, he couldn't get a hard-on if he taped a banana to his dangle.'

Thrippleton turned. 'I heard that, Sylvester,' he said, quite jovially. 'You want to be careful my lad or I'll show you what a hard-on's really like. You wouldn't sit down for a month.'

'Ooh, hark at him!' said Sylvester to the room in general. 'He should be so lucky.'

There was a general laughter which I joined in, whilst cringing a little inside. Elliott and I shared another mutually supportive look.

During the next twenty minutes the programme of entertainments was gone through in detail, a member of the Cruise Staff being assigned to each event to make sure it happened when, where and how it should. The morning, of course, would be taken up with embarkation, and I was assigned to sit with Wendy in the Grenville Lounge on Two Deck (which for the rest of the sailing would be for First Class only) inside the Information kiosk. A fat lot of use I was going to be in there. Things hotted up in the afternoon with Open Day, which lasted half an hour, where the passengers were enjoined to 'Meet your Hostess, Wendy, in the Hawkins Room, who will tell you . . . ' (and me)

'. . . everything you might want to know about the ship.' Elliott would go with Phil to set up and introduce a filmed lecture on 'The Art Galleries of the Big Apple'. Sylvester would oversee round one of the Scrabble Tournament in the Quarter Deck games room, there'd be Yoga for Beginners with Gavin on Boat Deck Aft while Benjamin would take care of the trap shooting. My brain started to seize up round about Boat Drill at three-fifteen. I was assigned position seven, this time with Phil, where I was supposed to instruct our trusting charges on the correct way to don a lifejacket. I'd never even seen a lifejacket, and on being told that position seven was Upper Deck outside the midships cardroom, all I could say was, 'Where's that?'

Phil said, 'Don't worry, I'll meet you at three and go over everything with you first. Where shall we meet? Where do you know?'

'Only my cabin and here,' I said, feeling overwhelmed and useless.

Thrippleton groaned. 'For God's sake, Phil, find the girl a map, will you?'

'And one for me too,' chimed in Elliott.

Another bond between us. The Cruise Director went rapidly on to the evening's entertainments. Phil and Benjamin would share the in-cabin radio request show, an hour each, starting at half past five. I pricked up my ears. Ah, a little touch of home. A radio show! Could I? But I thought I'd better leave it a few days before I suggested I took it over. After dinner we were to divide ourselves between the various dance floors to look after the musicians, the cabarets, and be generally pleasant, smiling and sociable.

'Right,' said our boss, 'any questions?'

I put my hand in the air. 'Yes. When do we officially go off duty?' I asked.

'When you retire for the night. So long as you're not in your cabin you're on duty. It works out at about an eighteen-hour day, all right?' Judging by the expressions on the faces around me he was deadly serious.

Elliott was next. 'Do we have a rota for days off, then?' he asked.

I thought it was a reasonable question but everybody else laughed.

'What days off?' said Gavin flatly.

'I think I'll run away to land,' I said.

CHAPTER THIRTEEN

Over the next two or three days my emotional and psychological imbroglio was echoed and reinforced by the physical world around me. I learned the full meaning of that phrase, 'all at sea'.

For one thing, I'd never realised exactly how big the Atlantic Ocean is, what that much water all in one lump really means when you're sitting on the middle of it. It's awfully big. It is also grey. It's a vast desert of grey water, no hills or valleys to relieve the sight. A liner takes nearly five days and nights to cross from our side of it to the other going at something like a steady twenty-eight knots. If you imagine doing about thirty-two miles per hour in a car on a straight road without any breaks for sleep and with no landmarks to look at, you get a rough idea of both the size and the monotony. The sighting of a bird, another ship or an aeroplane is a conversation topic. And the ocean is rarely calm, the wind hardly ever still, the sky hardly ever blue. Often there isn't any sky at all, just mist. It's a great, grey wilderness of a world, out there in the middle of the Atlantic Ocean.

The limits of your world are defined by the length and breadth of your ship. It's a self-contained bubble, impenetrable, with little, usually no, contact with the outside world. You get the feeling that civilisation could end and you wouldn't get to hear about it for days because there's no television out there in the middle of the water, no *Guardian* or *Times*, no morning visit from the milkman, no passer-by to swap gossip with.

And all those broken rules I'd become so aggrieved over during recent weeks? They were as nothing compared to what I collided with on the ship as, one by one, the normal laws of existence we take for granted got clobbered on the head. For example, because of the five-hour difference between New York and Greenwich, clocks and watches are adjusted by one hour each night, so the days no longer contain twenty-four hours, but twenty-three or twenty-five depending on whether you're travelling east or west. And even the seasons can pass without your noticing them because there's just grey, and water and sky.

The ocean lurched along its bed, the ship lurched along the ocean and I lurched along the ship, desperate for some sort of stability. I found it in Elliott. I fancied him as soon as he walked into the Cruise Director's office that first morning. Not a lot, but a bit – probably it was the clean-cut contrast he made standing next to Thrippleton. But Elliott, for his part, didn't fancy me at all. Sometimes you can tell that sort of thing right away. I wasn't too bothered though, because the last thing I needed right now was another bloody man in my life. But brotherly love I could cope with and Elliott, bless him, was radiating it. By the time the full meeting was over I knew that here was a Friend. Not friend with a little f, everybody has lots of those, but Friend with a big F, like Sally, the kind you're lucky if you end up with one of at the end of your lifetime.

A friend in my definition is somebody who you can see every day for months and yes, you can get bored or irritated by them but it doesn't matter. It's somebody you can see only once, twice a year and they're still your friend and you take off together like you saw them only yesterday. It's the person you'd call if your lover had left and left you pregnant, the one who says 'There, there, it'll be all right' and you believe them. If the floor of your world is falling away from under you a friend is the one who lies down and says 'stand on me'. Male or female, a Friend is to do with love.

I loved Elliott. He loved me. And all we'd exchanged were a couple of sentences and a few significant looks. But things like that happen very quickly at sea. It's something to do with the whole bubble-like existence, a nursery school for adults. The crew is the child, the shipping line is the nanny. You have so few real-life responsibilities that it really is like living inside a rainbow-coloured bubble. Meals are provided, served and cleared away. Your cabin is cleaned and tidied for you, the bed made and the washbasin scrubbed. You use the phone, turn on the lights with no thought of a quarterly bill dropping through the letterbox. Spending-money appears in your bank account miraculously at the end of each week and all you have to spend it on is yourself. So too, you form your friendships and other relationships with the speed and intensity of a five-year-old, helped along by the fact that even total strangers immediately have something very big in common – the sea, their vulnerability to it and their complete dependence on the ship. Everyone, from Captain to AB and from occupant of Penthouse Suite to tenant of Five Deck (inside, shared), is a prisoner for the duration.

My impression of having found a friend for life in Elliott was confirmed after lunch. The members of the Cruise Staff ate in the Collingwood Restaurant (tourist class) at our own table, set slightly apart from the others. I don't know whether this was organised as a luxurious respite for us or because we weren't quite good enough to eat with the passengers, and who cares? Once the trials of embarkation were over with, I was simply glad of the escape. In my mind the passengers had already metamorphosed into the 'punters'. I'm always fairly quiet at mealtimes with strangers because food is important and I prefer to take mine undiluted by polite conversation. I'm also very bad at making polite conversation, which made me a rotten prospect as a Cruise Staff hostess. During that first lunchtime on board I was even quieter than I might normally have been because it was the first proper hot meal I'd had in two days and it was the first time I'd ever eaten such a rich and extravagant repast on a moving ship. The task required all the concentration I could spare. I harvested impressions of my new colleagues and the job so far, and tried hard not to allow my growing apprehensions to show through. Occasional glances at Elliott showed that he, too, was quietly taking it all in.

We finished. Wendy departed immediately saying she had a headache and was going to lie down for a bit and that I should meet her for Open Day in half an hour in the Hawkins Room. Sylvester pointed out that it was good for the sanity to develop the habit of locking yourself away in your cabin whenever the opportunity presented itself, then he scurried off, smiling. Phil nudged Benjamin and said, 'I know that look. He's fixed himself a target already,' to which Gavin replied, 'Disgusting. He could at least wait until tonight. Anyone fancy a run round the deck?' His offer was declined. Phil and Benjamin sauntered off saying, 'May as well size up the talent,' which left Elliott and me looking at each other across the debris-scattered tablecloth.

'We've got half an hour then,' I said to him, feeling at a bit of a loss.

'Mm. Your place or mine?'

'Which is closer?'

'Who cares, so long as we can find one of them?'

'Mine, then,' I said with a show of decisiveness. Then I sneaked a look at the map inside my handbag (Thrippleton had instructed us that under no circumstances should we refer to them in public) to check on the home route. 'Come on, I think it's more or less directly below us.' And, miracle of miracles, I was right. In only a few minutes of fixed smiles and polite nods we were secure inside my cabin with the door firmly shut behind us. I flopped on one bed and Elliott perched on the edge of the other, facing me. 'So,' I said to him. 'What do you think?'

His smile had come unstuck. His face mirrored all the apprehension that I knew was showing in mine. 'In one word – help!' he replied.

'Me too.' Our hands met in the space between the two beds and squeezed tightly. With that brief, mutual admission, our friendship was sealed. The next logical step was confession, so when Elliott asked what a nice girl like me was doing in a place like this I thought briefly about the stock answers – excitement, glamour, seeing the world – dismissed them all and said, 'Running away.'

'You too, huh? What happened? Tell me about it.'

'Want a life story?'

'Yes.'

So I settled myself on the bed, feet up, hands behind my head resting back on the pillow, fixed my gaze at a point just beyond the ceiling, and told him. The lot. The radio station, Joe, Carol, Joss, quitting, hoping, despairing, everything. It was a series of brief, bald statements and I tried very hard to be unemotional about it and just state the facts but even so my voice was a bit quavery at the end of it and my eyes were pricking. Elliott didn't say anything at all while I was talking, which I was glad of. It kept him anonymous, which of course, to all effects and purposes, he still was. But when I'd finished he crossed to my bed, sat down on the edge of it next to me, pulled me up into a sitting position again and put his arm around my shoulders. 'Poor Alison,' he said.

I sniffed, then smiled. 'Oh, I'll survive.'

'Sure you will,' he said, giving me a hug. 'But it's still pretty rotten. I think you're ever so courageous.'

I shook my head, but didn't say anything to contradict him. If this guy wanted to apply words like courageous to this quivering mass of insecurities who was I to disillusion him? So I changed the subject. 'And what about you? Running away or just seeking excitement?'

'Both. And I promise I'll tell you all about it later, but if you're going to meet Wendy on time you'd better be off.'

I looked at my watch. 'God, you're right. Where the hell's the Hawkins Room?'

'And where's the cinema?'

Out came the maps and we spread them between us on the bed, poring over them like a couple of bank robbers over a floor plan. We found our respective routes then agreed to meet again at midnightish in the Frobisher Nightclub for a nightcap and a natter. I quickly dragged a brush through my hair and checked my make-up. 'Do I look okay?' I asked, still not used to the image in the mirror even though the short haircut seemed a lifetime ago.

'Beautiful,' he said, and I adored him for lying. He planted a brief kiss on the top of my head and then said, 'Good luck, friend!'

'And you. Friend.' Then I giggled. A slight touch of hysteria. 'Oh God! "Open House: Your hostess will tell you all you want to know about the ship". I feel like I'm heading for the execution block.'

'Me too. Oh sod it, come on, let's both go and lose our

heads.' Laughing, he grabbed my hand, and tangoed me head first out the door.

Actually, the afternoon wasn't nearly as bad as I'd been anticipating. I watched Wendy plug up the sound system in the Hawkins Room and relaxed when she got out one microphone, not two, then worried again when she said gaily, 'Of course, you'll be doing this on your own on the return trip. Jim'll probably want you to do the disco soon, as well. We all take turns at it.'

I'd noticed the little podium with double turntables on it in the corner of the floor. 'So this is where the discotheque is?'

'Every night. It's drinks and piped music in here till ten-thirty then Carousel do a set until half past eleven. Then they go to the Frobisher Nightclub for midnight and we take over with the disco.'

'How long for?'

'Depends on how soon the punters start wandering off to bed.'

I was beginning to understand Jim Thrippleton's comments about the working hours being 'flexible'. Wendy took a little sheaf of paper out of her bag as the passengers started to wander in and sit down looking expectantly at the two of us. 'I'll start by introducing you, you come on and smile and say hello, then I'll launch into the lecture. You can have my notes after. It's easier if you learn them.'

I nodded and prepared myself to watch and listen very carefully. She began with a huge smile. 'Hi. I'm Wendy, your hostess for the voyage, and this . . . ' she held out her hand and ushered me on to the floor for all the world as if she were compering at the London Palladium, ' . . . is Alison!' I walked over to her, feeling dead stupid, and smiled at the sea of unresponsive faces before us. I nodded at them, smiled harder, and said 'Hi, everybody.'

Silence.

'Hey,' Wendy continued, 'aren't you going to say hello? This is a *friendly* ship!' She sounded very enthusiastic and she suddenly reminded me of Carol. All I wanted to do was slink away into a corner, but I stood there, still smiling. 'So, Hi!' she said again.

One or two passengers said 'Hi' back, and then she launched into her spiel and I moved back to the sidelines as unobtrusively as I could. It turned out to be quite interesting. Did you know, for instance, that for each return crossing the ship carried one hundred and fifty pounds of caviar, fifteen tons of potatoes, nearly ten thousand jars of jam and marmalade, and seventy-nine thousand two hundred eggs? I found myself marvelling at it all along with the passengers and only when Wendy finished did I remember that it'd be me confidently spouting all those facts and figures in another five or six days' time. And she'd hardly referred to her notes at all. 'How on earth do you remember it all?' I asked when she was putting the microphone lead away.

'After three years, it's easy,' she replied.

Three years. Now there's food for thought. Why on earth would a girl in her twenties want to spend so long away from home, land, family, friends . . . real life? Either her mother was a mermaid or she must be running away from one hell of a problem, I decided, because surely nobody could choose to be a ship's hostess as a life career?

I quickly popped into the Ladies' Room so I could look at my street map in private, then successfully made my way without a single wrong turning to the midships cardroom on Upper Deck where Phil was waiting, already wearing his iridescent orange lifejacket.

'Ah, there you are. Where's your lifejacket?' he asked in surprise.

'Oh, haven't you got one for me?' I said.

'You're supposed to bring your own. From your cabin.'

'Oh, sorry. I didn't know. I don't even know if I've got one down there.'

He unstrapped himself. 'No time to go look now. You'll have to wear mine and I'll make do without. Here,' he handed it to me, 'put it on.'

I looked at it in wonderment, loose tapes dangling everywhere and not an arrow or label in sight to say 'front' or 'this way up'. The brief flash of pride I'd felt over the excellence of my navigational skill disappeared in a surge of helplessness, which made me cross. If the ship got into trouble *I'd* surely be the first to drown. It's no fun being an innocent abroad, and it's no fun for someone who's an expert in her field to be forced into showing total ignorance over such a seemingly simple and basic thing like putting on a lifejacket. So why wasn't he helping me?

'Well don't just stand there looking superior,' I said to him. 'Show me how! And in return, I might show you how to do a proper radio programme!'

He laughed. 'Oh yes? What would a little thing like you know about it then?'

'Quite a lot, actually.' I was fed up of being the underdog. I'd had enough. I summoned up every last dreg of pride in my former achievements and said firmly, 'It happens to be my profession. I've been producing and presenting a daily programme on commercial radio for four years.'

I've never seen such a quick change in someone's attitude towards me. It was lovely. 'Really?' he said. 'Proper radio, not toytown like ours? Where? How did you get into it?'

'At home. Up in Dringley.'

'Dringley. You mean 2D Radio? You're not the woman who does the late night show are you?'

'Was.'

'I've heard you! You're good!'

Fame at last. I laughed. 'Well, don't look so surprised about it!'

'I must talk to you about it later. It's been my ambition for years to be a real radio deejay. Ever since I used to listen to Luxembourg under the covers. Oh, wow! What on earth are you doing on here, then? Why did you leave?'

I wasn't going to go into all that again. 'Oh, I just needed a break for a while,' I said casually. 'Now are you going to show me what to do with this animal or not?' I asked, waving the lifejacket at him.

'Sorry, yes, here, let me help you.'

And he did. For the rest of the day, in fact. Through Boat Drill, Afternoon Tea, the Teen and Twenty Get-Together, until he handed me over to Wendy again at half past five to help set out the Upper Deck midships cardroom for the

Bridge Tournament. I was released at six to get myself showered, re-made-up, and resplendent in evening dress to report to Jim Thrippleton's suite at seven where I was supposed to be hostess to his host for the Cruise Director's cocktail party which was always held on the first day of the voyage as the formal encounter group for the star entertainers and guest lecturers.

When I left my cabin at five to seven it looked like the victim of a severe squall. I like to get dressed up in a leisurely manner. I had to learn very quickly to change the habit. I felt so rushed that I even forgot to listen to Phil doing his stint on the in-cabin radio show. I hesitated outside Thrippleton's door remembering the last time I'd entered it, so long ago that morning. Surely he wouldn't be sitting on the loo this time? But then again . . . I knocked and waited for permission to enter then went in with a swift glance at the bathroom door, which was shut. Thrippleton approached, saying, 'Come in, come in, Alison. Next time try and be here by ten to at the latest, you are supposed to be the hostess, that is to arrive before the guests . . . ' He was interrupted by another knock on the door. 'Only just in time, you see,' he said then called out, 'Come in,' and held out a welcoming hand to a sun tanned fellow in plum velvet jacket and dress shirt. 'Ah, Lionel, come on in, there's a good chap,' and in a stage whisper to me: 'Lionel Markham' as if that explained all. 'What'll you have?'

He ushered Lionel into the centre of the room and introduced me. We shook hands and I smiled while Thrippleton poured champagne into a couple of the glasses which were standing neatly to attention along the top of a side-unit.

I launched into my polite conversation opener: 'And what do you do, Mr Markham?' First mistake. Apparently he was billed in For Your Pleasure and Leisure as 'International Singing Star'. I'd never heard of him. Memo to Alison: in future learn its contents. Luckily my *faux pas* was covered by the arrival of more guests and I was too busy for the moment concentrating on getting the names right and introducing strangers to each other to worry about making any further attempts at conversation. Unfortunately the flood soon turned to a trickle and if I wasn't too careful I was going to be cornered and my glaring inadequacies as hostess would be spotlit again, so I filled one hand with a bottle of champagne, the other with a plate of canapés and started flitting from group to group with my ears open and smile in place. This earned me a nod of approval from the Cruise Director, and after managing to drink a couple of glasses myself I started to enjoy the whole thing, in a schizophrenic way – being in the middle of it, yet observing it all from a distance. The guests turned out to be quite human after all, even Lionel Markham.

I was released for dinner at eight. By the time I greeted my colleagues at the table I was utterly exhausted and feeling more like a bedraggled moth than a social butterfly. My feet were throbbing, legs aching, face stiff from smiling and head a little woozy and aching either from champagne on an empty stomach or from watching the grey horizon swing up and down outside the restaurant windows. I ate with a lack of enthusiasm that surprised even myself, moaned occasionally to Elliott, 'My God how do they keep this up?' and to the others, 'My God how do you keep this up?', then had time only for a brief freshen-up before being officially back on duty by nine-thirty at the latest with hair gleaming, evening dress floating, eyelashes nicely mascara'd and smile once more in place.

Elliott was paired with Wendy for the evening and I was allocated to Benjamin who accepted a bribe and handed me over to Phil. After tonight, though, Elliott and I would be expected to do the rounds solo like everybody else. Thrippleton directed Wendy and my friend to the Franklin Room with Sylvester, whilst me, Phil and Gavin were to take care of the Gilbert Room. That left Benjamin and Thrippleton to be MCs for the evening with the Cruise Director taking the Franklin Room because he always kept the First Class cherry for himself. I was released from under his eagle eye.

As we made our way to the Gilbert Room I studied the route very carefully because it was a new one on me, whilst keeping ears tuned to my companions' instructions as to what I was supposed to do for the rest of the night.

'While the dance band's on you just flit round being generally sociable,' said Phil.

'Sort of, "Hi, I'm Alison your happy hostess is there anything I can do to make your trip pleasanter", kind of thing,' said Gavin.

I groaned and Phil laughed. 'Just alter the phrasing to suit.'

'Find partners for people who look lonely.'

'Join in conversations between contented couples.'

'Sounds like you have to be either a pimp or a gate-crasher,' I observed. 'Isn't there a happy medium?'

'Only if you manage a pick-up for yourself,' said Benjamin.

'Oh, you'll be all right. It's only for forty-five minutes or so, then the cabaret starts,' said Phil.

'You mean then we can sit down and watch it?' I asked, hopeful.

'No chance,' said Gavin. 'Between the three of us we operate the sound mixer, the lighting board and help the dancers to dress – that'll be your job tonight.'

'Wonder why I never get to do it?' put in Phil. 'Right. We're here. Off you go, you can manage the first bit by yourself, and I'll see you backstage at quarter past ten.'

'Whoopee,' I said flatly, and set off towards the tables arranged round the edge of the dance floor looking for faces who looked lonely, lost, interesting or at least vaguely familiar.

I wandered around the room, smiling furiously, looking the occupants up and down and considering who was to be my first victim. I spied a chap sitting on his own, a solitary drink in front of him, ripe for the social Samaritan act. He looked apprehensive when he saw me bearing down on him and I wondered if perhaps my smile was a little too fierce. But, in for a penny in for a pound, it was what I was being paid for, so I drew up a vacant chair and sat down next to him. 'Hi,' I said. 'My name's Alison and I'm one of your hostesses for the voyage. Are you enjoying yourself so far?'

He stared at me blankly.

'I'm Alison, one of your hostesses,' I tried again, smile faltering slightly.

Again, a silent stare.

I hadn't picked on a deaf-mute, had I? Once more with feeling: 'Official hostess. Is there anything I can do for you?'

He opened his mouth and said something like: 'Xyrjash-sponj itchclick.'

My turn to offer the blank stare.

'Eesswaffyungoochklerf?'

Oh God, Norwegian, Polish, Outer Mongolian? Help! I took a deep breath, reinstated the smile and tried, '*Parlez vous Français*?'

It appeared he didn't, which was just as well because all I had left was *La plume de ma tante* and *Toto est dans la petite maison*. But he was beginning to show some sort of interest because with 'Zhbottekjidlveek hwahnng?' he reached across the table and caressed my forearm. He had a knowing smile on his face.

Now I may not have had this hostess business totally sussed out, but I did know when to make a strategic withdrawal. I stood up quickly, said, 'Well, it was nice meeting you. Hope you enjoy your trip,' and beat a hasty retreat to the ladies' where I locked myself in, had a cigarette and reviewed my progress so far. The appropriate comment had to be: 'Alison tries, but could do better.' I resolved to do much better. After all, the job wasn't exactly difficult, didn't particularly overstrain the intelligence. I was suddenly stabbed by the memory of Joe saying, 'You're so stupid. You have nothing to say. Talk to me. Talk. I want to see how you react.' Damn word association! Damn Joe! Damn these flashfloods of memory!

I threw the cigarette into the loo. It sizzled and turned from glowing red to soggy black, and I went out into the Gilbert Room again determined to sail through it. No more sit-down conversations, just nods and smiles and brief introductions and flit from punter to punter like an effusive butterfly asking if everybody was having a good time but not staying around long enough to be saddled with the answer.

It worked! I actually made it to Cabaret Time. Phil explained the lighting board then I sat next to him and watched it in operation as I'd have to handle it myself in a few shows' time. You don't have much to do with lighting effects when you're doing a self-op radio programme, but the basic principles of it were much the same as on a sound-desk. You operated faders. Fade up, fade down, fade out. This I could handle.

The dancers came to the end of their opening routine and Phil nudged me to get backstage to help out with the costume change while Benjamin filled with a brief comic routine. I hurried behind the curtains to be greeted by, 'There you are! Quick, where are my shoes, the silver ones? Where's my comb? Do up my zip. Who's got my wig?' from all directions. Nearly naked girls, slim with small breasts, yards of legs and sweaty, sheeny skin, fighting amongst ostrich plumes and spangled bikinis and hair lacquer and powder puffs, with me in the midst of it tripping over the hem of my long evening gown and getting in the way. Suddenly the confused tangle of legs, arms and sequins formed itself into a line. I heard a drum roll from the other side of the curtains, the girls switched on their eyes and teeth and off they went, high kicking out into a crescendo of applause. The whole mad, chaotic transformation had taken less than three minutes and I was left behind in a frazzled heap of ruffled hair and torn hem, suddenly engulfed by another tidal wave of despair for all that I'd lost. *I* used to be the entertainer, the performer, the star. Where, oh where was that lady on the radio who everybody envied? Where was my pile of glossy photographs to be autographed? Who was there now to ask for them? I half-heartedly set about tidying the debris. Would I ever again manage to make any waves of my own?

'Alison, just the girl I need!' said a male voice as a hand was correspondingly placed on my shoulder.

I nearly jumped out of my skin. I turned, and Lionel Markham was standing there holding his trouser fastening together. 'Help. I've lost my button. Got a safety pin?'

'Christ, you're on in two minutes and no, I haven't.' I scanned the dressing room hastily. 'Here,' I said, grabbing a red silk scarf from the floor. Use this. Tie it round your waist. Like a cummerbund. Come here, I'll do it.' He surrendered to my ministrations unprotesting, as I drew the scarf tightly round his waist and fiddled with knots and folds. My hands got a swift impression of hard, unyielding muscle. It was nice. 'There,' I said, standing back to survey the job. 'Looks good. Just don't move around too energetically, and you'll be all right.'

He looked in the mirror. 'Great. Thanks.' Then he put both hands on my shoulders, pulled me to him and kissed me on the mouth. 'I owe you,' he said. 'That was some quick thinking.'

It was a long time since I'd been properly kissed, and Lionel Markham was quite attractive in a darkly Latin sort of way, but there was no time to follow through my reactions because there was a burst of applause, the girls came tumbling through the curtains and Lionel took up his position waiting for the cue to go on and be an international singing star. I crept back out front while the lights were down and took up position beside Phil again.

Lionel's set wasn't bad; standard cabaret stuff like *My Way* and *It's Not Unusual*; and his newly fashioned cummerbund stayed neatly in place. About half way through his act the band played the introduction to Billy Paul's *Thanks for Saving my Life*, and Lionel dedicated it to, 'A special little lady who's very close to me.' He glanced to my side of the stage and winked. 'This could be interesting,' I thought and returned him a small answering smile. Phil leaned over and whispered, 'He means you. What's all that about? You don't waste much time, do you?'

'Shut up and mind your own business,' I whispered back and watched the rest of Lionel's performance with an appraising eye and 'Shall I or shan't I?' running through my mind. After all, hadn't Sylvester said that the sole aim of any trip was to get boxed off? When in Rome . . .

But by the time the dance band packed up I didn't feel like pursuing it. Not tonight, at least. And I still had to get tomorrow's programmes delivered to Thrippleton before I was free to find Elliott. Phil told me where to go, then asked if I'd like to join him after in the Hawkins Room for a drink because he hadn't had a chance to pick my brains about 'real radio' yet.

'Not tonight, if you don't mind,' I replied. 'I'm feeling a bit dazed. Besides, I'm supposed to be meeting Elliott. But soon, I promise, and you can put in a word for me with Thrippleton if you like. I'd love to have a go at the in-cabin thing. Keep my hand in. If you don't think I'd be stealing your thunder, that is?' I was learning diplomacy.

'No, really, I think you should be doing it,' he said generously. 'I'll see you tomorrow then. And don't forget to put your watch back. It's not really midnight. It's only eleven o'clock now.'

'Cheers.'

'I'll be off then. See if I can find that redhead.'

I made my way down to a little office near the Grenville Lounge on Two Deck where the For Your Pleasure and Leisure brochures were stacked. It seemed miles, and I wondered briefly if it would be quite the thing for a Cruise Staff hostess to be seen without shoes on. My feet were killing me. Two Deck was pretty deserted so I cast caution to the winds, took my shoes off and to hell with decorum. I found the office, picked up a handful of brochures and then went to the Cruise Director's suite by way of a crew only staircase. I put my shoes back on before knocking at his door. Didn't want to give the impression that I was willing to be undressed. I needn't have worried, though, because no one was home. I turned on the light and looked around. The boss had had a heavy day. The room smelled of stale cigarette ends and alcohol. There were empty and nearly empty glasses standing on practically every available surface so I cleared a space on the table, dumped the programmes and left quickly just in case Thrippleton decided on an early night. Back along the corridor, feet throbbing, hating the luxury of fitted carpets everywhere, up two flights of stairs at the end and emerged into the subdued lobby of the Frobisher Nightclub where the gentle rhythm of Carousel playing *One Note Samba* drifted through the doors and mingled with the background noises of engines and ocean waves. And I hadn't referred to the map once. I was dead chuffed with myself.

I went into the club, longing to sit down and quietly enjoy a brandy and a cigarette. Elliott was already there, ensconced in a corner and engrossed in a discussion with a very elegant looking middle-aged gentleman. Their heads were very close together. Interesting. It wasn't as if this were the disco in the Hawkins Room where you had to shout to make yourself heard. The whole atmosphere of the Frobisher – lighting, music, decor – was subdued, as befits the First Class only, after hours nightclub. I watched, wondering if I should interrupt. The older man smiled, nodded, wrote something on a slip of paper with a gold pen, passed it to Elliott then patted his knee and stood up. Elliott smiled back at him and nodded. The gentleman left. *Very* interesting.

I approached. 'Hi, Elliott! Hello, Friend! Sorry I'm late.'

'Oh, that's all right. I haven't been bored. Want a drink?'

'Do I want a drink!' I slid on to the bench next to him. 'Brandy. Quick.'

Elliott nodded at a steward who came over. We ordered, the drinks arrived, and Elliott signed for them.

'I didn't know we could do that,' I said. 'Handy.'

'Good isn't it? We settle up at the end of the week down at the Purser's Office.'

'Cheers,' I said, and sipped at the brandy, letting it trickle down my throat and burn all the way to my stomach. Heaven. Off duty at last. 'Do you realise we've been at it practically non-stop for fifteen hours? And the first day is supposed to be a fairly light one!'

'Mm. Not quite what I expected. Still it makes a change.'

A few more sips and it was Elliott's turn to spill his life story. It turned out he was a couple of years younger than me and a singer by profession, opera not pop. He'd recently finished a provincial tour doing extracts from Gilbert and Sullivan which he loathed. He was a frustrated Rodolfo at heart. He wanted to join the English National or the New York Met or the Vienna State Opera, anywhere, so long as he could become Pavarotti one day. 'Well, there's no sense in aiming for the bottom, is there?' he said.

'Hey, don't apologise for your ambitions. If you're going to go for it, then go for it.'

'Yes, but none of them will have me. Apparently my voice is too immature.'

'Don't worry. I'm a fatalist – if it's meant, then your voice'll catch up with the rest of you one day.'

He laughed. 'I'm not sure the rest of me is all that mature yet, either.'

'So who wants to grow up anyway?'

Elliott put his arm around my shoulders and gave me a hug. 'Oh I do like you!' he said, and followed it with a kiss on the cheek.

'And me, you.' I disentangled myself and turned to face him. 'Elliott, are you gay? I mean, if you are I don't give a damn, and if you're not I hope you're not offended by my asking, but I just thought I'd check before I decided whether to chat you up or not.'

Gay or straight he was a bit taken aback. I hoped I hadn't ruined a beautiful friendship. Then he laughed. 'You really meant it, didn't you – "if you're going to go for it, then go for it". Okay. Straight question, straight answer. Yes, I am, and how did you know? People usually don't with me. Even Sylvester hasn't picked me out.'

'Oh,' I said airily, 'just put it down to witchcraft. And a certain debonair gentleman who writes notes with a gold pen.'

'Oops.'

'Quite. A word to the wise from Sylvester himself: Golden Rule – Be Discreet. Particularly on a ship.'

'I will from now on. Thanks. Do you think anyone else knows?' He looked a bit worried.

'I shouldn't think so. You look too butch. But would it matter?'

He thought. 'I guess it would. I'm fairly new you see. What we were talking about earlier, running away, well I'm not exactly running away from it, not from myself anyway, but my family didn't handle it too well and it was all a bit difficult. Thought I'd best just leave for a while and let the dust settle.'

'Poor Elliott,' I said, and squeezed his hand under the table. We lapsed into a sympathetic silence, the sort shared by two people who've offered their separate vulnerabilities and then become one through mutual acceptance and protection. Pity he was gay.

The moment was interrupted by the approach of Sylvester. 'Naughty, naughty! Caught you. No use hiding under the tablecloth, I can tell a pair of joined hands from a mile away. I've got a nose for romance!'

Elliott and I looked at each other with a we-know-something-you-don't-know grin. Our hands stayed glued together forming a heterosexual armour for Elliott and a cover-all for whatever escapade I might decide on. The ultimate in discretion by using indiscretion with each other as a decoy. Perfect!

'Well,' he continued, 'I can see when I'm not wanted. Don't like playing gooseberry so I'll leave you to it. Enjoy, my darlings!' He blew us a kiss and left.

Elliott and I giggled. 'So what's your type?' I asked. 'Do you fancy him, Sylvester, for example?'

'You must be joking! If I want to camp around I'll get a tent, thank you. What do you think I am anyway, some kind of slut?'

'How should I know, idiot? Come on, let's find the disco and eye up the talent together. Then I might find out.'

'Wicked.'

'I know. But it's fun.'

So up we went into the thumping rhythms and flashing lights of the Hawkins Room where Gavin was deejay for the night, Phil was leaping around the floor with the redhead and Thrippleton was leaning against the bar chatting up a lanky blonde. He nodded an acknowledgement when he saw us and then went straight back to business, either not noticing or not caring that Elliott and I were together rather than circulating separately. We sat down and surveyed the scene, surreptitiously eyeing up the same blokes, comparing notes and impressions and giggling like a couple of schoolkids who'd just discovered *Lady Chatterley's Lover*.

'This is fantastic,' I said to Elliott around one o'clock in the morning. I was well under the influence of four brandies. 'I mean you're fantastic.'

'I know I am. And so modest too. Why am I fantastic?'

'Because you're the perfect friend. Every woman should have a gay, male friend. It's great. There's no real area of rivalry because the men I might make it with wouldn't fancy you anyway, and the men you make it with wouldn't fancy me. No clash of interest, you see. But you can still swap confidences. S'great. Doesn't always work out that way with female friends.' Just like that, smash. Another bloody great tsunami. Carol. 'Oh shit. I think I'm going to cry.'

'Come on,' he said and stood up, pulling me up after him. 'Time we got you into bed.' He led me quickly out of the Hawkins Room, gave me his handkerchief and hurried me down to Five Deck via the crew stairways.

'Sorry,' I sniffed when we stopped outside my cabin. 'It was just that suddenly . . . '

'It's all right, I understand,' he said. 'And it's been one hell of a day, too. You get a good night's sleep, Ali. You'll be okay. It'll all seem better in the morning.'

And the funny thing was, I believed him.

CHAPTER FOURTEEN

I said goodnight and went inside. Took my shoes off, got undressed, splashed my face with cold water, took the two pillows off the spare bed and got into mine with one propped against the other two behind me, and my arms cuddling the other to my tummy. I lit a cigarette and surveyed the day. The first day in a new situation is always the worst, so the first day of a 'new life/fresh start' is bound to be even ropier. How had the pros and cons balanced out? Well, I'd survived it. I hadn't thrown myself overboard, I'd made a good start at finding my way around and I'd memorised the life-support systems: ladies' loos, restaurants, bars. I hadn't come out with flying colours on the actual work side of it, but neither had I covered myself with shame. Lionel Markham had emitted signs of fancying me and I'd made a friend who showed signs of being the making of me. I'd sunk under two or three sharp waves of desolation but withdrawal symptoms were only to be expected – Joe was one hell of a dependency to kick. All in all it could have been a lot worse. I hadn't done too badly for a twenty-eight-year-old emotional wreck.

But oh, how I longed to be thirty. On my thirtieth birthday I was convinced that I would miraculously become a whole person. I would understand myself and I would understand the world around me. I'd be kinder to myself and all my feelings of inadequacy and guilt would vanish.

Think Positive, Alison. I considered writing it all down in my notebook but the book was in my handbag in the wardrobe and I was in the bed. Too much effort. I snuggled further down into the pillows and continued to develop a thesis, 'On Being Thirty'. I promised: I will emerge from my seething twenties like a butterfly from its chrysalis. The shell of self-doubt, guilt, self-dislike, indecision, inadequacy, bewilderment and insecurity will be discarded in triumph as I unfurl my wings, dry them in the sun, and fly away high above the world in the freedom of my self-confidence. It will be a magic day. When I'm thirty.

But as I smoked that cigarette in my narrow single bed in the early hours of a bound-to-be-bumpy day, I wasn't thirty. Even though I was approaching New York across the wide Atlantic for the first time in my life, I was still not thirty. I was only just approaching twenty-nine. There was still a year and a bit to get through before my fairy godmother would appear, waving a star on the end of a silver stick and showering glittery stuff over me to complete my transformation.

Still a year and a bit to go. Christ. Would I make it? I had my doubts. So I concentrated on little things, telling myself for example how wonderful it was to be able to smoke in bed and even fart or pick my nose if I wanted to, without Joe to complain about it. I was getting used to being mistress of my own bed. I was beginning to like it. There were advantages to the Victorian system of separate rooms and 'by invitation only'. I took a final drag on the cigarette and let the smoke seep out of me slowly through mouth and nose, drifting up and in front of my eyes. They began to sting and fill with water. I told myself it was only the smoke, and vehemently stubbed out the cause. Maybe I'd be able to give up smoking, too, when I got to be thirty.

As we pitched along towards New York time played mischievous tricks on me, sprinting and dawdling both together, telescoping the journey into an instant but drawing out instants into eternities. Days and nights, jobs and duties blurred into each other like the endless sea into the sky so that my friendship with Elliott stood out in relief like a shimmering island. Our colleagues naturally assumed that we were boxed off together and it suited us not to disillusion them. In fact we made a game of encouraging the notion. We held hands a lot and hugged a lot and were in and out of each other's cabins at every opportunity. Before long he told me the story of his conversion.

He'd first screwed (a girl, seventeen, randy) at the age of thirteen. Elliott had been a pretty boy, fair game for lusting older women, and had as he put it 'fucked like a rabbit' all the way through his teens and early twenties. Then, a few months ago he happened to be the last surviving guest after a somewhat boisterous party. The host had asked him to stay the night then proceeded to chat him up. Elliott had been very shocked and said no. The guy had been persistent and had said, 'How do you know you won't like it if you've never tried it?' Elliott, being a reasonable sort of bloke and smashed out of his skull at the time, had seen the logic of that question, tried it, and not merely liked it but loved it. 'It was as if,' he said without the slightest trace of self-consciousness, 'I'd suddenly found myself. I was really at peace with myself for the first time I could remember. Truly at peace. It was amazing.' He smiled. 'It still is. So I haven't bothered with women since. Not that way. I like them. But there's no sexual spark.'

'You make it all sound so easy. Weren't there any traumas at all?'

''Course there were. It wasn't that easy, not after the first few days when I came down to earth and it all sank in, what I was actually doing.' I was longing to know what they actually did do. He'd probably have told me. But I wasn't free enough of my own inhibitions to come right out with it and ask. 'I went through a terrible time then. Wanting it, but not being able to accept it because it was against everything that I'd ever been brought up to feel or think. My Dad's a Methodist minister, you know.'

'Oh dear. No wonder your family found it so hard to take.'

'Yes. It's very difficult. I wish I could be open and natural with them about it, like I can with you. But they won't let me.'

'No, I suppose not. But maybe one day, eh?' I squeezed his hand to offer comfort. 'So how did you come to accept it yourself?'

'I don't know really. Nothing *happened*. The anger faded and it just gradually stopped being important. I found myself thinking: "well, this is me, this is who I am," and it came not to matter so much, it was just a part of being me, like the colour of my hair or what size shoes I take.'

'Only more exciting, surely?'

He grinned. 'Not 'alf!'

Courage takes many forms. I wished I had his kind of strength, to be able to say: 'this is me. This is what I am, and I won't feel guilty or inadequate or ashamed.' Lucky Elliott, I thought, to be so comfortable with himself.

The night before we arrived in New York, Elliott and I parted early, no nightcap in the Frobisher Club, no prowling the periphery of the Hawkins Room discotheque. He had a farewell date with the debonair gent and intended to make a night of it. I wished him well. I also wished, briefly, that he was heterosexual and randy and going to bed with me. The delights of celibacy wear a bit thin when absolutely everybody around you is happily having it away. But it was only a brief thought. Our relationship was far too fraternal for that and it would only have spoiled a beautiful friendship. I wandered off alone to the Hawkins Room hoping to find an unaccompanied colleague, not ready yet to face another night with a good book. I wasn't exactly feeling sorry for myself, just enveloped in a mood of general despondency. I'd seen little of Lionel Markham since the first night because I'd had a run of being allocated to whatever room he wasn't appearing in. I'd been too bound up in the game Elliott and I were playing to make any significant inroads into friendships with my other colleagues. I was homesick for my Dringley cottage with its patch of grass, for the daily delivery of milk and newspaper, for my kettle and cups of tea on demand. Even the thought of at last seeing New York wasn't so wonderful anymore, because my naive excitement had had its edges blunted by the jaded attitude of my colleagues. And the job? Well, it was a doddle really. The challenge had worn off after about three days. My basic problem, I thought, as I entered the dark, sweaty, noisy and throbbing atmosphere which pervaded the Hawkins Room at that time of night, is that I'm bored. Simple as that. And I'm hungry. And I want a mug of tea. I don't want a brandy and I don't want anymore of those ruddy biscuits in my cabin. I want some good, honest, plain, real food and I want a cup of tea. And I want them now!

I saw a possible saviour in the shape of Sylvester who,

discreet as ever, appeared to be chatting up two middle-aged and intricately coiffured ladies at a table near the bar. I switched on a smile and approached. 'So sorry to interrupt,' I said to them with all the charm I could muster, 'but I must have a brief word with my colleague.'

Sylvester got to his feet a little too quickly for good manners. 'Do excuse us, ladies, but I'm afraid duty calls,' he said sweetly and then walked away towards the exit, me following. Once we were safely out of sight he clasped my arm in both his hands and said, 'Alison, you angel, I absolutely adore you. How did you know I was absolutely desperate for a rescue?'

'I didn't. What's up?'

'Oh God, these elderly divorcees! Stupid old bags were trying to get off with me. With me! Both of them my dear! Oh horror! Oh well. Chuck 'em all overboard tomorrow. Maybe the new batch'll be better.'

'Not a good trip then?'

'My dear, disastrous. It's all right for some,' he said giving me a knowing look. 'Where is he, anyway, that little friend of yours?'

'Elliott? Oh, just wanted a quiet night,' I said casually. I was getting very good at little white lies.

'I see. Too energetic for him, are you?' he grinned.

'I wouldn't say that.'

'No? Oh well, what can I do for you anyway?'

'Two things. One, you can recommend me a good kettle-shop in New York. I can't survive another trip without one. And two, is there anywhere on this barge I can get some decent food at this time of night? Real food. Like beans on toast or something?'

'Is that all? No problem. Ask and you shall be provided for. After all, one good turn deserves another. How does a steak buttie and chips grab you?'

My mouth began to water. 'You're not having me on?'

'Would I? Come on, my precious, it's time you were introduced to Taffy.' Taffy was the cook who did the all-night shift in the First Class kitchens. He prepared breakfast, supplied passengers with room service fodder and cooked a vat of stew or curry for the ABs on night duty.

He also provided for any other crew member who felt pangs in the middle of the night. 'Slip him a dollar,' said Sylvester, 'and he'll cook you anything you want. Fillet steak, egg and chips, whatever. He'll see you right. He's got the keys to the freezer.'

'I think I'm going to like Taffy,' I said. 'He must make a fortune on the side.'

'Earns more than the Captain, my dear. All the stewards do. They're the wealthy ones on this ship.'

We pushed our way back across the dance floor which was polished black marble and felt awfully hard to my still protesting feet. The floor gave a sudden lunge beneath us and people stumbled. Sylvester carried on walking as if nothing untoward had occurred, a stately prince among lurching passengers. I held on to his hand tightly. 'You'll soon get used to it,' he said. 'It can get far rougher than this.'

I began to wonder whether I was as hungry as I'd thought.

To get to the night kitchens you had to go down a deck and through the Nelson Restaurant walking towards the front. On our way through it Sylvester emptied a sugar bowl into his pocket and took a handful of small plastic tubs of marmalade from a plate, saying, 'May as well stock up, seeing as I'm passing.' Through two sets of swing doors at the far end of the restaurant and we entered another world. This was the first time I'd been properly 'backstage' where the carpeting and p.p.p. (possible passenger proximity) ended.

We entered a room which was about the size of a supermarket. It had bright white striplights, a lot of stainless steel and a floor which was very slippery when wet. The floor was wet. I lifted my long skirt to clear it of a pool of what could have been coffee mixed with diesel oil. A twenty-foot row of stainless steel sinks and draining boards was piled with dirty dishes, cutlery, cups and glasses, none of which had been emptied or scraped clean. Greyish lumps of steaks, black globules of caviar, wilted ex-salads and bits of potato congealed amongst the crockery.

'Remind me never to offer to wash up,' I said in passing.

A tiny man, not much taller than me and very thin, looked up from a steaming cauldron as we approached. He was somewhere between fifty and sixty with a pronounced squint, and long wisps of grey hair plastered sideways over the crown of a bald head. He grinned at Sylvester and showed gaps among teeth which ranged from pale yellow to dark brown. This was Taffy, who was to become the saviour and comforter of many lonely nights and to provide sustenance and extra sensual delights to some ecstatic ones. Sylvester introduced me as a new regular customer. Taffy wiped his sweaty palm on a grease-and-dry-blood-and-gravy-stained apron before offering it (the hand) to me. He also offered us beakers of tea from an urn to keep us going while he cooked me a fillet steak destined for chunky sandwiches with onion, and a plateful of crispy chips. Some takeaway!

Have you ever tried clutching a little evening bag, balancing a plate of chips on top of a plate of sandwiches, holding a mug of tea and keeping your hemline well away from the floor all at the same time? It's not easy. Especially when the floor won't keep still. Sylvester pointed out the quickest route back to my cabin via the crew stairways and left me to it, food, tea, evening dress and all. Down four flights of crew stairway, dirty, metallic and clanging with each footfall, through a double swing door (opened with my bottom) and I was in the corridor on Five Deck only a few yards away from my own little nest. I went in and locked the door behind me.

Bliss. Silence, food and solitude. Amazing what great changes can be made by tiny things. I'd swung from despondency to delight and all because of a steak sandwich. I stripped off, got into bed and into the attack. Nothing has ever tasted quite so delicious. There's something very naughty about stuffing yourself with food in the early hours of the morning and not having to worry about the crumbs in the bed – like the midnight feasts in the dorm at boarding school in the fourth form that you read about when you're a kid – and if it's naughty, then it must be nice.

Being a Yorkshire lass the flavour was vastly enhanced by the fact that the whole feast had only cost a dollar, and dollar bills are like Monopoly money – not real, they don't have a picture of the Queen on them. There's an old Yorkshire saying that goes: 'See all, 'ear all, say nowt; eat all, sup all, pay nowt; and if tha ever does owt for nowt, allus do it for thissen.' It's been my personal motto for years. Pay nowt or pay a dollar, it amounts to the same thing – fillet steak at its cheapest and most delicious.

Ah food! Panacea for an empty heart as well as a grumbling stomach. Steak sandwiches, chips and a mug of tea cured not only hunger but boredom and apathy too. I wiped my fingers on the sheets (no longer my job to wash the grease out) and turned out the light with words like Broadway, Times Square, The Empire State Building, Fifty-ninth Street Bridge and Fifth Avenue running through my mind. So up yours, Joe, back in dreary Dringley. Tomorrow *I* would be in New York!

But not until disembarkation sentry duty had been performed. Customs and Immigration officers came on board to process the crew before and during breakfast. I was duly processed and stamped, then sent to stand with Gavin at the top of the covered gangway leading from the Grenville Lounge, smiling at the passengers, most of whom were still total strangers, shaking hands and uttering commonplaces like, 'hope you've enjoyed your trip', 'hope you'll travel with us again', and practising, 'have a nice day.' I could hardly keep still, so eager was I to be rid of them so I could get my own release. We'd have about five hours free to explore the city before the new lot started to come on board. Five whole hours in public but off duty. It seemed like the gift of eternity.

'Go on,' said Gavin when the tide had reduced to a mere trickle. 'I'll finish up. Thrippleton will have gone by now. Run along and enjoy yourself.'

'Thanks, Gav.' I didn't hesitate, I was off. Back down to the cabin, rip off the smart clothes and slip joyously into flat pumps, denim jeans and a big, loose T-shirt. I felt like me again. Then I was off down below the waterline to Six Deck and along the crew corridor so there was no risk of bumping into any tardy passenger who might still be lurking around.

I passed little groups of smiling ABs, stewards and stewardesses, all incredibly smart and dolled up to the nines in reaction to their monotonous on-duty uniforms. Complete role reversal. I took the stairs two at a time and knocked, breathless, on Elliott's door. 'Come on! Are you ready? Let's go.'

He emerged looking as scruffy as me. We ran down the crew gangway on to the dirty, smelly, refuse-covered concrete floor of New York Dock, the bit that the passengers don't see because they use the marble-lined customs hall. I jumped off the bottom of the gangway on to the oil-stained concrete and said, 'I can't believe it. Is this it? Are we really standing on America now?' grinning, excited, hopping from foot to foot like a little kid.

And my friend, grinning even wider than me if that's possible said, 'Yes I know! Wow! Alison, we're actually in New York!'

We ran.

Yellow cabs instead of black taxis. Pot-holes all over the roads. Nine out of ten cars bashed and bent. It was incredibly glamorous. Is this how Americans feel when they visit London for the first time? It can't be. London could never be this exhilarating. The thrill of all those ridiculous numbers flashing by as you ascend at high speed in the lifts in the Empire State Building. Standing on the hundred and second floor of a building taller by half than our ship was long.

'Where next?'

'Broadway. I wanna be on Broadway!'

Nothing, nowhere in the world, could match it. The traffic lights that flashed 'walk' in green and 'don't walk' in red. Or the pillar boxes that looked like English rubbish bins. Or the van we saw that had a bullet hole: yes, a genuine, gangster-movie bullet hole, in its back windscreen. Or the policemen who wore guns who you'd never dream of asking directions from. Or the pavements that were sidewalks, the price tags that said $ instead of £. Or the sky that you could hardly see for the scrapers.

Culture shock. The second in less than a week. Like being on the ship for the first time, suddenly the world was the wrong way round again. In New York when we were there you had to go inside to get cool and outside to get warm. Very odd. Words didn't mean what I thought they meant. If you ask for a lager and lime they give you a funny look, tell you it's beer and stick a bit of fresh lime on the rim of the glass. If you ask where the nearest pillar box is they look blank and uncomprehending. Streets have numbers rather than names, and rounders is called baseball and played by boys. Lifts are elevators, an escalator is a moving stairway, fresh whipped cream is something that squirts out of an aerosol can. At last, I was in love again. Manhattan made me high.

'Hey, shall I send Joe a postcard?'

'Make him envious?'

'Something like "having a lovely time, glad you're not here"?'

'Ooh, you little bitch! Ali, I love you!' said Elliott, hugging me in the middle of Times Square.

I sent the postcard, opting for, 'hope you're well' instead of, 'glad you're not here', then we bought me a kettle and returned to the ship, exhausted, footsore, and high as a couple of kites, to shower and change ready for the trials of embarkation.

We sailed at sunset, and I managed to slip out on deck for a couple of minutes to see if Manhattan skyline viewed from the Hudson was all it was cracked up to be. It was. Towering columns of glass reflecting brilliant flashing gold as if the city were on fire, the sky behind dark enough to show off the asymmetrical geometry, still light enough to soften the harsh magic of it. I was securely trapped in its spell, longing to return before I'd even finished leaving.

We had an easy night. Because of the relatively late sailing the Boat-Drill, the Open Day meet your hostess get-togethers, the introductory cocktail parties, even the slick and glossy cabarets were scheduled for the morrow. Suggested dress for the evening was 'informal', dinner in both restaurants was 'open sitting', and entertainment was limited to resident dance bands and watching the other pasengers. I sneaked off down to my cabin at eleven-thirty having once more delivered For Your Pleasure and Leisure to Thrippleton's suite unscathed, taking a spare copy for myself to study in bed. Forewarned is forearmed.

I scanned through it quickly hoping against hope, but there it was, published, in print, unalterable. 10.30 a.m. Hawkins Room. 'Open Day – meet your hostess Alison who'll be delighted to tell you all you might want to know about the ship.' It's not as if I hadn't been warned. I knew that on the return trip I'd be flying solo, so to speak, fully trained, fully fledged and fully confident. I dug out the notes Wendy had given me five days ago (was it only five days?) and tried to memorise them. I gave up. Too tired, too full of New York and who cared whether it was two thousand bottles of pickles and six thousand pints of cream or the other way round? It all went down the same way. And came back up the same way if the sea wasn't feeling benevolent.

The next morning the ship was skimming smoothly upon the flat waters, the sun was shining its little head off and the floors upon which I walked were actually staying put. And I got seasick. I was standing in the middle of the polished marble dance floor in the Hawkins Room. The sun glinted on the mirror-like ocean outside the wave-proof windows and the room felt bright, airy and wholesome, so different from its night-time manifestation. I'd given a brief introductory talk – listing the various entertainments rooms, restaurants, bars, social areas, falling back on For Your Pleasure and Leisure with, 'comprehensive details of every day's entertainments are set out in here', and ending with, 'my Cruise Staff colleagues and I are here to help you in any way we can. All you have to do is ask.' Which led me nicely into 'any questions?' I was standing there, microphone in hand, hoping there wouldn't be any and grinning inanely. ('Smile a lot, make them think you're their friend. You are their friend. You're paid to be' – Thrippleton.) About half a dozen hands were instantly raised in the air. I picked on the most intelligent-looking, asked her to stand up and introduce herself, hoping that might put the others off, then ask away.

She did. 'Well, miss . . . Alison, did you say? . . . what I'd like to know is, do the crew actually sleep on board?'

Is this for real? It was for real. ('No, madam, we send 'em all back to England in a lifeboat at six o'clock every evening. Where do you think the crew sleep, when we get to be fifteen hundred miles from land in any direction, you silly cow?') I smiled harder and said, 'Yes, madam.'

'Am I correct in saying that this is a ship and not a boat?' a man in a check shirt fired off without standing, or even waiting to be asked.

I was in luck, I knew the answer to that one. 'Yes, sir, you are indeed. This is a ship, not a boat.'

'Then can you tell me,' continued check-shirt, 'why the train that meets us at Southampton dock is called the *boat* train? Why isn't it the ship train?'

'That's a good question,' I said, 'and to be quite honest with you, I'm not exactly sure. But I can find out for you if you like.' Hoping he wouldn't like.

'Do that, will you?'

So I took his cabin number and assured him I'd give him the answer before we reached England. I looked at my watch. 'Almost time for morning coffee or jogging round the deck with Gavin. Any last questions?' I smiled and hoped they'd all go away.

Up shot a hand. 'What do we do if we get seasick?'

'No need to worry about that, madam,' I said still smiling. 'We have an injection for it. Just pop down to the doctor, have the injection – just a little prick, it doesn't hurt . . . ' here beginneth the first lie, 'then you rest for a couple of hours and after that you feel marvellous. It lasts for days so you won't get seasick for the rest of the trip.'

'Sounds like sales jargon to me,' said the woman. 'Too good to be true.'

'Oh, I can assure you,' I said, 'it does work. I got seasick the first time I joined the ship but I had the injection and I've never been bothered since.' The lie continued. 'Believe me, it really does work. Look at me – living proof.' Smile fixed forever, lie completed.

How could I lie like that? How could I get away with it? I lied, I felt no guilt and I *didn't* get away with it. I paid, oh how I paid.

Seasickness isn't just nausea, it's complete disintegration

of mind and body and everything that ever held the two together. By lunchtime I'd disintegrated. It was so bad that I even overcame my lifelong fear of injections. I stumbled my way down to crew sickbay which was on Six Deck, the place for sick sailors, right down in the bowels of the ship below the waterline. I managed to convey to the nurse that I had terminal seasickness whilst rolling up my sleeve.

She raised an eyebrow at my bared arm while inserting a hypodermic about the thickness of a knitting needle into a bottle. She withdrew it, squirted it, tapped it and then said, 'Bend over.' I could tell she was going to enjoy this. She had a vindictive look about her, a sort of cold sparkle in the eyes. I didn't move. 'Come along now, don't be a baby. It won't hurt.'

Why do they always say that? They know it's going to hurt, you know it's going to hurt, so why do they always insist on the lie? I'm sure it wouldn't hurt half as much if only they'd have the honesty to say 'this is going to hurt like hell!' So up went my skirt, down came tights and knickers and up shot a pain like a stream of scalding lead through the right cheek and all the way up the side of my back.

'There,' said the nurse. 'All done. That didn't hurt a bit, did it? Now go back to your cabin and sit down for half an hour.'

Sit down, she said! I could hardly walk. Trembling, shaky and weak, with a desperate desire to vomit, I took the lift up from Six Deck to Five and stumbled to my cabin. I eased myself on to the bed, face down, convinced I was dying. I swore that I'd never lie again, not ever, not for anything. Not even the kind of lie which is designed to get me out of trouble – the one where I lie about saying no.

They hardly ever work anyway. It's men who cause the problem. They are congenitally incapable of believing the truth. When you say no to them they really are convinced you mean yes. They think you're lying. Unfortunately, it's usually the other way round that you're lying – you say, or at least intimate, yes when you really mean no. Like the times when you're flat on your back with a heaving sweaty body on top of you which you don't even like all that much, and you're thinking, 'oh God, hurry up and finish so I can get up and go home.' Saying, 'yes I want to' and getting it over with can sometimes be easier than the hassle of making him really believe you mean no.

When I have the strength to say no I will be a grown-up person. That's another thing that'll happen to me when I'm thirty. I'll say no a lot more often. I'll say no every time I mean no, and yes only when I mean yes. I'll stop using these two words the wrong way round, I'll stop lying with them. I'll stop lying, period.

The phone rang. I fumbled for it, took it off the hook and groaned into the mouthpiece.

'What the hell are you doing there?' It was Thrippleton. 'Get up off your pretty little arse and move it. Delia Jeffrey's doing her nut in the Grenville Lounge.'

Oh God, the cookery lecture. I was supposed to set up and assist. The last thing I needed right now. 'Sorry, sir,' I said, breaking my resolution with the first word I uttered. 'But I've been down to sickbay for an injection. Guess it knocked me out.'

'I don't care if it knocked you to Timbuctoo. You're on duty. So get out there. And smile, damn it.'

The line went dead. I put the phone down, smoothed my crumpled skirt and went back to work.

By tea time in the Franklin Room I was starving. For reference of any future sea-travellers, the injection really does work. My earlier lie had turned out to be a truth after all.

We skimmed along the ocean, turned around in Southampton, bobbed along back to New York, turned around and headed back home yet again. Once you've made one return trip across the Atlantic you've made them all – the scenery doesn't change much. The first voyage had been taking me away from Joe and into a new life. The second was taking me back to nothing but a big empty question mark. The trial contract was about to expire. I'd had no word of an extension, but neither had I heard any rumours of a replacement for me. We were a day and a half out from Newfoundland and I decided to find out. I had a life to plan, I'd at least like to know whether the immediate next bit of it was going to be spent on the ocean waves or sorting out the backwash back in Dringley. I tried all day to get Thrippleton to myself for a few minutes but without success. So when I made the midnight delivery of For Your Pleasure and Leisure I decided to wait for him, hoping he'd turn up unaccompanied, unlustful and reasonably sober. Two out of three isn't bad.

'Ah-ha!' he said on entering. 'I knew you'd relent one of these nights.'

'Sorry boss,' I said. 'Not tonight. Business before pleasure, I'm afraid.'

'Fair enough. Business first.' I didn't like the way he stressed 'first'. 'What's your problem? Tell Uncle Jim.'

'I was wondering about my contract. It expires in three days, when we get back to Southampton, and I wondered if you'd heard from Head Office at all? Whether I'm to stay on or not?'

'Ah, that. Yes. Well . . . it hasn't actually been decided yet.'

'Oh.' Still room for hope then. 'Any idea when I might know for definite?'

'Depends. Have a drink?' He unscrewed the cap from a bottle of Johnny Walker Red Label.

'No thanks.'

'Depends on my recommendations. Sure you won't have one?' He poured himself a large measure.

I gulped. Stick to your guns, Alison. 'No really, thanks.'

'Suit yourself.' He screwed the cap back on the bottle and sat down on the couch-cum-bed which the steward had already prepared for its night-time role. 'Sit down?' He patted the bed next to him.

Oh dear. He was being remarkably subtle but the message was coming over loud and clear: be nice to me and I'll be nice to you. Did I want the job that much? Did I want *any* job that much? 'No thanks,' I said, 'I won't keep you. I'm very tired.' I wasn't in the least bit. Lying again. 'I just wanted to know if there was any news, that's all. Can't you give me any idea when I might know?' I tried again.

'Not really.'

'So I just wave the ship goodbye, go back home and sit

waiting for another phone call?'

'Very succinctly put.'

'I see. Oh well. Sorry to have bothered you. Goodnight.' And I left. Quickly.

So. No decision. I seemed to have developed a remarkable talent lately for leaping from one state of limbo straight into another. And I didn't really want to go back home. That had now become the unfamiliar territory, the ship and Elliott the familiar base. I was walking along Five Deck corridor back to my cabin when Elliott called me from the other end. 'Hi. Fancy a nightcap?'

I waved and nodded, not ready for sleep, so I went along to his place and we had a couple of drinks while I told him my dilemma.

'You know what you need, don't you?' he said when I'd finished.

'Apart from a firm commitment from someone, anyone, about anything, what?'

'A damn good screw.'

'Chauvinist. You're almost as bad as Thrippleton.'

'No, really. I mean it, Ali. Not from him of course, you've got much better taste . . . '

'Thanks for that, at least.'

' . . . but the ship's bursting at the seams with talent this trip.'

'Is it? I hadn't noticed.'

'I know you haven't. And that's not like you. You might not participate – and I can't think why – but that hasn't stopped you from appreciating it before. What's up?'

'I dunno. Defence mechanism? The closer we get to home, the more it brings back Joe and everything I suppose. It was all right earlier, till we got past the half-way mark, I was kind of moving away from it all.'

'And now you're going back?'

'Something like that. I can't help hoping it might still work out.'

'Fair enough. But don't let it stop you enjoying yourself while you can. I'm not talking about falling in love and getting involved and that kind of thing, I'm talking about screwing. Having fun. Enjoying it for a night or so. Nobody said anything about dropping your defences or muddying your home pitch.'

'But it's not that easy! I'm out of practice, Elliott. I haven't picked anybody up for years. I'm not the type.'

'Rubbish. It's as easy as falling off a log.'

'It might be but I'm not.'

'Oh come on. Don't give me all that outdated moralistic crap. Besides, you're on a ship. Try conforming!'

I laughed. 'It's silly, I know, but . . . '

'Lionel Markham was asking after you earlier,' he said casually. Subtle as a signpost. 'There'd be no strings attached there. He's off to Europe at the weekend.'

'Really?'

'I've only just left him up in the Frobisher. All alone, he was, and asking after you . . . '

'Bully for him.' I kissed Elliott on the cheek and stood up. 'I'm off to bed. See you in the morning.'

'Coward.'

I smiled, wished him goodnight, debated briefly whether to head upstairs to the Frobisher or go straight to bed, then turned along the corridor and went back to my cabin. I fell asleep with my arms around the pillow wondering if I'd made the right decision. I woke up in the middle of the night convinced that I hadn't. All this time at sea surrounded by people, passengers and crew alike, whose only aim seemed to be how many times they could get boxed off, and all I'd done was wander around being invulnerably above it all, or squelch along aching for what I used to have with Joe with the rest of it going on way above my head. And now there were only three days left. Wasn't it about time I leapt in and found out what it was all about? For myself? Wasn't it about time I put into practice some of those I'll-show-Joe-he's-not-the-only-one-who-can-screw-around thoughts I'd had on my very first night? Talk about procrastination! With that, I thumped the pillow into a more manly shape, snuggled into it again, and went back to sleep.

It was, as my friend said, as easy as falling off a log. I didn't even have to do any deals with Wendy about swapping duties between the Franklin or the Gilbert because Thrippleton assigned me to the Franklin which, according to the programme, was Lionel Markham's gig for the evening. I was to be the lighting technician and Sylvester the backstage dresser. Couldn't have planned it better if I'd tried, because the lighting person had to meet the cabaret artiste at some point in the afternoon to pick up the cue sheet and go over the effects that were wanted. I rang his cabin after lunch and we arranged to meet in the Franklin's bandroom at five, when afternoon tea would be over with and the musicians would have cleared off. The bandroom was a 'secure' area backstage where the musicians left their instruments and where the microphones, spare leads, music stands, lighting gells and other such tackle were stored. I collected the key from the Purser's Office as soon as the tea ritual was completed, nipped back to my cabin to freshen up, added a dab or two of the Chanel No. 5 free sample that I'd wheedled out of a Macy's assistant last visit, and then let myself into the bandroom to wait. I didn't have to wait long.

He came in, dressed casually in slim fitting slacks and an open-necked shirt which showed off his tanned chest and gold medallion, and said, 'Hi. Where've you been hiding? How can two people be confined to the same ship for a fortnight and hardly see each other?'

'Well it's a big ship,' I said. 'And I'm not exactly free to wander where I will for most of the time. Not like you entertainers. Jammy lot. A gig a night and the rest of your time's your own, you've got it made.'

'Ah, but when we work, we work hard. We give our all!'

I decided neither to agree nor disagree. 'So give me your cue sheet.' He took a crumpled piece of paper from his pocket and handed it to me. I looked at it. 'You don't expect me to work from that, do you?'

'Everybody else has so far.'

'Exactly. It'll fall apart if I so much as sneeze. Come on, let's make up a proper one,' and I took an A4 notepad out of a cupboard, pen out of my handbag, and sat down. 'Pull up a chair,' I said as he hovered over me. He did as he was told and I went on, 'Right, entrance, what's this, I can't read it? Is it house lights or douse lights?'

'Douse lights. Then follow-spot as I come on, then fill-in reds . . . '

We went through the sheet, him giving instructions, me making alternative suggestions, him accepting most of them. He'd finish on *My Way*, do two curtain calls, and then do *Can't Smile Without You* as an encore.

'Suppose they don't want an encore?' I asked innocently.

'They get one anyway. It's standard. Part of the act.'

'I see. Like cheese and biscuits extra, but it's still part of the menu.'

He smiled. 'You could say that.'

I smiled back. 'I just did.' I stood up. 'Right then. I've got to go. Chief Purser's cocktail party at seven, so I'd better go put the war paint on.' I was already wearing plenty. It takes ages to get that unmade-up effect.

'You don't need make-up. You look gorgeous as it is.'

'Thank you,' I said. 'See you later then.'

'I'll look forward to it.' He said it as though he meant it.

'Oh, by the way,' I said, as I was locking the door behind us, 'how are your trousers holding up these days?'

'I'll show you later,' was the reply.

I smiled to myself. Guess that's me fixed up for the night. And I wondered which one of us was the pushover.

Playing the game for all it was worth we met at midnight outside on Upper Deck aft and watched the moon on the ocean, making all the appropriate, appreciative noises. Then he put his arm around my shoulders and asked if I'd like to go back to his cabin for a nightcap.

'What sort?'

'Brandy, whisky . . . whatever you like.'

'I have a better idea,' I said. 'Why don't you come to my cabin and I'll make you a cup of tea?' That clinched it. It's the kind of offer you don't refuse. Anybody, anywhere on the ship can provide alcohol, but a fresh cup of tea, well, that's a whole different ball game.

Twenty minutes later two mugs of tea stood beside my bed and two naked bodies lay within it. I'd never made love to an almost total stranger before and I found the experience quite interesting. A husband or a regular lover is familiar. You already know what their hands feel like, for example, or the shape of their head, the texture of their hair. But when it's somebody you don't know, you get a whole series of little shocks and surprises, even down to the way they taste when you kiss them. I'd forgotten that people don't all taste or smell the same. And I'd forgotten how restricting a single bed could be. Lionel was quite pleasant. A little over-enthusiastic and lacking in technique but I couldn't be bothered with teaching him the finer points of female anatomy because we were only, to use an appropriate phrase, ships that pass in the night. I ended up faking an orgasm, not to satisfy his ego but to get it finished, because he wasn't going to let up until I came.

Afterwards he said, 'Was that good for you?' which proves that either he was a bad lover or I was a bad actress or both, because nobody worth their salt should have to ask. After what I considered to be a decent interval I said, 'Come on, time you were going,' as I climbed across him and reached for my dressing gown which had started out on the bed and was now in a heap on the floor. I put it on and got out of bed. 'I'd ask you to stay the night,' I said, lying with practised smoothness, 'but making love in a single bed is one thing. Two people trying to sleep in it is another. And it's nearly three o'clock.'

He looked at his watch and said, 'It isn't even two yet.'

'Wrong. Westbound, remember. And I have to be up at eight. Unlike some.'

He smiled. 'God, how uncivilised.'

'I wholeheartedly agree. So come on, Mr Markham. Out.'

He got up, got back into his clothes, and kissed me muttering, 'How about tomorrow?'

'Maybe,' I said. 'We'll see. Goodnight.'

He left and I got straight into the shower. I felt dreadful. What had I done? Why? And talk about failure – why had I bothered? I didn't know him well enough to even decide whether I liked him or not and there I was, allowing him into my bed and my body. Maybe he had VD? Oh God! I turned the shower on harder and directed it upwards in an attempt to wash away any suspect micro-organisms. I wanted his sticky semen *out*. Why had I let him in? Joe might find out. The pill would fail and I'd get pregnant. Joe would take one look at me and *know* I'd been unfaithful. Then I thought: and serves him right. What about him and Carol? This made us sort of even. Then I thought: no it doesn't. What's a quick screw compared with a passionate love affair? And why can't I even stage manage a quick screw properly? Not even one lousy little orgasm. I couldn't even do that right. I dried off and got into bed angry, ashamed, guilty. I didn't like myself much that night.

At the Cruise Staff meeting the next morning Elliott raised a questioning eyebrow at me. I returned him the merest flicker of a smile and slightest nod of the head. He winked and mouthed, 'well done,' and I replied with a slight shrug of the shoulders which could have meant either, 'it was a doddle,' or, 'I don't know why I bothered.'

It had been easy enough, I suppose. Except why should my life suddenly get easy? Being on a ship might be like living inside a narcotic bubble but it doesn't provide painless remedies to pain that quickly. Going to bed with Lionel had, if anything, brought Joe all the closer, brought the loss of him into sharper relief. It had bolstered my self-confidence a bit in that it proved I could pick up a guy as easily as the next girl or gay, and there was a sense of satisfaction, revenge, call it what you will, in finally being unfaithful to my husband. But it didn't do much for *me*. I told all this to Elliott when he whisked me away for five minutes directly after the meeting in order to get all the juicy details.

'Oh, don't worry,' he said. 'All you need is practice. Who do you fancy for tonight? Lionel again, or somebody else?'

'Haven't decided. We'll see what the day brings.'

I must have been sending out some kind of telepathic signals over the waves because the day brought – Joe. He reached out across the ocean and clutched me firmly back again, just like that. It was as if I'd been quiescent in his web all this while, then last night had shown signs of struggling free so he sent out another squirt of sticky threads to catch me up again. A message from the radio room sent me hurtling from lunch table to cabin to receive a shore-to-ship-to-shore telephone call. Why couldn't he let me go?

It was a strained and strange conversation, struggling with time delays and uncanny echoes down the line, his familiar voice reaching directly into my heart across hundreds of miles of empty sea.

'Hello, it's me.'

'Hello, Joe, what's happened, what's the matter?' Hand shaking so I could hardly hold the phone. First thought, parents have died, house has burned down, why is he calling?

'Nothing. Everything's fine. Why?'

'Oh I just thought . . . I was being silly. How are you?'

'I'm okay.' Flat voice, little, sad. A pause. 'I miss you. When are you coming home?'

My heart missed a beat. He misses me! Oh, Joe, how I love you, please let me hope, let me come home, be there when I come back. 'I've missed you too,' I said.

'When do you dock?'

'Day after tomorrow.'

'Are you staying on or coming home?'

'Coming home.'

Tentative again, 'Would you like me to be here?'

A pause, then I said, 'Yes, I think I would.'

'I'll be here then.'

'Joe?'

'Yes?'

'Take care then,' I said.

'You too.' Another pause. ''Bye.'

The line went dead. I sat there trembling, still holding on to the phone that had connected me to him, but no Joe at the other end any more. I went over the conversation, trying to memorise it. What had he said? Not that he loved me, nor that he'd finished with Carol, nor that he wanted me back nor wanted us to try again. But he had called me. From Yorkshire, on the phone, all that way away over mountains and oceans, he'd needed to speak to me. And he said he missed me. Yes, well, you can miss a pain in the shoulder, a cosy armchair, a dead cat, a broken habit, I told myself. But it's something, to miss somebody. And Joe had missed me!

My newly launched experiment in one-night-standing was over before it had really begun. I was a married woman again with a husband waiting for me at home. But the next two days consisted of a series of small but unmitigated disasters. I rediscovered what it was like to be a pre-menstrual pubescent. My hair lost its lustre, pimple appeared on nose, two spots blossomed on my chin, fingernails suddenly became brittle and broke off in jagged edges. Joe didn't like my hands at the best of times. They weren't 'artistic' like his. And with short nails they just looked squarish and bony. To cap it all, I really was pre-menstrual. This wasn't supposed to happen when you were on the pill.

We docked during the night and Thrippleton released me from disembarkation duty so I could get an early train back up to Yorkshire. 'I don't know about a new contract,' he said. 'But you've done well. I hope we'll see you back.'

I hoped not, hoped I'd never need to run away to sea again. 'Thanks. I've enjoyed it,' I replied as we shook hands.

I said goodbye to Elliott feeling very buoyant, convinced that I'd never join the ship again but without a doubt that he and I would somehow remain friends. We hugged and I left him waving to me from the top of the gangway. I got a taxi to the station and bought a single ticket to Dringley, then went to a phone box to call Joe. It was about half past eight in the morning. 'Hello, it's me, I'm back,' I said brightly. Happy, excited.

'Oh,' he said. 'I wasn't expecting you so early.' Did his voice sound resentful of my return or was it my imagination? Or was it that I'd woken him up?

'The train gets in at four-oh-five,' still excited, but not quite so. 'Can you meet me?'

'I don't think so. Can't promise. Get a bus or something.'

There it was, the customary greeting thud. I'd come all the way from New York and was about to face a seven, but seems more like ten, hour train journey, changing at Sheffield, lugging a suitcase bigger than I was, and he wouldn't even take time out to pick me up at the station, in *my* car that he'd had free use of in my absence. 'But you'll be home this evening? After work?' I asked.

'Probably. I did have a meeting but I'll try and cancel it.'

'But I told you I'd be back today.'

'Sorry. I thought you meant tomorrow. I'll see what I can do. Have a good journey.'

'Thanks.' The pips started chirruping and I didn't have any more change. 'See you later then,' I managed before we were cut off.

I spent the whole train journey fluctuating between mild hope and severe depression and trying hard to will him to the station, to embrace me passionately. It was a waste of energy. I scanned the faces at the barrier fervently, but he wasn't there. I drooped off to the exit and joined the queue for a taxi. I spent the ride willing him to be at home when I arrived, but I needn't have bothered because I had to let myself in to an empty house. I dumped the luggage, made some tea then sat down to wait with a very strong feeling of *déjà vu*. I'd been there about an hour when Joe came home and we were not reunited. We merely met again. There was tension in the air between us, both very wary. He came into the room and I got up from my chair, crossed the floor, held out both my hands and took his in them. He didn't draw away, he didn't do anything, not even offer an answering squeeze. His hands were just there in mine, acquiescent, limp.

'You look very different,' he said. I'd have preferred a simple 'welcome home'.

My first impulse was to apologise but I restrained it. If I didn't live up to his expectations that was his problem not mine. We went out to get some fish and chips. We brought them back and ate, talking without saying anything, drinking and not being merry. Eventually we went upstairs to our double bed because we felt we ought to make love. But all we managed to do was screw each other and even that was not done well. Afterwards I lay there thinking: Oh, Joe, what happened? Where did it go so wrong, has it gone too wrong for any hope of rescue? But I didn't say it out loud for fear that he might answer. I wondered why he'd bothered to phone me on the ship, why he'd missed me, why he'd told me and raised my hopes, on the phone, over the water, stirring up the waves I'd been trying to quell. I didn't need to ask him because I already knew the answer: he'd missed me like a broken habit, that was all. Like giving up smoking or stopping taking sugar with your tea. You long for it, but if you try it again it only makes you feel sick.

Joe was sleeping. I left him there and went into the bathroom and spent about an hour soaking myself in the tub because the evening had left me feeling manipulated, used, despoiled. I knew that hadn't been his intention, and that it was only my hang-ups coming out, but so what? I still wondered if I'd ever be able to forgive him for it.

He moved out for good the next day. He took the rest of his belongings and handed over the keys. We gave each other a sad little wave as he got on his bike and I stood on the doorstep watching him as he rode away not looking back. He was as cut up as I was. I've never seen such hopelessness expressed in a pair of shoulders.

I spent the next few days readjusting, taking a cold-turkey cure for the habit that had been as strong in me as in Joe, and teaching myself that any hope of me and him together again must be eliminated from my vocabulary. Traumatic, yes, but this time I didn't get suicidal about it. I'd already been on that trip and come through it. Instead I settled into watching Wimbledon on the telly and the birds hopping about on the lawn, and I phoned the shipping line head office to ask about another contract. I'd passed the trial hadn't I? I could come back, couldn't I? The answer was yes I had, and I could.

In five more days the ship would be back in Southampton and I would be there to meet it clutching a new three-month contract in my de-wedding-ringed left hand, having spent a weekend with Sally en route.

CHAPTER FIFTEEN

This time it's going to be different, I promised myself as I walked up the crew gangway nicely balanced by a medium-sized suitcase in each hand. This time it really will be a matter of watch out world, Alison is coming. No more being the nice quiet little girl smiling all the time and playing it by the rules so she won't ruffle any feathers. No more riding the waves and going unquestioningly where told. This time Alison was going to be the best. And she was going to be it by being herself.

It was already a lot easier than the first time I'd boarded the ship. This time I knew my way around. This time it felt like I was coming home rather than merely running for somewhere to hide. I walked confidently to the Purser's Office filled with a ridiculous urge to stop every now and then, put the cases down and pat things. There was no one waiting to be attended to and young spotty-faced-half-stripe, the officer on desk duty, was sitting with his feet up on a chair, half turned away from the desk and involved in what was obviously a phone call of a personal nature. He was smirking fit to bust and saying things like, 'Mm. Darling. That's a lovely idea,' and, 'Ooh, you naughty little creature.' He glanced up, gave my impatiently tapping fingers a dirty look, then continued his conversation making no effort to lower his voice, or his feet to the floor.

It wasn't so long ago that I'd have simply waited until he was ready to attend to me, probably apologising profusely for the very fact that I needed attending to. But not this time. Right, I thought, may as well start as we mean to go on. And I put on the most imperious voice I could find, bolstering it with the thought that if this scene had occurred in Dringley a couple of months ago the little slob would have been drooling for my signature scribbled on a bit of card. 'My cabin number, please,' I said loudly.

He simply waved a hand in my direction then turned his

back. Cheek! 'Now!' I said. No response at all. I left the suitcases on the floor, went round to the side of the desk and into the office through a door marked 'Officers Only'. Technically, I wasn't an officer. Technically, young half-stripe was. Who cared? 'My cabin number and key, please,' I demanded. 'Immediately.'

'Just a sec,' he muttered into the telephone, then leapt to his feet and blustered, 'You're not allowed in here!'

'Neither will you be, I should think, if I report your discourtesy. I'd like my key please because I need a cabin because I need to unpack because I need to get changed because I have an appointment shortly with my uncle . . . Captain Lawrence.' I told the lie calmly in the knowledge that it was most unlikely the pimpled youth would ever find out my true relationship to the Captain, as the gentleman in question was a distant, Godlike figure to all but the First Officer. Half-stripe would have been honoured to polish his shoes. By the same reason I was quite confident that the Captain would never find out that he had acquired an extra relative.

'I'll call you back,' he said into the telephone, replaced it in its cradle and quickly consulted a list. 'Number 126. Up on Fluff Alley already.' He took a key from a pegboard and handed it to me. 'Here you are, ma'am.'

Fluff Alley was up on One Deck and was the name given to a for'ard portside corridor behind a door labelled 'Lady Officers' Accommodation. Private. No Thoroughfare.' I wondered how come I merited a cabin along there, but thought it best not to query the matter. I simply took the key and walked out.

'Shall I call a steward to help you with your luggage?' he said when I reappeared at the front of the desk.

'Not necessary,' I replied and added a superior little 'Thank you' for good measure, as Captains' nieces would surely have good manners. As soon as my back was turned I started grinning. Suppose the Captain should discover I'd been putting it about that I was his niece? Instant termination of contract, probably. Oh, what the hell, I thought, still smiling. Take it for all it's worth and enjoy it for as long as it lasts. That was going to be my *modus* vivendi from now on.

I was just approaching the door into Fluff Alley when I heard Elliott's familiar voice calling me. I turned, put down the suitcases and held out my arms to him, grinning. Dear Elliott whooped in glee, shouted, 'I knew you'd be back!' and then started running towards me, waving his arms in the air and crying 'Catheeee!'

I took the cue. 'Heeeeeathcliffe!' I called and started loping towards him in my imitation of a slow-motion run. We bumped in a giggling heap of arms and hugs in the middle of the ship. He picked me up and swung me round in the air, narrowly missing a dour-faced steward who appeared from nowhere with an armful of dirty towels and muttering darkly about 'bloody Cruise Staff', which only made us giggle even more. I told him about my victory at the Purser's Office and with his arm around my shoulders and mine around his waist we walked back along One Deck towards my new accommodation, him complaining bitterly that he was still garrisoned down on Five. 'Still,' he said, 'it keeps me away from the eagle eyes of Thrippleton. You're not going to have nearly as much privacy, you know, surrounded by all those nice young lady officers. Your "uncle" has probably commissioned them to keep an eye on you!'

'Well,' I said, 'you know what they say about being well-connected: "if you've got it, flaunt it." And if you haven't, lie through your teeth!'

'That's my girl!'

We were both very impressed with my new quarters. A little touch of how the other half lives. The single-occupancy cabin was considerably larger than my old 'double' down on Five Deck. That is, you had to move both legs to get from one side of it to the other. It had a porthole too. The bed, unfortunately, was the regulation small single. Lady Officers I assumed, were assumed to be Nice Girls, and we all know what they don't do. I started to unpack, taking out the New York kettle first so Elliott could brew up while I hung up my clothes. Then we settled down to a cup of tea and a good long natter. We had a lot to catch up on.

Of course I told him all about what had happened while I'd been away, and of course he came out with all the old platitudes like 'you're too good for him anyway', and 'you're better off without him', and 'you're free now and the world is your oyster', which were all highly acceptable and comforting because it was Elliott who said them. He was repeating practically word for word what Sally had been telling me, so between the two of them I was almost beginning to believe it myself.

'You're a cliché-ridden fool,' I said affectionately.

He replied haughtily, 'Clichés only get to be clichés because they're true,' and then we both agreed that getting straight to the point and cutting out all the corners, when you've laid your cards on the table and all's said and done, life's too short to spend worrying over spilt milk so we should eat, drink and be merry, and grasp at life's opportunities with both hands, putting our best feet forward and our noses to the grindstone, because it's only as good as you make it.

The ship was between-passengers, most of the crew were off doing whoever they did on shore and Elliott and I didn't have to be on duty until eight-thirty the next morning. We had the whole evening before us in which to explore the delights of fun-packed Southampton, so we decided to treat ourselves to fish and chips in a dockland chippie with red and white checked plastic tablecloths. Over real tomato soup – genuine Heinz tinned, not the squashed and sieved and creamed tomato mush that you get on the ship – Elliott told me the details of his sex life since I'd seen him last. It was beginning to get quite busy. He'd kept his secret from Sylvester, whose attempts at matchmaking between Elliott and Wendy had of course been doomed to failure, by pretending to have sworn fidelity to me. Meanwhile he'd been tiptoeing along corridors in the dead of night to the cabins of two First Class passengers and one Tourist Class, and had entertained a couple of times in his own cabin too – a brief fling with a holiday relief stylist from the men's hair salon and an even briefer fling with an AB from the engine room who he'd taken in sheer drunken desperation one night after chatting up a bloke whose wife had turned up.

'Oh dear,' I said. 'How embarrassing.'

'It was rather.'

Mouth full of fish and crunchy batter I said, 'Elliott, how do you do it?'

He actually blushed.

'No, I don't mean the clinical details you fool, I mean your success rate. Hunting and bagging the quarry. I've decided to broaden my experience, you see . . . '

'Good God! Don't tell me you're actually going to conform at last!'

'Yes, I suppose that's one way of looking at it. But I might need a few lessons. Pass the vinegar.'

He did. 'Nonsense. You did fine with Lionel Markham, didn't you?'

'Only because he was a pushover.' I doused my mushy peas. Mint sauce was better, but you couldn't expect that sort of refinement down south, so vinegar would do.

'What about that Joss chap you told me about? You had him at your feet pretty smartish by all accounts.' He speared a chip which had strayed on to the tablecloth, spearing me along with it.

Joss. A frisson of longing which I quickly subdued. 'That was different. We were thrown together by circumstance.'

Elliott nearly choked. 'Excuses, excuses. A pick-up's a pick-up . . . you can do it if you want to. And the ship's just teeming with people who want to be picked up. Otherwise they'd take a plane, wouldn't they?'

'I hadn't thought of it that way.' I beat the hell out of a tomato ketchup bottle. 'But I'm still not sure if I can do it. I mean it's years since I've been on the prowl. I just don't think I'm the type. Take Lionel, for instance. It was a washout really.' I lowered my voice. 'I didn't come. And I still felt guilty afterwards, and sort of dirty.'

'What are you whispering for?' He picked up his empty plate and licked it clean.

'The waitress might hear.'

'So what? What's she to us?'

As if on cue the waitress appeared and took away our greasy plates, leaving trifles in their place. She plonked them down on the table, little plastic tubs, fluted. We dug in.

'You're all hung up about what other people might think. I'll bet, while you were at it with Lionel you were thinking . . . ' he put on a squeaky voice which was supposed, God forbid, to be an imitation of mine, ' . . . "what's a nice girl like me doing in a situation like this? Oh dear, what would the neighbours think?"'

I giggled. 'I think it did cross my mind.'

'No wonder you were uptight then. But really, Ali, it's dead easy to get over that kind of hang-up. Believe me, I know. Think what *I* went through! I've said it before and I'll say it again: what you need is a bit of practice, that's all. If you don't use it, you lose it. The more you do it, the looser you get.'

'But I don't want to be loose, I want to be in love!' I declared, waving my spoon dramatically.

'Bollocks. Only two minutes ago you were saying you wanted to broaden your experience. Women! Listen. What you've got to do, my girl, is learn how to have some good, honest, mucky fun. And you'll do it if I have to break every bone in your body!'

I laughed. 'Thanks, friend.'

'That's quite all right. Any time.'

At the Cruise Staff meeting the next morning I volunteered for the jobs I wanted instead of waiting like the others did to be allocated to various duties. 'I'm an experienced broadcaster,' I said. 'So can I have a go at the in-cabin radio show please?'

'But the girls don't do that,' said Thrippleton.

Oh Christ, not that one again. 'You never read my curriculum vitae then?' I asked.

'Head Office do that. I just take what I'm sent.'

'Well this time they happened to send you someone with vast experience in producing and presenting radio programmes. Don't you think you should make some use of that?'

'Oh, all right. I'll give you a try out. So long as Phil and Gavin don't mind. Fellas?'

Phil couldn't very well object after all he'd said to me before about it and Gavin didn't look too bothered one way or the other. 'Okay then,' said Thrippleton. 'You'll have to do the first hour though because the Captain wants you for his cocktail party at seven. Specifically asked for you. Sorry, Wendy my love, you'll have to take charge of my little thrash.'

Wendy looked disgruntled. Hostessing the Captain's cocktail party was recognised as her duty, she being the senior hostess. And I didn't like the sound of that 'specifically asked for'. Oh well, cross that bridge when we come to it. Put on a sparkly dress along with a sparkly smile and hostess your heart out, Alison.

But first, to embarkation duty. I sat in the information kiosk alone and passed the time in between proffering information by reading the passenger list. You could pick up quite a lot from that, especially the separate VIP list which was marked 'Confidential'. If you're going to go prospecting among the passengers you may as well begin where the gold is signposted, I thought. I'd heard tales of incognito royalty, knighted ex-politicians, film stars and rock stars and the most surprising success stories from Sylvester. This might even be the trip when I'd meet the tall dark and handsome Venezuelan millionaire who'd whisk me off my feet and the ship and back to his palace to live happily ever after so I wouldn't ever again have to worry about anything more taxing than 'which jewels shall I wear today?' Such little fantasies grease the smile muscles quite nicely when they've been out of action for a couple of weeks. I must have presented quite a pleasant face to the oncoming passengers.

I scanned the list quickly but was disappointed. I'd never heard of any of these Very Important Passengers. I mean, who the hell cares about Mrs Irma Schwarzz who is socially prominent in Boston, Mass.? Or W. Harvey Butler III, Vice President, Weiss-Froom Corporation? Or Miss Susannah Tiffany, niece of the prospective Conservative candidate for Banbury (East)? How on earth did she get herself on the VIP list? Perhaps she was also a niece of the Captain? I allowed myself a little chuckle. I read on to discover the name of another person socially prominent in Boston, Mass. – one Boyd H.C. Ziegler – and I speculated as to whether he and the aforementioned Mrs Schwarzz were perhaps more than just good friends. And then, an entry that spoke volumes on 'class' one-upmanship: Clifford Stanton-Bruce (what, no middle initial?) had his name on the VIP list in bold type next to the description 'does not wish for VIP recognition'. Beat that, baby.

Lunch was followed by Open Day, again a solo mission, followed by Boat Drill, great fun in partnership with Elliott and first opportunity to recce the big game hunt. Afternoon tea and cakes was followed by quick dash to cabin to do face, hair and manicure for Captain's cocktail party, so when I finished the radio show at half past six all I'd have to do would be to change clothes. Then off to find the studio somewhere in the middle of Three Deck and make myself at home in a new version of my old niche.

What a let down. Studio? I couldn't believe it. The in-cabin radio show was slung out from a corner of an electrical repair shop. It wasn't even partitioned off. Doors might open, phones might ring, Harry and Lester might call to each other for soldering irons, Avo prods and signal diodes while I stood in my corner at an obsolete disco twin-turntabled thing held together by rubber bands and bulldog clips. At least it had pre-fade so you could actually cue up a record but that was where any concession to effective music presentation ended. Once you'd found the start point of the record you had to wind it back half a turn and hold it steady with your finger on a slip mat while the turntable spun merrily away underneath it. When you wanted the record to play you just let go. Fine and dandy except you needed another hand to turn the microphone on (with a big black knob not a sliding fader) and another one to fade out the other record. Three operations. Two hands. Tricky. Solved that one with a toothy metal clothes-peg which Lester assured me was called a crocodile clip, on the end of an Avo lead: tie end of lead to nail hammered in side of desk, fix croc clip to slip mat making lead taut and thus holding slip mat in place leaving hand free for microphone. Clever, huh?

But the microphone was a bit of a problem. My co-deejay Phil being somewhat taller than me, the microphone had to be adjustable for height. It was fixed to a gooseneck (one of those flexible bendy-toy type tubes) which had seen better days. If your link lasted any longer than thirty seconds you found yourself gradually following the microphone on its drooping journey floorwards. Maybe it was all a foul plot by Gavin to keep our spines exercised.

The record selection was an abomination – they hadn't even got evergreens like *My Way*, which was something of an omission, considering the brief was 'keep it nice and easy, none of this head-banging rubbish' – and what there was was in a disgusting state. Fingermarks, dust, scratches, even ring stains from straying coffee cups. And no headphones. And an audience, I should think, of about three. I prayed for a smooth crossing and wished I was back at 2D Radio.

I wished for much the same thing when the deific Captain Lawrence greeted my arrival with, 'Ah, Alison, my new niece, I believe. Pleased to meet you at last.' He was a man of contradictory appearance, stately but jocund, rounded but with a powerful, threatening dignity. I braved it out and apologised straight to his face. 'Ah. Yes. Er, sorry about that, sir. I'm afraid it was one of those situations where I needed to pull rank. And as I haven't got any I borrowed yours. I do hope I haven't caused you any embarrassment. I can't apologise enough.'

'Hm. Well, much as I wouldn't be disappointed to have you as my niece, please be a little more discreet when choosing your relatives in future.' He kept his face quite straight, but I detected the trace of a twinkle in his eyes. 'But you showed initiative. I like that. Apology accepted.'

'Thank you, sir.'

'And thank goodness you didn't say you were my daughter. I never married you see.'

I blushed. That would have been the end of my new career for sure. 'Should I put the record straight then, sir, and disown you?'

He laughed. 'I don't think that will be necessary. Come along and have a glass of champagne before our guests arrive. Tell me about yourself.'

It was a cracking good cocktail party. I hoped I'd be invited again. After that, dinner in the Collingwood, off out into the social whirl of small talk, small drinks and a small victory with the sound mixing board which elicited a compliment from the band leader after the show. Then wander down to the Frobisher and along to the Hawkins for a look at the talent with Elliott, decided one of Taffy's steak butties would be more appetising than anything else on offer that night. 'Scaredy cat!' accused my alter-ego, then off up to the night kitchens and so to bed.

I was off again. Somewhere, nowhere, parcelled up in a cushy little bubble and chugging across the great divide between the old world and the new, turn around and back again, turn around and off again, and find myself in bed with a saxophone player simply because I felt like it. And about time too. I felt like I'd lost a second virginity. The mental barrier against fornication had been breached never to be rebuilt – I began to look for another lay.

By the time I'd got rid of him in the early hours, I was still feeling good about it, unlike that earlier episode with Lionel Who? Elliott's lessons in morality must have been taking effect, because I wasn't feeling guilty and I wasn't feeling used. If anything I was feeling very pleased with myself, the cat who'd just licked up the saucerful of cream. The thought of having whichever men I chose hopping in and out of my bed like a succession of fleas with little chance of ever meeting any of the involved parties again once I went back to real life on land was taking on the allure of a most interesting and titillating intellectual exploration . . .

I thought back to Joe saying that sex itself was unimportant, 'like shaking hands only more fun'. I hated to admit it now, but he might have been right. My little saxophone player had indeed been fun. I took my notebook into bed with me and started a list of my lovers. It wasn't difficult. Up until now I'd never led a particularly promiscuous life – I could still count on my fingers the men I'd been to bed with – so I quickly jotted down the names, hesitating briefly after Joe because I wished I could put Joss's name there, then added Lionel Markham and . . . heavens, what was his name? Alec or Alex? I was catching up with Joe's attitude in more than just numbers.

I didn't get the opportunity to talk it over with Elliott until after cabaret the next evening. It was one of those days when our duties seemed always to be at opposite ends of the ship. By the time I got him cornered my conscience had done an about-turn. Typical. I grabbed my pal and dragged him off into the Frobisher Club where I knew we wouldn't be disturbed because the musicians were only allowed in there when performing and my saxophonist was down for the Hawkins Room. I wanted to avoid any confrontation with him that night because he'd expect a repeat performance and having said yes to someone once it's very difficult to say no the night after.

'Okay, what is it?' asked Elliott when we'd settled into a dark little corner with a couple of dark tall drinks.

'Elliott, I have sinned.'

His face lit up with delight. 'I don't believe it. You haven't!'

'I have.'

'When?'

'Last night.'

'Who?'

'The saxophone player with the Taylor Jones Quintet. Alec, Alex, whatever.'

'Can't even remember his name? Alison, I'm shocked.'

'So am I. Isn't it awful?'

'Totally shameful.'

'Elliott, you're supposed to just say "no". Comfort me or congratulate me or something. Absolve my conscience.'

'I can't. It's your conscience. I wouldn't feel guilty but then, I'm not you, am I?'

'It wasn't particularly wrong of me then, was it?'

'Here we go again. You can be really irritating sometimes, you know, Ali. Can't you think for yourself? You're not a child, you should have worked out your own rules by now. And anyway,' here he took a long drink of his rum and coke, 'I think you're just pretending. You don't feel bad at all, really. You just think you *ought* to.'

That was the trouble with Elliott. He could zoom right in to the middle of my inner confusions and point straight at the truth underneath them. It was like being naked all the time. 'Bastard,' I said, smiling at him.

'I love you too. Now drink up and piss off. I've got a date.'

'Sorry.' I gave him a peck on the cheek and left. Feeling very immature and foolish.

I lay in bed alone that night really trying to work myself out. The problem was in learning to disassociate sex from love. I never had. That was why it had always caused the big problems in my life, got me into all sorts of trouble including a couple of marriages I'd have been better off without. That was why the Joss thing had been so heavy. I couldn't sleep with him if I didn't love him, but I wanted to sleep with him so I must love him, but I still couldn't because I couldn't be unfaithful to Joe because I loved him although he had been unfaithful to me and therefore must love Carol. Sex and love. Separate the two, and bingo! Here I was, nobody to be in love with, nobody to be unfaithful to and lots of people to have sex with.

Next morning I woke up feeling bright and happy and saying: oh the hell with it. Screw the lot of 'em. Literally. The sun was streaming through my porthole which helped the euphoria nicely and besides, we were only a day away from New York and New York always gave me a lift. That reminded me. I had to see Thrippleton about the record library. I couldn't go on presenting programmes with such a limited choice of music. I couldn't bear being forced into doing a bad job if there was the slightest chance of improving it. I had to try.

I took him to one side after the morning meeting. 'We *must* have some new records, Jim,' I said. 'I could get them in New York tomorrow if you'll give the authorisation.'

'I don't know.' He thought about it, then said, 'You make out a list and show it to me first. I don't want you spending the company's money on a load of noisy punk stuff.'

'Jim, really. Have you no faith? I know the kind of thing

to get. Sinatra, Mathis, Streisand . . . trust me.'

He looked doubtful but he signed a piece of paper anyway. I glanced at it. Up to five hundred dollars. Wow. 'Guard it like you guard your purity,' he said, patting my bottom.

I slapped his hand away, and scurried off to make out a list. Christmas will be a little early this year!

The days and nights tumbled along, New York and Southampton forming fleeting landmarks along the journey, and I tumbled along with them, conforming for all I was worth.

'Elliott? I . . . er . . . went to bed with Gary last night.'

'Gary Anthony?'

'The same.'

'You little groupie.'

'You're only jealous.'

'Huh. Does he screw as badly as he sings?'

'No. Worse.'

'Poor little Alison. Didn't she enjoy it then?'

'Not a lot.'

'Then why did you do it?'

'Because I thought I might.'

'Fair enough. But you are a cow, you know. I fancied him.'

'Feel free,' I said. 'You're welcome to him. He wanted to . . . well, let's just say he's probably more your type than mine after all.'

I was reigning over the Captain's cocktail party when Sir took me to one side. 'I just wanted to say I've been enjoying your radio programmes, my dear. Lovely music you're playing.'

'Thank you, Captain Lawrence.'

'Perhaps you could do something about those dreadful noises in the discotheque? I'm sick to death of hearing *Tie A Yellow Ribbon*. Haven't we got anything a little more up to date?'

'I've been thinking about that myself, sir. How about if we bought the basic top ten singles next time in Southampton and New York, and then updated them each crossing

after that? We'd soon have the Hawkins Room throbbing.'
'Good idea. I'll talk to Thrippleton about it. Smart girl. You're turning out to be quite an asset to us.'
I soaked up the praise like a dry sponge.

A few nights later I was sitting on a bed in a cabin down on Six Deck belonging to a couple of the girls from the hair salon. They were giving a party because it was 'Susan's neighbour's cat's birthday'. It was very crowded, bodies squeezed into every available space, bottles and glasses and people all over the beds, drawers and floor. On the bed opposite me Alec/x and Gary Anthony were sitting squashed against each other. Elliott was one (male) hairstylist away from them, looking very pleased with himself. I gave him a significant look, glancing at the stylist and Gary then back to Elliott again with a questioning eyebrow. Elliott grinned across at me. He'd scored with both. Then he inclined his head slightly towards Gary and Alec/x and back to me again. My turn to grin. We met on the floor between the two beds on the pretext of filling up our glasses. He nudged me and said quietly, 'Hello, slut! I won't tell your two if you won't tell my two.'
I squeezed his arm and replied, '"Slut" yourself! Agreed. Or we could try a fivesome?'
'Too tired. Another crossing, maybe.' We kissed each other on the mouth, clinked glasses and drank a silent toast to our mutual successes.
Elliott nudged me. 'Hey, if only Joe could see you now!'
'Joe who?' I said.

The morning after the night before: 'Elliott, I've done it again!'
'Congratulations. You're really coming on. I'm proud of you. Who was it this time?'
'Dunno. I never asked.'
He looked at me in admiration. 'You *are* coming on! Passenger or crew?'
'Passenger.'
'First or tourist?'
'First, of course. VIP probably. Suite, not cabin.'

'Lucky you. And was it good?'

'Okay, I suppose. But nothing to write home about.' I yawned. My system was beginning to demand an uninterrupted eighteen hours' sleep. With nobody mucking about with the clocks in the meantime.

'Promiscuity's not always all that it's cracked up to be, is it, Ali?'

'Well, let's just say it can get to be a bit boring.'

'Mm.'

Boring. Whatever next? I didn't have to wait too long to find out.

CHAPTER SIXTEEN

It happened about three days out from New York and was a bit like being hit by a tidal wave. Three days out and just over a week since I'd decided that I'd got about all I was going to from sleeping around. I'd enjoyed it and it had been fun and I'd come a long way from the girl who'd scrubbed herself clean after the first one-nighter with Lionel. I'd even written a kind of essay under the heading 'Progress?' in my little black book: I was making it in the physical sense either because my responses had loosened up with practice or because I'd dismissed the guilt or because I cared enough about myself to make demands without feeling shy or embarrassed or worrying about the dents I might be making on the other party's ego. That was progress. My newfound expertise was eliciting complimentary responses. That was progress. And more often than not it was the bloke who did the chatting up rather than me, so my ego, sense of being attractive to the opposite sex, was much improved since Joe's demolition job. I'd tried it out, enjoyed it for a time and then rejected it – not from any external moralistic influences but simply because *I* wanted to. I wasn't particularly enjoying it anymore. I was bored, I was uncomfortable about it. Pure selfishness really. That was the biggest progress of all. I wanted something else now. I wasn't sure what but I was sure I'd know it when I saw it.

And I did. 'It' came straight out of a fantasy and had already been on the ship for three days before I was aware of its presence. That's not as strange as it might seem on a vessel that holds about three thousand people all told and contains such huge distances from points A to B. It's quite possible to meet somebody on the first day of a crossing and then never see them again, anywhere. It's even more likely that someone could be on the ship for the whole trip and your paths wouldn't cross at all, ever. By those standards, three days isn't bad.

'It' went by the name of Yuri Vladimirovich Monakhov. He strode into my life like a prince straight out of Tsarist Russia wearing a Cossack tunic with baggy silken trousers tucked into white leather boots, a jewel-encrusted dagger at his waist, a tasselled cape over his shoulders and a big furry hat. What a way to make an entrance.

I was sitting at the side of the cabaret platform in the Gilbert Room quietly minding my own business, which on that occasion was the antiquated lighting board and a secondhand cue sheet that was so straightforward there had been no need to go over it with the artistes beforehand. So the band struck up, I turned all the overhead spots up full white, and there was a rush of wind behind my back as three men in furry hats ran past shouting something like 'Oy!' at the tops of their voices. They leaped on to the dance floor and then stood there, absolutely motionless as if trapped in a single frame of a movie, to be admired in all their splendour. Then the three of them, in a single, uniform movement, strode forward and bowed the most arrogant bow I've ever seen. I always thought a bow was meant to be a gesture of humility. But not this one. This one said, 'I am God, fall down on your knees and worship.' The audience worshipped and I missed my next lighting cue.

Elliott was on duty next to me operating the sound control panel. He nudged me, I twiddled my faders and got the lights right, and he twiddled his knobs and stopped the speakers from humming. Then we looked at each other, looked at the Cossack Dancers, specifically the tall one in the middle, then back to each other again wide-eyed and open-mouthed. Neither of us said anything. What was there to say except that it was lust at first sight? Lust in its purest, if you can juxtapose the words, kind. How many times in my teens did I describe my 'type' of man, the ideal male? How many times in my whole life did I never meet him? Believe me, if you ever do stumble across a living, breathing, warm and throbbing incarnation of your ideal man, oh boy, are you in trouble. Oh boy, was I in trouble! In the nicest possible sense.

I was looking for an indefinable something one minute and looking on Yuri Vladimirovich Monakhov the next.

Oh, the music in that name. Typical of me really . . . could I fall for a Peter Briggs or a Harry Grimshaw or even a W. Harvey Butler III? Unlikely. But one Yuri Vladimirovich Monakhov, there, there was a name to be in love with. If ever a man matched the *idea* in his name, there, there was the man. I didn't actually want to love anybody. But to be *in* love, that was a different matter. And I was in it. Before we'd spoken one word to each other, before he'd even finished that first cabaret.

They leapt off the stage and disappeared behind the back-drapes with the same sudden magnificence with which they'd appeared. And I was manacled to the lighting board for another half-hour. When midnight came Elliott and I scampered off in search of our prize, rivals for the first time, wondering where he'd disappeared to and whether he'd turn out to be straight or gay. Oh, he had to be straight. He just had to. Nobody could be so obviously formed to delight the female sex and end up gay. It was unthinkable.

We tried everywhere. The Frobisher Club, the Hawkins Room, even went down to the sober Grenville Lounge and in desperation the gymnasium and the indoor swimming pool. We even circled the promenade decks starting at different ends, one of us going clockwise, the other anti. But nothing. Nowhere. We went back to the Frobisher for a drink to calm our jiggled nerves.

'Elliott, I swear to God, he can't possibly be your type, so you may as well stop hoping. And anyway, you couldn't possibly want him as much as I do. With you it would be just lust, another conquest, another scalp for your belt. But I swear, this time it's different for me. It's silly and ridiculous and crazy and wonderful and I don't believe in love at first sight, but I'm in love.'

'Just because you want him it doesn't necessarily follow that he has to be totally straight. Your radar went a bit astray with Gary Anthony didn't it?'

'That was different. That didn't matter. This time it does. It really does. And anyway, I was watching him. Nobody could look at women like I saw him looking at the women in the audience and not like women.'

'What's that got to do with it? I like women.'

'Not that way, you fool. Anyway, you wouldn't know. You're a man. It's something only a woman would notice. A feeling. So you may as well forget about him. He's not for you. Believe me.'

'I'll reserve my opinion until I've met him properly.'

'I don't know how you can sound so cool and collected about it! Ten seconds flat and I'd forgotten the meaning of the words! What am I going to do?'

Elliott shook his head. 'Oh dear you have got it bad. I've never seen you like this.'

'Neither have I.'

The next two days were agony. I was meticulous over make-up and hair just in case I bumped into him. I performed the various social duties like a robot with crossed wires – occasional jerky movements and a constant electrical fizzing inside. He seemed always just around the corner or just leaving a room as I entered it, the shadow of him but never the substance. I was consumed by the fact that he was on the ship and I was on the ship so we were bound to meet sometime if only the Cossacks' contract was long enough. Please, God, Fate, somebody, let them be long-term entertainers and not one trip wonders. We were destined for each other. We just had to get together.

I was nearly frantic by the time we reached Southampton. It hadn't worn off at all. But at least I'd discovered one optimistic rag of information and that was they were booked for at least one more trip. Time had not yet run out on me. I made myself sit down and think seriously how I could engineer a definite meeting. It had to be soon. And it had to be in the right circumstances where I'd be at my best. Preferably in public so I'd be forced to keep my dignity, but not too public so there'd still be the opportunity for intimate conversation. And bingo! I had it. Thrippleton to the rescue. Not that he'd be aware of it, of course.

We had only a brief meeting of the Cruise Staff on Southampton morning. All the boss had to do was allocate us to our different disembarkation stations and then we were free until the next day. I waited till all the others had gone and then said to him, 'Jim? Can I ask a favour?'

'Oh-ho, what's this then? So long as you remember that if I do you a favour I'll expect one in return.' He'd been remarkably unleery for the last few days so it's not surprising that the tide should turn again just when I could do with it least.

'Well it's not exactly a favour, Jim, I was just wondering if I could host your cocktail party tomorrow evening instead of the Captain's. Change and change around, you know.'

'Oh. What brought this on? I thought you enjoyed being Captain Lawrence's right-hand woman.'

'Well I do, of course, it's just that . . . your first night dos for the entertainers are so much more fun. Captain Lawrence is fine, of course, but, well, VIPs can be a bit stuffy. Go on, Jim, be an angel and let me hostess yours tomorrow. Besides, it's only fair that me and Wendy should take it in turns and she hasn't done the Captain's for ages now.'

Thrippleton looked quite happy at the suggestion. 'Okay. To tell you the truth . . . ' and he lowered his head to whisper in my ear, 'Wendy can be a bit stuffy too. So you be here by ten to seven all prettied up and we'll have ourselves a private little drink together first.' He finished by nibbling at my neck. I dodged. My mouth smiled its automatic polite response but I'm not sure if the rest of my face managed to be in accord with it. 'It's a date then,' he continued. 'Now move your pretty little bum out of here and get it down to the Grenville.' He patted my bottom.

I moved it out of the way quickly. 'I do wish you wouldn't do that, you know,' I said as a parting shot. 'One of these days I'll turn and grope you back.'

He spreadeagled himself and said, 'Do it, do it!'

'Sorry, haven't the time. I've got to get down to the Grenville Lounge! 'Bye.' And I escaped quickly. Mission accomplished. Roll on tomorrow evening.

I don't know why I bother making plans. He didn't turn up. Neither did the other two Cossack Dancers. I'd spent a self-indulgent time in dock doing a thorough overhaul – proper manicure, face-pack, leisurely shampoo and blow dry – and then I'd prepared for the Cruise Director's cocktail party with the sort of care and attention to detail I hadn't practised since I was about seventeen, and all for what? To spend forty-five minutes chatting up the most unprepossessing crowd you could imagine. A middle-aged hypnotist, an overweight operatic duo, a raggle-tailed magician, a female nightclub singer, and a husband and wife flamenco dancing team. Where was he? How dare he stand me up like this after all I'd been through? And to cap it all, Jim Thrippleton kept appearing at my shoulder saying, 'You're looking especially lovely this evening, Alison. Shall we meet for a nightcap later?' I resolved that Elliott, Phil, Wendy, anybody but me should make the night-time delivery of For Your Pleasure and Leisure even if I had to resort to breaking a leg. The only good thing that came out of the cocktail party was that I managed to read an outline of the whole trip's cabaret timetable. The Cossack Dancers were on it, due to appear in the Franklin Room tomorrow night. At least they hadn't fallen overboard, or been shanghai'd, or had their contracts cut short. By hook or by crook, tomorrow night I was going to be backstage in the Franklin helping with the showgirls. Then we *had* to meet.

Having settled that point with myself I managed to get through the rest of the evening with equanimity reasonably restored. It was around one o'clock and Elliott had scurried away to meet the AB from the engine room. Wendy, Phil, Gavin et al. were nowhere to be found but as I'd just seen Thrippleton in the Frobisher Nightclub with his arm draped around a skinny teenage girl in a skinny dress over which fell skinny long blonde hair, I deemed it safe to do the late night programme delivery girl routine myself. I was wandering back through the Hawkins disco, debating whether I should give it all up and visit Taffy for consolation when it happened.

He was there. He was alone. And he was leaning against a doorway looking as lost and not knowing what to do with himself as I was. A quick prayer: please don't let him disappear through that doorway before I get to him. I kept him fixed in my sights in the hope of glueing him to the floor. He must have felt it because he looked up, looked across the room and straight at me. And he didn't look away again.

That first look. My insides turned into melting blancmange. Of all the places on a ship sailing the romantic ocean for eyes to meet across, ours had to choose the noisy, sweaty, garish, throbbing crowded room of the Hawkins. No Albinoni organ playing softly in the shadows, no honeysuckled scent wafting past gauzy curtains, no watercolour sunsets or green wooded glades. Our eyes met and held fast over Carousel's abandoned drumkit in smoky, alcohol-smelly fog under red blue and green strobe lighting by the shiny marble dance floor. I was weaving my way through gyrating, disco-dancing bodies and obtrusive elbows totally unthinking, drawn to him by an invisible thread, reeled in like a fish on a line. Hooked. And suddenly I was standing before him. He looked down through the foot of space that divided the top of his head from the top of mine and said, 'At last, we meet.'

'At last,' I replied. This was no time to start playing coy.

'Aren't you little?' His arm fell around my shoulders.

'And you're so tall.'

'That is because I have long legs.'

'And mine are too short,' I said.

'If we sit,' said Yuri, 'we might be the same.'

'Let's try it.'

So we did. A corner table emptied miraculously as we approached. A table for two. We sat opposite each other, bringing our heads to almost the same height, and we talked, never once looking away from the other's face. We explored uncharted territories. We discovered enchanted lands. We wandered together lost and secure across a charmed and magical dominion while its ruler looked over us and smiled. We fell in love, Yuri and I, in the space of moments. Except that fell is the wrong word. Soared is better . . . we soared into love, up up and away . . .

Eventually we noticed that the music had dimmed into silence and the lights had become louder and all white. People were drifting away around us and the stewards began to collect empty glasses and wipe the ashtrays. But it was far too early. We were only just beginning. I suggested that we go out on deck.

'But it is raining, I think.'

'So?'

'You will get your pretty dress wet.'

'I don't care.'

'You will be cold.'

'I love the feel of rain on my skin.'

'So do I.' And he took hold of my hand and held it tight as if it was the most natural thing in the world to do and led me out on to the deck.

It was indeed raining. Stair-rods. The wooden slats of the deck were shiny and slippery. There wasn't a moon and there were no stars and it was windy and cold. It was a pretty rotten night, in fact, and there was nobody else but Yuri and myself foolhardy enough to venture out into it. We leaned over the rail and put our faces into the wind. It was difficult to breathe. The air came in great gulps so it almost hurt. The rain lashed at my bare arms and the wind blew our hair into tangles. Yuri put his arm around me and sheltered me with his body. 'What shall we do now?' he asked.

I loved his voice. It was like spun copper. Lambswool. Oceans. Perhaps it was only the Atlantic wind in my ears. But I loved his voice. I leaned against him pretending it was for shelter. He felt so hard. I put my arm around his waist and felt the warmth of him coming through the damp, tight cotton of his shirt. He reminded me of Joss. 'How about a cup of tea?' I shouted into the wind.

'Russian?'

'No, Tetley's.'

We walked back along the deck and inside again. This time I was leading him.

But as soon as we were alone in my cabin it was very difficult. Awkward. Polite. Superficial. To cover it I fiddled with the kettle and the tea things and asked silly questions like did he take sugar and how many? Then he sat on the bed and I sat opposite on a stool and we drank the scalding tea because it was the least awkward thing to do. We were in the middle of that uncomfortable space between initial attraction and real physical contact. He could finish his tea and go back to his cabin and it would be as if we'd never locked eyes or held hands or shared the same gulps of ocean air. Or he could stay and somehow cross that invisible but very tangible barrier between his personal space and mine.

I had a desperate need to go to the loo. But how could I when there was only one flimsy door between the lavatory and Yuri, and he'd be able to hear me in there and we weren't intimate enough for that? So I crossed my legs and asked him if he'd like some more tea.

'No thank you,' he said, and then he started to laugh.

'What are you laughing at?' I said, catching it from him and laughing myself.

'I laugh because we are like strangers. But we are not. Oh, we are *not*. There is only one thing for us to do. Come here please,' he ordered, so I naturally obeyed. He pressed my body against his and we clung to each other laughing and holding each other in the middle of the room, no space between us at all. And then, like in the long ago song, he kissed me.

Oh. Ohhh. Ooohhhhh.

His fingers were on the back of my neck, that secret warm little place at the top of the spine, under the hair. Yuri was kissing my forehead, my eyelids, my cheekbones, the bridge of my nose, and I was drowning in the dryness of his lips. But I had to pull away from him. Standing up, the pressure of gravity on my bladder was unbearable, damn it.

'Don't go away,' I said, 'but I'm dying for a pee,' and I went into the bathroom, sat on the loo and peed with passion, not caring anymore that he could hear. Is there anything quite like the ecstasy of relieving a stretched to bursting bladder? It's almost as good as coming. I flushed the loo and remembered to wash my hands.

Yuri squeezed past me as I came out. 'I also,' he said with a grin. He closed the door. I listened unashamedly, thinking how forthrightly he urinated. Not in silly noisy spurts like some men do but a steady stream of water hitting water, gradually ebbing into a little trickle. What integrity, I thought, he even pees with class!

'That is better,' he said when he emerged. He wriggled

his shoulders. 'Do you mind if I take off my shirt? It is still a little wet from the rain.'

'Take off anything you like. Would you like a shower? Are you cold?'

'Can I do that? I would like it.' And he began to unbutton his shirt.

'Of course.' I watched him. His movements were contradictory. They seemed specifically designed to make me want him at the same time as being totally natural, totally unconcerned whether I was watching him or not.

'Will you come with me? You shower also,' said Yuri taking off his shoes and socks then unzipping his jeans. Cool as anything, standing there barefooted, bare-chested, flies undone. I was glad he took his shoes and socks off before his jeans. Men look so silly in underpants and socks. 'All right,' I said, not moving, not taking off my dress.

Yuri stood before me in his underpants (brief ones, dark blue) and I wanted desperately to touch his skin, peel off his pants, stroke his tight buttocks, cup his balls in my hand. I didn't. Instead I looked at the floor.

'What is the matter?'

'It's silly,' I said, 'but I feel shy.'

'Then we will shower with the light off.'

'Silly.'

He smiled and touched my hair. 'You are very pretty, little one,' he said, slipping off his underpants quickly and pulling me against his naked body. I could feel his penis pressing hard against my abdomen through the thin cloth of my dress. Oh. Oooh. Ohhhhh, again. 'Come,' he said. 'Do not be shy. I will wait for you,' and he left me for the shelter of the plastic shower curtain.

I felt foolish. Virgin, shy, randy, confused. How come I suddenly couldn't cope with this? It was a simple enough situation – man in my shower, naked, waiting for me to join him, naked – it happens all the time. I took a deep breath, slipped off my clothes and went in.

True to his word Yuri had kept the light off. He was standing under warm jets of water, naked, in the dark. I turned the light on and stepped into the shower holding in my tummy muscles.

'Hello,' he said. 'Turn around and I will wash your back.' Very simply, like we were born together.

So I turned round in the tiny space of a shower built for one and filled by two and Yuri began to run his soapy hands all over me. As he soaped my neck his fingers slid round the sides and over my throat and I thought, plucked out of the steamy air: he could strangle me now and I wouldn't care. Still standing behind me he soaped my throat and across my chest then down and gently round each breast skimming my nipples with soapy bubbles. His hands slid gently over my tummy, over the little hillock of abdomen, then they left me and I felt suddenly orphaned. But not for long. Yuri knelt down and his hands caressed my armpits, my breasts again, and turned me round to face him. I felt his fingers roaming over my buttocks and down between my thighs, the insides of my thighs. Then he rinsed me all over carefully and methodically, everywhere he'd touched was sprayed with warm water running in drops and rivulets all over my skin. He was kneeling in front of me, his face sideways against my navel, then he began to lick me and catch the clean water drops from my pubic hair with the tip of his tongue. I looked down at the top of his head, his hair wet, dripping water drops, both of us wet under the shower, and I loved him. Love, not just in love. I knew it didn't make sense and that it was silly, but I did, then, that minute. Rising slowly and kissing me all the way up from my navel to each nipple he said, 'There. You are done now.'

I put my arms around him and we held each other, my head against his wet chest, his bent over to rest on the top of mine. We held each other so reverently, yet so close that even the water showering down couldn't get in between us. He felt so good. Smooth. The skin on his back like hot silk.

'Now you,' I said. My turn to enjoy his body. I didn't merely enjoy it, I anointed it, worshipped it.

Soapy smooth his body under my fingers, my hands over his skin. His neck, his shoulders, his back, his thighs, the hair on them wet, curling. His balls were so soft, so vulnerable, cool in my hands, cupped like a captured bird. His penis, hard, smooth, softly I drew back the foreskin, soapy I smoothed the palm of my hand over the sensitive part, round and over and away again and all the way over the front of his body. I smoothed my fingertips over his nipples and they became hard under my fingers; his nipples were sensitive, another way for me to pleasure him. I rinsed him all over, licked the water drops from his penis, licked it out of his navel, tasted the water, tasted him, tasted good. Yuri was just standing there with his eyes closed, completely given up to me. No embarrassment, no awkwardness, a child of nature naked under the water and my hands. I turned the shower off.

We dried ourselves back in the main part of the cabin. We didn't dry each other. No need, the offering had been made. We got into bed, the tiny narrow bed, and held each other, mouths together, skin against skin. 'Ohh,' I said. 'Yuri . . . '

He kissed my earlobe. 'I did not expect this,' he said. He sounded quiet, awed. 'Not this. Not that it would be like this.'

'Nor me,' I said. 'I know.' I moved my damp head slightly away from him so I could see his face properly, look at it with love in my eyes. 'Oh,' I said again. All I could say was oh. Oh, oh, oh, too sweet for pain.

'This is crazy,' Yuri said. 'It would be enough just to hold you . . . it is . . . '

'Oh, Yuri, yes, hold me. Hold me like you're never going to let go.' I squeezed my eyes tight shut because I couldn't bear to look on that face anymore, it was almost holy, and my body was echoing with 'Love me. Love me, Yuri. Please love me.' A new fire had been lit. It would take more than the Atlantic Ocean to quench it.

CHAPTER SEVENTEEN

'Are you happy, little one?' he asked later, much later. It must have been about five in the morning and we hadn't slept yet.

'Mmm,' I murmured. 'Yes.' It was the truth. This moment, right now, I thought, I'm happy. It felt good to be happy. I'd forgotten how good. 'You?'

Yuri pressed my head into his shoulder. His arm was under my neck and our bodies were very close together from affection and caring and delight in touching and from trying not to fall out of bed. 'Yes,' he said. 'This is happy.'

We cuddled for a bit, then we lit cigarettes, one Silk Cut, one Balkan Sobranie. The smoke from our two cigarettes mingled together in the air above our heads. I watched it and thought symbolic thoughts. I was really glad that Yuri smoked. Joe had always made me feel guilty about it. There's none so passionate as the converted sinner and Joe was a convert. He'd given up one morning, years before I'd met him, and never had a cigarette since. He objected to the sight, smell, and most important for our sex life, the taste of them. He was always telling me that my mouth didn't taste good when he kissed me. I was nagged all the time to give it up. I tried every now and then, even substituted a pipe for a little while but I never managed to stop smoking. So Yuri and me were lying there sharing cigarettes and smoky kisses and it was lovely to kiss him and be kissed back.

I had no particular desire yet to know about his past, or to tell him anything about mine. It didn't seem necessary for us to have pasts. It might have spoiled everything. What we had was 'now' and now was enough. I didn't really want to know about who he was or where he came from or how he came to be the person he was. We were each other's present and it was as if there had been nothing before and would probably be nothing after because the now was the important thing and now was going to last forever. Like the timeless places and magic forests in children's books. Yuri was my enchanted prince and I was his beautiful princess and it was just like in the fairy stories except there was no wicked stepmother.

'I am very tired,' he said.

'Go to sleep.'

'But I do not want to.'

'Why not?'

'If I sleep, this will be finished. You will disappear. I would wake up in my own cabin with Jack making snores in the other bed.' He kissed the end of my nose.

I smiled sleepily. 'No you won't.'

'Promise?'

'Promise.'

'This is very silly,' he said.

'What is?'

'This. I want to say that I love you and I do not even know you.'

'I know. Silly.'

'Yes. I love you.'

'And I love you.'

'That is good,' he said.

'Mmm.'

'I think I will sleep now.'

'Mmm.'

We both slept. There was no question of getting him out of bed and packing him off to his own cabin. This was different. This was already a relationship. I was 'his woman' and Yuri Vladimirovich Monakhov was 'my man', whose name I would learn to pronounce, whose body I would indeed worship, who would become the shining star on my grey horizon, who would fondly call me 'little one' and teach me the meaning of happy.

The Cruise Staff meeting next morning: nine-thirty and I'd managed about three hours' sleep. I was knackered and radiant. Elliott took one look and said, 'You little cow. You did it, didn't you? You've got him.'

I grinned.

'Oh well, I suppose the best woman won. Congratulations.'

'Thanks.'

'Happy?'

'Ecstatic.'

About an hour later I was sitting in the broad corridor between the Hawkins Room and the Collingwood Restaurant in charge of the Tote on the Ship's Mileage. I collected the figures from the Navigator's desk and a cash box and ticket book from the Purser's Office, then the passengers gambled at a dollar a go on how many miles we would have travelled since noon yesterday until noon today. The punters weren't feeling much like gambling that morning in spite of my enthusiastic accosts, and their dollars were only dribbling in. I was gazing out at the grey Atlantic thinking of Yuri still sleeping in my bed, and I was smiling at the sea, the sky, the plush carpet, the cash box, whatever my gaze happened to fall upon. Sylvester approached me with an equally indiscriminating scowl and I smiled at him too. He sat down opposite me. His manner was precise and prim. 'I want to talk to you, young woman.'

'Fire away, my love,' I answered dreamily. 'What's the matter?'

'To be frank, *you* are.'

'Why? What have I done?'

'And no use putting on that look of sweet innocence. I saw you. Me and the whole bloody ship.'

'What are you talking about?'

'Last night. Going off as bold as brass with that Russian excuse for a dancer. How could you? And Elliott's such a nice boy.' It began to dawn on me what he was on about. 'You could at least have been a bit more discreet about it. What did I tell you that first night I met you? *Discretion*, dear. And poor Elliott. What's he done to deserve it? You wicked woman, what are you after all of a sudden, your Gold Belt or something?'

I liked that 'all of a sudden'. If only he knew. 'But it's not what you think, Sylvester, honest.'

He snorted. 'Tell that to the marines, ducky.'

'And anyway, even if it was, you were the one who gave me my first lesson on ship morals, getting boxed off as often as you can.' How could I get out of this whilst keeping my friend's inclinations a secret? They were his to reveal, not mine. Oh the games we play. Lies again, getting me into trouble. 'And Elliott was quite happy himself last night, thank you very much.'

'You can't wriggle out of it that way. I saw him. He was no such thing. He was talking to a friend of mine from the engine room, know what I mean.'

'I mean after. He told me. We swapped notes this morning.'

'You never! Well, I must say. I've heard of open relationships but this is all a bit much. Well! Did you really?' He'd really perked up, ears agog, longing for the details.

'Mm. We have an understanding, Elliott and me.'

'You little scamps. Well really. That makes two each already this trip. That's supposed to be my prerogative.'

'You'll have to get used to the competition then, won't you?' I said not meaning a word of it. Fidelity was going to be my middle name.

He sniffed. 'My dear, you've a long way to go before you could get anywhere near *my* record.'

'Really? How long?'

'Ah-ha, discretion, dear! I'll never tell,' he said winking. He fished about in his jacket pocket, and a little smile shattered his face. 'But I was interrupted at a very awkward moment last night. My friend had to leave in rather a hurry.' So saying he placed a limp brown phallus on my cash box lid. 'Bananas to you,' he said and strutted off.

I laughed out loud. I was really very fond of Sylvester. He was so camp, so over the top, that you had to like him. At twelve noon on the dot I closed the Tote, locked up the cash box, and ate the banana while waiting for a message from the Navigator as to the actual mileage. It was 666 and there was only one mark next to it on the wall board. Somebody had the luck of the devil that day. I circled it, wiped the rest off the board and wrote 'please present winning ticket to the Purser's Desk' in big red chinagraph letters, then I took cash and ticket stubs downstairs, had my accounts checked and put the day's takings in an envelope to await collection by the winner, before scooting off back to Fluff Alley to awaken my lover.

I let myself into the cabin quietly but Yuri was already awake, sitting up in bed with his arms behind his head and only a single sheet to cover his glorious nakedness. 'Hello,' I said.

'Come here.'

Like I said, we soared. God, we must have been so boring. There's only one thing worse than being around two people who are madly in love with each other and that's being stone cold sober when everybody else is smashed out of their minds. We were high as a couple of kites, Yuri and me. Junkies. Our 'fix' was each other. Stoned on love and sex had never been so exciting. We wanted nothing but each other. Every aspect of my existence was lightened by either seeing Yuri or by the anticipation of seeing him. We were never apart for more than three hours at a stretch. Every opportunity, every five-minute break between one duty and the next I dashed back to my cabin or belted down to his, all for the sake of a kiss and a 'hello, I love you'. It was a breathless day.

And that night's cabaret, I got myself installed at the sound board so my ears could get on with the work while the rest of me revelled in the sight of Yuri in his silk and fur with the dagger at his waist. He danced and spun and cartwheeled and addressed the audience in Russian while I sat there at the side of the stage just watching him move, thinking: that body belongs to me. I know every beautiful nook and cranny of it and I also know that every woman in the audience would wish she were me if she knew about me and Yuri. I know that in an hour or so we'll be in my cabin in my bed guzzling Taffy's steak sandwiches and chips and each other and there'll be nobody else on the ship on the ocean on the world, except us. I sat there doing the sound mix, watching my lover, thinking my thoughts and smiling, like pregnant ladies are supposed to smile when they're happy about being pregnant and they haven't told anyone yet. I sat there smiling, watching my secret, the very special excitement of all his movements being for me, an occasional special look in my direction, the wonder of every moment being so intense, the now extending before me into a future of more of the now.

All right, I know it sounds like something straight out of a paperback romance. I know it's soppy and rosy pink and halos of light and exploding stars. But that's how I felt and how Yuri said he felt and it wasn't going to wear off, I knew it. The rosy pink cloud was soft, bubbly, warm and exciting and it wasn't going to go raggy round the edges. I wouldn't let it.

I woke up in the middle of the night, our second night together, thrilled by the fact that Yuri's body was curved around mine, the two of us in my tiny bed like a couple of spoons in a drawer. When you're happy you sleep well. When you're ecstatic you don't, because it's hard to have to forgo a single moment. My feelings for him, his professed ones for me, the amazing physical responses we awoke in each other . . . I mean, how long could it all last before it burned itself out? Which was a euphemistic way of saying 'before he saw through me and left'? How would I bear it when it happened? So much for my newly emerging self-confidence, I said to myself. Two nights of bliss and already I'm worrying about when he leaves me.

I hadn't drawn the curtains across the porthole because there's not much danger of peeping-toms on the Western Ocean, so the light of an almost full moon was reflecting up off the water and casting a translucence over the bed, silver ghost writing on the ceiling. Fey. It was like waking up in the middle of a dream and finding yourself still in it. Very real but nothing to do with reality. A bit like the man sleeping beside me, I thought. I wondered why I couldn't turn off my ceaseless philosophising and just enjoy the moment. I edged myself away from him carefully so's not to disturb, then got out of bed, wrapped myself in my dressing gown and pulled up the stool. I sat there and watched his sleeping face, studying it, loving it, etching it on my memory for future recall, this particular face on this particular night. I wondered at the classic line of his profile. He must have been created by Rodin and then sent here specifically for me. I marvelled at the fact that he was here in my bed in the total vulnerability of sleep, that he'd rather be here crowded in with me than enjoying a whole bed to himself. Yuri was totally unbelievable. Totally perfect, a miracle. He didn't even snore.

It lasted another day. And another. And another. All the way to New York and the magic was still there, getting stronger and stronger. I positively blossomed. Like I'd been a withered stalk, all bruised and dried up and then Yuri had waved his magic wand over me and turned me into the me I'd always wished I could be but had never quite managed on my own. Beautiful, witty, intelligent, lively, outgoing and sexy. That last one's important. I'd started a sort of repair job myself with a succession of nameless faces and bodies after the demolition job that Joe had done on my sexuality, finishing it off that last abortive night we'd spent together in Dringley, but it took Yuri to add the finishing touches. Okay, so his taste in women might be questionable, but so what? Here was this god and he worshipped me. What more could a woman want from a man?

Even Elliott noticed the change in me. 'If it had been anybody but you, Ali, I'd have been really jealous. That guy must certainly have something. You're positively glowing. It's quite sick-making.'

'Sorry. Can't help it.'

'Maybe not, but you could try sharing it. Especially with your best buddy. Come on, when are you going to lend him to me for a night?'

I laughed. 'No way! You keep your mucky hands off him. Find one of your own.'

'Funny, I thought you might say something like that. Oh well, it was worth a try. Fancy a cup of tea before the Scrabble Finals? We've got half an hour.'

'Sorry lovey, got a date.' And it was quick march back to my cabin to spend twenty glorious minutes with Yuri, revelling in each other's nakedness. He did have a beautiful body, slim, hard, well muscled. Broad shoulders, straight spine, would have looked incredible at a Wimbledon final except I don't think he played tennis too well. But the most amazing thing was that he thought *my* body was pretty o.k. too. He loved my round mound of belly and wouldn't have it flat. At last, a Rubens fan. He loved the way I smell and taste and he nuzzled all my secret places like he was licking a strawberry ice cream. And when he came he exploded inside me like he was a volcano erupting then afterwards he'd ask me how *I* did it to *him*! Dear, lovely, dreamed-of Yuri. You only had to look at him to know that he must have had a lifetime of women throwing themselves at his feet and he, this vision, wanted me, thought I was the one who was the gift from heaven. And he told me he loved it all – that's important, saying it.

The other thing about Yuri that became increasingly obvious and that I found terrifically thrilling was that he was passionately, excitingly, possessively, wonderfully, Russianly jealous. At first I wasn't sure if it was my imagination playing tricks on me again because in the evenings when I was doing my social rounds I thought I caught glimpses of him in the background. Wherever I was, whichever room I happened to be circulating, whoever I was smiling at, talking to, dancing with, I kept seeing Yuri's shadow, his face just turned away, his back just disappearing round a corner. But the night before we got to New York I was certain it was him and not some phantom conjured up by my longing. I deserted my duty during the cabaret, the showgirls could manage without my assistance for once, and sneaked away via the backstage exit, down a deck, along under the Franklin Room and up again to appear at the back of the room where Yuri was seated in a corner nursing a vodka. 'I thought it was you,' I said. 'Have you been following me or something, keeping tabs?'

His face lit up with pleasure. 'Little one! Why aren't you backstage?'

'Never mind that. What are you doing here?'

'I just like to be near you.'

'Well I can hardly run away, you know, not on a ship. What's the matter, don't you trust me?'

'Of course I trust you.' He picked up my hand and kissed it. 'But all the other men, them I don't trust. I don't like to see you dancing with them, smiling up at them. How can any man see you, talk to you, hold you in his arms and not want you for his own when you are the most desirable woman on the ship? I just want to be close to you, for you to know that I'm here if you should need me. I love you so much, my little one.'

That was quite mutual. I burned with agony if I saw him so much as smile at some elderly matron. I considered the situation and decided I rather liked the idea of his watchdog patrol. Besides, it meant I could keep an eye on him too. Not that I didn't trust him, of course, but he was the most desirable man on the ship! 'And I love you back,' I said. 'You're not jealous then?'

'Of course I am jealous!'

How wonderful! None of this 'screw who you like, I don't mind' that I used to get from Joe. No. Yuri *did* mind and he had the confidence to admit it. 'You've no need to be,' I said, sneaking a quick kiss. 'You're the only man I want,' hand surreptitiously squeezing his thigh. 'But tell me,' I said, digging for more ego boosting, 'what would you do if some bloke did start to seriously chat me up?' I was curious.

Yuri appeared to give the question serious consideration. 'I would probably kill him,' he answered casually, but his eyes glinting steel.

My man, my protector! I decided that from now on I'd restrict my duty socializing to couples as much as possible. Not that I believed him for a moment. But just to be on the safe side. 'Oh Yuri, I do love you!' I said before hurrying back to my duties.

I almost made it. I was taking the stairs two at a time concentrating on keeping my hem out of the way of my feet when I hurtled pell mell into the looming figure of Jim Thrippleton himself. 'And where the hell have you been?' He was thunderingly angry. 'It's been chaos back there with the dancers. Why weren't you helping them? I've enough on my plate trying to organise who does what and where with so few staff without any of them taking it into their heads to just wander off. Explain yourself.'

'I was . . . I was . . . ' Come on, girl, I told myself, stop blushing and faltering and think! I stopped blundering, pulled myself up straight, smoothed down my dress and looked him straight in the eye. 'I had to go back to my cabin. For personal reasons.'

‘What “reasons”?’ he asked scathingly. ‘Another quicky with your fancy-man?’

‘No!’ I said, outraged, horrified that he should be so close to the truth. Had Yuri and I been that obvious? Oh dear.

‘No? Why then?’ His tone was such that whatever I said he was most unlikely to believe it.

‘If you must know,’ I said with all the dignity I could manage, ‘I had to go back because my period has just started unexpectedly and it was either that or go round all night with a red stain at the back of my dress. Sir.’

He actually blushed. ‘Oh. I see. Well then, er . . . ’

Get yourself out of that one, boss. Pity though. It’s the kind of fail-safe excuse you can only try on once and get away with. ‘So if you’ll excuse me, I’ll get back on duty then?’

‘Yes, yes, of course. Sorry.’ And he hurried away.

Saved by the curse! I settled myself in a corner backstage again and wondered, out of interest, when exactly I was due and if it would put any kind of damper on Yuri’s and my intra-mural activities. Somehow I doubted it.

We arrived in New York. Solid ground together for the first time. Why is it so difficult to remember the little details of joy, I wonder? With pain it’s easy – every word that hurt, every mood, even whether it rained or was cloudy or clear. Pain is vivid. It’s a lot of individual little knives, every sentence, every look, remembered both for itself and the sum total of unhappiness that they made. But joy? Joy is just remembering being joyous. You can’t picture, after it’s gone, the when, the why, the how, the details of it. Only being pervaded with this thing labelled joy. Being with Yuri in New York was like that. Being with Joe once upon a time had been like that. A feeling of running through sunny cornfields in slow motion. Wind in hair. Sun in our eyes. Seeing things in technicolour instead of black and white. Or warm sepia, old photographs. Then Joe became synonymous with pain, the hurt at the end of it blotting out the joy at the start. Poor Joe. It’s not fair that memory should do that to him. But then Yuri came and blotted him out altogether. Puff, he was gone.

Sunshine again and giggling in Central Park. Showering each other with cut grass. Yuri and me standing on top of the World Trade Center giving everything we could see to each other to keep forever. Burger Kings and foamy beer moustaches. Taking photographs. Squinting at the sun in our eyes. Again, you see, the whole cycle of it. Joy/pain/joy – each shuttering out the other for its space.

We were an established couple, by the time we set off for Southampton, living together, each of us half of a pair, primary definition of Alison, Yuri's woman: primary definition of Yuri, Alison's man. Boxed off. Boxed in? No matter. How could something so positively delicious be in any way bad for me?

But I just wasn't very good at being happy. Not too much practice of late. I handled it the same way as I handled despair – leap right in there with both feet and lose yourself in it and to hell with independence. Who wants it when you can have a man instead? To hell with getting fulfilment from your work. Who wants that when you get all you need from your man? I was rapidly heading for another series of S-bends and the danger signs were winking on again but this time I didn't ignore them so much as simply not see them. I was too dazzled by my fiery, costumed Cossack.

'No, I won't let you go yet. There are five more minutes before you need to go.'

'But Yuri, I have to get dressed. My hair, my face!'

'You have never looked so beautiful. Please, if you love me, just one more kiss!'

I complied, wantonly and was ten minutes late for the Teen and Twenty Get-Together.

The phone ringing in the middle of the night. Reach out a fumbling hand. Answer it.

'It's nine-thirty. I'm waiting to start the meeting,' a cold Thrippleton-like voice.

'Oh Christ.' Wake up very fast. 'I'm sorry. I overslept. Give me two minutes.' Phone clicks dead and I whizz through the cabin like a tornado. It knackers me for the day.

*

'Southampton tomorrow, little one. What would you like to do?'

'I don't mind. Whatever you want to do. You decide.'

'Then we will just stay here in our little cabin and make love with each other. The whole day and the whole night.'

'Sounds good.'

We rehearsed.

We didn't stay on the ship the whole time in Southampton though. I dragged him into town with me when I went to collect the chart new-entries for the disco and I got sidetracked by the aroma of fish and chips leaking from a side street so we bought two portions. Even though it was pouring with rain we ate them out of the newspaper walking back to the docks, then licked each other's fingers clean. When we got back to the ship the crew mail had been delivered. There were three letters for me and one for Yuri, from Blackburn. 'Who on earth do you know in Blackburn?' I asked.

'My family. I come from there,' he said, as if it was the most natural thing in the world for a Russian Cossack dancer to say.

'Pull the other one,' I said, not believing him for one minute.

He looked puzzled. 'What is the matter, little one?'

'You mean you actually mean it? But I thought . . . But you're Russian!'

'That is also true. My parents, their parents before them. From the very edge of the USSR, Zhdanov, on the shores of the Azovskoye More. But alas, me I was not born there. I shall go there one day, see my motherland . . . ' his eyes and voice took on a dreamy expression.

'Yuri Vladimirovich Monakhov, you fraud! No. I refuse to believe it.' Talk about fantasies going up in smoke. 'Your accent, your bearing, your looks, everything about you, you're so . . . well, Russian! You can't be from Blackburn! Lancashire, for God's sake!'

'I have been brought up in a very close-knit Ukrainian community. I feel Russian. I *am* Russian. I am merely the victim of an accident of birth.' He sounded a bit hurt, on the defensive.

'Confidence trickster! Fake!'

'I'm sorry, little one. Are you very disappointed?' He took me in his arms and cuddled me close to him kissing my face, my neck, my hair. 'Do you not love me anymore?'

'You fool!' I thumped him playfully. 'Of course I don't love you anymore.' I pushed him away from me and forced him backwards on to the bed then sat astride him, pinioning his arms with my knees. Then I started to tickle him mercilessly. That was a mistake.

He pulled his arms free effortlessly and reciprocated with double measure until we collapsed into each other laughing and gasping and I begged for mercy.

'Am I forgiven?' he demanded.

'Never!'

He renewed the attack.

'You're forgiven!' I yelped.

But he didn't stop. 'On your word of honour?'

'Yes, yes, stop it!'

He stopped tickling, clasped both my wrists firmly in one hand while with the other he started to undo the buttons of my shirt. 'Kiss me then. Tell me you love me.'

Well, I hadn't any option, had I?

If anything, the fact that my fairy tale Russian Prince turned out to be a lad from Lancashire added to the intensity of my feelings. The sprinkling of reality that it cast made the dream easier to grasp, to hold in my hands, making it spread over into real life. It wasn't confined anymore to the protective amniotic sac that I'd been inside since I'd cast off from my old life and embraced the ocean waves. The Yuri dream now had something to do with Alison, from Dringley in North Yorkshire, married to Joe, unrequitedly embroiled with Joss, the girl who had a friend called Sally and a Mum and Dad and a little house with a patch of grass outside it and bills which dropped through the letterbox and a whole cartload of complications which would have to be faced and sorted out sooner or later.

All this went through my mind as I was making us a cup

of tea much later that afternoon. When Yuri wasn't Cossack dancing around the world, he was based in Lancashire. When I wasn't hostessing my way across the Atlantic I was based in Yorkshire. Fifty or sixty miles and a few measly Pennine bumps were easy enough to cross. Oh boy. It opened up whole new vistas which I found just a little too scary to explore just yet. Too soon. I pushed the thoughts away and decided to concentrate for the moment and for as long as I needed to on the fiery costumed Cossack whose roots were in Stanoff, Zhdanov, wherever it was he said. I handed him a steaming mug and he pulled himself up out of the tangled mass of sheets and blankets that had once been a neatly regulation made-up bed. I sat on the edge of it up where the pillows had been and nestled into his shoulder. We drank our tea and opened our letters.

I read the one from Mum and Dad first. Everything was fine at home, the family were all well, how was I and was I still enjoying myself and they may be taking a little holiday soon so would let me know when and they'd come to Southampton for a day when we were in dock.

Sally's letter was next. Great news. She'd got an assignment. Her first, real, actual, professional assignment. She was temping for an estate agent who wanted her to go round and photograph the new properties. 'Expenses and fifty pence a shot,' she wrote. 'Extortion, an out and out insult, but it's still a commission! So when are you bringing your randy Russian to see me? Any chance of me doing a layout on him for *Playgirl?* Sounds gorgeous. I hate you. Has he got a brother?'

And the third letter was from Joe. He was living in a bedsitter, still looking for a reasonable flat to rent, work was going well, he hoped I was happy and that we could be friends, not lose touch. He didn't say whether he was happy or not and I was glad of it because he might have said he wasn't and that would have intruded upon the happiness that I'd found. I didn't want him to be unhappy, of course, not anymore. I could afford to be generous, leaning my head back upon Yuri's strong, broad shoulders.

I looked up at him and kissed his jaw. 'Hey, Cossack. I'm hungry again. What are you going to do about it?'

The next six weeks passed in a sensual, bleary-eyed addiction, mainlining on each other. Torpid days in which the wild Atlantic turned benign, a mother-figure gently rocking us in her arms, her face a smiling silver in place of the erstwhile grey, while I got on with my job, a mildly irritating inconvenience that had to be put up with in order to cover the bill for our feverish nights. Oh, those nights! Surfriding a tsunami, harnessing white horses, every wave we made was Big Wednesday, the surfers' dream.

But every wave ends up on the shore, every rider eventually gets washed up with it, and at the end of six weeks there were only two more before the end of my contract and three before the end of Yuri's. After that was a great big blank that I tried not to think about too often. Little questions like where would I go next? Back to my cottage in the north? Back to 2D Radio? And where would Yuri go next? His parents in Blackburn? Another job? On a ship? He didn't know. And what about us, Yuri and me? Would we be together somehow, would our magic be sustained or would it last only as long as we were both on the same ship? Was it only a part of the rest of the strange bubble existence at sea, would it burst as soon as one, other or both of us was forced ashore? We never got the chance to find out.

In keeping with my fairy tale lovelife I was half expecting either a fairy godmother or a wicked witch. Wouldn't you just know it, I got an amalgam? But at least she granted me Elliott and I'm thankful for that.

Her spokesman was Jim Thrippleton.

'Your contract's up in a fortnight, isn't it?'

'Yes. I've been meaning to ask you about that . . . '

'Good news for you.'

My ears pricked up. Extended contract? Another precious week to be with Yuri? 'What?'

'How do you fancy the Caribbean?'

'Pardon?'

'One of our girls is getting married. She's taking two

months' leave as from the nineteenth. We need a replacement. Interested?'

I was thinking rapidly. All I came up with was, I won't have Yuri. I'll be on my own again.

'I know it's short notice,' Thrippleton went on, 'and you'll have to leave your young man behind, but quite honestly, my girl, I think it would be the best thing you could do. Your work's been going downhill recently and to be frank, if you hadn't been the last resort I wouldn't have put your name forward . . . '

It was a slap in the face. A short, sharp shock. Had I really sunk so low again and so quickly; me, the Captain's pet, the one who was going to hit 'em right between the eyes?

'It'd give you just four days from docking in Southampton to flying out to Puerto Rico. Think you could do it?'

'I don't know.'

'Think about it. And I want to know by this afternoon.'

'Okay.'

'Oh, and could you find Elliott for me? Tell him I want a word. Now.'

'Right.'

I fetched Elliott and sent him in then waited for him. I needed to talk.

He emerged grinning. 'Wow! How about that, Ali?'

'What?'

'Barbados! And the Virgin Islands, Venezuela, Puerto Rico, sunshine, palm trees, coconuts, little black boys!'

'They're not sending you too?'

'Yup!'

Snap decision. Say now, pay later. I knocked on the Cruise Director's door. 'Jim?'

'What?'

'The answer's yes,' I said.

'Good girl.'

Elliott picked me up and swung me round in the air. 'Wheeee! Isn't it fantastic?'

'Put me down. I have to go find Yuri.'

'Oh. Yes. I'd forgotten about him. Sorry. Oh well, chin up, maybe he'll come and visit, or the new Cruise Director will sign up the Cossacks or something. You never know.'

I gave him a half-hearted smile. 'Yes, you never know,' I said, already knowing full well that it would never happen. I went to look for Yuri, all the while telling myself how sensible it was to accept the contract – two more months' work, money in the bank, a bit more breathing space in which to plan a life for when all this ocean nonsense was over with. All those places I'd never been, never get such a chance again. And Elliott would be there to hold my hand. Yes, it was the right decision. And it would be a sort of test for us, Yuri and me. If we could survive a two-month separation . . .

I eventually found my lover out on deck by the choppy swimming pool. He was leaning over the ship's rail, looking out to a grey horizon, the wind blowing in his hair. My heart contracted at the sight of him, I couldn't bear to love him so much. One look at him and I regretted the decision. I went up to him, touched his elbow and told him what I'd done.

'So. It has come. You are going to leave me, little one?'

'Don't put it like that. I'll be coming back. Will you wait for me?'

'No, I will not wait.'

'Oh.'

'I could not. I will have to follow you.'

I hugged him, regardless of the passengers milling about on deck. But he wouldn't really. I said, 'No you won't. That's silly.'

'But I will try. This new ship of yours will need cabarets. We are a cabaret. I cannot see my two friends denying themselves a few weeks in the sunshine.'

'Oh Yuri, I do love you.'

'And until I am with you I will send you letters every day.'

I couldn't believe it would ever happen, that he'd come out there to share the sunshine with me. 'But it isn't as easy as that. They book acts in advance. They'll be booked up. You won't come.'

'Listen to me, little one,' he said, putting his hands on my shoulders and looking very serious. 'I know that you are right. But you do not have to say it out loud. It might not happen but that does not mean I cannot try. I love you. I want only to be with you. And if I do not succeed, it is . . . well, it is only two months . . . ' his voice trailed away.

'Only! I'll say I'm not going, I've changed my mind, I won't go!'

'You *will* go. You are being foolish. You are going and you will be happy. And I will be here when you return.'

'Will you?'

'Do I have to swear it for you to believe me?'

'But two whole months!' I looked at him, how beautiful he was. It could never happen. 'You'll meet somebody else,' I said. I was panicking again. Why, oh why had I said I'd go?

He put his hand on top of my head. 'No,' he said. 'But you, you might.'

'No I won't.' I won't, I know I won't, I don't want to, I only want you.

'Promise?'

'I promise.' I studied his eyes studying mine. I touched his face. 'Special one,' I said.

And then there were only ten more days. One more outward journey to New York, one more return to Southampton. We wandered around like Romeo and Juliet, sentence of exile hanging over us, approaching too rapidly, except it was Juliet who was going into exile. Our time was precious, sweet, and passed all too quickly because the days could actually be counted. Our 'now' had had a time limit set on it. Nine more, eight more, seven more, and very, very quickly, one more day, one more night. We were both terrified to let the other out of our sight not knowing when or where we'd see each other again, only wanting it, needing it. Yuri talked about 'when I come out to you', and I talked about what we'd do together in Barbados, knowing it wouldn't really happen. Yuri talked about 'when you come back', and I asked, 'Yes? What? What then? Will we be together, will we?'

Clinging to him, afraid to close my eyes in case I should open them to find we'd been cheated of our last hours and it was tomorrow already. We talked about getting a big house somewhere together. In October, when I came back. Keeping each other warm through the coming winter. I pictured open fires and sheepskin rugs and Yuri in a big chair, me on the floor hugging his knees and a Borzoi in the picture somewhere. They hurt me, all those last hours. But it was a sweet pain. Happy, sad, laughing, crying, all at once, all rolled into one. Not sad, not happy, but both together, a double intensity.

We didn't sleep at all that last night, couldn't bear to. There were too few hours left to squander by sleeping. We tried to make the night longer by staying awake, even make it last forever. But we couldn't. We were already back in Southampton. The ship had docked. The creaking was silenced, the floors stayed put and we watched out of the porthole as the black sky slowly changed to dark blue then grey, till the grey faded into dreary, dirty Southampton off-white. I, forgetting the past, thought: this is the first time in my life that a dawn has spelt anything other than new birth and hope.

To spread the hours a little further Yuri hired a car at the docks and insisted on driving me back to Dringley. I let him. I was grateful for the extra time, happy for the care it showed, pleased that I wouldn't have to face that nightmare journey alone. We were both stunned by tiredness, lack of sleep. We no longer talked much, a silence between us saying much more than any words could have done. After all, there are only so many ways to say I love you. After that it's just repetition.

But I was lucky: I was the one who was going. Yuri had to contend with the ghosts that would haunt familiar, now empty, places. I had new places to look forward to. Yes, they would be empty places without him but at least they would be new and different. They would hold no memories, only discoveries. I took little solace from the thought.

At last, Yuri was sitting in my house in the big chair in front of the fire, in the room that had seen so much of my life. And now he was here, a part of it. A seal of reality, if only for an hour or two. His head was back and his eyes closed. I watched him. Did he look right here or didn't he? Was he a piece out of another jigsaw puzzle or was he a perfect fit? The phone prevented me having to answer. It rang harsh and shrill and very loud. A violent intrusion. Yuri opened his eyes.

'It's all right,' I said. 'It'll only be Joe.' It was about ten o'clock and I knew it had to be Joe. Nobody else ever phoned at that time. How on earth did he know I was back? So different, this, from the last time I'd gone home, Joe wanting me. So different from the last homecoming, me finding Joe intrusive.

'Shall I go away?' asked Yuri. 'You will not want me here if it is your husband.'

'Stay,' I said, bending to kiss him. 'I love you.' I hoped the phone would shut up of its own accord. It didn't. I wanted to ignore it but I've never been able to do that. Yuri closed his eyes again but I noticed his face remained alert, listening. I picked up the phone. 'Hello?'

It was Joe. He'd phoned the ship this afternoon and they'd told him I'd left. So he phoned here on the off-chance. He asked how I was, if he could come round, see me, now, tonight? He'd missed me. He said.

And I said no.

I didn't say it just because Yuri was there with me. I would have said the same had I been alone. It was late, I was tired, I was missing Yuri already even though he was still there. Emotionally the parting had been faced. There was only the physical one to go through, the parting of bodies. And Joe was no part of it. He didn't belong here. I had spent the last four years being there when Joe wanted me and waiting for him when he didn't. And now, for the first time, Joe did the beckoning, Joe reached out to me, and I said 'No'.

All too soon it was time for Yuri to leave. The only way to bear it was to treat it lightly, make-believe we'd see each other tomorrow or the next day. We kissed. We looked at each other for an aeon. I even smiled. 'Take care of yourself,' I said. I thought my voice was just a fraction higher than its normal tone.

'And you,' he said. Then we kissed and he got into the car and the night air whipped at me with its emptiness. I watched his profile as he drove away, then he slowed down and stopped. He looked back. I stopped breathing. I wanted to run to him and keep him from going away, keep myself from going away. I almost did. But then Yuri set off again, drove away, and I watched the car until it disappeared and for long after, imagining that I could still see it. Then I sat on the icy cold stone of the doorstep and looked up at the dark sky. The world was empty. I thought I would never see him again. I was wrong.

CHAPTER EIGHTEEN

In the three days between arriving home and setting off again for what seemed the other side of the world, I saw my parents, I saw my friends, I opened all the post, paid some bills, washed and ironed my clothes, ignored the layer of dust everywhere, wrote some letters and I saw Joe.

It hardly touched me. My mind, my emotions were pointed in another direction. He said that he and Carol were no longer seeing each other, she'd finally settled for Simon. He said he'd thought a lot about us – Joe and me – and he knew he'd made some terrible mistakes, caused a lot of damage. He said he'd missed me.

I told him I hadn't missed him at all. 'You were a big part of my life, Joe, but I've changed direction now.' That was as close as I could get to telling him about Yuri, because when it came to it, looking at Joe's face, into his eyes which were soft again like they used to be once upon our time, I couldn't manage more than a hint. What am I trying to do by my cowardice, I asked myself, keep both options open just in case? I felt I was being unfaithful to both Yuri and Joe (and myself) all at the same time.

'You've changed, Alison,' Joe said. 'You're not a bit like you used to be.'

'I'm glad,' I said. 'Look where that got me.' I didn't mean it to sound so bitter.

'Can I write to you?' he said. Such tiny, tentative, frightened-of-being-rejected advances he made, but advances none the less for all that. He was reaching out his hand. I couldn't smash down on it but I couldn't take hold of it either.

'If you like,' I said without much enthusiasm.

'Will you write back? Tell me what it's like, what you're thinking, feeling?'

'All right.'

'There're too many barriers between us now,' Joe said.

'I'm not sure if they're yours or mine. Maybe on paper we can learn about each other again.'

'I'm surprised you want to.'

'Don't,' he said. 'Don't be so hard. It's not you.'

'I'm sorry,' I said, meaning it, 'but I'm not the same person who went away. I've seen new places . . . formed new relationships . . . I'm different now.'

'Not *so* different. People don't change that much. We'll write?'

'I said okay.'

Joe got up to go. 'Take care of yourself then.'

'And you,' I said.

'I'll see you in October when you get back.'

Or should that have been *if* I get back? I, like thousands of other people, am scared of flying but still do it. I cling, white-knuckled, onto the armrests thinking, Dear God, only let me land again safely and I'll believe in you forever. Every time I fly I tell myself that this time I'll be sensible about it, but as soon as I'm strapped into the seat and feel that great surging energy as we rush towards take-off, and that stomach-lurching tilt as the horizon tips to forty-five degrees, I forget all the safety statistics and start praying. It's not so much a fear of death but the manner of it.

The flight to the Caribbean was no exception. I kept the seat-belt fastened and chain-smoked for the duration while the voice in my head chanted: I do not wish to die yet. I do not wish to die gazing upon formica and row upon row of too close for comfort seats of panicking humanity. This is too plastic a place for death, too mechanical, too man-made. I would be happy to die under a herd of stampeding elephants if I have to, Lord, but not under a runaway articulated truck; I would rather be crushed by a falling tree than the drum of a steamroller; chopped up by a samurai than by the wheels of a train; if I must die by falling from a great height, let it be off a mountain top and not inside a plunging DC10. Please.

Someone must have been listening because we landed safely in Puerto Rico and I got on the bus that took me to the ship which would take me round and round in circles for the next two months.

We sailed from San Juan at midnight and I stood out on the deck in the hot, humid night air holding on to Elliott's hand and watching the lights of the town glimmer into tiny specks and then go out. I felt empty-headed and light-hearted. Or possibly it was light-headed and empty-hearted because later, in bed, I had quite a strong attack of the 'what the hell am I doing here?' syndrome. It was the distance. I'd been picked up and plonked down again about four and a half thousand miles away from any familiar place or person except Elliott. Home, Sally, parents, Joe were in England. Yuri and even Thrippleton were bobbing along on different waters somewhere a long way away. I had no letter from Yuri to read over and over again, and because my New York films hadn't come back from the processor's before I left, not even a snapshot of him to look at and kiss before going to sleep. I missed my Lancashire Cossack's warmth and his smell and his voice and the sound of his breathing in the night. I crossed one day off a calendar left on the wall by a previous occupant. I worked out there'd have to be sixty-one more crossings out. Whichever way I calculated it, it added up to an eternity and only Elliott and the sunshine might possibly keep me sane.

I had this terrible sense of insecurity. And the new ship didn't help. It was a lot smaller than the one I'd become used to and to compare the two was to liken a tin shack to a brick and mortar building. The word was definitely 'tinny'. The carpets on the floors and stairways didn't do much to dull the noise of reverberating metal underneath. I didn't like it much. I counted the lifeboats and memorised their positions.

The Caribbean cruiser did have one considerable advantage over the transatlantic liner, though: it called into a different port every day except Sunday. Now the basic theory behind a Cruise Staff job is that so long as there are passengers on the ship you are on duty and working. But when ships call into exotic foreign ports passengers have this delightful tendency to go ashore exploring and spending dollars. So the passengers are no longer on the ship, therefore you're a bit redundant. The Caribbean Cruise Staff system had a duty roster worked out whereby just one member would stay aboard to keep an eye on the unadventurous few while the others were released for a few hours to head for the nearest beach. Not a bad way to earn a living.

What can you say about the Caribbean islands in August? They're everything that any travel brochure shows you, except better. Lying on a white coral beach with a sun beating upon you so hot that it feels you're two inches away from a blazing fire. The sky above you the kind of blue that can't be natural it can only have come out of a paintpot. The sea matches it only with sparkles. If you open your eyes and look upwards you see palm fronds and clumps of green coconuts. You lie there burning amidst vivid colours and dazzling sands and if you want a coconut you give a little local boy a dollar and he'll shin up a palm tree and get one for you. Little brown children with thin hard bodies and a sheeny skin, running in and out of the water with 'little brown dangling wet rubbery willies' (Elliott's description). Sometimes they came and begged from you or tried to sell you shells and bits of coral, staring at your whiteness with the heavy gaze of a calf. Sand between your toes and under your fingernails, the salty taste of sweat and sea-water and suddenly fine hot needles of spiky rain and a mass exodus to the bar made of bamboo and palm leaves. A glass of rum punch made of 151° proof rum, squeezed fresh limes and nutmeg picked from the back garden that morning. White bodies turning lobster pink and smelling of Coppertone. The shock of sea-water which is practically blood heat. The randiness creeping up on you because you're lying there nearly naked in the hot sun. The emptiness because your special person isn't there to lie beside you and put oil on your back.

There's nothing quite so poignant as beauty that you have to enjoy alone. It doesn't matter how many people you're with, how many friends are around you, or even if there's a special Friend there – if you're in a place like that and your lover isn't, you are horribly alone. The beauty of it hurts.

It was a week and a half before I got any letter from Yuri. I ran the whole gamut from 'he must be dead' through 'inconsiderate sod' to 'he's found someone else', before his first letters arrived. I used to go into the crew office every day we were in port as soon as the port agent came aboard, to scour the pigeonholes. It seemed that everyone had letters but me. It was totally unreasonable to feel like that because I'd given everybody the Barbados address so I couldn't logically expect a letter in any other port, but I still looked. Eleven days in a strange part of the world on a strange ship with a lot of strange people is an awfully long time to go without a letter from your lover. But I forgive very quickly. When the port agent eventually brought some envelopes with my name on, I found four from Yuri and one from Joe. I looked at the postmarks. Yuri's first letter had been posted from Southampton before I'd even left England. That meant it must have been waiting for me in Barbados for a whole week, must have arrived last Wednesday just as the ship sailed, just in time to miss me.

I didn't open the letters immediately. When you've waited a lifetime and the letter finally arrives you don't rip it open there and then, you savour it. I turned it over and over. I stroked the envelope, even sniffed it. I carried it round with me enjoying the anticipation for at least five minutes and when I could stand it no longer I found a secret place, a bolt-hole and locked the door. I lit a cigarette. Then I sat down and looked at it again. And then, at last, I opened it. There was a split-second of fear before I looked at the first sentence, knowing that it would begin something like, 'I'm sorry to have to tell you in a letter but . . . ' and then I grinned from ear to ear when I saw the words, 'My little one, how can I put into a letter how much I am already missing you . . . '

I devoured that letter. Then I read it again more slowly. I could hear Yuri's voice with every word I read. Then I breathed it and put it to my cheek and stroked it trying to take into my body any physical trace of him that may have been transmitted to the paper as he wrote. Then I opened his other letters and kept on smiling. Yuri loves me. Yuri misses me. Yuri is as empty without me as I am without him. Oh, we will be together, we will! And there are only fifty more days to go. I stuffed all the letters into my bag and scurried off to find Elliott so I could hug him in my joy, then we went to Discovery Bay and sweated in the sun.

Nothing is private when you work on a ship. If you receive letters, everybody else has rifled through them before you get there. Everybody knows how many you had and who they were from. Lying flat on our backs in the sand with eyes closed and limbs heavy with heat Elliott said, 'What did Joe have to say?'

I sat up. 'Christ. I forgot all about it. I haven't even opened it yet.' I was overwhelmed with guilt.

And when I read it I felt even worse. It was such a nice letter. All anybody has to do to win a place in my heart is to show me a little genuine affection. I'm a sucker for it. It doesn't matter what they've done to me in the past or what they might do to me in the future, if they care about me, even ever such a tiny bit, I can't think badly of them. It's part of the same syndrome as 'I love you', never failing to make me randy even when I know it's a lie. And Joe had written such a lovely letter. It wasn't effusive or anything. That wouldn't have been true to himself or to the way he expected me to receive it. It was simply a letter which used quiet words to say hello, how are you, are you happy, you're in my thoughts and I care for you, that you should be well and happy. He wrote about his work, his life, the new flat he'd found and the colour of the leaves on the chestnut tree outside his window. I felt homesick for the chestnut tree I'd never seen and the autumn that was about to creep over the England I wasn't in. I put the sandy letter back into my bag along with the four from Yuri and felt vaguely unsettled.

'What's up?' asked Elliott.

'Oh, nothing. It was just a nice letter, that's all,' said I, gazing out at the horizon and wondering if England was over the edge of it.

Elliott shook his head. 'Thank God I'm gay,' he said. 'I'll never understand you women.'

'Gay or straight, it might be worth learning how. I think we might just be here to stay, you know.'

'Come on, roll over and I'll put oil on your back. You're looking a bit cooked. Just lay down in the sun, woman, and close your eyes and think about nothing. Bide your time, there's no hurry. You'll sort yourself out. Anyway,' he continued, rubbing logic into my skin along with the oil, 'what's the point in worrying about anything when you're stuck out here for at least another six weeks?'

'I'm here so I may as well enjoy it?'

'That's the kind of idea, yes.'

'Mmm.' His hands felt delicious. I love being stroked. I closed my eyes and decided to spend my next life as a cat. 'Elliott?' I said, face buried in my arms and hidden from the glaring sand and Elliott's eyes. 'Why the hell aren't you straight? We'd make a lovely couple.'

He stopped and slapped my bottom. 'Why spoil a beautiful friendship?' Wise man, my friend Elliott.

In about an hour we packed our things together and walked back through the hotel grounds to the road. One day, I promised myself, taking it all in and trying to look as though I had a right to be wandering through the formal gardens which edged the hotel pool, I'll come and stay here as a legitimate paying guest. With a lover.

Back at the ship there was just time to shower and change into something appropriately bright and informal before hosting the rum-punch party out on deck where it was my duty to make sure that every passenger was garlanded with a plastic lei. The word is pronounced 'lay' and I had to approach countless strangers asking if they'd like one. How different from the cocktail parties of dear Captain Lawrence! I found it difficult to hold on to any impression of reality.

'7.30 a.m. Meet Alison and Elliott on Boat Deck aft for a before breakfast jog and some simple exercises to keep you in the pink' says the St Lucia edition of Funfare (the downmarket equivalent of For Your Pleasure and Leisure).

'Elliott? (Pant, pant) Joe says he still loves (puff) me.

'That's fan (wheeze) tastic!'

'Yes,' tone of voice belying the word.

'How do you (huff, puff) feel about it? Will you go back to him and (gasp) try again?'

'I really don't (gulp) know. Suppose it didn't work. I couldn't, you know (pant) I'm really beginning to hate this job (wheeze) go through all that again.'

He addresses our equally unfit keep-fitters, 'Okay, now stand still, feet apart and bend over from the waist. Flop!' Then upside down he says to me, 'So you're not sure then?'

Blood rushing to my head I reply, 'No.' I can't take it anymore so I then say, 'Now slowly straighten up and stretch! Touch the sky!'

'That means,' his voice straining along with his muscles, 'that you're not definitely against the idea either?'

'Now let yourself go and relax!' And to Elliott, 'S'pose not.' I expire.

Later that morning I brewed up in my cabin while explaining that Yuri wanted me to live with him. 'He says he's looking for a flat. A big one, for the two of us.'

'Will you?' asked Elliott.

'Don't know.'

'You might?'

'I might.'

'What about Joe, though? Your husband, remember him? After all, he's swallowed his pride, admitted his mistakes, and he wants you back. Don't you owe it to him to at least give it a try?'

'Hey, just whose side are you on, Elliott?'

'Joe loves you.'

'So does Yuri.'

'And you still love him?'

'Yes.' I said it with confidence, being none too sure anymore.

'Then go with Yuri.'

'But what about Joe?'

'You said it, Alison.'

Still the same St Lucia day, but at sea again in the evening. Standing at the back of the Americas Lounge with a couple of special 'crew only edition' pina coladas because it isn't our turn to do lighting or sound or undress and dress the ubiquitous showgirls. Ricky Sundae (real name, I discovered, Richard Church) is on stage carbaret-ing his little cotton socks off in a passable imitation of Tom Jones.

'I wish I knew what to do, Elliott,' I whisper. 'Joe says he's going to make it all up to me if I go back to him. He says he'll find us that big house we always used to dream about and take me off to Canada to visit his relatives and anywhere else in the world I'd like to see because he's making money and he wants to spend all his repeat fees on making me happy again.'

'Wow. Is that all?'

'No, there's more. His letters are just like he used to be, when it was all good.' Coconut milk is supposed to be an aphrodisiac and I drink down the pina colada remembering just how it used to be between us when it was all good. There is a warm feeling in the region of my groin. 'Do you think he's really changed? I mean, *can* people? Maybe we could make it together again. Do you think he means it or are they just words on paper? After all, he's a writer by profession, he knows how to use words for his own ends.'

'Ssssh!' A passenger turns and scowls at me.

Ricky Sundae finishes a song. During the applause Elliott says, 'How should I know? I never met the bloke, remember. How do you feel about it? And what about Yuri, I thought you said you loved him?'

'I do.' The applause ends and Ricky Sundae turns into Dean Martin before our very ears singing *Memories are Made of This*. 'But Joe's still my husband,' I agonise, *sotto voce*. 'Doesn't that count for anything?'

'That's for you to decide.'

'Fat lot of help you are.'

'Ssssh!' says the passenger again.

I concentrate on drinking quietly.

I'm rostered for ship duty on St Thomas day. It's a good day for ship duty, very quiet, as St Thomas is the island of cheap gold, cheap diamonds and cheap booze, the last chance for our passengers to have a credit card spending spree. So I'm sitting by the swimming pool out on deck, eating a hamburger, drinking a glass of iced lager and sheltering under a striped awning from a sudden rain. A few adults and a small army of screeching children leap out of the pool and head for shelter. (Why do people always get out of the water when it rains?) I'm trying to compose a letter to Joe on damp-spotted air mail paper. I write affectionately because I can't help it, it just comes out that way because I'm replying to a letter from the Joe I used to love. I sign it 'love, Alison'. I almost add in brackets after it 'please'.

Grenada day. Island of spices and revolutionaries. Ignoring both I get a smiling-faced taxi driver to take me to Grand Anse Beach where two miles of pure white sand are edged by palms against a backcloth of emerald green hills. I go to the beach alone, with only a bag full of letters and photographs for company. I lie down on my tummy with a bottle of coke pushed into the sand in front of my face, sipping its contents through a straw. I'm hypnotised by the searing heat on my back and a humming bird using wing speed beyond sight to hover motionless in the bushes before me. It's tiny, with plumage of an iridescent green, yet it's as common as an English sparrow. Beauty in microcosm.

I take out all of Yuri's letters and read them again, in order, although I practically know them by heart already because they don't actually say much. They're fairly boring if you read them all in one go like that, because he's run out of different ways to say 'I love you', and 'I miss you', and 'I'm longing to hold you in my arms again'. Pages and pages and pages of it. And his spelling isn't too good either. I put the letters back in my bag and take out the photographs. Mum went over to Dringley and spent a fortune forwarding my mail – packets of photos of Yuri laughing at the camera against backdrops of Central Park, a smooth silver Atlantic, a stormy grey Atlantic, rumpled sheets on a tiny bed and a swirling blur of Cossack costume. I study his pictures, glossy paper turning crisp and curling under the sun, and I think: so who needs perfect spelling? Christ, he's so beautiful.

I burrow my foot right down into the scorching sand and wish I could do the same with my head. How wonderful it would be not to need other people.

A cruise liner operates on much the same principle as an airliner, i.e. if you offer them enough drink and enough food at frequent enough intervals they won't have time to notice if they're feeling a bit bored. Our days began and ended with food. Literally, with the midnight buffet. No wonder passengers and crew alike always put weight on, in spite of the half-hearted morning jog. There was breakfast, morning coffee and biscuits, lunch, afternoon tea and cakes, dinner, all topped off with the midnight buffet and supplemented by the poolside hamburger stand open from ten till ten. And all included in the price.

Whatever our duties or his score-card, Elliott and I had a standing rendezvous at the midnight buffet, corner table, portside, aft. I arrived to find a glum-faced Elliott already seated behind a plate piled with fried chicken pieces. I asked him what was the matter.

'I'm miserable, Ali. I think I must be in love.'

'Oh God, not you too. Who is it this time?'

'Remember that chap crossing the Atlantic, the one you used to call my middle-aged gentleman? Well I've had a letter from him.'

'You never told me you were writing to each other.' I felt hurt. And after all those confidences I'd shared with him.

'We aren't exactly. We swapped addresses, so naturally when I knew we were coming out here I just dropped him a line saying where I'd be. And he's booked on. He's joining us on Saturday in Puerto Rico for the week.'

'Hey, wow. Sounds like he's really smitten. So why are you miserable?'

'Because I'm scared. Here, have a drumstick.' He thrust one at me.

I took it. 'Why? Because it sounds like involvement?'

'Maybe. I don't know.'

'Don't be silly. A bit of involvement is just what you need. All this promiscuity can't be good for you. It's time you found yourself a settled relationship.'

'Huh. Look who's talking. Settled relationships don't seem to do you much good. And you've had hardly anything else. There was . . . ' he started eating and using his bit of dead chicken to count off on his fingers, ' . . . your first husband. Then a lover, or was it two? Then you married Joe, then got yourself involved with Joss, and then you fell in love with Yuri and now you're dithering back to Joe again. Involvement! You can keep it.'

I considered what he'd said while dunking a second chicken limb in a dish of barbecue sauce. 'Doesn't sound too healthy when you put it like that, falling from one to the other.'

'I agree. And I want to stay healthy. I like being footloose and fancy free. I don't need to have another half before I consider myself a whole person.'

'Meaning I do?'

He didn't answer that. Just kept on gnawing at an already naked bone.

'Well?' I challenged.

'Well . . . ' He wiped his fingers on a paper napkin. 'You know what they say about a woman without a man . . . '

'Go on. What?'

'A woman – or a homosexual for that matter – without a man . . . ' he said ever so seriously, 'is like a fish without a bicycle.'

'I don't get it. What does a fish need with a bi . . . ?' Then I got it.

'Precisely.'

I giggled.

'So stop choking and have a pickle.' And he pronged one with a fork and shoved it into my mouth.

'You changed the subject very neatly,' I mumbled around the onion. 'I still think you should give yourself a chance with your middle-aged gentleman. I know I've had one or two little problems but . . . '

'One or two!' he interrupted. 'Little!'

'But it's better than not having love at all,' I went on, determined to say my piece.

'Is it?' he said.

And those two words were enough to shut me up.

CHAPTER NINETEEN

I never thought I could be jealous of Elliott. But I was for the next seven days. Green eyes positively smouldering while he quietly glowed. I wondered if he'd felt so left out of things and rejected during all the time I was wrapped up in the arms of my Cossack. Poor Elliott. He really did let himself go overboard for the middle-aged, debonaire gentleman he'd lovingly renamed 'Uncle'. I was happy for him, of course, but I didn't half feel lonely all of a sudden. The week skipped by and I volunteered to take over Elliott's ship-board duty day as well as my own so he could have a few hours on a private beach in St Lucia where Uncle had a friend with a villa. I must admit to being envious of all that business too. When I fall in love, I have to choose either a struggling writer, a penniless cub reporter or a wandering Cossack dancer, but when Elliott does it he hits jackpot first go. Uncle certainly had money to burn. He burned a fair amount of it in St Thomas on a discreet little parting present in the form of a solid gold wristwatch and equally solid strap. Did I say 'poor' Elliott? I take it back.

Saturday in San Juan again. The last but one before all the sixty-one little marks would have been made on my calendar. Elliott said goodbye to Uncle in the privacy of his cabin and then bravely waved him off in public along with all the other suntanned and smiling passengers. I tried to cheer him up by saying 'Only another week, old mate, and we'll be back in England too. You'll see him again then.'

'Will I?' he replied, disheartened. 'He never said anything. I don't know.'

I squeezed his arm. 'It'll be all right,' I said. 'You'll see.' I shook more hands, smiled at more peeling pink faces. One more week and then I, too, would disembark suntanned and sweaty to get the crew flight back to Heathrow. Only one more circular trip to make and I was no nearer solving the dilemma over Joe and Yuri than I had been a month, six weeks ago. From Yuri all the way round to Joe and then all the way back to Yuri again. Round and round the garden, like the proverbial teddy bear, one step, two steps and tickle you way up – where? A recurring circular cruise.

When the passengers were safely off Elliott disappeared to be alone for a while and I went back to my place and took out all of Yuri's and Joe's letters to re-read in the search for something, anything, some sort of guidance as to what I should do, who (if either) I should choose. But admitting the third possibility – of choosing neither of them – although a sign of progress on the surface, wasn't much help in practical terms. It just gave me a three-way dilemma instead of a two-way one.

Yuri's letters, loving and passionate as they were, didn't really say anything of any help. They told me little of his life, of what he was doing, what he was thinking, what was going on around him. They were full of dreams. How can anyone be so irresponsible when major decisions like what are we going to do with our lives hung in the balance? Joe's letters, on the other hand, were almost too full. He said what he thought, what he felt, what he was doing, where, what his plans were. He told me about his work and his worries and his joys and about the chestnut tree outside his window which was just beginning to show hints of autumn gold. I longed to see the burnished chestnut tree, to smell a touch of coldness in the air.

I loved Yuri and I loved Joe and I hated the pair of them, but I had to do something, because today was the last opportunity for me to post letters to arrive in England before I did. I sat down at the chest of drawers and wrote to Yuri: 'I'll seen you soon, my love.' Then I wrote to Joe: 'I'll see you soon, Joe.' I went out and sent them express from the main San Juan post office then resolved not to think about it for the rest of the week. Fate, I decided, would make the decision for me.

And perhaps she did. There was a knock on my cabin door. Probably Elliott, I thought. 'Come in, it's open.'

Hugo the Cruise Director entered. 'Ah. Glad I caught you. Not going off out today?'

'I've already been out. Like some tea?'

'No, no, can't stop. Saturdays are busy days for me, you know. Thanks anyway. No. What it was . . . ' he waved what looked like a telegram at me.

My heart plummeted into my feet. A telegram. Somebody's gone and died. Who? For someone who wasn't even conceived while the War was on why is my first reaction to a telegram always so morbid? 'What is it, Hugo?'

'It's from Jim Thrippleton via Head Office. Their girl Wendy's gone and resigned. Want the job? Lucky girl, you'll be just nicely in time for the Christmas in the Pacific Grand Cruise.'

'No thanks,' I said.

'Are you sure?' asked Hugo, almost as amazed by the answer as I was.

'Mm,' I heard a voice say, 'I'm quite sure.'

'Oh. I'll wire back "no" then.' He turned to go. Then he turned back again. 'I really think you should consider it a little more carefully, Alison. Look, come and find me after lunch. It'll wait till then.'

'No, really, Hugo. I don't want it, honestly. The bubble burst, you see.' He obviously didn't. But I did. At last. 'It's time for me to go home.'

It's funny how answers come when you're least expecting them. Whether I was meant to take the offer or reject it, who can say? All I knew was that I wanted to see a chestnut tree. Not necessarily Joe's particular one, any old English tree would do. I wanted to go home, meet real people again and not have to smile; pick up the pieces of my interrupted career, find out if that girl who sat on the steps of All Souls' outside Broadcasting House once upon a time would ever make it through the portals. I'd had enough of drifting around on the oceans. I might sink to the bottom or rise to the top but whichever place I ended up I had some splashing around of my own to do. I wanted to go home.

Of course, as soon as I'd got Hugo to believe me I stopped believing myself. I almost called him back. Almost.

Tuesday in Grenada. The last time. Ever in my life,

probably. Of all the islands we visited my heart belonged to this one. Just as Yuri had fulfilled my vision of the ideal man, so Grenada was the fantasy island paradise come true. I lay on its beaches day dreaming of getting money from somewhere and coming back to Grenada to buy some land and build a little house and live out the rest of my life in solitude except for my hi-fi and visits from lovers, Elliott and Sally.

We were lying on the beach watching yet another iridescent green humming bird hovering inside a bush.

'Elliott?'

'Yes, my love?' he sounded drowsy. He was rubbing his cheek against the sand with all the sensuality of a cat.

'I've just had a thought.'

'Well, stop it. Far too energetic on a day like this.'

'No, I'm serious.' I sat up and hugged my knees.

Elliott turned over on his back and squinted at me. He sounded resigned. 'Go on then. What is it?'

'Are you being met at Heathrow?'

'Ah, who knows? I wish I did. What about you?'

'That's precisely what I'm getting at. What about me? Suppose . . . just suppose . . . Joe came to meet me.'

'Nice for you.'

'Or, just suppose, Yuri came to meet me.'

'Okay, I'm supposing. What are you getting at?'

'Stop being thick. Don't you see? Suppose they were both there?' Panic was rising in my voice.

'Mm. I see what you mean. Could be interesting. But it's not very likely, is it? They've not said, have they? You haven't asked either of them to, have you?'

'No, but . . . '

'Well then,' his voice had a confident finality about it. 'And anyway, how would they know what flight you were on? You haven't gone and told them have you?'

'No. True.' I paused, feeling comforted. It didn't last. 'But suppose they find out? They could, couldn't they? I mean all they'd have to do is ring up Head Office.'

'Well yes, I suppose so, but come on, Alison! The odds against it must be millions to one. One or the other of them maybe, but not both. Anyway, what would you do if one of them is there? Have you made up your mind yet?'

'No. I don't know. Oh sod it, let's go for a swim!' I ground a half-smoked cigarette into the sand and ran off down the beach.

But the seed had been planted. I began to count the days left to me. My exile had become my refuge and I didn't want to leave it. I had four days left and I couldn't, like Scarlett O'Hara, keep putting it off until tomorrow because my tomorrows were running out. And I had no one to blame but myself.

I've always been annoyed by the nasty habits of time. Inconsistent myself, I can't stand inconsistency in something that's supposed to be constant. The way it goes slowly when you want it to rush. The sneaky manner in which it speeds up on you when you want it to slow down a bit. It was fairly sprinting. Barbados came and went. St Lucia followed hot on its heels. St Thomas disappeared in a flurry of sunshine and cheap booze, and suddenly we were in San Juan.

I sat on the edge of the bed looking at my bulging cases and at how desolate the little cabin looked denuded of all my bits and pieces. Only the waste paper bin was full. I was feeling quite calm by now. I imagined this must be a bit like the condemned prisoner feels on the eve of his execution. Elliott came in. 'Are you ready?' he asked.

'Ready as I'll ever be,' but I made no attempt to move. I merely sat there looking up at him with my chin in my hands.

'Oh, don't be so mopey,' he said, striding over my cases and ruffling my hair. 'You're being daft. Only three things can happen.'

'Three?'

'You'll get to Heathrow and nobody will meet you so you'll simply get on the train, go back to your cottage, make yourself a cup of tea and get a good night's sleep.'

'So tell me about the other two possibilities.'

'Or Joe will meet you and take you home. Now that would be nice, wouldn't it? No struggling with cases and trains. Somebody to hold your hand. And when you've seen him again, it'll all become clear. You'll know whether you want to try again or not. Simple.'

I grunted.

'Or, number three, Yuri might meet you – I only said might – he's probably leaping around the Working Men's Clubs in Outer Mongolia or somewhere – in which case he'll take you straight to bed somewhere, you'll spend the night and not get a good night's sleep before you toddle off back to the cold and windy north to sort out your affairs. And once you've seen him again, you'll know how you feel. Okay? Whichever way, no problem.'

I wished I could believe him.

CHAPTER TWENTY

Nine hours after boarding the plane at New York and an indeterminate number since leaving San Juan, Elliott and I were to be found jolting along English tarmac in the airport bus in the rain. I was still telling myself, and Elliott still patiently confirming, that it couldn't happen, not in a century of Sundays. But the thought stayed with me, sucking at my brains like a limpet: Yuri my lover, Joe my husband, both of them waving at me in the arrivals lounge.

The bus jerked to a stop and we struggled off it. We followed signs saying British Passport Holders Only, and Luggage Reclamation, and eventually Customs with 'Nothing to Declare' in green.

'Oh God, Elliott, what am I going to do?' I whimpered.

'I've told you, nothing will happen. Stop panicking.'

'I'm not panicking!'

Through customs, looking innocent, with an extra bottle of booze each in our cases and Elliott's gold watch strapped under his sock. Round a fence and out into an unprotected world. Clamouring, eager faces searching for loved ones. Were any of them looking for me? I desperately hoped not. We stopped and looked.

'Well?' said Elliott, knocked against me by the unstoppable stream of fellow travellers. 'Where are they then? Didn't I tell you?' He sounded really smug. 'Is that one Joe? Or that one? Oh, and isn't that Yuri over there?'

'I suppose you think that's funny.'

I looked around trying to keep hidden behind Elliott's protective form just in case, and I couldn't believe that the coast was really clear. And then it happened. The sledgehammer landed. Splat. I ducked back behind Elliott and said, 'Shit.'

'What?' he said. 'Where? Which, *who*?'

'Both,' I squeaked. 'Don't let them see me.'

'Well well well. Who would have thought it?'

'*I* did, remember?' I muttered into his back.

'So you did. Mm. What are you going to do now?'

Before I could think of an answer I heard a voice screeching through the clamour, 'Elliott! Elliott!'

'It's Uncle!' said Elliott in a soppy voice. 'Oh gosh. Sorry, Alison, but I'll have to go. It's Uncle!'

'But you can't leave me like this!'

'Don't worry love, things'll work out. Look, I must go.' He gave me a hasty kiss on the cheek. 'Write and let me know what happens,' and my shield disappeared into the throng.

Sheer, cold, clammy panic. I froze for all of two seconds. Then I ran. Bastard, I thought. Deserter! I fought my way through the flooding river of bodies, causing God knows what injuries with my flying suitcases, back in the direction of the customs men. How could Elliott *do* this to me? Joe and Yuri, standing expectantly right out there in the front line, only bodies apart from each other and both looking blissfully unaware of the other's existence. Both looking for me. What else could I do but run?

And then I saw a little sign twinkling away at the periphery of vision. It glowed at me like a star on the horizon. It said shelter, it said respite, it said funk-hole, it said hide here, Alison. The sign said 'Ladies'.

I don't know how long I sat inside that little cubicle with the bolt securely fastened and my cases piled up against the door as an extra barricade. It was probably only a few minutes but it seemed like hours. It was long enough, anyway, for my hot sweat to turn into a cold and clammy dampness and for me to make use of the facilities, seeing as they were on hand, so to speak.

I sat there thinking: What the hell do I do now? But you can't spend the rest of your life sitting on a public loo with your knickers round your ankles, can you? Not when there's a small but rather pressing problem of husband and lover waiting outside the door somewhere. I remembered all that I'd ever told myself about being brave and doing what *I* wanted to do and not telling lies and I knew there was no way out of this one except the straight and honest way. (Pity.) I was overwhelmed with the thought that I didn't actually want to be bothered with either of them. Not now, and not particularly ever. I was fed up with being cluttered. What was the point of coming home to make an attempt at getting a new, independent life together and then handicapping yourself right at the start with a couple of leftover complications? Because in that moment of seeing them, that's what they'd suddenly become. Yuri was nothing to do with *now*, he was moonlight on the ocean, a sparkling passion, a whirling dance and I wasn't in the mood to be made dizzy again, I'd got more important things to get on with. And Joe? So he wrote nice letters. So what? He was still the bastard who'd shoved me under and seeing him in the flesh brought it all back again. A few clever words on paper weren't enough to make me wipe the slate clean. They almost had been in the sunny Caribbean, but not now, feet on the ground, surrounded by rainy realities. Joe. Yuri. Me. Time I got the priorities right, not the time to take the easy way out. Start as you mean to go on, my girl.

Then I heard my mother's voice whispering inside my head: Alison, you don't want to end up single. If you get divorced you might not find anybody else. Can't you and Joe get back together again? You'll end up middle-aged and alone. Have you got another boyfriend yet?

But it was only a brief moment of doubt. I closed off my ears and told the voice to shut up. This fish needs no bicycle. I'd rather be whole by myself than a half depending on another, drawing my sustenance from somebody else's root. Time to put down some roots of my own even if they do turn out to be a bit straggly. With that thought I took a few steadying deep breaths, then I hitched up my knickers, flushed the loo and strode forth.

PART THREE

CHAPTER TWENTY-ONE

That was the easy part. What followed wasn't quite as.

Joe was still waiting, and he saw me and waved. He looked just the same as ever – bumptious, crumpled and not giving a damn. Yuri was still waiting, and he saw me and waved. He was nothing like the fiery, magical Cossack prince I remembered – this guy was wearing slacks, sweater and tweed jacket. He looked so clean-cut and *nice* it was positively revolting. They both walked towards me smiling while I stood my ground and attempted (not too successfully) to smile back. They arrived in front of me almost simultaneously and gave each other a suspicious look.

Another deep breath. 'Hello, Joe,' I said. Then, 'Hello, Yuri. Yuri, I'd like you to meet Joe, my husband. Joe, this is Yuri, my lover.'

They looked at me, then they looked at each other again and then two pairs of eyes fastened accusingly on me. There was a terrible silence.

'I'm sorry,' I said to fill it. 'Er . . . look, why don't we all go and have a drink?' I suggested chirpily but it came out as more of a squeak. 'Then we can all sit down and have a good long talk about this, I'm sure there must be one or two questions, and anyway my feet are killing me,' I rattled on. Smiling a lot and not meeting either pair of eyes. I picked up the suitcases and started walking towards the nearest bar hoping against hope that one or preferably both of them would turn around and walk away from me leaving me and my conscience free.

They both followed.

'Let me take those for you, little one,' said Yuri taking a case from my hand and making a direct hit on my heart with the way he said 'little one'.

'Give me your luggage, lovey,' said Joe grabbing the other one and underlining how different he was from the old Joe at Dringley station.

I surrendered a case to each of them and continued to walk, feeling heavier, husband on one side, lover on the other, anonymous amongst the milling crowds which were callously oblivious to the steamy drama being enacted before their eyes.

The bar was packed. We stood, an uncomfortable and cumbersome *ménage à trois*, on an empty bit of floor at the end of the counter. 'I'll get them. What would you both like?' I asked, fishing in my bulging handbag for English money and mettle.

'No, I'll get them,' said Joe and Yuri in unison.

Impasse. Someone ought to take charge here so it might as well be me. 'Joe, you get the drinks, I'd like a brandy and lemonade please. Vodka, Yuri? You see if you can find us a table and I'll stay here and guard the suitcases.'

Incredibly, they both did as they were told. I wondered how long it could last. And the next thought was: run for it! Now, while you've got the chance. But I refused the temptation. No more running away. Lay it on the line, cards on the table and all that. Just tell them where I stand and where they stand. Shouldn't be too difficult, should it?

I shifted my weight on to the other foot. Please, Yuri, be a miracle worker and find a table for me to lay my cards on. Or at least some chairs. Or at the very least one chair, for me.

The miracle was wrought. Yuri captured a table empty of all but a regiment of used glasses. And there were just three chairs around it. We all sat down. Joe passed the drinks around. I raised my glass and said, 'Cheers,' and Yuri and Joe reciprocated. We drank. We put our glasses down. And all at once the distracting fripperies of politeness were all used up. That terrible silence descended on us again. I took a deep breath, held it and prepared to dive, probably with a resounding belly-flop, right into the middle of it. 'Well, I guess I have some explaining to do . . . '

The words came fumbling, tumbling out of me, every one of them making me feel more grubby. 'You see, when I was out on the Atlantic I fell in love with Yuri . . . ' He reached out and took my hand in a proprietorial manner. Turning to Joe I went on, 'It was on the rebound from you and Carol, I suppose. And then, out in the Caribbean, when your letters started coming, it reminded me of how things used to be between us before it started going wrong and I, well I guess I started to love you again, too.' Joe took hold of my other hand and I felt in imminent danger of becoming the rope in a tug of war. This wasn't going at all as planned – I was supposed to be getting them both out of my life, not embedding them more firmly in it.

'How can you say this?' asked Yuri. 'You cannot love both. You must choose between us, little one. I will not share you. If you are going to be mine, then you will be mine alone.'

'Oh, no,' said Joe slowly. 'That's my wife you're talking about.'

I pulled my hands away from both of them. 'Now just hang on a minute, the pair of you,' I said. 'I haven't finished. And we'll have less of this "mine". I'm not a possession, I don't belong to either of you.'

'Well you needn't think I'm going to take you back while you're carrying on with this oaf,' said Joe. He suddenly sprang from his seat and flung his arms in the air. 'My God, you don't change a bit, do you? You little hypocrite. All the while you were writing me those letters you were just stringing me along, keeping your options open . . . '

'Me a hypocrite! What about you and Carol?' I cried.

'That's different!'

'No it isn't!' And here we were again, the old Joe and the old Alison, and strangers in the bar were beginning to stare.

I wanted to crawl under the table. I soon wished I had because Joe took hold of my arm, none too gently, and I thought he was going to hit me. Yuri, who'd been pretty quiet through this little exchange, pushed back his chair and stood up. His lithe body seemed to tower above Joe as he reached across and roughly grabbed him by the shoulder. 'Take your hands off my woman,' he said in a quiet but threatening voice.

Joe laughed and yanked me towards him. 'Or else what?' he said scathingly.

And to think I'd once been naive enough to revel in

Yuri's jealousy and wish Joe would show a bit. But, my God, I didn't want any of this. Or either of them. I was scared – I thought they were going to belt each other. And then me.

I was also acutely embarrassed. I struggled out of Joe's grasp and said, 'Stop it, both of you!' through clenched teeth. 'People are staring at us.'

'So?' said Joe.

'Let them stare,' said Yuri.

'At least, sit down,' I said. 'Have you any idea how foolish you both look?'

A wound to their manly pride. It did the trick. They sat down again and I took a deep breath and a gulp of brandy. 'I was trying to find some way of saying this tactfully but I guess I'm not very good at tact these days. All I can say is I'm very sorry for everything that's happened and . . . I think it's best if I don't see either of you again. Ever. You're better off without me,' I added as a sap to their pride. And my conscience.

Another bruising silence.

Then Joe said bitingly, 'Well that's just fine by me. But let me know where you'll be staying. My solicitor will need an address to write to.'

'And I,' said Yuri, 'do not wish to know anything of your whereabouts. You have betrayed me and this I cannot forgive.'

I must admit I felt rotten. I almost wished they *had* hit me because then I could have felt righteous and justified. As it was I just felt like a worm. And I wriggled even more when, with a burst of masculine dignity, they rose and walked away from me together.

I watched them go and wondered if they'd start comparing notes. Then I lit a cigarette and slowly finished my drink. Eventually I headed for the exit alone, humping both suitcases and stopping every few seconds to hitch my bag back up on to my shoulder. I was decidedly frazzled round the edges and already heartily sick of being an independent woman. So I dumped the cases on the floor, looked around, rustled up a bit of self-confidence and flagged down a porter. He loaded my bags on his trolley and I followed him wondering why I'd spent all those other journeys struggling with my luggage alone. So I drew back my shoulders, stuck my head in the air and waited while the hired help found me a taxi. Then I tipped him. He grinned at me and said thank you so I must have given him enough. I climbed into the back seat of the cab.

'Where to, lady?' asked a cockney voice from the driver's seat.

I thought: that's a very interesting question. 'Chiswick, please,' I answered, and gave him Sally's address.

I didn't collapse until early evening. Whether it was from jet lag, sheer exhaustion or overindulgence in alcohol I don't know. Probably all three, with rather more than a smattering of the latter as Sally welcomed me with not just open arms but an open bottle of wine as well. Then we started on the duty-frees. Oh boy. And then I must have skipped a day because the next thing I remember it was Tuesday morning and Sally was flying around with a mascara brush in one hand, a cup of coffee in the other and a piece of toast in her mouth. 'Ah! So you're not dead then,' she mumbled, spitting a crumb or two over her dressing table. 'I was beginning to wonder.'

I moaned. 'I've got it,' I said. 'You must be Sally.'

'Right first time.' She grinned and came over to give me a hug. 'Welcome back to the land of the living.'

'Is that what you call it?' A small groan accompanied the words.

'Feel a bit rough still, huh? Never mind. I've emptied the shower for you. Enlarger's in the living room and don't knock it over. So get up, wash yourself down and I'll see you this evening. Got to dash. 'Bye honey.' On her way out she called, 'Spare doorkey's on the table with a shopping list. Ta-ra,' and the door slammed.

I was alone. Beginning to wake up. Becoming aware of stiff joints and aching muscles and little sore patches from sleeping God knows how many hours in a bag on the floor. Sally's hospitality is sensible rather than self-sacrificing. One bed equals her bed. Wise lady. I crawled out on to the carpet on all fours and slowly hauled myself into anthropoidal stance. About half an hour later I was back in the land of the living . . . or at least washed and dressed and in my friend's living room gulping down a second mug of tea and pondering what to write next on a piece of paper which so far had only the words 'Plan of Action' to mar its pristine surface. I underlined the heading while waiting for inspiration. I underlined it again. Then I doodled round the underlinings.

The list slowly took shape during a piece of dry toast and a third mug of tea: 1) bank to change leftover dollars/get statement of my account. 2) Sally's shopping. 3) Train back to Dringley tomorrow. 4) Sort out cottage – pay bills, check place over, unpack, re-pack, leave secure, return to London in car. 5) Earn money – temp agency? 6) Find somewhere to live. 7) Write to BBC, Capital, Radio South, LBC, Radio London, Anywhere Else.

I read it through. Amazing to find only seven things on it. Can a whole future life boil down to a list of seven and one of those be only 'Sally's shopping'? I circled points six and seven as being priority essentials and then folded it and put it away.

I'd become so accustomed to sunshine, American accents, American money and permanently smiling black faces that I found Chiswick High Road in the rain and all its sullen, pasty white faces with only a smattering of black ones a rather alien and slightly intimidating place. I even had to convert the prices into dollars before I knew how much things cost. Most unpatriotic to lose one's innate understanding of pounds and pence so relatively quickly. I walked along thinking: well this is it, girl, real life, feet on solid ground – what do you think of it so far? Not a lot, was the immediate reaction.

But one good thing had come out of those irresponsible months at sea – my bank balance appeared to be almost healthy. I let myself back into the flat, switched on the light, unpacked our dinner, put the kettle on and settled down to a proper accounting session. If I set aside so much for the unseen Dringley bills and so much as a contingency fund, I reckoned I had enough for about three weeks of paying half

Sally's rent, bills and food money before the account would be empty. Whether the friendship account would run out before then I wasn't sure. Probably. Staying for a few nights in a friend's one-bedroomed flatlet is one thing. Moving in for an indefinite period is something else altogether . . .

I pottered through the rest of the day doing housework, making my presence useful. I made Sally's bed, vacuumed the dusty carpets, swabbed out the shower/darkroom, cleaned the kitchenette, dusted the visible parts of shelves and things then settled into a bout of cordon rouge, blanc et bleu cookery which resulted in beef stew and dumplings with treacle sponge and custard to follow. Cooking was still a luxurious novelty for me.

Sally was delighted when she came home. 'Something smells good,' she said as she came in the door sniffing the air appreciatively. Then she noticed the rest of the flat. 'Wow. Hasn't looked this clean since I moved in! Wanna marry me?'

'Don't let it go to your head. This is just a one-day aberration.' As we tucked into the meal I told her of my preliminary plans.

'You can stay with me as long as you like, you know,' she said.

I smiled at her across the table. 'I know. And thanks. But it's not really practicable in the long term, is it?' But it was good to know that the offer was there. What would we do without our female friends? 'I'm going back home tomorrow. I'll probably stay up there for a few days, could do with a bit of a holiday . . . I want to just flop around for a bit, not see anybody, you know?'

'Sure. Don't blame you. And then what?'

'Well, if it's okay with you I'll come back Sunday and borrow your floor for a bit longer while I see about finding a flat and earning some money. What's your temp agency like? Think they'd take me on?'

'Depends on your typing. They'll give you a test.'

'Whoopee.'

Almost twenty-four hours later, to the minute, I'd paid off

the taxi and was standing outside my little house in Dringley. I turned the key in the lock and pushed on the door. It didn't open. I kicked it. It juddered and stayed shut. I kicked it again. This time it opened with a protesting screech of damp-swollen wood. Cases inside, me inside, I kicked the door back into its frame and wondered if I'd ever be able to heave it open again or if I was going to be forever imprisoned. Cocooned. I rather liked the idea.

I turned on the lights and the fire. Good. Electricity and gas still working. Turned the water on at the mains and heard satisfactory noises of activity from upstairs as the cistern filled up. I flung myself with glee into the big chair in front of the fire but it didn't take more than thirty seconds for the cold and damp of it to penetrate my clothes. I took the cushions off and propped them up in front of the fire and watched the gentle mist begin to float out of them, smelled the musty aroma of it and thought: home at last! I smiled. But I can never really settle back and relax unless things are in a reasonable state of order. The suitcases were accusing me from the corner of the room as were the spiders in the other corners and, horror of horrors, a couple of woodlice crawling over the hearth! I dreaded to think what might have made its home under the duvet upstairs.

Still, if I was going to be a successfully independent woman then bravery, like charity, must begin at home, so I took the cases and a feather duster upstairs, shook out the bed and with a small prayer to the patron saint of electric blankets, switched it on and stood well back. Nothing happened except that the little orange light came on. I relaxed slightly. Electricity, to me, is High Magic. Black or White, I'm not sure, but either way you don't fiddle with it or you might conjure up a demon in a blinding flash of red smoke. I dusted down the cobwebs, opened the window a crack to let the fresh-damp in, gingerly gave a cursory sweep under the edges of the bed with the duster-on-a-stick and then set about unpacking.

Downstairs, the room was beginning to feel warmer and dryer. The steam had stopped rising from the chair cushions so I put them back, turned on the TV for a bit of background company and then went into the kitchen intending to attack the black mould that had started its invidious journey along the back of the sink. I settled for making a cup of tea instead. Then I settled myself, slippered feet up on the hearth, body cuddled by cosy chair and tummy warmed by tea.

Immediate question: if I'm going to start a new life, new base, new career in London, should I sell up?

Immediate answer: sheer panic at the very idea.

Push the panic away and think about it objectively: the money would be useful. No it wouldn't. The price of a one-bedroomed cottage (cottage is a euphemism – hovel is more honest) in Dringley would hardly pay for the deposit on a garden shed in London. Try again: the place would be like a millstone round my neck, a burden, a responsibility, a constant worry I could well do without if I'm to make my way down south. No it wouldn't. It would be security, a private place of escape, somewhere to run to. Okay, one more try: let it, rent it out, take the money and rest easy that someone would be living in it, looking after it, keeping it warm. No good. Three reasons for rejecting that idea. A month's rent on this place would get me a day's rent in London if lucky; I couldn't bear the thought of strangers living here because they'd wreck the place rather than look after it or at least would never love it like I do, and if someone else was paying me so they could live here then I couldn't live here. Bang would go the bolt-hole.

Isn't human nature wonderful, the way it's so easy to talk yourself into doing something you want to do, keeping something you want to keep? Pity it's not quite so easy when it comes to actually achieving things.

I spent three glorious days not doing much at all. I wrote out a few cheques and up-rated the house insurance but after that it was painless. I made the duty phone call to Mum and Dad but didn't bother with anyone else and nobody bothered with me. I revelled in being incommunicado. After months of ship-life where there's virtually no privacy and where you're at the beck and call of the world and its aunty for almost twenty-four hours a day it was sheer heaven, a sort of convalescence, refuelling myself before the grand attack so that by the time Sunday dawned

I was raring to go. I loaded up the car, locked up the past and set off for the M1. I felt brave and intrepid, ready to take on all comers, conquer all resistance, establish a new base, a new career. 'London, I'm going to love you!' I promised.

It's a pity the feeling wasn't mutual.

CHAPTER TWENTY-TWO

I joined the mad scramble for accommodation. Waiting at the corner shop for the bale of *Standards* to be delivered, buy the paper, skim the Accommodation to Let column on the way to the telephone. Ring every number, suitable or unsuitable, only to be told, 'Sorry, it's taken.' Study the postcards in corner shop windows where rooms to let were hidden amongst 'French lessons' and 'exotic massage' and 'ZX81 for sale, offers' but again the same result. Spend the afternoons hiking around local accommodation agencies thinking: so what if their fees are a rip-off, I have to find somewhere to live. Sitting in dingy waiting rooms waiting to be interviewed about my suitability for a slum which is totally unsuitable for me. And foundering always when we get to the rocky bit about what's my monthly salary. Awkward one, that, when you're unemployed. But I stuck with it, clinging on there, round and round on the not-so-merry-go-round.

I eventually acquired walls and a ceiling of my own by resorting to that well-tested technique, telling a whopper. I felt no guilt. I wanted that flat. It was small, made the cottage into a mansion by comparison, was not too squalid inside though the setting was dubious, but it was only a three-minute walk from Sally's place. And the rent sounded just about affordable. So, working on the principle that if the only way of achieving your ends is to lie then do it through your teeth and make sure you turn it into truth before you get found out, when the woman at the agency asked my monthly salary I simply took the rent figure and quadrupled it.

She looked slightly surprised, but she wrote the figure in the space provided on the questionnaire she was filling in. 'And what's your actual job?'

'Freelance,' I said without hesitating.

'Freelance what?'

'Broadcaster and journalist,' I replied, hedging as many bets as I could.

She seemed quite interested. 'Broadcaster? Will I have heard you on the radio then?'

'Quite possibly.' It wasn't really a lie – she might have been to Dringley.

She smiled. 'Lovely. Well that's settled then. Would you like to take another look at the flat before you sign?'

'No, I'm quite satisfied,' I said. 'It'll do nicely to tide me over until I find a suitable property to purchase.' I signed on the dotted line and wrote out the cheque for one month's rent in advance along with an equal amount as deposit, refundable, against damage and breakages. I handed over the cheques with a smile on my face and an empty feeling in my heart and bank balance. It just about cleaned me out, previous calculations having been, shall we say, a little on the optimistic side. The secretarial agency's typing test could be put off no longer.

It was Friday afternoon and already dark as I re-emerged into Chiswick High Road with the keys to my new base tucked firmly into the bottom of my handbag. I could either turn left and go back to Sally's to start getting my stuff together, or I could turn right and attack the temp agency. I dithered. Wasn't crossing off one main item on my life-plan list quite enough of an achievement for one week? Didn't I deserve a little treat now? So how about turning neither right nor left but going into the off-licence directly opposite for a celebratory bottle of something instead? No. I was firm with myself. Take advantage of the winning streak while you're on it. You haven't the time to put things off till Monday. I turned right and walked briskly.

You know the old saw about experience being worth more than paper qualifications? Rot. And the paper qualifications don't count for much either. When it comes to signing on with a secretarial agency all that counts is what you can actually do with your fingers. University degree, irrelevant. Work experience as radio producer/presenter, irrelevant. Travel-broadened mind, irrelevant. 'Very nice, dear, but what are your speeds?' asked the bespectacled, picture-of-efficiency female in tailored suit who must have been all of twenty-five going on seventy.

'A hundred words a minute shorthand and fifty typing,' I answered confidently. (Somewhere up in Dringley or maybe in my parents' garage in Lancashire there were certificates to prove it.)

'Good, good. That would put you in pay-band C. Come with me then and we'll just give you a straightforward little practical test.' She smiled like a dentist.

Oh-oh. Try bluffing your way through a practical, Alison.

We went into a back room where there was a table on which were two typewriters, a pile of clean A4 paper, a spiral-bound shorthand pad and a pencil. We both sat down. I picked up the pad and she began to dictate. I managed 'Dear Sir, thank you for your letter,' before my Pitman's packed up altogether. The humiliation.

'Well, let's try the typing shall we?' she said with a tighter little smile than the last, and gave me a hand-written sheet of paper covered in crossings-out, arrows, asterisks attached to balloons and other such 'corrections'. I started on the electric and she started a stop-watch. The machine sprinted off and jammed.

'Can we start again?' I asked. 'I think perhaps I'd be better on the manual.'

This time the typewriter was dyslexic. When I'd finished she went over my effort with a little red crayon infecting the paper with measles. Each error counted as a whole word to be subtracted from the final speed-per-minute. I watched her mark it up with sinking heart and wondered if I'd be the first person in the world to officially register a negative score. The mortification.

'Oh dear.' She shook her head at me. 'Audio perhaps?'

I shook my head back at her. 'But all I need is a little practice,' I said hopefully.

'Perhaps. Very well, we'll take you on, but you'll have to start off as a straight copy-typist. That'll be on band E.' We went back out into the main office. 'I can't offer you anything at the moment, but ring in at ten on Monday morning. Something might have come in by then.'

'Thanks,' I said and left totally humbled, all thoughts of

buying a bottle to celebrate the flat mangled and murdered by a typewriter keyboard. By the time I got back to Sally's I'd calculated that on pay-band E I'd have to clock up something like ninety hours a week simply to cover the rent – and that was before deductions.

'Never mind,' said Sally later. 'It's only a stop-gap, isn't it? Pretty soon Ms Gimson will be kicking herself because she didn't get your autograph while she had the chance!' She knew it was a lie and I knew it was a lie, but friends are the people who lie to you to keep you whole and you love them for it. 'Come on, let's go out and celebrate.'

'Celebrate what?' I said sourly.

'Lots of things. No more sleeping bag on my bedroom floor, for example, darkroom back in one piece, no more dying to go to the loo when you're installed on it . . . '

'Okay. Enough. I get the message.'

'So where shall we go?'

We parked in a sidestreet off Bayswater Road, locked up and then walked back the way we'd come. The wine bar Sally had in mind was an ex-cellar decked out in olive green upholstery and candles in bottles and the menu chalked up on a blackboard. We settled in at a table for two in a corner and ordered a bottle of Mateus Rosé and a couple of slices of game pie with salad. We ate fast, drank slowly and made plans of action. I got out my notebook and wrote lists. Sally had to stop messing around and decide one way or the other between the typewriter and the shutter button because as things stood at the moment she had neither the time nor the energy to devote herself properly to either, therefore she'd never be properly successful at either. I had to stop mucking around with daydreams about being a national radio star and actually *do* something to get a foot in the door, make the powers that be aware of my existence, nay, my talent. 'You're beginning to sound just like Joe,' I told her.

'Which only goes to show that no one can be all bad. He was right. So what are you going to do?'

'Write letters. Keep my fingers crossed. See what happens.'

Sally considered. Then she said, 'Okay. But I know you, you need a deadline. New Year's Eve! If you haven't got yourself established on the radio – any old station will do for starters – by December thirty-first, you'll owe me . . . '

'Not New Year's Eve,' I said quickly. 'It's too significant. Look what a rotten year this one's been – how much has changed, how far removed I am now from everything I had on January first.'

'Like what? A lousy husband? Some loss.'

I took a long drink, marshalling my thoughts, trying to be articulate, concise. 'Yes, but I had labels: marriage, career, home, planned future. They've all been ripped off me. I feel like a battered old suitcase stuffed with dusty souvenirs that nobody wants to take on holiday anymore.' The wine was making me maudlin.

Sally giggled.

'What are you laughing at?' I was aggrieved.

'Sorry.' She gulped at her drink to steady herself. 'It's just me and my pictorial imagination. An old bag you might be, but an old suitcase!' She spluttered again.

'Rotten cow.'

'Sorry.' She calmed herself. 'Anyway, you're ducking the challenge, you superstitious old . . . suitcase!' She nearly choked.

But she wouldn't let me wriggle out of it so in return I threw the challenge back at her. By the end of the year she had to establish some sort of footing as a freelance, rather than hobbyist, photographer. 'And the forfeit if we don't succeed?' I asked.

'Don't worry,' she said. 'Of course we'll succeed!'

I raised my glass. 'Okay, you're on. To New Year's Eve!' We clinked glasses, drained the dregs of the wine and left.

I steered us carefully back to Chiswick, looking out for police cars through a rosé-coloured windscreen, then parked outside the Victorian monolith which housed my new abode. We got out of the mini and stood looking up at it. There was a stone plaque in the wall just above the ground floor that proudly stated in scrolled letters: 'Dewsbury Court. AD 1906'. The plaque was the only grand thing about the building apart from its name. The whole block seemed to lour down at us in the dark.

'You mean this is it?' asked Sally.

'Mm.'

'Oh well, you can't judge a book by its cover. Lead on Macduff.'

I led. We climbed the stairwell. Cold, bare, stone steps, brickwork naked but for peeling, once cream-coloured, gloss paint, three anonymous doors to each landing with a variety of mismatched locks and knobs, three dustbins on each half-landing protected from the elements by a hardboard-covered railing, the rest of the aperture open to the sky, wind and rain. One lightbulb per landing, dimly nestling inside a wire cage on the wall.

'Cosy,' said Sally.

'Ah, but wait till you see inside,' I said, panting outside a third floor door. 'This is it.'

'Number thirteen. Hmm.'

'So?' I said defiantly. 'It's quite nice inside, honest. And it's self-contained, fully furnished and cheap at the price.'

'Yes, dear.'

I opened the door, switched the light on and went in singing 'Da-der!' for a fanfare.

The door opened straight into the living room. Sally stood in the middle of the floor, looked around and said, 'Well, could be worse. But I thought you said it was fully furnished? Talk about the bare essentials!'

The living room contained a round drop-leaf dining table with a black telephone on it, two wooden dining chairs, a coffee table and two wooden-armed 'lounge seats'. A built-in cupboard by the door which housed shelves and the electricity meter, an ancient gas fire hung loosely on a wall and the coin-in-the-slot gas meter was over the door so I'd have to pull up a chair to stand on before I could put money in it. Oh yes, and there was a carpet on the floor. 'Come on,' I said, 'there's more.' I took her into the kitchen which was a sort of corridor leading on to the balcony. It was just big enough to hold a cooker, sink unit and tiny fridge. Two knives, two forks, two teaspoons, two dessert spoons, two tablespoons. A shelf on the wall over the fridge held the rest: two tea plates, two cups, two saucers, two dinner plates, two cooking pans and two dishes.

'Great dinner parties you're going to have! Looks like tomorrow we hit the junk shops, eh?'

The bedroom was bigger than the living room. And again, the bare essentials: one single bed, one chest of drawers with a mirror on top to serve as dressing table as well, and a bedside lamp standing on the floor. One naked pillow and two blankets were provided. 'Where did you say you got that cheap sheet you painted all over?' I asked. The 'built-in wardrobe' was a narrow cupboard in a corner with hooks inside, no rail. In the opposite corner, not built-in but standing proud, was a big white metal box with a curtain across the front. 'The shower,' I explained.

'No bathroom?'

'No bathroom.'

'I'm not sure I dare ask . . . where's the loo?'

'Ah. Come this way.' Back into the living room, through the kitchen, out on to the balcony, which like the half-landings on the stairwell was open to the elements apart from a bit of painted hardboard, and through another door.

'My God,' said Sally, a sudden gust of wind ruffling her hair. 'An outside lavvie in a third floor flat!'

I grinned. 'Different, isn't it? I think it gives the place character.'

'Bet you won't be saying that when you get up in the mornings in the middle of winter. What'll you do, get dressed first or get a potty for under the bed?'

'It'll be character building,' I said briskly as the wind started howling around us.

I designated Sunday a business day. Letters. Disc-jockey, newsreader, continuity announcer, anything at all I could think of to do with broadcasting in its widest sense. National radio, World Service, commercial radio, BBC local radio, BBC television, Thames, London Weekend, you name it, I wrote a letter to it. The blitz system had paid off with the shipping lines so why shouldn't it this time too? I fell asleep in the little bed on Sunday night to the accompaniment of the most glorious fantasies about fame and fortune on Radios One, Two, South or Capital, enacting delicious little scenes of visiting 2D Radio with the chauffeured Rolls parked outside the door and me with an oh-so-gracious smile peeping out from the hood of a mink-lined cape.

I woke up on Monday morning as an unemployed temp copy-typist with a phone call to make.

But the gods had decided to be on my side – by lunchtime I'd already progressed to being a fully fledged 'secretary', albeit impermanent and only promoted to pay-band D. Ms Gimson had sounded surprised at my landing 'such a plum job so quickly', but I was the only one she had at such short notice who fulfilled all the requirements: 'shorthand not essential, engagement three weeks but probably longer, older woman preferred.'

'Great,' I said into the telephone feeling decidedly ambivalent about the older woman tag. 'What is it and where?'

CHAPTER TWENTY-THREE

Shit,' I said under my breath at twenty-five past four on 'riday afternoon and not a sign of a letter for me all week. Shit. Piss. And bugger.' It was that buzzer again. Two horts and a long. My call-sign. But being only a humble emp who was I to criticise Mr Whitlock's infernal buzzer? 'd had a hard job not to smile when he'd explained it all on ny arrival in those long gone days of optimistic yore a week go. Poor Mr Whitlock, a small, grey-haired, dowager's ump of a man, was so obviously proud of it, regarded it as ne ultimate in office efficiency. But by the end of that first veek I was ready to scream when I watched the others in ne office look up expectantly at the first buzz or blip, then it was their code abandon whatever task or even elephone conversation they were engaged in to jump utifully to the summons. It grated on my nerves and ubbed up like sandpaper against all my notions about the ignity of humanity. It made us all seem like animals in an xperimental laboratory undergoing behavioural conditioning.

The Supplies Department of St Gabriel's Infirmary had s own little pyramid of power with Mr Whitlock sitting nugly and smugly at the top, the Deputy Supplies Officer, Ar Knight, next, and then the Supplies Clerks, of whom here were six, each one responsible for a particular type of ospital supply. In terms of status I apparently came omewhere in between Mr Knight and the clerks.

The daily routine of the department was quite straightorward. Requisitions were submitted, Mr Whitlock anded them to whichever clerk looked after that particuar category, the clerk processed them, they went back to Ar Whitlock for approval and then went on their way to entral stores.

The entire correspondence of the department was moniored by Mr Whitlock. Even when a letter was addressed directly to Mrs Fahey or marked, Attention of Mr Tims it was still opened and read by the Supplies Officer. Then he'd come into the general office and deal the letters out like a headmaster returning essays in class. The clerks wrote the replies in longhand, as did Mr Whitlock, for me to type up (remembering to put the appropriate reference at the top) and then at the end of the day Mr Whitlock read through them all checking my typing against the originals to make sure I hadn't sneakily altered a sacred word, then he signed his own name at the bottom. I'd only been at St Gabriel's a day or so when I suggested to him that I should begin the day by opening the mail for him. His response had been simple: 'Thank you, my dear, but I think not. You just get on with that specification for flock pillows. Quick as you can, dear. You're coping all right with the tabulations?'

But I stuck with it. And caught the clock-watching syndrome. An impatient two shorts and a long buzzed across the office noises again. 'That's you, Alison,' called Mrs Fahey kindly but with a worried look on her face.

I picked up the pile of finished letters and envelopes with their longhand originals clipped to them, knocked on Mr Whitlock's door and waited.

'Enter,' came a call from within after a suitable delay. 'Ah, Alison!' he exclaimed looking up and smiling as I went in, his voice implying that it was an unlooked for but very pleasant surprise to see me.

'You buzzed, sir?' I said like a servant.

'Twice. Would you be a little more prompt in future? Now, I'd like you to get me a couple of numbers please. I want Mr Rogers, Mr McIntyre and Mr Slinger. Mr McIntyre first. Quick as a flash, dear.' He issued his orders in the nicest possible way, slowly and very patiently as if talking to a backward ten-year-old.

'Right-oh. And here are your letters.' I put them on his desk.

He rifled through them. 'Only eleven? You'll have to be faster than this, my dear.'

It would help if you made your own phone calls, I thought, but didn't say. It was one of his many annoying habits, this refusal to use his own telephone dial even for internal calls. I suppose it gave him some kind of feeling of one-upmanship, enabled him to make a telephonic grand entrance after I'd put the caller on hold. Then, when I switched it through he'd say 'Ah, so-and-so!' in just the voice he used to say 'Ah, Alison!' I decided he must have a massive inferiority complex. And why not? He certainly had all the right qualifications.

I kept my face expressionless as I stood before his desk. 'Anything else?' I asked.

'No, that's all for now, Alison. I'll buzz for you when I want you again.'

I was already making sabotage plans for that disgusting buzzer. It wasn't part of a standard intercom system between boss and secretary but a self-designed contraption (God knows how many requisitions and tenders it must have taken before the thing was installed) with a button at Mr Whitlock's end fixed to a leg of his desk within measured reach of the left hand. The buzzer itself was out in the general office on the wall above his door, a bit like the Victorian system of bells that you sometimes still find in old houses for summoning the staff except that instead of a board with a visual indicator Mr Whitlock had worked out a personalised Morse code. As I returned to my desk it went off again, a long buzz followed by a blip. Mr Knight leapt to his feet and knocked on the inner sanctum door.

I looked up McIntyre's number, made the connection and switched it through to Whitlock. My new motto: just do as you're told, fill in the time sheet and take the money.

But I couldn't do it. I just could *not* faithfully type out: 'Model B.2003 exactly approximates Model A.1006 in all its specifications . . .' even though it was a Whitlock original in writing as clear as a tax demand. So I missed out the word 'exactly' and didn't think anybody would mind.

Two more phone calls for the boss and another half-dozen letters brought me to the five o'clock deadline for depositing the typewriter's regurgitations on his desk so he could check them, sign them and hand them back to me for the distasteful business of licking and sticking (self-seal envelopes hadn't yet arrived at St Gabriel's) in good time for the five-thirty internal post collection. In good time, that is, so long as there was nothing to be re-done. Whitlock didn't allow more than one hand-written error correction per letter.

I sat opposite him as he read through the day's outpourings and watched, satisfied, as he signed one letter after another without criticism or correction. 'Very good, my dear,' he said looking up and smiling. 'I can see that with a little bit of practice, once you get quicker, you could soon be another Leslie.' She was my predecessor and it was meant to be the supreme compliment. I felt a little surge of gratification but caught hold of it and strangled it quickly. God forbid I should ever want to be another Leslie! But it's so easy to be moulded, to let yourself slip into the least difficult course of action, to let action wait until another day. 'Ah, but maybe not that soon,' he said. 'Look.' He held a letter across the desk. 'You've missed out a whole *word* here, Alison.' He sounded terribly pleased about it.

I glanced at the letter. 'I left it out on purpose. You can't say "exactly approximates". It doesn't make sense. It's a contradiction in terms.'

He shook his head. 'You leave me to worry about the grammar, Alison. Just type what I dictate.'

I opened my mouth to argue the point but decided I couldn't be bothered. If he wanted the egg on his face, that was his choice. 'Shall I do the letter again then, Mr Whitlock?'

He glanced at the clock. 'No, I'll let it pass this time. But in future don't make any alterations without consulting me first, all right?' He signed the letter and passed it across. He hadn't 'corrected' it.

At twenty-five past five I started to tidy up my desk and get my things together. I suppose the first week could have been worse, apart from the buzzer, and Whitlock's allergy to the phone dial. And his constant references to being 'quick'. And his fanatical checking of every word and figure. And his finger (or signature) being in everybody's pie. Hmm. 'Three weeks probably longer' the engagement was for. Oh please let there be some replies to the can-I-be-a-radio-star letters soon. That was what I was thinking when Whitlock came into the general office, I assumed to bid his staff goodnight. Of course I assumed wrongly.

'Leaving early, Alison?' he said with his clown grin. 'Not five-thirty yet, you know.' He perched himself on the edge of my desk. 'Let's do a quick sum, shall we? If you were to do this every day for a fortnight say, start packing up your things at twenty-seven minutes past five, that would be ten lots of three minutes, that's a whole half-hour wasted, a whole half-hour we would have *paid* for. Do you see? So remember, dear, that in this office you work until half past five and then you clear up and go. All right, dear? And of course, the same thing applies in the mornings. You don't arrive at nine o'clock, you start working at nine o'clock.' He was still smiling. 'I can't sign your time sheet for hours worked if you haven't actually worked them, now, can I?'

I saved the scream for when I got back to Dewsbury Court and then I stamped on the floor wishing it was Mr Whitlock's toes. Fingers. Balls. I thought about lighting the fire and doing the washing up and peeling some vegetables and cooking a gourmet meal for one but I only managed the first before I sank into a chair and a mild depression. I phoned Sally, wanting to ask her if all temp work was like this and how on earth she'd stood it for so many years, but she was either not back yet or already out for the evening.

Half past sevenish on a Friday evening seems a little late in the week to be severely infected by a dose of the Monday Morning Feeling but I wasn't quite prepared to succumb to it just yet. I forced myself out of the chair and into the kitchen to try Panacea Number One – make a nice cup of tea. That didn't work. My dearly beloved, well travelled, world weary electric kettle, sprang a leak. So I set a pan of water to boil on the gas and waited for the tea to do its duty. Unfortunately its magic wasn't strong enough to combat a Friday evening in a Chiswick backstreet. So I gave up the effort, and gave in. When all else fails try the final solution.

I call it the Temporary Suicide. What you do is this: lock the door and put the chain on. Close the windows and draw the curtains. Take the phone off the hook. Switch off fires, radios, lights and anything else then close the bedroom door firmly behind you. Set an alarm clock for when you absolutely have to return to the world, then get into bed with a hot water bottle and burrow in as cosily and comfortably as possible. Then comes the difficult bit. You have to concentrate hard on keeping your mind's eye cinemascope screen a total blank of reddish-black or whatever colour the back of your eyelids happens to be. It's not easy but if you can do it, that is think positively of nothing at all, then it's a talent worth cultivating because it's a great cure for insomnia too. What you're doing, in effect, is saying to the rest of the world: 'Up yours. Who needs all this?' You give up the struggle, give in, succumb, stop fighting, retire from the battle. Just like suicide, you see. Only it's much better because no one has to discover the body afterwards and you can change your mind and re-emerge even before the alarm clock goes off if you want to. The Temporary Suicide! I sank into self-imposed oblivion.

The alarm woke me at seven the next morning and I got out of bed feeling full of energy. The Infirmary Supplies Office and its Officer had better watch out because if I was going to work there, be it only for three weeks or shorter, then I was going to work there properly, make it work properly. Not for me to take as long as I can to mechanically do as little as I could get away with just because I was being paid by the hour. Tempting, of course, but not an attitude to let myself slip into. I thought: if I'm going to take life by the throat and shake it around a little then I may as well start at the Supplies Office and get in some useful practice.

I passed the weekend in paperwork of one sort or another – planning reforms at the Supplies Office, cutting pictures out of magazines to stick on the wall with a few choice Sally-prints intermingled, writing follow-up letters to radio stations then tearing them up again because I didn't want to appear too pushy, and on Saturday night me and Sally went to explore the riverside pubs along the Strand by Kew Bridge and spent a fortune playing Space Invaders. The Invaders won.

On Monday morning the postman entered my stairwell at Dewsbury Court just as I was leaving it. 'Morning,' I said brightly. 'Anything for number thirteen?' not really expecting anything but hoping anyway.

He glanced through the packet of envelopes in his hand and gave one of them to me. Not a word, not a flicker of expression crossed his face as he continued past me and up the steps. Didn't he realise he could have been holding my whole future in his hand? I said 'thanks' to his receding back then gave him up as a bad job and turned my attention to the outside of the envelope. I studied and savoured it all the way to the station. It wasn't from Mum and Dad or from Elliott because it was typed. And it was in a white envelope, postmarked Friday and sent first class. Could it be . . .?

I bought my ticket and as I couldn't bear to wait any longer, ripped open the envelope as I was going up the steps to the platform.

It was a bill. From the accommodation agency for their services. Great. Isn't it amazing that when you move into a new place the first things you get through the post are always the bills? I shoved it down into the bottom of my handbag and decided to ignore it at least until the red one arrived, or if necessary the one threatening legal action unless settled by return. I refused to let it destroy my mood of optimistic determination. Only a week had gone by, after all. Who knows what tomorrow might bring, or the next day?

CHAPTER TWENTY-FOUR

Unemployment. It was Friday afternoon, two weeks since posting the 'please let me have a job or at least an audition' letters and here I was, unemployed again, and it was entirely my own fault. I'd walked out of Whitlock's office, picked up my bag and coat, left a half-finished letter curling in the typewriter and stomped down the long corridors of St Gabriel's and out into the street. It had been light-headedly easy at the time and infinitely preferable to having the Supplies Officer's blood on my hands. But how could I expect the agency to keep me on after this? Time to stop waiting quiescently for letters and start accosting the career dispensers in person. I literally couldn't afford to let the postman pass me by any longer.

It's easy to think all that when you're walking along a street under a blue and white sky with the sun glinting gold off the rusted leaves and the air has a crisp and cleansing smell to it. It's not quite so easy to keep it up when you're sitting on a Chiswick-bound tube train. And it's damned near impossible by the time you're standing in the shadows cast by the battlements of Dewsbury Court. I looked up at the place and picked out the two dirty windows which belonged to number thirteen then looked along the street at my even dirtier, once white mini perilously squashed between a transit van and a dented Ford Cortina. Every time I left or entered the building I looked along the street expecting my car to have been stolen – it was that kind of street. I looked at my car again, feeling a surge of affection. Dear little mini. Then I took another, closer look and my stomach lurched. Oh no. I may have kept it dirty but at least I'd kept it undented. Had. Until now. But sometime during the morning my poor little car had finally been initiated, become a fully paid-up member of London Transport (Private Branch) with the scars to prove it. Someone, something, some monstrous other vehicle, had made space for itself in the most brutish way. A deep furrow had been gouged along the passenger side from front wing, across the width of the door, stopping in a hollow just before the back wheel. A furrow which left a thin streak of shiny, naked metal glinting in the bottom of it and a signature of blue paint at one end. Oh my poor little car, who could have done this to you? I wanted to fling my arms around it and comfort it. Rapid calculations followed. Panel beating, respray, no claims bonus . . . and for what? So some other villain could make a dent in the other side, probably. I patted her nose and left her alone to lick her wounds.

Weary and thoroughly pissed off I climbed the three flights of steps up to the flat thinking about throwing all my possessions into the car and heading off up the M1 for Dringley and for good. Up yours, London, I don't like you much, and I'm getting the feeling that you don't like me. Then I pictured an imaginary Joe gloating: I told you so, knew you'd never make it on your own. I thought of Mum and Dad saying: all right, you've had your fling, time to come home and live with us again, we'll sort you out. I remembered Digby saying, 'Why don't you have a baby, dear?' meaning, that's about all you're good for. And suddenly, unbidden, came a picture of Joss. Dear, sweet Joss sitting next to me on the steps of the church outside Broadcasting House asking for my autograph and calling me Alison Wonderland and me saying, 'one of these days . . . ' I put the key in the lock and tears were pricking at my eyes and I thought: no, sod it, I'll be *damned* if I'll admit defeat!

I pushed open the door and in my longing to slam it firmly behind me, a barrier between me and the hostile world, I almost trod on the envelopes that were sitting there on the mat. Two of them. All hail to the GPO and its glorious second delivery. One was squarish and brown and had a window in it and I didn't feel much like opening it. The other one was long and slim and white and franked not stamped and had BBC in red on the top left-hand corner. Oddly, I didn't much want to open that one either. Sealed, it could contain my heart's desires. Once opened I knew they'd all fly away . . . I picked them up and put them on the table side by side, edges parallel, then I remembered Mr Whitlock's precision neatness and mussed them up a bit. First things first, spread out the hope and anticipation for as long as you can and get off down there to the agency. Open the letters later.

Ms Gimson wasn't very pleased with me. But she didn't strike me off the books, just said that she couldn't assign me to anywhere for the beginning of next week at least because she'd expected me to be at St Gabriel's but if I were to ring in on Monday just in case something had come in . . . She handed over a cheque for the last week's purgatory with a stony face which I accepted just as stonily then I ran all the way to the bank and got there just before they locked the doors. After I'd paid it in I hurried home wondering what on earth had possessed me not to open the BBC envelope as soon as I saw it. But again, when it was in my hand I didn't want to do the deed. It was like the long ago letter with A-level results in it. It can only be one of two things: good news or bad news. That makes it a fifty-fifty chance, I told myself, no worse than spinning a coin. So here goes. I took a deep breath and stuck my thumb under the flap and ripped it open, leaving untidy ragged edges. I glanced over it quickly to know the worst straight off. At least it was a proper typed letter, and not a standard polite but printed rejection. Then I read it through properly. It wasn't good news. But it wasn't altogether dismissive. It came from the Presentation Editor, Radio Two and he wrote: 'We don't have any staff vacancies at the moment but I've listened to your tape and perhaps you'd like to make an appointment to come in and have a chat.' So it didn't exactly offer a deal of hope but neither did it close the door in my face. A true middle of the road letter.

I picked up the phone and rang the number. Would Monday at three-fifteen be convenient, asked a secretary? 'Yes, that'll be fine,' I said, not letting on that so would any other time, any other day for the rest of my life. I put the phone back on the hook and yelled 'Yippee!' at the top of my voice. Maybe, just maybe, I thought, Fate was working on my side again. Ah, but 'no staff vacancies', what about that? Did 'staff' imply that there might be a 'non-staff' – temporary contract, holiday relief, that kind of thing? But probably not. 'No vacancies' were the operative words, staff or not. Then again 'a chat', I liked the sound of. 'Interview' is a horrid, negative, nerve-racking ordeal of a word. 'Chat' is definitely much friendlier. So I entered the weekend optimistically.

Most of it was spent in conference with Sally, going over my wardrobe deciding what not to wear, trying things on, taking them off, putting them on again. Broadcasting's a funny sort of world. 2D was all jeans and T-shirts, but the BBC? They didn't really still wear dinner jackets to read the radio news, did they? The rest of the time I spent getting my voice back into condition. I cut down on the cigarettes and stalked back and forth across the living room reading aloud from the *Standard* with Sally for an audience and alone to myself. I read out jokey bits from magazines, practised reading the backs of record sleeves so it sounded as though the information was being spouted off the top of my head, borrowed Sally's camera tripod and tied my little cassette recorder microphone to it with string then talked into it as though to a live and listening audience. I played back the tapes, hated them, tried again, stared at the microphone for ages, staring it out and daring it to make me feel nervous, because it's amazing how quickly you lose your familiar ease with pieces of hardware, how off-putting they can be. And of course I listened to an awful lot of Radio Two trying to imitate everything from music introductions to the football results and, 'It's one o'clock and here is the news read by . . .'

Monday arrived with no more post, no booking from the agency and me a nervous wreck. And all for the prospect of 'a chat'. I was just putting the finishing touches to my hair and wondering if I had time to iron my jeans again, when the phone rang. I went to answer it knowing that it would be the BBC to cancel everything.

'Hi, it's me. Break an arm or whatever it is you showbiz people say on these occasions!' It was Sally. 'I'll come straight to your place from work and if you're not back I'll camp on the doorstep, then we'll go out and drown your sorrows, okay?'

'It's a date,' I said. 'Thanks for the optimism.'

'S'all right, anytime. See you later,' and she was gone again, leaving me smiling.

I didn't feel much like smiling as I walked up towards Portland Place from Oxford Circus tube, though. I was far too early, had a sore throat from too much nervous clearing of it, was desperate for a pee and utterly convinced I was wearing all the wrong clothes. Talk about nerves. For someone whose career has been Dringley local radio, Broadcasting House and its national networks is something like the Temple of Jerusalem, or Mecca or Vatican City. Maybe it's not like that for everyone but it was for me. It was still only a quarter to three so I went into Wendy's, ordered a tea and a burger with small fries, carried the tray downstairs and pigged the lot. That was a mistake. I spent the next five minutes burping. So I chain-smoked a couple of cigarettes and practised deep-breathing to calm myself down a bit. I called in to the ladies' on my way out, did a final check on my reflection, hating it, and then set off up the road telling myself I wasn't a typist aiming for pie in the sky, I was a professional broadcaster temporarily resting between programmes and the BBC would be lucky to have my services. Desperately searching for the right label to attach round my neck. It worked quite well. I believed it right up until I was sitting inside the vastly marbled reception hall waiting for someone to come down and get me. Get me. I felt I ought to escape while I still had the chance.

My guide was the epitome of everything the words 'BBC Secretary' bring to mind – totally unlike the kind of BBC secretary I'd been all those years ago – tailored grey suit, cream blouse, high-heeled shoes, immaculate from head to toe. I wanted to ask have I got time to nip home and change, please? I felt short, too big for my newly washed denims and too old to be wearing denims in the first place. She was the Nine o'Clock News, I was Coronation Street. She smiled, shook my hand and said things like had I ever been to Broadcasting House before and yes it's a lot bigger than people imagine, as she led me up stairs, through millions of swing doors and along miles of carpeted and uncarpeted corridors until we came to a jolly-looking lady with a tea trolley. 'Would you like a cup?' asked my guide. 'I'm afraid Alan's a bit behind because the meeting with the Controller overran so it might be another ten minutes or so before he can get round to you.'

I said yes please, and she dispensed tea from a huge urn into three polystyrene cups, then paid the lady. 'That's Madge,' she explained as we continued along the corridor. 'Next to the DG she's the most important person in the Beeb!'

I smiled in reply and looked at the photographs displayed along the corridor wall. Faces that until now had only been voices and names: Robin Boyle, Friday Night is Music Night; Alan Dell, The Dance Band Days; James Alexander Gordon; Jean Challis; Tim Gudgeon . . . suddenly they were real people and I wondered if I'd ever be up there on the wall with them.

We went into a small office in between Colin Berry and Liz Allen, and Miss Grey Suit indicated a chair for me to sit on while she took one of the teas in for her boss. I looked around trying to look as calm and confident as my surroundings and wondering why my 'inner woman' felt more like an inner jellyfish. She came back, holding the door open. 'He's caught up. Would you like to come in? Bring your tea with you,' she said.

I went in. She introduced us. He stood up and leaned over his desk to shake my hand. She left and closed the door on us. I sat down and prayed I wouldn't spill my tea. My hands were shaking. He was in his late forties, early fifties probably, spoke with the original dark brown voice of the BBC and was absolutely gorgeous. It didn't help. 'Have you ever done any newsreading?' he said with no preamble. I got as far as 'I'm afraid not, Mr . . .' when he went on, 'Call me Alan. Do you smoke?' and he offered me a cigarette.

I relaxed a bit. Smoking is akin to a social disease these days so we were suddenly members of the same club. We talked for a while about what I'd done so far and he somehow managed to turn it into a conversation rather than an interview. 'Chat' was coming true. It was absolutely great until he said, 'Well, shall we do a voice test, then?'

My easy smile got itself stuck. He handed me a two-page script, a test piece cobbled together with very out of date news items no doubt littered with pitfalls for the unwary, and left me alone for a couple of minutes to have a glance at it while he popped across the corridor to set up the recording. I read through it, heart sinking further with each sentence. The Ayatollah Khomeini was in there along with Galtieri in Buenos Aires, Chernenko and Ustinov in the Soviet Union, Lech Walesa doing something in Bydgoszcz, and there was an item about the Monte Carlo rally and a German chap called Rohrl, and even the home news wasn't so good being mainly concentrated in the Welsh outback and Wimbledon.

'Ready?' he said, poking his head round the door.

'Er . . . no.' I might have been able to get away with the old trick of taking a deep breath and saying it with panache back on 2D Radio where most of the audience didn't know how to pronounce the names either, but no way was I going to risk that in front of a critical expert. 'One or two names here I'm not sure of the correct pronunciation of. How do you say this?' I asked, pointing to at least one name out of each story.

'Good girl,' he said. 'A lot of people just try and muddle through. First rule at the BBC: if in doubt, check it.'

I breathed a little sigh of relief inside. I'd passed the first test then. He came and stood behind me leaning over my shoulder to look at the script. I caught a discreet whiff of Eau Sauvage as he told me the pronunciations and I scribbled them in phonetically with a pencil. Then we went across the corridor into a small studio where I was introduced to another chap who was to operate the equipment while Alan settled himself into a corner and said, 'Just start when you're ready.'

Great. Just what I didn't need. A live audience. I neither looked nor felt much like a newsreader and my hands had started shaking again, a fact made very obvious to all and sundry by the fluttery sheets of paper I was clutching. Come on, girl, I ordered mentally, you've faced worse than this in your time. All you have to do is pretend to be a newsreader, act it out and remember to take it slowly and at least try to sound a bit posh.

I launched into it and never have two minutes seemed so long. I wasn't happy. When I finished Alan said, 'Would you like to have another bash at it?' So obviously he wasn't too happy with it either.

'Yes please,' I said. They spooled back the tape and I did it all again, this time I thought, much better.

'Okay, let's go and have a listen to it.' The engineer, whose name I'd already forgotten, spooled back again and handed it over to Alan then we retired to his office and he played it back. In twenty-second bursts with comments and criticism and two 'now that was nice's. Then he took the script back and read it out himself. He was so good it was positively embarrassing.

'Hmm. I see what you mean,' I said. 'Can I have another go?' He'd made it sound so easy once you knew how. It wasn't a question of reading the words clearly without fluffing them, it was more to do with tone, pace, pitch, variety, authority and what he called 'lifting the words off the page'.

He handed it back, although I felt I practically knew the summary by heart now, saying, 'And see if you can use your voice better. It's good but it's a bit too light. You sound like a little girl and I want you to sound like a *woman*. Use your lower registers. Remember you're the one with the latest news and you're going to tell it to the nation. About eight million of them, anyway.'

Christ. Eight *million*. Not cosy little thousands like with local radio. If that last comment was supposed to inspire me with confidence and make me feel big and important it didn't work. I started reading with a squeak. 'Sorry,' I said and cleared my throat. Forget the nation, Alison, just do it for this one man.

'Much better,' he said when I'd finished. 'You're speeding up too much now but you're beginning to get the idea. You take direction well. I think I could do something with you . . .'

And me with you, I thought, watching his hands playing with the cigarette lighter on his desk because it was safer than eye to eye contact. He had the kind of eyes you'd gaze at rather than look at.

'. . . and that's rarer than you'd think,' he went on. 'I see hundreds of hopefuls a year pass through this office and some of them are hopeless, most of them mediocre. There's only a handful I'd consider taking on my team. And I don't waste people's time, by the way, if I don't think they stand a chance I tell them so. But you've got the makings of a good broadcaster.'

I was disproportionately chuffed considering he said I'd only got the 'makings of' rather than already being one. But I sat there, grinning like an idiot and thinking: okay, go on then, when do I start?

'So I'll keep you on file,' he finished.

Thud.

'As I said in my letter, unfortunately there just aren't any vacancies at the moment, I have a full complement.' The disappointment must have been blazing on my face in spite of all efforts to keep on smiling because he went on, 'And I'm not trying to fob you off, believe me. I'd like to have more women on the team anyway . . .'

'You mean at last it's an advantage being female?' I quipped.

He grinned. 'Believe me, darling, if you were a black, one-legged lesbian you'd have it made! Times are changing!' Pity nobody had told that to Frank and Digby and all at 2D. He looked at his watch and stood up. End of chat, end of my fantasies of being a BBC star. For the moment.

I stood up too. 'Well, thanks for giving me your time, and for the encouragement.'

'It's been a pleasure,' he said. 'And if I do get the opportunity to use you I'll be in touch. Maybe in five or six months . . .?'

'Yes,' I said. 'Well, thanks anyway. I'll keep my fingers crossed.'

I sat on the tube going back home racking my brains for

ways to get hold of and introduce a mysterious but voice-wrecking 'flu bug into the ranks of BBC announcers . . . break in one night and spray all the microphones with an aerosol, sabotage the tea urns, send a psychosomatic message down the telephones? Or maybe just start a new career as a sci-fi spy writer?

By the time I got back to the flat disappointment had set in as firm as concrete. It wasn't until then that I realised how much, stupidly, I'd been pinning my hopes on that one little invitation to the BBC. It was hard to forget about it and put it away in a little box labelled 'good audition experience'. In a way it would have been easier if I'd screwed it all up, been dreadful, totally blown it. But the guy had genuinely thought I had talent, something to offer. I'd done well, sod it, so why no reward? It wasn't fair. So close, but so far away. What good's a 'maybe' and only in five or six months' time? I wanted it, needed it now.

CHAPTER TWENTY-FIVE

The rest of the week brought a three-day booking, starting Wednesday, as a copy-typist at a little firm in a house down by the Thames and a few more job-query replies in varying degrees of the let down easy variety. But they all boiled down to the same thing: thanks, but no thanks. I crossed them off my file copies one by one until only Radio South, LBC and ITN were still to come.

I also suffered my first severe attack of the London bedsitter land syndrome – which you can summarise as crushing loneliness. All those brave old words about making your life's base yourself instead of someone else are all very well in theory but a base is supposed to be something you can build on and for that you do need one or two bricks – acquaintances, social gatherings, hobbies, friends. I had Sally of course but she had her own life to get on with and I didn't like to lumber her with a lame dog, in the shape of me, too often. But visions of the two of us in later life sharing a house comfortably, a pair of slightly eccentric Hinge and Bracket spinsters, still loomed somewhat forbiddingly before me along with the rapidly approaching prospect of my next decade. But I also found the idea of finding new friends, making new relationships, all that trial and error business right down to the basics of things like do you enjoy the same television programmes, somewhat daunting. Too much like hard work. I mean, that kind of exploratory probing is for your teens when you've got the energy and optimism for it, not for the jaded pushing-thirties. I felt I couldn't be bothered with it all, wanted something instant and ready-made. I even, God help me, suffered a pang or two for the familiarity of Joe. Or at least for the fantasies of what he and I might have been together if things had been different. Perhaps I should go up to Dringley for the weekend?

I drove to work on Friday morning filled with an

enervating lethargy which put all thoughts of a couple of days in Yorkshire out of my mind. It seemed so far away. I didn't even bother to call in at a newsagent's shop to buy a copy of *Time Out* so I could spend the weekend composing an advert for the lonely hearts columns or sending off for a computer dating application form. I drove along Chiswick Mall, where my latest office was situated in an elegant house which had a walled garden overlooking the river, and the marrow-deep lassitude I felt even prevented me being pleasantly surprised that for once I could actually park along there without any difficulty. I walked along the higher than normal pavement, up the step and through the door into the garden, up more steps and along a short path to the house. If only I were rich, what I couldn't do with a place like this, elevated just enough from the road to maximise the view over the Thames from the house, yet with the garden wall just high enough to afford maximum privacy from pavement-level prying eyes. How unutterably sad that it should now house offices instead of the love and laughter of a family.

I spent the morning doing more window gazing than typing, watching the incoming waters gradually rise up the banks of the Eyot which was just on the edge of the view, and thinking how pretty it was. In between that and working I kept an eye on my watch which seemed to have joined a go-slow conspiracy with the electric wall-clock. It was one of those lonely jobs – just me and the typewriter in one room and a boss who appeared every hour or so to collect one sheaf of typewritten paper and deliver another of hand-corrected proofs. It was some kind of publishing firm, a tiny subsidiary of an American conglomerate which churned out travel guides on the National Parks of the USA. The clock hands eventually arrived at twelve-thirty and I stopped typing in the middle of the Grand Canyon somewhere in Arizona. I called through, 'I'm going for lunch now,' put on my anorak and left without waiting for affirmation or acknowledgement. It was a mildish day, but raining, so with hood up and head down I negotiated the slippy, mossy garden steps, opened the garden gate and stepped out . . . straight into the river. Ankle deep. Where was the pavement? Under water. Where was the road? Deeper under water. Where was my *car*? You've guessed it.

Obviously the locals knew about the tides. That was why it was so easy to park that morning. But of course nobody had bothered to tell me about it, nobody had even been interested enough to wonder whether I arrived by wheel, foot or parachute. Three small children in a rubber dinghy were paddling around my bumpers and two men, one in fisherman's waders, the other on higher ground in wellington boots, were surveying the scene and smiling as I waded carefully to my poor little mini. The water was lapping around the top of her hub-caps and just over the door sill.

'It'll never start,' said one.

'Hardly even worth pushing,' agreed the other helpfully.

'But it's on the turn,' said the first. 'I think it's gone down a bit. If you wait a few hours and then perhaps a hairdryer?'

'Battery'll be wet,' rejoined the second, shaking his head.

I could manage nothing more than a stony glare. So much for British chivalry. I ignored them, stepped deeper into the water and went round to the driver's door which I unlocked and opened gingerly. The floor inside was divided into four black lakes by the seats and the transmission hump. The seats were dry. The pedals had their noses peeping above the water level. I sat inside, carefully pulled the door closed, put the key into the ignition and wiggled my toes inside their soaking leather cladding. My jeans were clinging wetly cold all the way up to my knees. I patted the dashboard, mentally said, 'Come on, baby, you can do it. Show the bastards what we Yorkshire folk are made of . . . ' then held my breath and turned the key. The engine spluttered twice, turned over and caught. I could have kissed it! I gave it a couple of slow and gentle revs, put her into first gear, let off the handbrake and then praying, 'Don't stall, don't give up now, baby,' I slowly let out the clutch. We moved at snail's pace, trying not to make any waves that might splosh up inside the bonnet and wet the electrics, whilst I gritted my teeth, battled hard not to shut my eyes, and hoped and prayed that we weren't going to be drowned in any submerged pot-holes. I turned a corner into an uphill slope and then, miraculously, we were on dry land, water gushing out from the bottom of the doors. I didn't look back in triumph at the men or the children. I would have liked to but I didn't dare stop in case we never started again. I just patted the dashboard once more, said, 'That's my girl! Well done!' out loud, and headed dripping for the main road. We offloaded more water going round the M4 junction roundabout and by the time we'd limped back to Dewsbury Court there were only about a couple of inches of Thames and silt left slopping around under my feet.

I managed to park her only a few yards away from my stair-hole. I turned off the engine, flopped back in the seat and just sat, thankful to have arrived. But not for long. If I was going to have to walk back to work this afternoon, and that would take a good half-hour, then I had barely ten minutes to get myself changed and dried, let alone doing something about mopping out the car. I went inside and phoned work saying I'd be late because you can do that sort of thing when you get paid by the hour. (Walking out on Whitlock and now this! What on earth was happening to the conscientious person I used to be?) Then I changed into dry clothes and raided the kitchen. Ten minutes later I was to be seen crouching on the pavement with a sponge, a chipped mug and a roasting baster, doing my best to bail out the car while pieces of dripping, dirty carpet hung over the railing getting wetter in the rain. And suddenly, all of London turned friendly. Of the six people who walked past on my side of the road, two grinned, three said words to the effect of: 'Cleaning the car? You can do mine too when you've finished!' and the other commented, 'Could have chosen a nicer day for it.' I smiled back at them all, murder in my heart. When I'd finished as best I could I tried to start her up again but she'd had enough. Damp and condensation had set in so any remaining hope of bolting for the cottage expired along with the engine. My private escape route to sanity cut off. Stranded in an alien city, damp, miserable, hanging on to solvency by a knife edge, and career prospects getting dimmer with every day's post. It was all too much. And a disabled mini was the last straw. I'd had enough!

So I got angry.

I stomped, rather than walked, back to work that afternoon. Once there I typed with a fury that punched holes in the paper every time I made the letter o. I finished at four-thirty on the dot, not caring much that I was in the middle of a paragraph and still stuck in Arizona. I made it to the agency in record quick time, practically threw the time sheet at Ms Gimson with the words, 'I'm in a hurry. I'll pick up the money on Monday.' Then ran from there back to Dewsbury Court and tried to start the car again. I'm not really sure what I had in mind – flight up to Dringley, escape to anywhere? But my friend the mini failed me. I got out again, slammed the door, kicked the tyre and hurt my big toe. I limped up the stairs, weary and out of breath, heard the phone ring, fumbled with doorkeys, dropped them and eventually got inside just as the blasted thing stopped ringing. Talk about wanting to scream! I settled for slamming yet another door and then turned on the radio. Volume maximum. It was tuned to Radio South.

Anger can sometimes be constructive. The radio stopped me dead in my tracks for a moment and then spurred me to a flurry of titivating activity – change clothes, check face, brush hair and out again speeding for the tube in the dark and drizzle of late afternoon.

By six o'clock I was standing outside Lisson House near the Marylebone flyover (dreadful pun, to place a radio station in a tower block called Lisson House) wondering whether to bother going inside or if it would be better to find the nearest reasonable-looking pub. I was working on the principle that a radio station has a pet pub. Like 2D and the Admiral. By now all the somewhat manic physical action had ousted the anger I felt towards the world leaving a residue of quiet determination in its place. Not quite determined or courageous enough, though, to go marching off on a solo pub crawl looking for someone who I knew by title only. I'd look pretty daft standing inside a pub doorway and yelling, 'Is anybody here the Programme Controller at Radio South?' So I pushed through the smoked glass doors that seemed second only in importance to the big brass ones of Broadcasting House and walked determinedly up to the reception desk.

I found myself face to face with a receptionist who was straight out of *Dallas* from the tips of her beautifully lacquered nails to the outermost strand of her carefully dishevelled auburn mane. She looked up, unsmiling.

I drew myself up to my full height, not much at the best of times and I wished I'd worn higher heels, and with the full force of a very recently acquired BBC broadcasting voice I said, 'I have an appointment with your Programme Controller but I'm afraid I was unavoidably held up. I do hope I'm not too late and that he hasn't left yet?'

'What name please?' she asked, destroying the *Dallas* image in three syllables. 'Just a moment,' and she picked up a phone and pressed a button on a switchboard. 'Dorothy,' she said quietly into the mouthpiece, 'there's a girl here says she had an appointment with Stewart.' A conversation ensued during which I could tell, even from this monosyllabic end of it, that my bluff was about to be called. The receptionist replaced the phone and then turned back to me. 'There seems to have been some confusion, a mistake perhaps, but the Programme Controller's secretary can't seem to find your name in the diary. If you'd like to take a seat for a moment, she's on her way down.' The girl obviously wasn't sure whether there'd been an embarrassing mistake on someone's part or whether I was just trying it on and I had to give her ten out of ten for diplomacy in the way she handled me. I settled into a chrome and mock-leather armchair and studied the posters of the station presenters which were mounted on screens dividing the reception lounge into a series of none too intimate booths.

I didn't bother to wonder if my face would ever be up there among them, not like when I made that all too brief excursion to Radio Two. I had far too many other things to distract me, like: how am I going to bluff my way past the secretary, and whatever got into me that I should find myself in this situation anyway? Why hadn't I just sat politely at home and waited for the man to reply to my letter? Bravado was sloshing out of me like the muddy Thames from the car this lunchtime. I regretted not staying in bed all day.

A stocky, bespectacled, furry man came down the staircase at the far end of the reception foyer. He had a brief exchange with Miss East-End-Dallas who nodded over in my direction. Till then I'd just been watching him casually, as a fairly pleasant part of the scenery, but now my heart started to thump audibly. He was walking over to me. God almighty, not the boss man himself? What happened to Dorothy the secretary? More important, where's my nerve escaped to or my confident smile? I cleared my throat praying: voice, don't desert me now.

'Sorry to have kept you waiting,' he said, holding out his hand. I shook it and stood up so's not to continue at too great a disadvantage. 'I'm afraid there's been a bit of a mix up at our end,' he continued. 'I'm Dave Channing, Stewart Brennan's deputy. He had a slight accident last week – nothing too serious, broke his ankle – so he'll be laid up for a while. Obviously in the confusion he forgot to mention your appointment to our secretary . . . '

He went on apologising and I couldn't believe my good fortune. A broken ankle! Oh, jolly rotten luck, Mr Brennan, Programme Controller, well done old chap! Suddenly I was *bona fide*. Dave Channing led the way past the security guard, up the stairs and I followed, feeling ridiculously VIP-like, into a pale wood and hessian office on the first floor. He helped me off with my coat, gestured me to an armchair by a coffee table and then settled himself into another chair to one side of me. My can-I-be-on-your-radio-station letter and its accompanying sample programme tape had been fished out from somewhere and were lying on the table next to a pristine ashtray. Oh, what I wouldn't have given for a cigarette, but I know my interview etiquette. The Deputy PC picked up the letter and glanced through it quickly. 'I take it this is why Stewart wanted to see you?'

I nodded.

'Fine. Well I've listened to your tape and I agree with the notes he made . . . '

I tried to hit a compromise between being too eager for compliments and certain of insults. I settled for an alert expression.

'We could certainly use you – good women broadcasters are hard to come by . . . '

I didn't like the way he was hesitating. 'But,' I said. 'You're about to say "but".'

He grinned at me and we had a delicious moment of eye to eye contact. 'Actually, I was going to say "however". You see it's a bit difficult with Stewart being away. I'm not authorised to hire and fire.'

'Oh, I see.'

'And anyway, we're fully staffed with jocks at the moment.'

I sighed and smiled. 'Same old story. They told me exactly the same thing at Radio Two just the other day.'

'Radio Two?'

'Mm.' I relaxed into the chair and lit a cigarette. What the hell. Now there was no likelihood of this man giving me a job I could start treating him like any other member of the human race. 'Sorry,' I said, 'I'm so used to people saying they don't smoke and making me feel guilty that I forgot to offer. Would you like . . . ?' and I proffered the cigarette packet.

'Thanks, yes. Stewart's a bit of a health freak so I've sort of got into the habit of not smoking in his office.' He took a cigarette.

'But while the cat's away, the mouse will play, eh?' I said.

'Well, not . . . ' He grinned. 'Yes!' He lit the cigarette and inhaled with deep satisfaction. We both laughed. Laughter suited him. He wasn't a strikingly attractive man but with those brown eyes twinkling behind the spectacles and the profusion of hair and beard there was a definite teddy-bearishness about him. He was nice. Comfortable. I almost wanted to come clean and confess all to him about the bluff and not really having an appointment with the absent Programme Controller. Almost.

'So tell me about Radio Two,' he went on. 'Who did you see? How did you get on?'

I complied, skipping over the criticisms and concentrating on the good bits, ending with, 'and he offered me a six-month contract but not until sometime next spring.' Strange how precise meanings can become subtly altered in the précis.

'Will you take it up?'

I appeared to consider the question seriously. 'I don't know really. It has its attractions, of course, national radio, BBC kudos, and it would be a way in, I suppose. But programme presentation is what I'm best at and what I really enjoy doing. I don't really see myself as a newsreader/announcer. So it depends. If nothing better crops up in the meantime then of course I'll jump at it. Six months on a national radio station isn't to be sneezed at . . . '

'Naturally. But you'd turn it down for a programme on local radio, ILR?'

'Not any old local radio station.' I hoped I wasn't hinting too hard. 'I've already done my apprenticeship up in Dringley and I don't believe in retrograde steps. It would have to be a big station. Established, respected, big audiences . . . '

'So if we could offer you a programme, or Capital?'

He was nearly hooked. How much further could I push it? 'Well, the money would have to be right, of course . . . and it would have to be full time, none of this one show a week and only at the weekend business . . . '

'That's understandable,' he said with brow furrowed slightly as if in full agreement.

Could I take it even further? Oh what the hell, why not, it's all make-believe anyway. 'No, what I'd really like – and what Radio South needs, if I can be blunt . . . '

'Go on.' He was sitting forward in the chair now, hands clasped around his kneecap.

'Well what you could do with is a woman on your station during the daytime. Lunchtime or afternoons, maybe. Hell, look what Gloria Hunniford did for Radio Two, for example.'

'You're absolutely right, of course.'

I know that, I thought. The point is, do you think I'm the right woman to do it? He didn't answer my thought waves.

Instead he looked at his watch, stubbed out his cigarette and stood up. Damn, I've blown it, I thought.

'It's been interesting talking to you. But time's getting on and if I don't make a move I'll end up in the divorce courts.'

And another one bites the dust. Married men should be compelled by law to wear a wedding ring.

'PTA meeting tonight so I mustn't be late.' He handed me my coat and led me downstairs again saying all the appropriate things one says on these occasions like, 'Thanks for coming in,' and, 'Sorry I can't offer you anything,' and ending with, 'We're not sure yet exactly how long Stewart is going to be away but either he or I will be in touch and we can perhaps talk some more.' Big deal. We shook hands and the security man unclanked his bunch of keys, unlocked the main doors and let me out.

I waved goodbye and walked quickly away. I was on Marylebone Road going east. Radio South at one end, Capital at the other and me, jobless, in the middle. I didn't really think about where I was going until I realised I was at the turning into Park Crescent. No wonder my feet were protesting. I stopped there for a moment and just looked. How long ago was it now, a year, eighteen months, somewhere in between, that night with Joss? I wondered what had happened to him, hoped he'd managed the time between then and now a little better than I had. I looked up at those Regency columns and thought: well, Joss, here I am again. Why aren't you here too? If that night were tonight, or if tonight had been that night, think how differently things might have turned out for us. Possibilities without end instead of an end with no possibilities. I smiled at myself for a sentimental fool. Life changes things, just as the way you look at them changes things. Take these buildings for an example: once they had been dream-castles washed over by the setting sun. Now they were just . . . wet.

And me with them. I pulled my coat closer across my chest and hurried on towards the tube station, head held down against the rain.

I'd just nicely been home long enough to strip naked and let a nice, hot shower finish off the soaking that the rain had started when the phone rang. I reached for a towel and dripped through to the living room and for once, first time all day, something turned out totally right – I got there before whoever it was rang off.

It turned out to be Sally, sounding very excited. 'At last!' she cried. 'Where have you been? I've been trying to get you for hours.'

'Don't ask,' I said. 'It's a long story. And I'm dripping wet and practically starkers. Can I call you back?'

'No you can't. Get dried and dressed, I'll be round in five minutes. No "buts" . . . ' and she rang off.

I sighed. There are times when she can be just a little too forceful. This was one of them. I wanted to fall into bed and quietly ruminate until sleep came. I wanted to be insular, self-indulgent, continue the daydream about what might have been with Joss my teenage lover, and there were one or two scenarios I wanted to explore which had Radio South as the setting and me in the starring role. After all, Dave Channing had said they *would* be in touch, not they might. But the best laid plans of mice and Alison . . . it looked like today was just destined to be one of those days. I went back into the bedroom and got dressed again wondering if my bio-rhythms were on a triple critical. Then I felt guilty for being so selfish. And towards Sally of all people. She was obviously excited about something. The least I could do was to be here to share it.

When she banged on the door a few minutes later she was clutching a bottle of wine in one hand and flapping a photography weekly at my face with the other. 'Hi!' she said exuberantly, 'do you want my autograph now or later? Or shall I ask for yours first? Where's the corkscrew, the glasses?' She was rattling around in my kitchen before I'd even closed the door behind her. 'Isn't it wonderful?' she called out. 'I didn't want to say anything before because I'm superstitious, but . . . '

'Sally, what *is* it, what are you burbling about? Are you pissed? What's happened?' I demanded, laughing and bemused.

'Look for yourself.' She flung the magazine in my

direction but it flapped wings of its own accord and missed me by miles. 'Pages sixty-four, sixty-five and sixty-six,' she said coming back into the living room with the opened bottle and two glasses. 'A three-page spread no less!'

I still had no idea what was happening. I picked up the magazine and flipped through it looking for the right pages while Sally's eyes were on me, eager and anticipatory. I'd never seen her so lit up before. She was like a Christmas tree that's just been plugged in. It was infectious. I had no choice but to grin along with her. Then I saw it, or rather, saw some of my own faces, staring back at me.

'Well – what do you think? You don't mind? But they are some of the best pictures I've made and they must have helped clinch it . . . '

'Just shut up and pour, woman, while I read! Perhaps then I'll have some idea of what's going on around here.' I sat down and studied the article. '*Through Fresh Eyes*' said the headline, and under it: 'continuing our occasional series highlighting tomorrow's top photographers'. Beneath all that, Sally's name and a selection of the portraits she'd taken of me earlier this year, the time when Joe and I were beginning to split up. I hadn't realised just how good they were till now, seeing them grouped together like this. I looked up at her, thrilled by her achievement. 'One of tomorrow's top photographers, hey? But didn't I always say it?'

She gave me a playful thump. 'No, I can't recall that you ever did. Here.' A full glass was handed to me. 'Now drink up and read on. You haven't got to the best bit yet. There, look.' She stabbed at the closing paragraph with her finger.

I read it out loud. 'Sally has accepted a commission from Faces Cosmetics to produce a calendar – theme, obviously, "Faces" – as the first thrust in the publicity campaign which will launch a new line of skin care products.' I dropped the magazine on my lap. 'My God,' I said slowly, 'you've actually *done* it! It's . . . Oh, Sally! And it's nowhere near New Year's Eve yet!' And I leapt to my feet spilling wine all over the place and gave her a hug that even a grizzly would have been proud of.

We celebrated. My friend the Professional Photographer. 'And you should see the studio I'm going to use! And they're going to try and get Gene Nocon to do the printing. And . . . ' and Sally bubbled on.

And so she should. Who wouldn't when a long-standing, hard-worked-for dream of an ambition is finally being achieved? I'd have been just the same of course if I'd been in her shoes. Worse, probably. And of course she could use my face to practise on any time she wanted. And of course she should let her childlike excitement about it spill all over me because of course she had to show a confident professionalism to everyone else involved in the project. And of course it was bound to lead to lots more work and the opening up of all sorts of prospects. I was thoroughly chuffed to pieces for her. And I felt more than a twinge of jealousy.

CHAPTER TWENTY-SIX

The golden days of autumn were finished, dark afternoons and misty rains gave way to mornings brightened and hardened by frosts. I'd never spent winter in a city, not a proper city like London. Up in Dringley you can always escape into the beauty of the soft whitenesses of the Dales or go and look at the awesome barrenness of snow-covered moors or the craggy Pennines with bare, black patches of steeply naked rock. But in London? I imagined snow would start out grey and melt into brown sludge on the pavements. I wasn't looking forward to it. I was sorely tempted to pack up and go home because if I was going to be stuck as a permanent temp I could do that just as well up there as down here, with the added attraction of being in my own place, where I fitted and where everything fitted me. Hope springs eternal, they say, but I felt as if my own particular spring had frozen over.

Oddly, my friend's success had acted as a damper on my own ambitions rather than as a spur. And yet I was so close to goal myself: two maybes were a hell of a lot better than a hundred straight rejections. So, although optimism and energy were doused for the moment I wasn't quite ready to give in. What I was ready for was a week off – a few days away in my special private place where the cold northern air invigorated rather than slowed you down and where the tap water didn't taste as though it had already been processed through a thousand different urinary tracts before it reached yours.

The mini had recovered herself after a generous application of a magic aerosol spray which the garage attendant round the corner from Sally's had assured me was just the thing for damp engines. I went back and bought another can of the stuff as a standby as well as filling up the tank to see me at least as far as Leicester Forest. Then I packed the bare essentials and set off for home feeling happier and more optimistic with every mile north so that by the time I let myself into the cottage I was convinced that every 'maybe' has a 'definite' in it somewhere if only you work at it hard enough.

The elderly couple next door kept a spare key to the place in case of emergencies and they must have looked in recently because there was no post on the porch floor and only a small heap of it on the table. It all looked a bit puckered up round the edges. I made a note to hang something behind the letterbox to catch things before they drop to the floor – a lot cheaper than buying a new door which would be the only permanent cure for the puddle inside every time it rains. I rifled through the envelopes in a desultory way. But right at the bottom, written in ink that had run and then dried out again in great big pale blue teardrops was a postcard. From Elliott! So he hadn't abandoned me after all. I felt instantly warmer. The writing was just about still legible if I angled it under the light and squinted, and he wrote that he'd lost my new address in the flurry of packing. I turned the card over and looked at the picture. Pyramids. Ye Gods! He was still with Uncle and having a glorious time. Here was their phone number in London and I was to ring in the New Year because they should be home by then. 'I'm a veritable courtesan, my darling, but madly in love and enjoying every depraved minute of it!' he wrote, and signed off with, 'a million hugs'. I propped the card on the mantelpiece to smile at every now and then, threw the junk mail into the bin, then put my feet up on the hearth and settled myself in front of the telly. Bliss.

Those few days did me the world of good. Home was like an enormous, tatty teddy bear which cuddled me every night and grinned at me every morning. There weren't many memories of Joe left in it because I tidied and rearranged furniture and bought a large can of 'Misty Mushroom' paint which I applied liberally to walls and doors because it's easier than washing them down. It was more and more *my* place – special, safe, private – and I wondered if I'd ever become close enough to anyone again to want to share it.

In the middle of the week I decided it was time to stop being insular, so I got myself together and took myself out for lunch. To the Admiral. It was still the only pub in the world that I felt comfortable entering alone, although I must admit to nearly funking it after I'd parked the car. I could always just carry on down the hill and go shopping instead. I mean, suppose all the people I knew at 2D had moved on by now, or maybe they wouldn't recognise me, or even worse, remember me? I told myself not to be so stupid. A lot of water might have passed under my bridge since those days at 2D but for those who'd remained there, only months not years had slipped by. So I went in.

The same chap was serving behind the bar. The same brasses hung on the wall. The same hatstand stood in the same corner. It was like walking into a time warp.

'Hello!' said the barman. 'Long time no see. Thought you were off gallivanting in America somewhere.'

I smiled. 'I was, sort of.'

'Well now you're back what'll you be having – the usual?' he asked, already turning for the whisky optic.

'The usual.' Just like that. Nice. He poured me a scotch and lemonade, ratio 1:2, without asking me to say 'when', and I paid for it, sipped it and said: 'Just right. A usual.' I don't think I'd even had a whisky since I was last at the Admiral but I must admit it tasted good.

'Your muckers are over there,' he said, pointing to a couple of tables over in the corner.

'Ta,' and I pushed my way across the room wondering if I'd be welcome but too late now to turn tail and run.

It was Frank who looked up and saw me first. 'Alison! Well I'll be damned. What are you doing here? Come and sit down, nice to see you,' he said, half rising from his seat in an unfamiliar gesture towards chivalry.

'Good Lord, talk about bad pennies,' said Mick, one of the engineers.

So I said, 'I can see you haven't changed much!'

'No I haven't. Come here,' and he grabbed my arm, plonked me down on his knee and gave me a smacker of a kiss.

'Gerroff, Mick!'

'You haven't changed much either,' he said, shuffling along the bench to make a space for me beside him, and I thought: that's what you think, mate.

I had a lovely time. When Frank asked what I'd been up to since I left and what I was doing now I revelled in exaggerations. It was ever so easy to say I'd been 'in charge' of the in-cabin radio shows while cruising the Caribbean, 'a sort of nautical Programme Controller' I continued happily. And now, I told him, I was taking a brief holiday while making up my mind between Radio South and Radio Two, both of which were showing interest. And of course, neither of the statements were strictly untrue – just not strictly the *whole* truth. It's great fun if you can get away with it.

'Well, if you ever decide to move back up here, Alison, the late night show hasn't been the same since you left . . . '

I smiled sweetly. 'South are thinking more on the lines of lunchtime or afternoons.' (Oh please, let it be true one day, and soon.)

Two more drinks and I decided it was the right time to leave. I didn't want to end up the wallflower alone in a corner after they'd all gone back to work. Hugs and kisses all round and then Frank said, 'Keep in touch, Alison, and good luck. The way things are going I might be coming to see you for a job one of these days.' He said it in an only joking, never in a month of Sundays kind of way. Bastard.

I gave him my most brilliant smile. 'If ever that happens, Frank, you can rest assured that I'll give you exactly the same kind of consideration that you've always shown to me in the past.' If only . . . I thought. After all, they say there can be no sweeter revenge than being more successful than one's old antagonist.

It certainly was a day for bumping into old friends and acquaintances. I was raiding W.H. Smith's a little later in the afternoon, studying the paperback best-sellers stand, when I felt a tap on my shoulder and a voice said, 'It is you, Alison, isn't it?'

I turned. To stone. Carol. She was smiling prettily and had the gall to be looking absolutely fantastic. The rodent-coloured lanky hair had been transformed into a highlighted urchin cut which made her look gamine and sexy. The scruffily casual student stereotype had been replaced by a *Vogue* day-wear individual and I could swear she'd grown at least two inches taller and three slimmer. I have to admit, I did not handle the situation too well. Okay, so Joe had eventually wanted me back and ultimately I'd rejected him but that's hardly the point. What is the point is that the unexpected sight of her flourishing before me reduced me to a churning pulp of helplessness in micro-seconds. I was shocked by the force of it. The wound might be long healed but I bitterly resented the scar, still hated the inflicter of it. The memory of all that desperate and humiliating grovelling throbbed inside me with a vivid clarity. I felt totally vulnerable again, utterly naked. She must have seen it in that instant before I turned away from her and walked out of the shop. I had to because I couldn't trust myself to speak or to stay in her presence for a moment longer without slapping her face or thumping her in the stomach. And that would have demeaned me much more than injuring her. So I just walked away. It's a good job I didn't have any books in my hand at the time or I'd have been had up for shoplifting for certain.

So, the best revenge is in being more successful than your enemy, is it? Bollocks! Even supposing I was, all that would do would be to give her a chance to appear magnanimous and say: 'Oh, I'm so glad she's managing to make a go of things at last.' No. Straightforward, honest to goodness, cold-blooded retribution's the thing. And there's an appealing openness about the idea. Cleansing. Wholesome. The problem is in finding exactly the right way to achieve it.

I fled home. Cursed myself all the way for not having the hauteur to hold a cuttingly polite conversation with her. So once more the battle honours had gone to Carol rather than to me. I felt that I'd never really be free to go properly forward until I'd settled that particular score from the past. But I couldn't for the life of me think of any way I could do it apart from useless things like physical violence or silly things like infecting her with a plague of warts.

When I'd recovered sufficiently I settled down with a cup

of tea to make a list of requirements, revenge for the wreaking of. Just writing it all down helped, made me believe that at least I was doing something about it. One: it would have to be both painful and humiliating. Two: it would have to be emotional rather than physical. Three: she would have to suspect but never know for certain that I was the perpetrator. Four: it mustn't be too nasty, because I'm a nicer person than she is. Five: but it must still be nasty enough to be termed a just revenge. And six: it musn't be illegal.

I read through the list. It made one hell of a specification. I'd never be able to think up anything that would fit the bill. Was there anything? How much easier life would be if magazines ran help columns on the most tasteful way of getting your revenge as well as the most tasteful way of getting your house redecorated or your face made-up. Oh well. A little face was saved just by making out the list. So having settled the point with myself if not with her, I finished with it for the moment and put it away for further study at a later date.

The next morning I woke to find that someone had stuck icy doilies all over the inside of the bedroom window panes. The water pipes made a threatening rumble like severe indigestion when I turned the bathroom cold tap on and at first only dribbles came out. Then it coughed, spat and finally threw up a few little brown lumps of ice before running freely. The basin filled rather quickly considering I hadn't put the plug in yet. And what's that little drift of white stuff doing on the inside of the windowsill? Who was it who came out with all that romantic nonsense about northern winters being so much more beautiful? Suddenly my little rooms in Dewsbury Court began to take on a very cosy aspect and for the first time in what seemed like ages I felt ready to rejoin the fray. Decision: tomorrow, albeit earlier than planned, I'd head south again.

To be successful in life, or at least to have an opening shot at it, I've come to the conclusion that the one thing you need is good timing. As it happened, and through no particular aptitude on my part, for once my timing was spot on. Quartz crystal micro-chip perfect. That's why, on Friday morning when Dave Channing phoned, I was in Chiswick to answer the call instead of being tucked away up in Dringley. And if I hadn't been there, he'd have had to ring someone else. It was that kind of problem for him, that kind of so-easily-missed opportunity for me.

'I may not have the authority to hire and fire,' he said, getting straight down to business without even a hello, 'but I can employ last minute emergency stand-ins. Are you free tonight?'

Me: 'Yes.'

Him: 'Good. It's not a lot to offer, I'm afraid, but our all-nighter's got the 'flu and no voice. The programme's from one till five, mainly library stuff and tapes, minimal needle time and no phone lines. Tonight, tomorrow and probably Sunday night as well. Will you do it?'

As if there were any question about it. Me: 'Yes.'

Dave: 'Good. Sorry to chuck you straight in the deep end like this, no rehearsal, no practice on the desk, even. I'll leave your name with security – come in around midnight – and there'll be a folder for you with requests and things and the odd pointer. The engineer on with you is called Geoff and he's a helpful sort of chap . . . '

'Don't worry!' I said. 'I can handle it.'

'Good girl. Best of luck then and I'll see you sometime Monday afternoon to go over it.'

Now there's another example of Fate in action: if I hadn't decided to spend the night driving, my body clock would have been upside down for a through-the-night show and I'd have been useless by two o'clock in the morning. As it was . . . best get myself off to bed and get a good day's sleep because if I was going to be working off my wits all night a solid eight or ten hours' kip was the best possible preparation for it.

Sleep? That's a laugh. Well would you have been able to? No, me neither. I hadn't been to bed for who knows how many hours and I was too knackered to count them but I was so wound up with the thought of all that might hinge on the next two or three nights that sleeping seemed as much within my capabilities as running a three-minute mile. And there was all that technical jungle to negotiate. I hadn't worked a proper self-op desk for months and months, and all desks are different. Where was the pre-fade going to be, which fader belonged to which deck, were the carts on fader-start or push-button, what sort of tape decks did they use at Radio South and how did you lace them up, or would this Geoff person be dealing with the tapes leaving me with just the grams, and did they take a feed off IRN, and . . . Why did I say yes? Why didn't I think first? Look what happened the last time I said yes first and thought second – I ended up in the middle of the Atlantic.

Oh well, I thought, flinging myself over in bed again trying to get comfortable, that escapade didn't turn out too badly, did it? And ocean waves, radio waves, what's the difference? Come on, woman, to sleep! And if you can't do that then at least try and lie still and turn your mind off.

With that instruction I got out of bed, took the phone off the hook and put the kettle on the hob. It wasn't a good start.

I didn't make a particularly good start to the programme, either, in spite of having propped little labels against the faders and tied up the ones I wasn't going to need with rubber bands and having half an hour to play with it all before we went on air. I clipped the front off IRN because I'd hit the wrong pre-fade key, I came out of IRN with the news introduction jingle because I didn't know there were both 'in' and 'out' versions, and then, absolute mortification, fell into the oldest and easiest trap in the book by starting the opening record at forty-five r.p.m. instead of thirty-three which in turn, although I made a quip about, 'okay, slow down, let's have the long version shall we, boys?' messed up the voice-over timing so I crashed all over the vocals. Whoops. Geoff looked at me through the double glass with a mixture of sympathy and wondering pity as much as to say 'what sort of moron have we got here?' and then said on the talk-back, 'Never mind, petal, everybody gets nervous the first time.'

He was trying to be helpful, I know, but I felt so mortified that I wanted to yell back, 'Mind your own bloody business.

And it's not my first time, I'm an experienced professional!' But the anger was for me, not for him, so I just shrugged then took some slow deep breaths and went through a checklist in my head for the next record while physically pointing at each item. Check speed. Fader shut, check cueing up on pre-fade. Cancel pre-fade key. Open fader. Leave biro on desk pointing at start key. Left hand on gram one fader, ready to close it. Right hand on mic fader ready to open it. Ready? Fine. Now what are you going to *say*?

Radio is a funny business. It can be the most intimate or the most lonely occupation in the world. If you can't get that gut certainty that people are listening and that those people are friendly then you feel about as relaxed and at ease as you would if you were sitting in an empty room trying to have a meaningful conversation with the wall. Conversation is the keyword. Even though you can't hear the other end of it or see the faces at the other end of it you've got to hold a conversation. You can't just talk *at* a microphone because it picks up every nuance, every falsity or insincerity, it magnifies the slightest hint that you might be ill at ease and that makes your listener ill at ease, uncomfortable with you. Which means you've failed in your basic duty because a radio is supposed to be a friend.

Five minutes into the programme and so far I was proving to be a pretty poor acquaintance. I could feel the hostility, worse, the apathy, coming back at me. Oh, I know it's all in the mind but what you feel is echoed in how you sound. And you start with a built-in disadvantage when you're a stand-in, no matter how good you are, because you're a stranger. They don't even know your name unless you keep on saying it and you can't do that too often or you sound like you're an ego maniac. You're a sneaky intruder, too, because all the letters you read out are addressed to somebody else, contain references to something they said that you never heard. It's like butting in on a private joke – you can't help but feel a bit awkward about it.

Worst of all I knew that Dave Channing would be glued to a radio somewhere, at least for the first half-hour. He must be going through agonies, I thought, as the first record began a long and gentle fade and my nerves built to a crescendo in converse proportion. And I so desperately wanted not to let him down, let myself down.

I was getting into a state. If I wasn't careful everything would disintegrate around me. Only one thing to do – think 'sod it', pretend the audience is only Sally and Elliott, and then just be myself. Love me or loathe me that's all I can be. The record ended and I grinned at the microphone. 'Well,' I said. 'That wasn't a very good beginning, was it? Hang on a minute, I think I'll start again. Won't be a sec.' Then I left the microphone open on purpose while I clattered around, mumbling, found the jingle I should have come out of the news with and shoved it noisily into a cart machine. Then I said, 'Right, here we go.' I switched to a posh newsreading voice, said very formally, 'Independent Radio News, it's seven minutes past one.' Then I played the jingle, introduced myself over it and did another 'opening' link, started the next record, talked over the intro and did the whole thing perfectly leaving just half a second before the vocals came in. With the next link I just carried on as if nothing had happened and, convinced they'd never have me back after all that, started to enjoy myself.

I saw Geoff give a couple of apprehensive glances towards the control-room telephone (which was an ex-directory, direct line phone, by-passing the switchboard out of office hours), but it didn't do anything other than sit there blind and silent. 'You've got a nerve,' he said appreciatively, 'but I think it's going to be okay. Bosses must all be asleep.'

'Thank God for that,' I said into the talk-back mic. 'Hey, is there a kettle around here? I'm absolutely parched.'

'Sure thing, petal. Tea or coffee?'

'Tea. Tell you what. You come in and stand in for the stand-in for ten minutes and I'll make it if you like.'

He gave a friendly V-sign and disappeared.

We made it to five o'clock without too many more mishaps. And every time there was one I left the mic open and did it all again properly with a running commentary. A sort of exposé of radio. I was exhausted by the time it was all over. A four-hour programme is one hell of a stint. But we got the news on okay, I flopped over the desk and then the Saturday early show took over from the other studio. I cleared away my clutter and carried it through into the control room. I was just about to ask Geoff where I should leave all the records when the phone rang. We both stopped dead in our tracks. 'Oh-oh,' I muttered. 'Well, Geoff, it's been nice knowing you.'

He patted my shoulder and then answered the phone. He listened for a moment, nodded and said, 'Yes, she's still here,' then he covered the mouthpiece and said to me, 'It's Stewart Brennan – the Programme Controller. He wants to talk to you.' He handed me the phone.

CHAPTER TWENTY-SEVEN

'And who the hell are you, to be tramping all over my radio station in hob-nail boots?' He sounded a bit feverish. 'Who's responsible for this? Channing, I suppose?'

'Yes, er . . . '

'The *middle* of the *night* and you sit there sounding like it's beer and skittles and workers' playtime,' he shouted. 'I've never heard anything like it!'

'I'm sorry.'

'Sorry? It was a breath of fresh air, girl! You're hired. Come and see me Monday, four o'clock and we'll talk. Goodnight.' The machine-gun voice disappeared. The line went dead.

I stood there, mouth open, still holding the handset and looking at it, puzzled, till Geoff took it from me and replaced it quietly on the receiver. My face must have been showing something closely akin to shellshock because he put his arm round my shoulder and said, 'Sorry, kid. It's known as Brennan's bark. Baptism by fire, eh? Pity. Never mind, petal. I thought you were good. There'll be other jobs. Come on, I'll make us a drink.'

'No,' I said. 'No, it's okay. He . . . Christ, I think he liked it!'

But when the Programme Controller had said 'hired' he hadn't exactly meant hired. Or not for a while at least. By the time I saw him on Monday his excitement had gone off the boil a bit and he talked in terms of a three-month contract starting in the New Year when he was planning to implement one or two programme schedule alterations. He hadn't actually finalised his plans yet but he was thinking on the lines of either a lunchtime spot Monday to Friday of an hour or maybe an hour and a half, or possibly two shows at the weekend instead. It was all going to happen at last. Oh, roll on the New Year!

'How would you feel about that?' he asked. He fired all his questions like a cork out of a pop-gun. Convalescence didn't sit on him well. For a man with one leg in plaster propped up on a footstool he radiated a disturbing amount of energy, as if he were longing to be up and pacing the room. He made do with twitching a pencil instead.

Working on the honesty is the best policy principle I told him that I'd prefer Monday to Friday and a three-hour show in the afternoons with live star guest interviews and perhaps a phone-in as well. 'But whatever you say, of course,' I went on. 'Just so long as you find a spot for me somewhere, I'll be happy.' Then I added, 'For a while, at least. Till we see how things work out. On both sides.' I wanted him to know that Radio South would be on trial as well as me. God knows what got into me but why give the impression I was desperate to work there just because I was desperate to work there?

And that's how we left it. Up in the air. He'd be in touch again in December by which time he expected to have his plans finalised, then I could sign a contract and have a couple of meetings with my producer to go over the programme format. A producer was a species I hadn't come across much in ILR before. This is really coming up in the world, I thought, impressed.

'Till December then,' he said. 'I'm looking forward to working with you . . . and in the meantime I assume I can call on you as a last minute relief if anything untoward crops up?'

To which I answered graciously, 'As long as it's not too last minute,' while silently asking Fate to provide another convenient bug to which I alone would be immune.

'And you must come along to our Christmas party,' he said. 'Give you a chance to meet the crowd before you start.'

'Thanks. I'll look forward to it.'

And how! More and more. As the dark days passed and their accompanying succession of miscellaneous temporary typewriters succumbed to the pounding of my fingertips the Radio South office party took on the aspect of social event of the year as far as I was concerned. I seemed to be living in a social vacuum. Occasionally there was a cosy evening round at Sally's or she'd come round to my place and we'd drink lots of tea or lots of plonk or lots of both, but that was about it. We'd discuss our exciting futures, the not quite so exciting hard slog realities of the present and what did we want to get out of it all eventually anyway.

'Everything,' I said one evening at the beginning of December. It was one of those dreadful nights, rain bucketing down, cold and gusty enough to elicit a severe weather flash on the radio with warnings of possible structural damage. Just the kind of night when all sensible people are tucked up in a cosy chair in front of a cosy fire somewhere. So Sally and I had gone out. We were in a little Italian place in one of the backstreets of Notting Hill Gate delighting in having practically the whole place to ourselves. 'Everything,' had been my answer to Sally's question: 'What do you want to have by the time you're thirty-nine?'

'So specify,' she said.

'Okay.' I put down the fork which was not too successfully twined about with spaghetti and started to list off the requirements on my fingers. 'A terrific career . . . fulfilling and very well paid but not so demanding that it doesn't leave time for a home-life as well. That's one. Two . . . ' I picked up the fork again and ate a cool mouthful while organising the vague desires into words. 'A nice home to spend the home-life in. A house with enough rooms to spread about in and a garden to sit in in the summer and grow lettuces. Third, a man in it to be comfortable with, to share things with . . . somebody who loves me and worries if I'm home late. And a child, perhaps, and a couple of moggies to warm my lap and enough money not to have to worry about where the next mortgage payment is coming from. Then there's respect. I want that too. Not just at work from my peers but at home as well, for me simply as who I am even if I've got a headache and I'm moaning about it . . . '

'You've stopped counting.'

'It was too much like hard work.' My spaghetti had gone cold and I'd eaten enough anyway so I pushed it away and picked up the wine. 'I suppose it all boils down to independence with roots.'

'Mmm. I think I know what you mean,' said Sally, swirling red liquid around in her glass. 'Sort of like when I use a tripod. Gives you a solid base, but lets you swivel round in any direction you want.'

'That's it. Exactly.' I raised my glass to her. 'Here's to tripods, then!' We clinked glasses and drank. 'But anyway,' I said. 'What's all this "by the time I'm thirty-nine" business? Stuff thirty-nine! I want all of it. *Now!*'

She laughed. 'You'll have to work a bit harder on this Brennan chap then, won't you? What's he like anyway? Single? Your type? My type?' She had a wicked glint in her eye.

'Down girl! Besides, I shouldn't think so – too spiky. Now Channing, the Deputy, he's much more my type. Yours too, I should think. But he seems very married.'

Not that I was all that sure these days just what 'my type' was. As we change and grow so do our aims and desires. Once upon a time Joe had been my type of man, or at least I'd thought so which amounts to the same thing. Then Yuri had come prancing along like some sort of thoroughbred to match up with a vague fantasy figure I must have carried around since fairy tale and Father Christmas days – lovely for a while but not too practical when it comes to fitting in with real life. The other important person in recent years, delicious, delectable Joss, had fitted nowhere really. I still had regrets when I allowed myself to think about him, which seemed to be happening more and more these days. If only I'd known at the time what was in store for me and Joe I wouldn't have hesitated, I'd have gone flying off with Joss into the wild blue yonder when I had the chance. But that's the trouble with hindsight – it's always bloody late.

The days and nights dawdled along filled up in about equal measure with boredom, frustration, anticipation, panic and the ever present teetering-on-the-edge-of-poverty feeling. At least Radio South promised an end in sight to the latter, though not so sharply focused that I could afford to quit the agency yet. That joyous release seemed a life-sentence away. When I'd officially signed up with South, when I had the contract in my hand, then I'd decide whether to stick it out to the bitter end or not.

The Contract. My own radio show again, back in my niche. And at Radio South too – next to the BBC nationals, one of the two biggest stations in the country! I was looking forward to it with exclamation marks as if it were the gateway to much more than just a career and money and a satisfactory label to tie round my wrist and wave about saying: 'Look, this is me, this is who I am. Somebody!' It would fill in all the other blank spaces of my life too, be the open sesame to a wonderland of ready made friends, or the ticket to a never ending joy-ride of social engagements. Not a very healthy attitude but I was sick to death of going home to an empty flat, horrified at how difficult it was to meet real people in a city that seemed to be teeming with cardboard cut-outs. I reasoned that it must be partly due to the contrast between what I didn't have now and what I'd had a surplus of in those heady months at sea, but surely somewhere there must be a happy medium? But this was London, where people disappear or get mugged or murdered and where nice girls definitely do not make overtures to strange men even if they don't look in the least bit strange. But the nagging question remained: how come no strange men had made any overtures to me? Not even a wolf-whistle. The closest thing I'd had so far was the chap who tried to open my passenger door when I was waiting at a red light just a little bit too near to the kerb. Luckily the door was already locked and the lights switched to green so I drove off like I was in pole position at Brands Hatch before I could find out what might happen next. I guess I just wasn't giving off the right sort of vibes.

And there was another problem. Christmas. It loomed ahead most unfestively and I couldn't put off making some sort of decision about where to spend it for much longer. When I looked at all the twinkly bits of tinsel creeping over the shop displays I did my best not to notice and when that became impossible I tried not to mind it instead, but it was difficult. The lights were up and winking along Oxford Street and Regent Street, Woolworths had racks of plastic Christmas trees and boxes of shiny plastic baubles for sale, people more organised than me had already bought up all the nicest charity cards, the high street greengrocers had started to sell mistletoe and sprigs of red-berried holly and butchers had splattered Order Your Turkey Now messages all over their windows. Talk about depressing.

I couldn't decide whether I should go and hide alone at home in my cottage with the television and a frozen duck or give in to family supplications and spend Christmas with Mum and Dad. Neither alternative is particularly appealing when you're twenty-nine and used to cosy Christmases with husband and friends. I was too old to go back to childhood. Sally wasn't much help, either. I listened smiling, with envy in my heart and empty echoes resounding from my coffers, as she outlined her all-expenses-paid trip to Gstaad to photograph a selection of glowing, frosted, beautiful ski-people for the 'December Face'.

So when, in the second week of December, Stewart Brennan phoned from Radio South with his offer I was literally saved by the bell. Not that I ever doubted he would, eventually. How did I feel about working over Christmas and the New Year, he asked? 'I know it's lumbering you with the short straw but it'll be a good way of introducing you to the listeners so you don't have to start absolutely cold in Week One,' he went on. Oh how it warmed my heart to be speaking in week numbers and quarters again and dispensing with the names of the months. 'Christmas Day morning,' he said, 'from ten till one, then Boxing Day afternoon from one till four and New Year's Day one till three. That'll be your proper slot, we've decided, weekdays, one till three. Suit you?'

Did it suit me? Hell, if my fairy godmother had waved her magic wand I couldn't have asked for anything better! It's odd. You can get so accustomed to always falling flat on your face into a dung heap that you forget what it feels like to land in a bed of rose petals. So after the immediate euphoria of it I started to wonder about the hidden thorns – it was too good to be true, he'd change the schedules again and bung me on in the middle of the night, the job wouldn't last, the challenge would be too much for me, my producer and I would take a pathological hatred to each other, the audience wouldn't like me, and all that kind of thing. Daft, isn't it? Why spoil the enjoyment of today by worrying about what probably won't happen tomorrow anyway?

So I went along to Lisson House to sign up and had my first production meeting. That was one worry, at least, that could be crossed off the list – my producer turned out to be the Deputy Programme Controller himself, the furry Dave Channing, a man I already felt comfortable with. Our 'production meeting' lasted all of twenty minutes and a mug of tea at a desk in a corner of the large communal presenters' office, a room known as the Playpen. I would be given a running order for each programme which was strictly formatted and divided into half-hour segments. Each segment would have its proportion of records from the Top Ten, the bottom half of the charts, new releases, oldies and album tracks. All the chart records and new releases that had made it as far as the station playlist were in boxes in the studio for use by every presenter and were to be played in strict rotation regardless of personal likes and dislikes – you take the one at the front, play it and then put it at the back. 'And no cheating,' said Dave. 'All the different formats have been precisely worked out so that airplay is even but staggered across the week.'

It all seemed very restrictive after my unfettered nights at 2D. 'What does this mean then?' I asked, pointing hopefully to the words 'free choice' which appeared next to last in each segment.

'Means exactly what it says. Except it mustn't be from the studio boxes. And, for the first few weeks anyway, it'll be *my* free choice rather than yours.'

'You mean old sod,' I accused. 'That's not fair.'

'Listen you little Yorkshire Tyke, for all I know you might be one of those cloth caps and clogs and trooble oop at t'mill traditionalists.'

'Your accent's lousy,' I said. 'But you're right. It'ud be t'Brig'ouse n'Rastrick Brass Band playin' Ilkla Moor Baht 'at every 'alf hour if'n I 'ad me way, sithee lad.' I put on as thick a Yorkshire twang as I could remember.

'Exactly what Stewart's afraid of,' he said, laughing.

'Seriously though, Dave, will you listen to suggestions?

It doesn't half buck up my performance if there's the odd all-time favourite record to look forward to.'

''Course I will. So long as it's not too odd. But I don't think we need worry too much about your performances,' he said. I was about to say thank you and accept the compliment with grace when he went on: 'Not after that Oscar-winning show you put on the day you bluffed your way in here to see Stewart and ended up twisting me round your little finger instead.'

I suspect I blushed.

But Dave was smiling. 'Come on then, Tyke. Time for a guided tour and introductions.' And that was how I got a new identity along with my official ID card. He introduced me to everyone qualifying it each time with: 'she's a Yorkshire Tyke, you know, so watch out,' and I was nicknamed Tyke from then on. Thank God he hadn't latched on to Yorkshire Puddings.

The place seemed very big and flashy compared to my memories of 2D but nothing like so monstrously huge as Broadcasting House, and as I already knew my way round at least one studio and the control cubicle it didn't seem too intimidating. Faces were another matter entirely. I forgot most of them, along with the names and jobs that were attached to them, as soon as the next one came along. It all seemed very pleasant and friendly apart from one heart-stopping moment when we looked into the newsroom and I was convinced I saw Joss disappearing into a Tardis-like recording cubicle in the far corner. Of course it couldn't be him. It's not *that* small a world. I never found the appropriate moment, or nerve, to ask. At least half a dozen people asked me if I was coming to the Christmas party and I said yes to all of them before I remembered to ask exactly when and where it would be held.

'The twenty-third,' said Dave. 'It starts off in the pub round the corner at opening time and then moves into the Playpen.'

'Which opening time? Lunchtime or evening?'

'Well,' he answered, tugging at his beard and looking surreptitiously over his shoulder towards the Programme Controller's office, 'that depends on whether you want the official version or the unofficial one.' Then a bit later as I was gathering bag and coat together he said, 'By the way, feel free to bring your boyfriend along.'

I just smiled for a reply and thought: if only.

CHAPTER TWENTY-EIGHT

The more I thought about taking someone along with me to the party the more I stopped thinking 'if only'. Suppose Joss really was working at Radio South? Stranger things have happened. I had such a wonderful time enacting various grand reunion scenes that before long I really had convinced myself that it would all happen – Joss would be there, our eyes would lock across a smoky room, we'd move towards each other oblivious of everything going on around us and then he'd say . . .

And then I'd spend just as much time telling myself not to be so stupid and infantile, he was probably a war correspondent in Lebanon or somewhere by now. Nevertheless, I resolved to go alone and be a free agent, just in case.

After all that looking forward and the secret hope that Joss might have found his way through the small world of broadcasting to Radio South, the party left little to look back on. I spent half an hour being briefed by Dave Channing on the Christmas programmes and danced a couple of times opposite to, rather than with, Geoff the nice engineer from my first stand-in through the night programme. He was between girlfriends, apparently, and did I have any nice friends, were there any more back home like me, he asked? I watched a bit of the evening phone-in through the double glass from the control room and took a glass of wine in to the presenter who was feeling a bit left out of the mainstream fun going on in the Playpen. At one point I even collared the News Editor, took a gulp of wine then a deep breath and asked, 'Does a young bloke called Joss Jordan work here?' I forgot to breathe while he answered.

He repeated the name slowly then said, 'No. Does ring a bell though, sure I've heard of him from somewhere. Let me see, Capital or LBC? No. No, I've got it. BBC. Network, not Radio London.'

Really?'

'Yes, almost positive.'

I started breathing again and my heart rate slowed down. So we were both in London. But as for the likelihood of our paths ever crossing with him making news for the Beeb and me making programmes for ILR he might just as well have been out in Lebanon. Joss at the BBC. There's a turn up for the book. He must have grown respectable in his old age. And just to think that only a few weeks ago I too had been walking the corridors of Broadcasting House. We might have been only yards away from each other and never known it. We might have missed bumping into each other by milliseconds, he opening one door just as I closed another . . . Trust me to get the wrong contract. 'And is there much co-operation between you and them?' I asked. 'You know – all journalists together or is it rivalry to the death?'

'Depends on whether there's an NUJ dispute in the offing,' he replied. 'Can I get you another drink? Red or white?'

'White please.'

He took my glass and disappeared. I perched myself on a desk and wondered if he'd come back replenished or if it was an easy brush-off line. I wasn't familiar with the rules these days. I was just rewriting my BBC audition so it had the firm offer of a job and Joss in it when Stewart Brennan hobbled over. 'Well, what do you think now you've seen the mob?' he asked. 'Glad you joined us or are you regretting it now?'

I hitched along the desk a bit to give him and his walking stick some leaning space. 'Ask me again in a month. If you haven't already fired me by then.'

He patted my shoulder. 'You're feeling nervous.' It wasn't a question.

'A bit.'

'No need, you'll be all right. Don't worry. Just go in that studio, relax and enjoy it. Dave's a good producer. Let him do all the hard work.'

That shows how much you know about programme presentation, I thought. I smiled. 'That's all very well, tewart, but if the listeners don't like it it's *my* face with the gg on it, not his.'

'You'll be fine. Don't worry. That's an order.' He ointed a stern finger at me then hobbled off again saying, And happy Christmas.' That was an order too.

o I obeyed. He was right. Everything *was* fine, I did ave a happy Christmas and once I got behind the nicrophone and the red light went on I didn't worry in the lightest. It was one of the best Christmases I've ever spent, ne and the mic and the music during the day and feet up in ront of the fire and the television in the evening. Alone, es, but not in the least bit lonely.

Isn't it odd how as soon as you stop looking for omething it suddenly lands on your doorstep? You know he saying: it never rains but it pours . . . well, it didn't xactly start pouring, more of a slight drizzle, but it was ery refreshing after so long a drought. And I'm not talking bout the weather although, come to think of it, if it hadn't een bucketing stair-rods on Boxing Day I might not have umped into Terry. Literally. What could I do but pick him p – in all senses of the phrase? I thought I'd be able to find parking place easily enough when I got back home after he Boxing Day programme but the whole world and its randmother-in-law was visiting my street in Chiswick for ea so the best I could manage was back wheels just kimming the edge of the double yellow lines at the other nd of the road from Dewsbury Court. I slammed the car loor, hunched my coat up over my head and belted for the tairwell, shoulder bag joggling and record box bumping gainst my thigh. I went hurtling through the slush, turned harp right, leapt over the puddle at the bottom of the tairwell and crashed straight into this guy who was on his vay out. Talk about bowling someone off their feet! I ffered to buy him a drink by way of compensation for his ruised shin, but the pubs were shut so we agreed on a cup f tea instead. I sat him down in front of the fire while the vater was heating, propped his foot on a cardboard box nd rolled up his trouser leg. The damage was superficial – razed skin, bleeding a bit and beginning to turn purple round the edges – but it necessitated a bathing with cotton wool and warm Dettol solution. He protested. I insisted – was still on a high from doing the programme and anyway it was a very nice looking, hard-muscled calf with golden hairs glinting over a faded tan. Very strokable. He gave in to my ministrations with good grace until I got the elastoplast tin out, whereupon he hastily rolled down his trouser leg and said, 'No, no, it's all right, it'll be fine just as it is, really.'

'Sure?' I asked, looking up into his face and really noticing it for the first time. It was a pleasant face. Not particularly handsome, not particularly not. I went off to make the tea and came back with two steaming mugs, gave one to him then sat myself down in the other chair. 'I'm awfully sorry,' I said for the nth time. 'I mean I've heard of pick-ups but I've never had to do it literally before.'

'Can't say I've ever been picked up quite like that either.'

I looked at my watch. 'This must have made you awfully late. Can I give you a lift to wherever you were going?'

'No, that's okay. I wasn't going anywhere special, just fancied a walk.'

'In weather like this? You must be mad.' I was sure he was just being polite, not wanting to put me to any trouble.

'My secret vice,' he said. 'Ever since I saw Gene Kelly do it. You should try it sometime, it's great fun.'

'All right, drink your tea and come on then. No time like the present!'

And that's how I met Terry who lived two flights further up in number twenty-one. We got thoroughly soaked, parted for separate hot showers, joined up again when the pubs opened, ended up eating curry at the Taj Mahal in the High Road and suddenly it was past eleven o'clock, time for a nightcap back at my place and then to our separate beds. Or just one bed? The question did cross my mind and Terry made it fairly obvious that it crossed his too.

It wasn't that I didn't want to – his goodnight kisses were delicious and his hand sweetly tentative on my breast. But something held me back. It wasn't anything to do with all that 'nice girls don't, especially on a first date' business because I'd got rid of those hang-ups in the salty waves of the Atlantic. And an easy lay with no strings attached would probably do me the power of good, get this rusted old heap lubricated and back into gear. Fine for Alison, the girl who lives down in number thirteen. But what about Alison the radio star? I didn't like the possibility of Terry switching on his radio and preening, remembering me only as a recent casual screw. Best leave it till I knew him a bit better.

We agreed on lunch together the next day at his place and then he left without further resistance. As soon as I locked the door I wished he was on this side of it, not the other.

I rectified the situation the following afternoon, though in his bed on his sheets rather than mine, and I enjoyed it immensely. On a scale of one to ten Terry scored about five for sexual proficiency but considering I'd been chaste rather than chased since somewhere out in the Atlantic, five translated as pretty good. That's the great thing about sex, somebody said once: when it's good it's very very good and when it's bad it's still not bad. And the more we practised together, the better it was bound to get. Stands to reason. So what about all that casual screw business? All a matter of attitude. I was the one who was preening and Terry was my casual lover rather than me his. If he felt differently, so what, because it's what I feel that counts. And I was feeling good. I was at the centre of the world again and looking outwards. The vista was expanding rather than closing in on me.

I was actually looking forward to New Year's Eve.

Next year and the start of my programmes-proper was only days away and I was dying to get stuck into it, not feeling apprehensive anymore as to whether I'd cope. Of course I'd cope. If the Christmas shows were any indication I'd do more than that, I'd be terrific, or at least, reasonably good. After all, I'd already been given Terry by way of reward so I couldn't be doing too badly, could I? And I was earning real money again instead of peanuts, enough to allow the thought of finding another, nicer flat to rent, one with a proper bathroom and an inside loo. And there was

Joss as well. Somewhere. Here we were, sharing the same city, and there was no reason on earth why I shouldn't just ring him at the BBC one day and say hello just for old times' sake. There was Sally too. She was due back from Switzerland in a couple of days, in time for New Year's Eve. I could have a small dinner party and invite Terry and Sally and . . . maybe Geoff the engineer? It would be nice to have another couple to make up a round half-dozen so I wondered about inviting Dave Channing and his wife but decided it would be a bit forward as I'd only met her briefly at the party and me and Dave would end up talking programmes and they'd probably have made family plans anyway.

But I phoned Geoff and he accepted. Then I thought about phoning Joss but that was a secret treat to be held in store for sometime/later/never and anyway I wouldn't want him to be with a girlfriend and I'd hate to meet him again while I had Terry or anyone else in tow. So, resigned to it being a foursome, I tried Elliott's number just on the off-chance that he and Uncle had shaken the sand out of their shoes and returned.

And they had! And they'd be delighted to accept. I was over the moon. To see in the New Year with both Sally and Elliott at my side and then on New Year's Day to really get stuck in at Radio South with the first of my Alison-in-the-afternoon shows. Talk about happy. I was in transports of delight, so contented that even the crunchy puddles and frosty pavements outside Dewsbury Court seemed tinged with pinky-gold round the edges. I was independent, self-sufficient, confident and optimistic for the first time in . . . how long? I thought about it. For the first time ever, really. And I liked it very much.

Those few days between Christmas and New Year were a hiatus between two distinct phases of my life and as the shops were open again I remembered the Boy Scouts' motto and bought myself a little present on New Year's Eve in the sales. A big present actually. In the shape of a double mattress. Terry helped me tie it on the roof of the mini and we had a chilly drive back with all the windows open where the washing line went through, then had to double park outside the stairwell entrance while we offloaded it. Have you ever tried heaving a double mattress up three twisting flights of stairs? Don't. Buy a winch or let the men from the shop deliver it. The thing took on a life of its own. We lugged it through the door of my flat then heaved it into the bedroom. 'And don't let this go to your head,' I said to Terry. 'I haven't bought it for your benefit, you know.'

'No?'

'No. Go and put the kettle on while I re-park the car, there's a good lad.'

Then it was moving the single bed into the living room. Whoever invented castors should have got a peerage. We rearranged the furniture so the bed could go up against a wall and a corner, threw a few cushions along the back of it and then sat. It made a very comfortable sofa.

'Looks really good,' said Terry. 'And just in time for the party tonight.'

'I've got an idea,' I said and led him back into the bedroom. 'Let's start the party early.'

He grinned. 'I thought you said this double wasn't for my benefit,' he said as I started to unbutton his shirt.

'It isn't,' I replied, peeling it from his shoulders then kissing his chest. 'It's for mine.'

CHAPTER TWENTY-NINE

The first day of January. About three o'clock in the morning and alone in my bed. Through choice. I was sleepy but not yet ready to switch off either the light or my thoughts which were still lingering deliciously over landscapes of lazy consciousness. It had been a damned good night. And it was going to be a damned good year.

I'd switched on the radio just before midnight so we could all listen to Big Ben doing his duty, then everybody yelled 'Happy New Year' and hugged and kissed everybody else. So much good spirit had been flowing that Geoff and Terry had even submitted to being kissed by Elliott and Uncle. Sally had returned from her trip with about fifty rolls of exposed film and a marvellous snow-tan. My benevolent match-making scheme looked like paying off because Geoff and Sally left hand in hand shortly after midnight replete and smiling after a relaxed infusion of roast beef and claret with conversation and coffee to follow. Elliott and Uncle departed soon afterwards and Terry stayed behind long enough to share the washing up and my bed. It had all been extremely satisfactory. Now that I was alone again I stretched out languorously under the new duvet and spread my limbs across the unrestricted space of the double mattress..I was content to linger over memories of the evening.

Elliott had practically smothered me in hugs the moment he arrived and then we'd picked up from where we left off as if it had only been a day or so since we'd seen each other. When Sally turned up we hugged each other as if we'd been parted for months. The two of them seemed to get on quite well together in spite of the fact that they both held the title Alison's Best Friend. Anyway, towards the end of the meal, that delightful stage when the table is covered in crumbs and fruit peelings and remnants of cheese and the contributory causes have lapsed into a momentary and congenial silence, Sally pushed back her chair and stood up. 'Lady and gentlemen – and you two as well,' she said wickedly nodding towards Elliott and his lover, 'I give you a toast.' She cleared her throat ostentatiously. 'Here's to friendships new and old. And to success. And to . . . tripods. And to radio's newest and brightest star, our hostess, Alison!'

There was a chorus of hear-hears and a general clinking of glasses which were quickly drained and refilled. I stood up to reply. 'Thank you,' I said with a bow. 'I too would like to propose a toast.' I raised my glass. 'To the New Year! May it bring everything that you want it to and nothing that you don't and God bless all who sail in her!'

Glasses were clinked again and Terry put his arm around my shoulder saying, 'Boy, for someone who makes her living out of stringing words together, that was really original!'

'Don't be cheeky. I'd like to see you do any better,' I replied with a hiccup.

'Now then, children, no squabbling at the dinner table,' said Elliott.

'Who's squabbling?' I asked. 'Terry knows damn well that if he argues with me I'll simply thump him or shove him down the stairs.' I smiled sweetly at Terry and raised my fist in mock attack.

'She would, too,' he confirmed. 'I surrender!'

I grinned. 'That's a good boy. I prefer my goods undamaged.'

Later, when everybody else had gone home, I was lying in bed watching him undress and analysing our relationship. There was certainly no danger of me falling in love with him. Usually I didn't agree with him, had discovered over the last few days a surprising number of things we didn't have in common, and I found him quite amusing – usually when he was being utterly serious. But I did find him physically attractive. The face that I'd first labelled 'pleasant' had evolved into 'quite good looking', probably because the body which supported it was uncommonly good. I wondered if I'd ever find a man who had mind, face and body to make a matching set. Then I ran my hand lightly over my own body and thought ruefully: who am I to demand perfection? I made a quiet resolve to get myself fit and in trim this year. My eyes went back to Terry. He did look delicious standing there in just his underpants. 'Have I told you recently that I think you're very pretty?' I said to him.

He laughed. 'I'd rather you said handsome and ruggedly macho!'

'Oh, I think I'd need a much closer study before I could say that . . .' and turned back the duvet for him.

Later, when he'd gone, I luxuriated in the emptiness of my bed. Although I liked making love with Terry I didn't particularly want to sleep with him. That would be much too intimate. And one of the advantages to being a single woman again is that you don't have to sleep with someone if you don't want to. And there are no arguments about who gets the wet patches either. I reached over for the alarm clock and set it, with a little groan, for nine o'clock.

At approaching three minutes past one I was sitting in Studio A with the lights dimmed and listening for the out-cue from IRN. It came. I fired the news jingle, opened the microphone and was off and running. This was it. No more a last minute stand-in presenter or holiday relief, but my own programme, my name on the billing not just Alison doing The Somebody Else's Show. And broadcasting to a six-figure audience. Good old Radio South. The programme flashed by and it seemed only minutes before I was saying, 'I'll be back at one o'clock tomorrow so I hope you'll be able to join me again then . . .' Back tomorrow. And the day after. And the day after that. And next week. At least for the next three months. Guaranteed. What a high!

I closed the mic, listened to the start of the news and stayed in place until transmission went safely next door to Studio B. Oh, the luxury of having two on-air studios and no more hot-seat changeovers. I was just reaching under the desk to unplug my cans when a voice came through on the talk-back from control room, 'Alison, your phone's flashing. Will you get it or shall I take it from in here?'

I surfaced, mouthed a thanks at the double glass window and picked up the phone. The girl on the switchboard said, 'It's someone called Sally phoning from Chiswick. Will you take the call or shall I get rid of her?' Wow. Protected from the listening public by the switchboard operator! Just like I was somebody special, important, a star even!

'That's okay, I'll speak to her, thanks.' She connected us.

'Alison? Hi. Happy New Year again. Hey, you did okay.'

'You mean you actually listened?'

'Well I thought I ought to. First opportunity and all that. You're not bad, really, are you?'

'Not bad? Can't you do better than that?'

'Sure I could. But you're big headed enough already! I was really ringing to say thanks for last night and why don't you pop round on your way home. We've a lot of notes to compare.'

'You and Geoff . . .?'

She chuckled. 'I'll tell you later.'

It sounded good. I said I'd be round, put the phone down and it flashed again almost immediately. The operator had put this one straight through to me. It was the boss man himself, Stewart Brennan: 'Happy New Year. Nice one, Alison. Just ringing to say if you carry on like this I might let you stick around.'

A couple of minutes later, by which time I'd got the singles back in their boxes and half the LPs into the right sleeves, it flashed again, and again the caller was put straight through. This time it was Dave Channing. 'Hi there, Tyke. Now then, about tomorrow's programme . . .' And it was down to work with a vengeance.

I finished getting my stuff together and cleared away the accumulated programme flotsam, emptied the ashtray, swilled out my mug and took a final glance round the studio. I like to leave it the way I'd like to find it, though it doesn't seem to be a habit too common among broadcasters. Then I went through to the Playpen, sat down at my desk and attacked the music logging forms while considering what I planned to do. Well, it wasn't so much a plan, I just knew I was going to do it. The logging was just by way of putting it off for half an hour or so. Even that wasn't much of a plan because I'd hardly begun it when I found myself stopping in mid-duration, going back to Studio A where I could dial nine to get a direct outside line, and picking up the phone. I knew the number. I dialled it. It rang for ages. Long enough for me to dismiss the whole idea as stupid. But one of those miracles of timing happened because I was just about to put the phone down and funk it when they answered. 'BBC good afternoon what number?' said the female voice in a monotone.

'Newsroom please,' I said.

Click. Static. Click. Silence. Click. 'Newsroom,' said another anonymous voice, this time a male voice, rushed, curt.

'Joss Jordan please,' I said.

'Hang on.'

I hung on.

'Sorry, he's not on duty. Can I help?'

'No, it's a personal call. Can you give me his home number please?'

'Sorry, can't give that information. Can I take a message?'

'Yes, tell him . . . no, never mind. Could you tell me when he's next on duty please?'

A sigh. 'Just a minute.'

I was ready to funk it again and hang up rather than on. But I wasn't quick enough.

'He'll be in tonight. Ten o'clock. Radio Two summaries desk. Who shall I say called?'

'Thank you,' and I rang off. Ridiculous. My hands were trembling. I lit a cigarette and gulped the smoke down. And I'd so nearly got a job as a Radio Two newsreader. Choices, options, to phone again later or not to phone at all? Or to lie in wait, lurk behind the pillars of All Souls' and ambush him on his way in? Or to go straight round to Sally crying 'help'! Or to knock on Terry's door? I went back to my desk wishing I knew the right answers.

I sat down and tried to apply all my energies to finishing the logging but it was no good. My mind kept dashing off to open up lots of different little boxes. One was labelled 'was

Joss listening to you this afternoon?' All I found inside it were more questions like: 'if he was, did he realise it was you?' and 'if he was and he did, would he care?' and 'would he be listening to the opposition anyway?' and 'would he be listening at all or out at the pub or in bed asleep or . . .?' Amongst all those different questions and scenarios one thing was certain: even if I wanted to I couldn't just sit back any longer waiting for something or nothing to happen. Old ghosts have to be laid (one way or another) if you're ever going to be able to go forward. And I *was* going forward, and I was going to keep on going that way. Under my own steam.

I got through the logging, though with no guarantee as to its accuracy, and dropped it off on the presentation secretary's desk on my way out. I'd just reached the Playpen door when my phone rang. I went back to answer it. It was our receptionist. 'Glad I caught you. There's a reporter bloke down here wants to do a piece on you. Shall I put him off?'

My heart skipped a beat. Telepathy, thought transference? The way my mind had been zooming in on Joss the last hour it wouldn't surprise me at all. 'What's his name?' I asked, trying to sound casual about it.

'Dunno. Says he's *Daily Express*. Got a tape recorder with him.'

I felt really let down. Just for a moment I'd really let myself believe it might be him. Stupid cow. Then I thought: why the hell am I feeling disappointed? A national daily, and wanting to interview me? 'Tell him I'll be down in five minutes,' I said, then went into the ladies' and quickly tarted myself up. If only I'd known. I'd have done my hair, put more make-up on, worn smarter clothes. Why the hell hadn't he made an appointment? God, they must be short of news, the usual bank holiday lull, time for the funnies, the return of wandering puppies, a new voice on the radio, anything to fill up a column inch. I brushed my hair vigorously then shook my head to get a bit of lift into it, blotted the shine on my nose with the roller towel then pulled in my tummy, glanced at my profile in the full length mirror and was glad that at least I'd put tight jeans on which held in more than they gave away.

I smiled at the security guard at the bottom of the stairs and had a quick glance round reception but all I could see was a pair of feet and some chair legs beneath one of the poster boards (my poster still wasn't up there amongst them. I hadn't had the photo done yet. I wondered if they'd employ Sally to do it if I asked them nicely). I went up to the receptionist and she pointed me in the direction of the feet. I approached, polite and friendly professional smile already in place.

CHAPTER THIRTY

'You know you've still got the sexiest backside I've ever seen,' said a familiar voice as its owner emerged from behind the screen.

I think my heart stopped. All the well-rehearsed scenarios fluttered out of my head like a flock of startled birds and the only thing I could think of to say was, 'You're supposed to be the *Daily Express*!'

'I wasn't sure you'd want to see me if you knew it was me, so I lied,' he said simply, shrugging his shoulders, for all the world like a small boy modestly admitting to a successful scrumping raid. The same, dear Joss.

I smiled at him, not sure whether to shake his hand or catapult myself into his arms. I did neither, just shook my head and said, 'You haven't changed a bit.'

'Older but no wiser, I guess.' He paused. 'Not over some things, anyway.' Oh, the way he looked at me when he said that. I hoped it meant what I wanted it to mean.

Without any spoken agreement we were heading towards the door together and I wondered how on earth I made it without falling over. My legs felt weak and I knew my hands were shaking so I stuffed them firmly in my pockets out of sight. Neither of us said anything more until we were outside. There were so many questions I wanted to ask, like: had he married, got engaged, got a girlfriend, a lover, did he still want me or was this just a curiosity call? So I tried to ask them all with, 'Well, how are you, how've you been?' and tried to read all the right answers into his 'I'm fine. You're looking well.'

By the time we reached my car we were firmly stuck in a muddy rut of polite and inconsequential small-talk. This wasn't at all the way it was supposed to be.

'Still the same old mini then,' he said and patted its roof. 'A few more dents in it, though.'

Just like its owner, I thought. Like Joss, too. He looked

leaner, older, more character to his face – as if he'd done a fair bit of living in the time between now and that night at King's Cross station when I'd last seen him. But it suited him. I couldn't stop looking at him. Memories often glamorise people but mine of Joss did no justice to this man standing beside me. All my old images had suddenly shattered and blended together again into a new reality. I wanted him so much more than I'd ever imagined.

But there we stood, facing each other in the middle of the pavement, and we looked at each other in silence, not touching, not smiling anymore, and not moving. It seemed all we could do was gaze at each other like a couple of kids trying to stare each other out. The world might have stopped, everything around us seemed so quiet, so still and misted over. Only Joss was in sharp focus.

I was the first to break, to give in. I couldn't cope with it any longer, had to take the risk. 'For God's sake, Joss, don't just stand there! Kiss me. Please.'

Then his mouth was on mine, his hands in my hair, then firm against my back pressing me into him as if he'd never let go of me again. And I was holding on to him just as tightly and there was the well-remembered feel of his shoulders, his back, the muscles tense and hard under my fingers. I think the world really did stop for a while.

Eventually he said, 'I tried to find you, you know. When I heard that you and Joe had split up. But all they said was that you'd gone to America. Did you? Why on earth didn't you come to me?'

'I didn't know where you were. And besides, I don't think I was ready to.'

'And are you now?'

'If you want me.'

'Oh, I want you.' He put his hands on my shoulders and looked straight into my eyes. 'So long as there's no chance of you going back to Joe? Or America?'

'No chance,' I said and gave him a quick précis of what had happened over Joe, Carol, running off to sea, coming back, coming here.

He laid the back of his hand lightly on my cheek and said, 'My poor Alison. Sounds like you had a rough journey.'

I smiled and shook my head. 'Oh, I wouldn't say that. Not all of it.'

'But it was an awfully long way to go just to travel two hundred miles.'

'I suppose so. Let's just say I took the scenic route.'

Joss laughed and hugged me. 'Oh, you really are something, woman! The same irrepressible Alison Wonderland.'

'You remember that?'

'Of course. You autographed my arm and I swore I'd never wash it.'

'And did you?'

'I'll never tell,' he said and we laughed at the memory.

'Well at least today you won't have to bribe the cab driver,' I said and unlocked the mini. 'Come on, hop in. Where shall we go?'

'Any enchanted castles nearby? Preferably with a turret I could climb. After all your travels I've got to impress you somehow.'

'You already have,' I said. 'But I know just the place.' With the thought of having Joss inside it, even Dewsbury Court had its magic.

We bundled ourselves into the car and then he leaned across and kissed me again before I could get the key in the ignition. It was a very long kiss. Eventually I said, 'Come on. We'd better go or this mini might just turn itself into a pumpkin and then we'd be in trouble!'

'No chance,' he said.

'Why not?'

' 'Cos the glass slipper still fits you,' he said softly.

Oh Joss.

I put my finger to his lips. 'Be careful, love. We mustn't mix our fairy tales.'

'It doesn't matter,' he replied. 'They've all got the same ending.'

Ar.d you know, he might just be right.